Praise for Kathleen

'A MUST READ in my

'Utterly perfect … A timeslip tale that leaves you wanting more … I loved it'

'I may have shed a tear or two! … A definite emotional rollercoaster of a read that will make you both cry and smile'

'Oh my goodness … The pages turned increasingly quickly as my desperation to find out what happened steadily grew and grew'

'Very special … I loved every minute of it'

'Brilliant … Very highly recommended!!'

'Touched my heart! A real page turner … The perfect read for cosying up. I can't recommend this gorgeous book enough'

KATHLEEN MCGURL lives in Christchurch with her husband. She has two sons who have both now left home. She always wanted to write, and for many years was waiting until she had the time. Eventually she came to the bitter realisation that no one would pay her for a year off work to write a book, so she sat down and started to write one anyway. Since then she has published several novels with HQ and self-published another. She has also sold dozens of short stories to women's magazines, and written three How To books for writers. After a long career in the IT industry she became a full-time writer in 2019. When she's not writing, she's often out running, slowly.

Also by Kathleen McGurl

The Emerald Comb
The Pearl Locket
The Daughters of Red Hill Hall
The Girl from Ballymor
The Drowned Village
The Forgotten Secret
The Stationmaster's Daughter
The Secret of the Château
The Forgotten Gift
The Lost Sister

The Girl from Bletchley Park

KATHLEEN McGURL

ONE PLACE. MANY STORIES

This novel is entirely a work offiction. The names, characters and incidents portrayed in it are the work of the author's imagination. Any resemblance to actual persons, living or dead, events or localities is entirely coincidental.

HQ
An imprint of HarperCollins*Publishers* Ltd
1 London Bridge Street
London SE1 9GF

www.harpercollins.co.uk

HarperCollins*Publishers*
1st Floor, Watermarque Building, Ringsend Road
Dublin 4, Ireland

This paperback edition 2022

5

First published in Great Britain by
HQ, an imprint of HarperCollins*Publishers* Ltd 2021

Kathleen McGurl asserts the moral right to be identified as the author of this work.
A catalogue record for this book is available from the British Library.

ISBN: 9780008480837

MIX
Paper from responsible sources
FSC C007454

This book is produced from independently certified FSC™ paper to ensure responsible forest management.

For more information visit: www.harpercollins.co.uk/green

Printed and Bound in the UK using 100% Renewable Electricity at CPI Group (UK) Ltd

This book is dedicated to all the health,
care and key workers who have kept us
going throughout the pandemic.
Thank you.

Chapter 1

Julia, 2019

Four hours. On waking, Julia checked her sleep-monitoring app as always. Not too bad a night. She'd had a lot worse. She groaned slightly as she hauled herself out of bed, leaving Marc beside her still snoring gently. He had another hour before he'd need to get up and head out to work, but Julia had a list of jobs she wanted to get done before the working day began. As she showered, she ran through the list in her head. Put a load of washing on. Before that, put the previous load into the dryer. No, before that, take the load out of the dryer and put it away. Some of it needed ironing. Where was Ryan's football kit? He needed it today. Hopefully it was in the washing load that was in the dryer. Empty the dishwasher. Or could Oscar be persuaded to do that? Probably not before school. He had a school trip today, so Julia needed to make sure he had a suitable packed lunch. He was fourteen – surely old enough to take control of his own lunch-making? But he wouldn't, and she'd worry, so better that she should sort him out. Ryan had football practice after school. Marc would be late home, no doubt, so dinner needed to be ready for seven. Oscar would probably go round to a mate's house after school for a bit.

She showered efficiently, towelled herself dry, dressed in black trousers (not jeans, never jeans on a workday) and a cream shirt. Make-up could wait. The washing was sorted while a slice of bread toasted and the coffee-maker did its thing. Meanwhile, her mind turned to work. Team meeting at eleven that she needed to prepare a few slides for. Annual appraisal with Tulipa that afternoon. The girl was doing well – a real asset to the company. She had to find out whether Ian had followed up on that new business lead she'd shoved his way a few days ago. Then she needed to check in with Barry – he always worked best if he spent a bit of time talking through his work with her. Then get on with her own project. There was a tricky technical problem she needed to find a way around. Barry might have some ideas.

Toast eaten, and a possible solution to her work problem ticking away at the back of her mind, she glanced at her watch. Not quite seven o'clock. There was time to unload the dishwasher, clean the kitchen sink and hob and possibly also vacuum the sitting room where Marc had dropped crisp crumbs all around the sofa the previous evening. She donned an apron and got on with the chores, and was halfway through a batch of ironing when a scowling Oscar and still sleepy Ryan stumbled down the stairs and began organising their breakfasts.

'Ah, watch what you're doing – I've just cleaned up there!' Ryan had slopped milk over the counter as he poured it over his cereal.

'Sorry, Mum. Do you know where my football kit is?' the twelve-year-old said through a mouthful of cornflakes.

'It's just out of the dryer. In the washing basket.'

'You should do your own washing,' Oscar said. 'Only way to make sure it's done on time in this house.'

'Unfair, Oscar,' Julia replied. 'I do a good job of keeping on top of the washing and you know it. But if you really feel like that, then feel free. Do your own washing. You know how. Programme Four is the best one.'

'Not got time.' Oscar pushed back his chair from the kitchen table, left his cereal bowl by the sink and headed out to the front door.

'Bye, then. Dinner at seven,' Julia shouted after him as she loaded his bowl into the dishwasher and tucked his chair back under the table.

Ryan was eyeing up the drizzling rain that had just begun. 'Can I have a lift to school?'

'Only if your dad does it,' Julia snapped. 'I've got to get to work.'

'Huh. You mean you have to walk all the way across the kitchen, through the hall, and through a door into the office. It's not far, Mum. Takes you about ten seconds. You can drive me to school then start work.'

'I mean, I need to get going with work. My business doesn't run itself, you know.' She glanced at her watch. Eight-fifteen. Tulipa generally arrived for work at 8.30. Julia liked to be in the office by then.

'Morning, all.' Marc had come downstairs at last. 'Fry me an egg, would you?' he said to Julia, while he poured the last of the coffee she'd made into a mug and sat down, scrolling through news items on his phone.

'No time. Sorry.'

Marc pouted. 'I only asked as you're so much better at it than I am.' He gave her a cheeky smile and a wink.

Julia couldn't help but smile back. 'Can you take Ryan to school?'

'Can't he walk?'

'It's pissing down,' Julia said, leaving before she ended up agreeing to do it anyway. She picked up her now cold coffee and went through to her office, to get started with the day's work.

The office was housed in an extension to the house, originally intended as a 'granny annexe'. There were two rooms, a neat little kitchen and a tiny bathroom. Perfect for the small IT company Julia had set up with her old university buddy, Ian. Julia and Ian used the room – originally intended as a bedroom – as their office, while other employees had desks in the sitting room. One end of the sitting room was kitted out as a break-out space. The kitchen allowed them to make coffees and store sandwiches. Currently only Barry and Tulipa came to the office each day and were on permanent contracts. Other than those two, they employed IT contractors as and when the workload required it.

With Julia taking care of the technical work – designing and coding the systems for small retailers – and Ian managing the financial and sales side of the business, they'd built up the company from nothing and now were both able to draw decent salaries from it. It was a success, and Julia was proud of all that they'd achieved, even though running a business and being a mum and homemaker meant she had little time to call her own. Sometimes she wondered if her work-life balance was out of kilter, but she never dared dwell on this thought for too long. Who knew where it might lead? She had it all – living the dream of many, with a family and a successful business. Life was good. Mostly.

She sat down at her desk, opened up her laptop and had a sip of coffee, grimacing as she realised how cold it had become. While the laptop booted up, she went to put on a fresh jug in the office kitchenette. Through the door that connected the office with the rest of the house she could hear Marc and Ryan laughing and joking in the hallway. It seemed Marc had been talked into giving Ryan a lift after all. Good. Julia didn't have to do everything. Back at her desk, she began putting together a to-do list for the day.

'Hey, good morning!'

Julia looked up as Tulipa came in through the side door, shaking droplets of rain off her umbrella. 'Hey. Still raining, is it?'

'Yeah. Chucking it down.' Tulipa fetched herself a cup of the coffee Julia had put on and settled herself at her desk. 'When's our meeting? Ten? I've time to get on with those changes you wanted, adding the new company logo into the style sheet.'

'Eleven. Great. We'll talk later, then.' Julia smiled. Tulipa had been a fabulous addition to the company. Julia was planning to give her a pay rise soon. Tulipa often talked about wanting to buy her own flat, and how she was saving as much as she could. A pay rise would certainly help, and she deserved it, Julia thought. Tulipa was that rare combination of technically competent but also artistic. Her screen designs were attractive, intuitive, stylish and a large part of the reason they'd bagged a number of new contracts recently. Small companies which had struggled along for years using spreadsheets and outmoded databases, which could now upload their data to Julian Systems and manage their entire business through one easy-to-use portal, that covered product information, stock control, ordering, receiving and sales reporting.

Julia had barely got started with her work when she had a text from Marc.

Hey, sweetheart. Hate to say it as I know you took a casserole out, but there's a leaving do tonight I'd forgotten about. Won't be home for dinner. Sorry, see you later. Luv M.

She felt a surge of annoyance. There would be too much for three people, and it couldn't be reheated again. Why couldn't Marc have told her sooner? She read the text again. OK, so he forgot. Well, it couldn't be helped.

*

Halfway through the afternoon Julia had another text, this one from her brother. Bob Whiteley was a long-haul airline pilot, working irregular shifts, living out of hotels around the world, although he did own a flat in Paris that he managed to stay in for about three or four weeks of every year, and a house in south Devon that he'd inherited from their grandparents. Julia sometimes wondered if he'd ever settle down.

Hey Sis. Owing to a bit of last-minute rescheduling I have a few days off. Got news to share, and something for you. Are you free tonight?

She smiled and texted back. The perfect solution. *Sure. Actually, got some spare dinner with your name on if you can be here by 7.*

He sent a thumbs-up and a smiley face in response, and Julia sat back, looking forward to the evening. Bob was always good company, and a frequent visitor, as their house in west London was a convenient place for him to stay if he flew into Heathrow. She wondered what the news he had was; her mind instantly flew to the possibility that maybe at last he'd met someone he wanted to spend the rest of his life with. And what did he have for her? She had no idea but was looking forward to finding out. Maybe something simple like flowers or chocolates but knowing Bob it'd be more interesting. He'd probably need to stay the night, she guessed. The spare room was made up, so that would be no problem.

*

The last meeting of the day was a catch-up with Ian, who'd been out all day. He arrived just in time, looking flushed and a little flustered. 'Appalling traffic,' he said by way of explanation. 'And actually I've not got long. Promised Drew I'd be home early tonight, and I daren't disappoint him.'

'Sure, well, just give me a quick update. Or if you prefer, you rush off now and drop me an email when you have a moment. Just wondered what Mannings and Co thought of your pitch, and whether there's any more feedback from those other potential clients?' There was so much on these days. As so often, she felt like a juggler, keeping so many balls in the air at once. Or perhaps a plate-spinner, dashing quickly across the stage to give an extra spin to a plate that was beginning to wobble. Not just work, but home-life plates as well.

'It's OK, I have fifteen minutes to spare.' Ian flashed her one of his wide, gorgeous grins that never failed to cheer her up and make her smile back. It was one of the things that had first drawn her to him when they met at university, in a bar during Freshers' Week. That infectious smile, his charm and infallibly cheerful outlook, his cheeky-boy demeanour that made everyone instantly like him – all had attracted her to him, and they'd quickly become best friends. They worked well together, and the business they'd set up a few years after leaving university, once they'd got a bit of real-world experience under their belts, had been a success.

It had been Ian's idea to set it up. Left to herself, Julia would have continued working for other companies, in nine-to-five jobs. That might have given her an easier life, but running your own company was most people's dream, wasn't it?

'So go on then,' she said, opening a notebook to a blank page ready to jot down anything she'd need to follow up on. 'Shoot.'

'OK, well, Mannings were positive. I left them with the slide pack and they're going to look through. They were a little iffy on the licensing fees, but I said we might manage a deal if they signed up for a longer period. They won't take the current version, but they're excited about our planned new release which meets their needs perfectly.'

She nodded and made a note. 'Sounds promising.'

'As for the other two: nothing yet but I'll chase them tomorrow. I'll draft some answers to the questions from Mannings and will run them by you to check I have the technical bits right, then with luck they'll sign on the dotted line by the end of the week.'

'Good stuff.' Another client almost in the bag. Just what she'd hoped for.

'So, I'm going to head off again – sorry for the flying visit! Drew wants a romantic night in. You know what he's like.' That flashing grin again, all white teeth and twinkling eyes.

'A romantic night – what's one of those, then?' Julia asked wryly.

'Aw, Jules, you should try it. I'll babysit if you want to go out.

Or you could send the boys over to stay with us if you wanted a night in, just the two of you. Any time, Jules. Just ask.'

'Thanks. The boys are old enough to be left on their own if we're only out for a few hours in the evening. I guess … we just don't ever have the time.'

'Make time. It's worth it. Offer stands, anyway.'

'Cheers, mate. See you tomorrow – you're in the office, right?'

'Sure, yeah, see you.' Ian leaned over to kiss her cheek as he shrugged his coat back on again and then left.

Her gay business partner kissed her goodbye when he left; her husband of seventeen years didn't. Julia shook her head sharply to stop herself brooding again, and got on with the last small jobs she needed to do before leaving the office for the day. At least she had the promise of a fun evening with Bob ahead of her.

*

Ryan arrived home, his legs caked with mud from his after-school football session. Julia suggested he go and have a shower, but he headed into his bedroom and a few minutes later the sounds of an online game were echoing down the stairs.

Bob arrived shortly after 6.30, when Julia had closed up the office and begun peeling potatoes to go with the defrosted casserole that was now bubbling away in the oven.

'Hi, Sis. Good to see you,' he said, plonking a bottle of good wine on the table and giving her a kiss. 'I've some chocolate for the boys. Are they in their rooms? Where's Marc?'

'Hey, Bob. Ryan's upstairs. Oscar will be home in half an hour or so – at least he'd better be. Marc's got something on, so he won't be joining us for dinner. It's why I had enough for you.'

'Ah, all right. So, let me take this up to Ryan, then I'll get the cork out of that bottle.' He went up the stairs two at a time, while Julia put the potatoes on to boil and set the table. She smiled, knowing Bob loved having a bit of family time on his sporadic visits. He got on well with his nephews; probably better than he got on with his brother-in-law, she thought. Marc and Bob had a prickly relationship. They were too different, perhaps. Or was it that Marc always seemed a little jealous of the close relationship she had with Bob – the lifelong friendship, the shared memories from childhood, the easy camaraderie they had always shared?

Bob returned a moment later. 'Ryan's deep in battle with some sort of alien army,' he reported. 'I got a grunt as thanks for the chocolate which I suppose is better than nothing.' He laughed. 'They get so involved with their computer games, don't they?'

Julia made a face. 'Sometimes I think it's all they're interested in. I'm sure I liked to go out at their age, but this generation's different.'

'Hmm.' Bob looked thoughtful. 'I went somewhere recently that might interest them. Bletchley Park – you know, it was the British headquarters for code breaking during the Second World War. They do tours. It's fascinating.'

Julia smiled. 'I'd love to go somewhere like that.'

'You should take the boys. It's amazing what they achieved there. They reckon the work that went on at Bletchley Park had a huge impact on the outcome of the war. Imagine being a part of that!'

'I'd have loved it.'

'You'd have been good at it, you with your logical computing brain, Sis.'

She flashed him a grin and went to the bottom of the stairs. 'Ryan, make sure you have your shower before dinner! You have thirty minutes, all right?' She turned back to Bob who was uncorking the wine and pouring out a couple of glasses for them.

'So. My news,' he said, as they clinked glasses and he took a seat at the kitchen table. 'I'm selling up in Devon. Going to buy a smaller house, probably in Sussex. I fancy Brighton, or Hove. Somewhere within easy reach of Gatwick as mostly I'll be flying out of there for the foreseeable future. I like the idea of being able to get home after a flight, even if it's only for half a day. Devon's too far.'

'Makes perfect sense,' Julia said, nodding. She'd always wondered why he'd hung on to the big rambling house their grandparents had owned, and which he only managed to visit for a handful of weeks each year.

'Yeah. I should have done it long ago, I suppose. But I love that house and always wondered if one day I'd want to stop flying and settle there. Now, I've decided I won't ever do that. It's too big for just me, anyway.'

Julia opened her mouth to say that maybe one day he'd meet someone, but he held up his hand to stop her. 'Don't. I'm happy being alone. Anyway, that's not the point. What I wanted to tell you about is that I've begun the process of clearing the house. I know you won't want any of the old furniture, but there are a few things … memorabilia, really, that I wondered if you'd take. You're the family historian.'

'Am I?' Julia considered. It was true that she'd compiled a family tree on Ancestry, and had hung on to the boxes of photos their widowed father had wanted to ditch when he decided to move to Spain a few years before. One day, she'd sort through them. One day, when she had time.

'Well, more than I am, anyway. So, I've brought you a few things. Some old photos of Grandpa's. A box of old books. I know you love anything that smells musty and has pages falling out.'

'Ha! I do if they're interesting books!' Another activity for when she had more time: browsing second-hand bookshops, collecting and reading old books.

'They're in the car. Shall I bring them in?'

'Go on, then. I'll sort through it all sometime.' When she'd have opportunity, she had no idea. But the house had a big attic so there was plenty of space to store it until that mythical future time when her life was organised and weekends were free.

'Great.' Bob was already on his feet, and a minute later came back through the front door carrying two boxes, a smaller one balanced on top of a larger one. The bigger box contained books, and the other was photographs. He dumped the boxes on the floor in the hallway.

'What's this?' Julia tugged at a brown canvas case with a worn leather strap that was on top of the photos.

'An old camera,' Bob said. 'A Box Brownie, by the look of it.'

'Must have been Grandma's. Grandpa had that old Leica that he was so proud of.'

Bob nodded. 'I remember. Probably Grandma's, then. It's a pretty old model, probably pre-war.'

Chapter 2

Pamela, 1943

There was an hour to go before dinner time. Time enough, Pamela thought, to look through the latest set of photographs she'd picked up from the chemists and arrange them in her album. She adored her old Box Brownie camera that her father had passed on to her, when he'd bought a newer model. Hers worked well still, and she loved capturing happy moments with her friends. 'A reminder,' she'd said to her brother Geoff, 'that we can look back on, and see that despite the war we still had fun.'

And these photos certainly proved that. Pam chuckled as she flicked through them. There was Geoff, silhouetted against the sky on a hillside near their village. Her friends Ada and Emily, clutching each other and laughing at something – Pam couldn't remember what, but the photo made her laugh all over again. Ada and Emily again, along with Joan, sitting on a rug on a fine day they'd had two months ago when they'd bicycled miles and then had a picnic. And another one, of herself, that Ada had taken on that same day, her legs astride a bicycle and her mouth open wide. She was calling out instructions to Ada on how to use the camera, she remembered, and Ada must have taken the snap at just the wrong moment. Pam had wanted her to wait until she was cycling, and try to get an action shot.

She looked carefully at each photo and picked out the best ones to go in her album. The others she tucked back in their envelope. She had one more spare film to put in her camera, so she opened up the back of the camera, pulled out the end of the film and wound it on ready for the next photo. It was becoming harder to buy film, so she'd have to make this roll last.

'Pammy! Dinner's ready, love,' her mother's voice sang up the stairs.

'Coming.' She put her photos, album and camera back onto the shelf she stored them on, and hurried downstairs. Mum was putting dishes on the table – a pie, a dish of mashed potatoes, another of boiled carrots. The vegetables had been grown in their garden. Pam took her place at the table alongside Geoff. Her dad came through from the sitting room and took his place at the head while Mum served up the food.

'Everyone have a good day?' Dad said, looking around the table.

'Just the usual,' Mum replied.

Pam nodded. 'Yes, a good day.'

'Only another week to go, eh, Pammy? And then you'll have left school for good.' Dad smiled at her across the table.

'Still thinking of going to university?' Mum asked, with a frown. Pam had been offered a place at Somerville College, Oxford, to read mathematics. Her mother had never been very comfortable with the idea – thinking that a girl should do secretarial work, find a man to marry, and then keep house for him. As she had. But Pam's father, a schoolteacher, had encouraged her to make the most of her talents and apply to Oxford. She'd been amazed and delighted to be accepted.

'Yes, of course. I can't waste the place I've been offered.'

'But when you find a husband and have a family, it'll all be for nothing. I'm sorry, I just don't see the point.' Mum shook her head, and then lifted a forkful of pie to her mouth.

They'd been over this so many times. Mum was from another generation, and things were different now. Women had more opportunity. Especially during the war, when women were taking on so many jobs that had previously been open only to men. Pam smiled at her mother. She didn't want to start an argument over the dinner table. 'Maybe I won't find a husband. Maybe I will, but won't have a family so I can continue working. Who knows, Mum, what the future holds? For now, I want to make the most of my brain.'

'And you're right to do so,' Dad said. 'Elsie, we just need to accept that the young want to make their own choices nowadays. Let Pammy go to university and study mathematics. If she ends up a blue-stocking all her life then so be it. As long as she's happy, that's the most important thing, isn't it?'

Pam glanced at her mother. She'd have to agree that her children's happiness was of paramount importance, and indeed, Mum nodded in response. Pam reached out a hand to her. 'Thanks, Mum. I want you to be happy for me, and not worry.'

'I'm happy for you, Pam,' her brother Geoff interjected. 'And actually, I have a bit of news of my own today.'

'Oh yes?' Dad looked at him expectantly.

'I've signed up. Been thinking about it for ages. I've signed up with the RAF. I'm going to train to be a pilot.'

There was a stunned silence at the table as everyone let that news sink in. Pam's first thoughts were that her brother was the bravest man she knew, and she was proud of him for doing his bit for the war effort. Her second thoughts were of the multitude of pilots and crew who never made it back from their missions. Every day the newspapers gave more numbers of those who were lost.

At last Dad answered him, positively, although his voice sounded a little strangled as though he was forcing the words out. 'Well done, son. Proud of you.'

'Yes, I'm proud too,' Mum said. 'But you'll take care, won't you? I mean …' Pam noticed tears glistening at the corners of her eyes.

'Of course I will. I leave next week for training. It'll be three months before I'm trained up. Maybe the war will end by then.'

'Not much chance of that, I'm afraid.'

'Geoff, I think you're jolly brave.' Pam turned to smile at her brother. 'I'm also very proud of you.' But his news had made her wonder … was she being selfish by going to university? Should she be doing something for the war effort too? Emily was planning on moving to London and driving ambulances. Ada had a job working in a canteen on a nearby air base and was thinking about joining the Women's Auxiliary Air Force. There were land girls working on the local farms. Pam felt a twinge of guilt that she'd be doing nothing for the country, and merely indulging her love of maths.

She switched her attention back to Geoff, who was talking about his experiences signing up, and the reaction he'd had at his job at an engineering works when he'd told them. 'They all understand it, you know. Even though we're in a reserved occupation, they really understood my need to do something that could really make a difference. I'm young, I have fast reactions and perfect eyesight. I could be really good as a fighter pilot.'

'It's just so dangerous, love,' Mum said, but she whispered it quietly, pushed away a tear and then smiled at her son. 'But you will certainly be good at it, I know.'

*

That last week of school, before study leave began, was full of mixed emotions for Pam. Excitement that a new stage of her life was soon to begin. Trepidation about the forthcoming exams and worry that she might not get the grades necessary to take her place at Oxford. Sadness at leaving school, saying goodbye to friends and teachers she might not see again. Fear, when the air-raid siren went off in the middle of her last maths lesson and the entire class had to hurry to an air-raid shelter, where the teacher, Miss Osbourne, tried her best to finish the lesson.

It was after that lesson, when the class emerged blinking into the sunlight and headed homeward (it was the last lesson of the day), that Miss Osbourne took Pam to one side. 'A quick word, please, before you leave, Pamela.'

'Of course, miss,' Pam replied, feeling a pang of nervousness. Had she done something wrong? Why was she being kept back? Miss Osbourne led the way back into the school building, and to her deserted classroom. She bade Pam take a seat, while she perched on the edge of her desk.

'You will no doubt do very well in your maths exam,' Miss Osbourne said. 'You are one of the brightest pupils I have ever had the pleasure of teaching. You will do brilliantly at Oxford, I am sure.' She hesitated, and Pam frowned a little, sensing a 'but' coming.

'Thank you, miss. I will work hard, to make you proud.'

'I'm already proud of you. So, there was just one thing I wanted to talk to you about ...'

Here was the 'but'. Pam felt dread clutch at her stomach – was Miss Osbourne going to tell her some reason she couldn't take her place at university, even if she passed the exam? 'What is it, miss?'

'My father works, erm, for the government. I met up with him last weekend, and he was talking about a recruitment drive. They need young people who are good at maths, especially if they also have an aptitude for languages.' The teacher smiled at Pam. 'He could have been describing you. I hear from the other staff that you excel in both German and French.'

'I ... I do all right in them, I suppose.' Pam felt herself blushing. She managed well in all subjects, she knew, but maths had always been her favourite. This was due in part to Miss Osbourne, a teacher she'd always loved and looked up to.

'You are too modest. Look, this work my father does, it's for the war effort. I don't know what he does exactly, actually I don't really know what he does at all. He's very cagey about it. But he did ask me if I could recommend anyone to him. They're taking girls as well as boys.'

'But what about Oxford?' Pam was confused. It had been Miss Osbourne who'd encouraged her strongly to apply to the university.

'They will defer your place. When all this is over you will be able to go. Listen, you don't have to apply. You can just take up your university place as planned. But if you did want to do something for the war effort, this could be just the thing. Not everyone has your brain, and from what Father says, your brain would be put to very good use.'

Pam was silent a moment, considering. She had been wondering about doing more for her country. Now here was something she could do – whatever it was. And if she could defer her place …

'What do you think?' Miss Osbourne tilted her head to one side, the way she so often did when waiting for a student to give the solution to a question she'd posed them.

'I … I don't know …' Pam shook her head. 'What would you advise?'

'It has to be your choice, but I can't help but think, in your shoes, I would want to feel I'd done my bit. There's an opportunity here, to help your country. Just for a year, maybe. And then go and take your place at Oxford.'

'Are you sure they'll defer the place?'

'Absolutely. In these circumstances, there is no problem at all with putting it off for a year or two.'

Pam scratched her chin. 'And what about this project – the work? What would I be doing?'

Miss Osbourne shrugged. 'That, I'm afraid, I cannot tell you. It's all very hush-hush. But to my mind, that sounds exciting, don't you think?'

Pam had to admit that it did. Helping the war effort on a

secret project, that she could do because of her mathematical ability. She made a snap decision. 'Yes, it does. And I'd like to try … what do I need to do?'

Miss Osbourne grinned at her. 'That's my girl. I will put your name forward to my father. Then we'll see what happens next. I'd imagine there's some sort of interview process. It'll be away from home, you understand. My father lives in Buckinghamshire, so I suppose the project is based somewhere near where he lives.'

'I'd have to leave home to go to university anyway,' Pam said thoughtfully. She'd spent the last few months imagining herself among the spires of Oxford. Now she might be going to Buckinghamshire, which was not a county she was familiar with. But it all depended on getting through this interview process Miss Osbourne spoke of, of course. 'Yes, miss. Please put my name forward. Of course I would like to take my exams first, though.'

'Of course. I'll make sure my father knows you're not available until they're over. What date is your last one?'

'Tenth of June,' she replied. A date she'd had circled in her diary for a long time. She, along with Ada, Emily and several other girls, had planned a cycle ride that afternoon, after the final exam. A bike ride along a canal towpath, then a picnic beside some woodland. That evening there was due to be a dance in the village hall, to which they were all going. Pam had made herself a new dress for the occasion – well, she'd taken an old one of her mother's apart and remade it in a more up-to-date style. It was better than nothing.

'All right. Then I shall pass on your details.' Miss Osbourne stood up, and then as though on impulse caught Pam's hands and hauled her to her feet and into an embrace. 'Best of luck, Pamela. With the exam, the interview, the job, the degree course, and with the rest of your life. You deserve to do well, you know. It's been a pleasure teaching you.'

Pam was astonished to hear a slight crack in her teacher's voice at these words. She'd always thought teachers saw their pupils as nothing more than sausage meat to be processed, not individuals, but here was Miss Osbourne sounding genuinely emotional.

'Miss, we can stay in touch. I'll see you at the exams, and then I'll write and let you know how I get on.'

'I'd like that, Pamela. Well, I must be off now. Don't forget to do plenty of revision. You'll pass easily, but revision will be key to you getting top grades.' The older woman released her and stood back to let Pam leave the classroom first.

'Bye, miss. And thank you, for everything.'

Pam walked home with a skip in her step. Now she had two possible futures: one in which she went straight to university, and one in which university was deferred until after the war was over, while she did top-secret work for the war effort. She, little old Pamela Jackson, working for the government against the Nazis! Who'd have thought it! She couldn't wait to tell her family … but then she stopped, thinking … no. She couldn't tell her family. Not now. She should wait and see what happens, take the interview, see if she got the job, before telling them anything. If it was all as hush-hush as Miss Osbourne had implied, then it'd be better if she said nothing at all for now.

*

The weeks of study leave passed agonisingly slowly and yet at the same time, sped by. Pam spent her days revising hard, only meeting up with Ada and Emily for short periods to give herself a break. Every day when the post came she wondered if there'd be anything for her, about this mysterious secret work. A note from Miss Osbourne, perhaps, or from her father, or someone else who'd been given her details. But as the weeks wore on and nothing happened, she began to forget all about it. Perhaps, after all, Miss Osbourne's father had not been interested in an eighteen-year-old girl who happened to be good at maths. Besides, there were the exams to keep her mind occupied.

At last the tenth of June rolled around, and with it the last exam, and the long-awaited bike ride and picnic at which she took more photographs of her friends, and the dance in the evening. Her exams had gone well, Pam thought, and she was hopeful of high grades. Not so Ada, who was bemoaning her lack of revision. At a dance earlier in the summer Ada had met an American airman stationed nearby and had spent far too much of her study leave with him.

It was a good day, all in all, and Pam fell into her bed late that night exhausted and happy, looking forward to the summer before heading off to Oxford in the autumn. A bright future awaited her.

The letter came the following morning. It was on official, headed notepaper, and invited her to an interview at a place named Bletchley Park in Buckinghamshire. It referenced a Charles Osbourne, who, Pam realised, must be Miss Osbourne's father. So her name had been put through, and now she had an interview! After so many weeks of hearing nothing she'd given up on the idea of doing secret war work but now here was a chance again. The interview was scheduled for early the following week. She might as well go, she decided. It would be an interesting experience even if they didn't offer her a job. She sent Miss Osbourne a note to tell her, but decided against mentioning it to her family or friends until things were more settled. It might all come to nothing yet.

But every time she thought of it, she felt a surge of excitement. The chance of doing useful war work, mathematical work that she was suited to, was a thrilling prospect.

Chapter 3

Julia

Julia opened the worn fabric case and removed the camera, a black box with a tiny viewfinder on the top and a small round lens on the front. It looked nothing like any camera she'd ever held before. A marking on the back said it was a Kodak Brownie No. 2.

'Sounds like quite an early model,' she said, turning it over in her hands. She looked through the viewfinder on the top. The image was reversed. There was another little window on the back of it with a number displayed. 'Look at this, Bob. Does that mean there's film still in it?'

'Let me see?' Bob leaned over to see what she was looking at. 'Yes, I think there might be.'

'Wonder how you open it? Hold on.' If there was one thing Julia had learned in recent years, it was that you could find out anything on the internet. She quickly grabbed her laptop and typed in how to change a film brownie no 2 and with delight found a short YouTube video that showed her exactly what to do. 'Right, so you twist this …' She turned a key on the side of the camera which advanced the film. 'And then open the back.'

There was a clip at the back and once the camera was open, she could see that there was indeed a film still in it. 'I'd love to know what's on this.'

Bob grinned. 'Probably more snaps like these ones.' He picked up a handful of the little black-and-white prints that were loose in the box. They mostly showed scenery – distant mountains, lakes, a few buildings and statues. Some showed people – young women with 1940s hairstyles, men with baggy trousers and Brylcreemed hair, sitting on picnic rugs or playing cricket on a lawn.

'Wow. I don't know who any of these people are,' Julia said. 'Although, is that Grandma?' She pointed to a young woman who was sitting astride a bicycle, her head thrown back as though she was laughing.

'Yes. Think so. Well, I'll leave them with you to sort through, Sis. You might be able to get that film developed, too. I bet there are companies who still handle that type of film. Google, and you'll find one.'

'Yes. I'll do that.' Lord knew when she'd find time, but she would, eventually. Julia followed the instructions on the YouTube video for removing the film, tucked the film into an envelope and put the camera back in its case. 'Come on, then. Dinner's almost ready. I'm going to have to text Oscar to hurry him along; he loses track of time when he's round at his mates.'

'Ha. I was just the same, remember? Only I'd come home late, to a cold dinner left on the table, that I'd have to microwave.'

'You were a terror,' Julia agreed, laughing. 'Thankfully Oscar's so fond of his food he'll hurry back.' She picked up her phone and sent a text, then busied herself setting the table for dinner. Bob immediately got to his feet and began arranging cutlery, fetching plates and glasses. Julia couldn't help but compare him with Marc, who would have just carried on sitting while she laid the table around him, unless she specifically asked him to help. It was usually easier to just do it herself.

Oscar arrived home just as Julia was dishing up the dinner. 'Hi, Mum. Oh, hello, Uncle Bob. Where's Dad?'

'Out,' Julia said. Oscar shrugged in acknowledgement and sat down to eat. Over dinner, Bob asked both boys about their lives: the football teams they supported, their music tastes, the computer games they liked to play. Julia listened quietly, storing away tidbits of information. The boys were of an age where it was considered uncool to have any kind of conversation with their parents, at least with their mum, but Uncle Bob was still cool, being an airline pilot. Also, he was well up on the latest gaming consoles and games, which impressed them. He'd once explained to Julia that when he was stuck in hotel rooms around the world between flights, he'd pass the time by playing on his Nintendo Switch. Julia had at least heard of this console; Oscar had been clamouring for one for ages.

It was a pleasant evening. The boys disappeared up to their rooms along with the chocolate Bob had brought them, and Julia and Bob spent a little more time flicking through the photos and letters and books from their grandparents' attic.

'She was quite a looker in her youth, wasn't she?' Bob said, looking at a wedding photo from the late 1940s. In it, Pamela was holding on to her new husband's arm, gazing up at him, while the expression on his face was one of total adoration.

'She certainly was. Grandpa was punching above his weight, bless him. But they were very much in love, even in their eighties.' Julia wondered whether she and Marc would be that close, at the ends of their lives. They had been, in the early days. And then bringing up children, work, running a business, looking after a large house … had it all got in the way of their love? Was that what had gone wrong between them? Because she had to admit, if only to herself, that things had gone wrong between her and Marc. Maybe it was her own fault, taking on too much with the business and everything, when she ought to concentrate more on her family. Perhaps she was guilty of trying to have it all. She earned more than Marc, far more. She paid most of the mortgage and financed all the holidays and latest gaming consoles for the boys. Sometimes Marc acted as though he was jealous of her earning abilities. His own job, in local government IT, was never likely to command a high salary.

'You all right, Sis?' Bob had somehow picked up on her concern.

She shook herself and forced a smile. 'Yeah, I'm all right. A bit pissed off with Marc, if I'm honest. He could help a little more, around the house.'

'Perhaps you need a rota. The boys could do more as well. In fact ...' Bob got up and went to the foot of the stairs, calling for Oscar and Ryan to come down. They came immediately. They wouldn't have done so for Julia, she realised.

Bob muttered something to them that Julia couldn't hear. The boys glanced at her as he spoke, and then dutifully trooped into the kitchen where Ryan began loading the dishwasher while Oscar washed saucepans in the sink.

'Every day, right, lads? If your mum's cooked for you, you clear up after. And it'll be worth your while come Christmas, like I said.'

'Yeah, great, thanks, Uncle Bob. Chuck us that tea towel, Ryan,' Oscar said, and Julia watched in astonishment as Oscar proceeded to dry up the pans he'd just washed. Whatever Bob had bribed them with had worked.

'Report back to me if they slacken off,' Bob said to Julia.

'Oh, I shall. Thanks.' It was a small thing, but one less job for her to do herself.

The boys finished and went back upstairs, but a moment later Oscar came back down, with an armful of washing. He went out to the utility room with it. Julia grinned at Bob. 'You are amazing. I'm not even going to ask what you said to them.'

Bob just smiled and tapped the side of his nose.

*

The following evening, with Bob gone and Marc at home, the boys once more cleared the table and loaded the dishwasher after dinner without being asked.

'What's all this?' Marc said, watching them. 'Oy, careful!' Ryan had clattered a couple of plates together as he worked. 'Maybe let your mum do it, eh?'

'Marc, no. They're old enough to help out. Bob suggested they do some jobs around the house, so I don't have to do it all. They're perfectly capable.'

'Not if they smash all our plates. Those cost me a tenner each.'

'Cost me a tenner each, I think you mean.' Marc knew perfectly well that Julia had bought the new crockery, after a business deal had brought in a large bonus.

'I don't need reminding that you earn more than me, thank you, Julia.' Marc left the room leaving Julia staring after him. The boys sniggered a little, sounding embarrassed.

When the kitchen was cleared she went through to the sitting room where Marc was lying stretched out, taking up the whole sofa, a rugby match playing on the TV. She perched on an armchair. 'How was the leaving do?'

'Hmm? What leaving do?'

'Yesterday. The one you were at yesterday evening, the reason you missed dinner.'

'Ah yes. It was OK.'

'Whose was it, anyway?'

'Oh, er, Mike's. Chap you don't know.'

'Oh. Well, the boys and I had a fun evening with Bob. He brought me a few old things that used to belong to our grandparents. Photos, and an old camera. It has an undeveloped film inside. I'm going to see if …'

'YES! What a try!' Marc twisted round to a sitting position and clapped his hands loudly.

'What?'

'Munster just scored. I'm not a fan of theirs but that was spectacular.'

'I was talking to you!' Good God, the man could be infuriating. Julia stood deliberately in front of the TV. Marc craned his neck to look around her.

'Get out of the way. I've missed the replay of that try now!'

'You've seen it once. Come on, Marc, I was talking to you. Didn't see you all day yesterday, you missed seeing Bob, and now you're just ignoring me and watching a game you don't even care about.'

'Glad you had a nice evening.' Marc was still trying to look around her, his concentration 90 per cent on the TV.

'Bob asked after you. He'd have liked to see you too.'

'Right. I was ... GO ON, MY SON! YESSS!!' Marc punched the air.

'Fuck's sake, Marc! I'm trying to have a conversation with you!'

'And I'm trying to watch the rugby. Maybe pick a better time, hey? I was back from work by 5.30 today, but you were still holed up in your office till nearly seven. That might have been a better time.' He turned towards her, finally giving her his full attention. 'It works both ways, Jules. We both need to make more time for each other, I suppose. We will. But right now ...' He gestured towards the TV where the teams were just setting themselves up for a scrum very close to the try-line.

If she said anything more it'd turn into a full-blown row, and anyway, he was right. They did need to make more time for each other. Date nights, as Ian had suggested. But God only knew when that would work out. She turned and left the sitting room, went to the kitchen and poured herself a glass of wine left over from the previous night with Bob. She was breaking her own rule of no drinking on a 'school night' unless there was a good excuse such as a visitor. 'Oh, who cares?' she muttered, raising her glass to herself.

She glanced at the office door. Normally she didn't work in the evenings, preferring to keep that as family time, but with the boys upstairs doing homework or, more likely, playing video games, and Marc clearly not wanting to spend time with her, she might as well. She was part way through the technical design of a new part of the system, designed to handle debits to suppliers. A couple of hours on that before bed would put her in a good position to go through the design with Barry the next day. He was good at spotting potential pitfalls in what she suggested. She unlocked the door and went through to the office, taking her glass of wine with her. Sometimes a little alcohol freed up the creative side of her brain, and system design definitely involved a bit of creativity at certain stages.

Soon she was deeply immersed in her work, the argument with Marc forgotten and the wine half drunk beside her desk. The time passed quickly.

'What on earth are you doing? Isn't working dawn till dusk enough for you? Got to work all evening instead of spending it with me now?'

The rugby match must be over, she thought. Marc was standing in the doorway to the office, glaring at her.

'You didn't seem interested in spending time with me earlier, so I thought I'd come in here and do something useful.'

'Could have ironed my shirts if you were that desperate for something to do.'

He had to be joking, didn't he? Julia stared at him for a moment, until he burst out laughing. 'Had you there, didn't I? Your face – all that righteous feminist anger bubbling over. I've done my shirts myself. Since you were closeted in here and the match was over. So, another glass of wine?' He produced a newly opened bottle from behind his back and without waiting for an answer crossed the room and poured it into her glass, on top of the dregs of the old bottle. It was on the tip of her tongue to snap at him for this – he knew she preferred to finish one glass first and not mix the wines. But she was grateful he'd done the ironing. One less job for her.

'Cheers, Marc.' She clinked her glass against the bottle he was holding. 'I'll just close this down and then I'll come and join you. It's only 9.30. Plenty of evening left.'

'Yep. Don't be long, then.' He smiled and winked at her, and she was reminded of the man she'd married. They'd been good together, in those early days.

*

They'd met a couple of years after Julia left university. She'd been at a party thrown by someone she worked with, drinking warm white wine in a crowded kitchen. She was being chatted up by someone who was probably very nice but who had such bad breath she found herself flinching away from him every time he spoke. Eventually, unable to bear it any longer, she'd made an excuse, gone to use the downstairs loo, then made her way through the sitting room where the party was spilling out through patio doors into the garden. It was a cool night but she had enough alcohol in her bloodstream not to notice. She wandered to the end of the garden, tipped her head back and breathed in the fresh air. Above her, the constellation of Orion stood tall and proud.

'Lovely clear night, isn't it?'

She turned to find a good-looking man of her own age, holding two glasses and a bottle of wine. 'Fancy a drink? My name's Marc.'

'Yes, why not? And I'm Julia,' she answered. She'd left her last drink in the kitchen, beside smelly-breath man, and certainly didn't intend going back to retrieve it.

He smiled and poured her a glass. It was a Pinot Noir from Martinborough, New Zealand, and ever afterwards they would drink a bottle of wine from that region on the anniversary of their meeting. 'Cheers. So, Julia, you're a star-gazer?'

'Not usually, but I needed some air.'

'Plenty of it out here.' He took a step back. 'Oh, did you want to be alone? Let me know if I'm intruding. I'd hate you to think …'

'No, it's all right.' She smiled in what she hoped was a welcoming way. 'So tell me, Marc, what's your favourite constellation?'

'Do you know, I have never given that question a moment's thought before now. Let me think ... oh yes. Has to be Cassiopeia. It's like a big M for Marc. Also M for Morrison, my surname. Look, there.'

'And I always thought that was a W. Well, you live and learn.'

He'd laughed good-naturedly at that, and she'd thought that here was a man she'd like to see again, a man she'd like to get to know. They'd married three years later.

It had been fun, back then, getting to know each other. Building a life together, establishing little routines and habits. When they'd had time for each other. Before the demands of home-owning, family life and running a business, before everything else took over and squeezed out what they'd had together.

If they worked on it, they could get back to how things were, surely? It was just a case of coming up with a better split of household chores, and making sure the boys began picking up their share of it. Making time for each other.

But a niggling voice at the back of her head reminded her that it was more than that; Marc needed to give her more respect for her job and her contribution to the family finances. She didn't mind doing at least half of the chores – what she resented was doing all of the chores, even though she worked the same or often more hours than Marc. She saved her work and closed her laptop, then followed him through to the sitting room. He had indeed done some ironing. The board was still out, and the iron cooling down. The laundry basket was on the sofa and almost empty – he'd done the boys' school shirts as well as all his own things.

'Sorry I haven't done your blouse. It's silk, isn't it? I'd probably wreck it.' He looked contrite, as though regretful of his earlier grumpiness.

She'd been as bad as him, if she was honest. 'Thanks, love.'

Marc moved the laundry basket to the floor. He sat down and

patted the sofa beside him for her to join him. She snuggled into his arm, enjoying what seemed increasingly a rare cuddle. 'This is nice,' she murmured. 'We should do this more often. Perhaps we should book in date nights or something? The boys are old enough to leave at home alone.'

'Typical Julia,' Marc said, though there was amusement in his voice. 'Always wanting to plan, to get something in the diary. Didn't we used to be more spontaneous?'

'We did, yeah. Then life got in the way. Hey …' She twisted in his arms and kissed him. 'We could be spontaneous tonight … get an early night together … it's been a while.' She stroked his thigh with her hand as she spoke. Now that she'd had the idea, suddenly she found she really wanted him. It had been ages – a month, or more – since they'd been intimate, she realised. They were letting that side of their relationship slip, and maybe that was half of the problem?

Marc put his hand on top of hers and held it. 'Let's just sit here a while and drink this wine. Not sure I'm in the mood for anything else. It was a tough day at work, Julia, and now I just want to unwind a bit, with no demands on me.'

'Oh. Another time, then.' Disappointed, she turned away, removed her hand and picked up her wine. She resolved to make more of an effort. Perhaps she was working too much and should put her husband first for a while. It was difficult though, given that she ran her own business. It wasn't something you could just switch off from at five o'clock.

*

It wasn't until Sunday, when Marc had gone out for a run, that Julia had time to research where to send that old Box Brownie film. The boys were both at friends' houses, and Marc had declared he was doing a long run, and would be out for a couple of hours, so Julia was alone in the house. There were, as always, chores that needed doing – the bathrooms to clean, the stairs to vacuum – but right now she wanted to investigate what she could do with that film. She made herself a cup of tea and settled down to a spot of Googling.

Within minutes she'd found a company that would develop her film, and it was a quick job to print off an address label, package up the film and get it ready to send. The prints wouldn't come back for at least a week.

'I wonder what's on it,' she muttered to herself. Probably more snaps like the others Bob had brought her. But maybe there'd be ones of their grandfather as a young man, or of Grandma's parents. It'd be interesting to see what the previous generation looked like – Julia's great-grandparents. She wondered too, why this film had been left in the camera and never finished or developed. Perhaps Grandma had forgotten all about it. Well, Julia could pop out during her lunch break the next day and take it to the Post Office.

Chapter 4

Pamela

On the day of her interview, Pam told her family she was going up to Oxford to research accommodation. That was something she'd need to do soon anyway, if the interview wasn't successful, but she'd worry about that later. It was over an hour and a half by train to Bletchley, as from her home in Reading she had to go into London and then out again, but she'd caught a train with plenty of time to spare. The letter had told her she'd be met off the train at Bletchley station, so on arrival there she stood on the platform looking up and down it, wondering who would be meeting her.

She wasn't the only one doing this. There were a number of other girls looking as lost as she felt. Pam took a few tentative steps towards the nearest, but at that moment the train whistled loudly, making her jump, and then it pulled away. She waited for it to leave and the noise and steam to subside, and then realised the girls were gathering near the station exit, and there was a young man in a brown suit standing among them. He had a clipboard and seemed to be ticking names off, so she approached him.

'Excuse me, I am expecting to be met; is my name on your list?'

The young man smiled at her, his eyes crinkling in a friendly manner behind his spectacles. 'If you tell me what your name is, perhaps I'll be able to check it for you?'

She blushed. 'Oh, of course. I'm Pamela Jackson.'

He nodded and made a mark on his paper. 'Yes, you're here. And now I think we have everyone. I'm sorry, there was no transport available but it's only a short walk and the weather's fine. If you'd like to follow me please, ladies.' The young man led the way out of the station and a short distance along a road. Pam noticed a good-looking fair-haired man strolling casually along the road in the opposite direction. He smiled at them as he passed, and doffed an imaginary cap.

A little further on was a gated driveway. A sentry box stood to one side, and at their approach a guard stepped out. Pam noticed that the boundary to this property, whatever it was, was marked by a double barbed-wire fence.

'This all looks a bit serious,' a girl who'd been walking alongside Pam whispered. 'All this security.'

Their escort was showing the sentry a pass, and his list of names. The sentry counted them, checked them all off against the list, and then opened the gate to allow them to enter. They were then led up a tree-lined drive that passed a small lake on the left-hand side. It was all very pretty, but then Pam looked to her right, where several large, ugly concrete blocks had been built. Behind them was a large Victorian country house with a gravel forecourt. There were people everywhere, coming out of huts and into other ones, cycling around, carrying folders or boxes of papers. Some were in uniform – she spotted girls in the uniform of the Women's Royal Naval Service, affectionately known as Wrens – but most were not.

'What on earth is this place?' she whispered to the girl beside her.

'I suspect we're about to find out.' The other girl smiled at her as they followed their escort into the old house, where they were led into a large room where rows of chairs were placed facing a trestle table, behind which a man wearing round glasses was sitting. He stood as they entered, and bade them all take a seat. Once they were all sitting down, he stood in front of them to address them.

'Welcome to Bletchley Park. You've all been asked to come here for an interview, I hope. Some of you are in the Women's Royal Naval Service, some of you are civilians. All of you are here on recommendation – because you have the right sort of brain, that we here at BP can make great use of. The work we do here is highly secret, so I'm afraid I cannot at this point tell you very much about it. We're going to interview you individually, and should you be successful and want to take the job, you'll be required to sign the Official Secrets Act. Only then will you learn what your role here will be, and even then, it's only on a "need to know" basis.' He paused, and gazed around the room, catching everyone's eye. Pam forced herself not to look away – it made you look guilty if you couldn't hold someone's gaze, she thought, even if you had nothing to be guilty about. 'Anyone who does not think they are able to keep secrets, or who does not think they'd be able to work under these conditions, should make themselves known to my assistant Edwin Denham, who will then escort you back to the railway station.' He indicated the young man with the pleasant smile who'd brought them from the station.

There were a few murmurings among the girls, but no one got up to leave, and the man in glasses smiled as though he was pleased to see it. He then nodded at his assistant and went through a door into another room. Pam guessed that was where he would be conducting the interviews, and indeed, Denham called out a name and showed the girl into that room.

There was nothing to do now but wait for her turn. Pam felt her palms grow sweaty. She turned to the girl beside her, a studious-looking young woman with thick spectacles and her hair pulled into a tight bun. 'Hi. I'm Pam. I'm pretty nervous, how about you?'

The other girl looked her up and down. 'Not at all. And if everything here is so secret, you probably oughtn't to give your name out like that.'

Pam's mouth dropped open in astonishment. She'd only given her first name, she wanted to retort. And presumably all who'd been called here for interview must have been checked out first, before they were invited?

'Don't mind her.' The girl on her other side was speaking. 'I'm nervous, too. But we'll be all right, I'm sure. Are you in the Wrens?'

'No, I've just finished at school.'

'I finished last year. I was working on my parents' estate for a while, but then decided to join the Wrens, you know, to do something useful. As soon as I'd finished my two weeks' basic training they suggested I come here. I'm fluent in German. I think that's why they wanted me. I'm Clarissa, by the way.' The other girl held out her hand, and Pam shook it gratefully, glad that not everyone was as unfriendly as the bespectacled girl on her left. Clarissa's accent was cut-glass. And that mention of her parents' estate suggested she was from an upper-class family. Yet she seemed down-to-earth and friendly and Pam immediately warmed to her.

'Clarissa Morton?' Denham called out, scanning the room.

Clarissa jumped up. 'Oh! My turn. There you are you see, it's all right to let everyone here know your name.' She cast a dazzling smile at Pam and went off for her interview.

*

Soon it was Pam's turn. The interviewer introduced himself as Max Newman, and explained he was head of a section at Bletchley Park that was expanding, and they needed bright young women to work in it. 'As I explained, I can't say exactly what you'd be doing yet. But I see here' – he tapped a sheet of paper in front of him – 'that you have a natural flair for mathematics, is that right?'

'Erm, yes, sir, I think I am reasonably proficient.' She blushed. Blowing her own trumpet, as her mother would put it, had never come easily to her.

Mr Newman smiled. 'You are too modest. I have here a report from your maths teacher that suggests you are the ablest pupil she has ever taught. In addition to this you've studied German, I believe?'

'I have, sir, yes, but I can't say I'm fluent in it.'

'French too. So, an ability with languages. And can you keep secrets? Even from your parents, your siblings, and your friends?'

'Sir, yes I think I can.' Pam hoped she hadn't sounded too hesitant.

Mr Newman smiled and leaned closer across the table. 'Could you even keep secrets from people you are working alongside? I mean, if you were instructed to do one task, and the girl at the next table was doing something different, would you be able to keep from her exactly what it is you are doing, and refrain from asking her what she was doing?'

'Sir, if that was the requirement, yes I think I could do that. Though if both of us were employed on different aspects of the same problem, I think it might be better if we were able to discuss it and share ideas.' She mentally kicked herself as soon as she'd said this. It was probably the wrong thing. Too outspoken. She was supposed to be reassuring him she could keep secrets.

But to her astonishment Mr Newman laughed and put out his hand to shake hers. 'Capital, young lady. That's just what I want to hear. We have to keep secrets here, but we also have to share our knowledge and ideas, in order to gain the best results in the quickest time. I am all for discussion among my staff. Miss—' here, he referred to his piece of paper once more '—Jackson. I think you will fit in very well indeed.' He scribbled on a piece of paper and handed it to Pam. 'So, if you are happy to take up a place here, go through that door and hand this to the Wren sitting at the desk. She'll go through the Official Secrets Act with you. Then Denham will escort you back to the station, and we'd like you to report here to work on Thursday if possible, next Monday at the latest.' He looked up at her. 'That's all right, is it? We will arrange a billet for you then. You'll be joining the Wrens. Pack a suitcase of enough clothes for a few months. Although we do allow a couple of days' leave every now and again.' He smiled and waved her away.

Grinning, she went through to the other office he'd indicated and handed over the slip of paper. To her delight Clarissa was sitting in that room too, along with a couple of others. 'You've got the job, then?' Clarissa said, and Pam nodded.

'Yes, and I've to start on Thursday!'

'Same here. They're wasting no time at all.'

'We're certainly not,' said the Wren sitting at the desk. 'Jerry's not going to hang about waiting for us to recruit enough staff, is he? Now I need you to wait until the interviews are over, so I can cover the OSA once for you all. It's essential you pay the closest attention to what I have to say.' She fixed Pam with a stern stare. 'Of course, nothing you hear or see here can be communicated to your friends, family or anyone else. The penalties for doing so are extremely severe.'

'I understand,' Pam said, terrified her voice sounded shaky. She took a seat beside Clarissa who grinned at her.

'Well done. I'm so glad you got the job. I think it could be a lot of fun here – even if it does turn out to be hard work.'

Pam thought so too, but then she remembered that taking this job would mean she'd have to defer her place at Oxford University. Defer the dream that she'd held for so long. It was odd to be voluntarily making the decision to put it off, but it felt like the right thing to do. If she could help her country, then that's what she should do.

Twenty minutes later the interviews were complete, and those who'd been successful were seated in front of the senior Wren ready for their induction speech. Pam was quietly pleased to see that the unfriendly girl was not in the room so presumably had not been put through. She listened intently as the Wren went through their employment details and read out the Official Secrets Act which they would all need to sign before leaving. It was all very serious but at the same time, exciting. A whole new world was opening up!

As they left the hall, Edwin Denham was on hand again to escort them off the grounds of the park, and back to the station. The unsuccessful girls had already gone, so there was an air of excited anticipation as they walked back along the driveway and out through the security gates. Denham smiled shyly at Pam as she passed him. He looked like a decent chap – the kind that would do anything for you, she thought.

Clarissa nudged her elbow after Denham looked away. 'I'm thinking there might be chances of romance for us here as well, what do you think?'

Pam gasped. 'I ... I hadn't thought about it at all!'

Clarissa chuckled. 'All we girls, and all these men around. There's bound to be dances and clubs and social events. There'll be opportunities everywhere, and unless I'm very much mistaken, a certain young man has already set his eye on you.' She nodded towards Denham.

Pam shook her head. 'I don't think so. But I do like the sound of dances and social events. Well, we shall find out in a few days, won't we?'

As they entered the station, Pam saw the same fair-haired chap she'd noticed earlier outside Bletchley Park. He seemed to recognise her too, for he smiled and winked at her, making her blush. Clarissa nudged her. 'You'll have your pick of boys around here, by the looks of things. That's two of them giving you the eye, already!'

'Oh, what rubbish,' Pam said, but she felt herself blushing.

Throughout the train journey home, Pam made lists of things she needed to do by Thursday. Write to Somerville College to defer her place. Send a note to Miss Osbourne to say she'd been successful. Pack her clothes. See Ada and Emily, and tell them … what? Come to think of it, what was she going to tell her family? She looked at her watch. There were forty minutes before her train reached its destination, and in that time she had to work out how to tell them what she was going to do, without actually telling them anything. It would be the first time she'd kept secrets from her parents and brother.

*

The moment came over dinner that evening. Mum had been asking Geoff when he'd be leaving to join the RAF.

'Another couple of weeks,' he'd said, before turning to Pam. 'Then there'll be just Pammy here with you two, until she goes off to Oxford.'

Pam coughed. 'Ahem. Yes. About Oxford, there's something I need to tell you.'

'What? Have you changed your mind?' Mum's expression was a mix of worry and delight.

'You're still going to go?' Dad said. 'After all your work …'

'I'm still going to go,' Pam confirmed. 'Just, not this year. I'm going to defer my entry.'

'Why? What will you do instead?'

'Join the Wrens. I – I went for an interview today. They want me to start very soon. I'll be living away from home.'

'The Wrens! Well, that's … that's … marvellous,' Mum stuttered, and Dad looked pleased too.

'War work, then.' Dad nodded. 'Where will you be living?'

'Somewhere in Buckinghamshire. I'll write as soon as I'm there and let you know the address.' This was fair enough; she didn't yet know where she'd be billeted.

'And what work will you be doing?' Geoff asked.

Pam felt the heat rush to her face. So far she had not had to lie or obfuscate but this was the question that she'd dreaded. 'Well, I don't know exactly. I suppose I'll find out when I get there!' Still no lies told. She was feeling pleased with herself.

'This is all very sudden.' Mum put down her fork and stared at Pam. 'You didn't even tell us you were applying to the Wrens.'

'I didn't want to say anything until I knew I'd been accepted.'

'But they're accepting everyone who applies, love. Especially girls like you.'

Pam shrugged. 'I suppose … I just wanted to be sure it was all settled first.'

'Did you think we might talk you out of it?' Dad asked, a small frown between his eyes.

'Maybe, I don't know …'

'We're very proud,' he said. 'Aren't we, Elsie?'

'Yes. Proud of both of you.' Mum reached across the table to take a hand of both Pam and Geoff. 'Worried, but proud. Keep safe, both of you. Do your bit for your country, but please, stay safe.' She looked primarily at Geoff as she said this.

'I'll try my best to. Pammy will be all right; Wren stations are usually in the countryside and wouldn't be targeted in any way. Well, there could be bombs, but no more likely than anywhere else.'

'There was an air-raid alert on my last day of school. I was just glad there were none during the exams. Imagine having to go to the shelter halfway through taking an exam!' Pam was glad at the change of subject and seized upon it.

'I suppose they'd have to make sure the exam hall was secure, so no one went in while you were in the shelter. And they'd have to make sure you didn't refer to any books or notes while you were away. And check the time so you had the right length of time for the paper.'

Pam smiled. Dad had immediately begun planning how to

manage an air raid during the middle of an exam. That was just like him.

'Anyway, when are you leaving us?' Mum asked. 'We'll need to make sure we give you both a good send-off.'

'Thursday,' Pam replied.

Mum gasped. 'So soon? I thought there'd be a couple of weeks, like Geoff has. But … just three days? Well, we shall have to have our send-off on Wednesday evening, then. I'll use the meat ration to buy a decent joint of mutton, if I can find one. We'll have trifle as well – there's some strawberries doing nicely in the garden, and I've just enough sugar. When will you be able to come home on leave?'

Pam laughed. 'I've no idea yet, Mum! I haven't even got there. I'd have thought not for a couple of months though. As soon as I know, I will write and tell you.'

'I've got a few months' training then I have a short leave before my first posting,' Geoff said. 'So you'll probably be doing useful war work before me. And maybe if you're able to take leave at the same time as me, we'll see each other then, back here.'

'I'd like that.' Pam smiled. It would be a wrench leaving her parents and brother. Geoff had always been there for her. It would be hard for her parents too, she realised, with both their children leaving home at the same time. She glanced at her mother, who was smiling brightly but there was also a tell-tale glistening in her eyes, as though she were fighting back tears.

Chapter 5

Julia

'We're going to need, let's see, an extra coder and a testing specialist. Wouldn't hurt to take on someone else too, an all-rounder who could help with any of it. Otherwise it's going to be tight delivering the new version of the system by the date required.' Julia was poring over a set of estimates Barry had compiled for her. He was good at estimating how long something would take to code and test, though how he did it no one was quite sure, and he could never explain it himself.

'You want three more people on this?' Ian frowned at her.

'To be sure of meeting our deadlines, yes.' Julia tapped a pile of folders on her desk. 'We've promised several clients the new functionality by the end of June, and some have said they won't renew their contracts without it. And what about those new leads? Mannings and Co – didn't you pitch it to them on the basis of the updated system being ready?'

'Um, yes, I did.' Ian looked uncharacteristically worried, which surprised Julia.

'There's not a problem, is there? I mean, we can get contractors in at short notice. We could probably manage with just the coder and tester, but an extra pair of hands would give us plenty of contingency.'

'Three people. At that daily rate.' He stabbed his finger at a figure on the PowerPoint presentation they were working through. 'That's a lot of money.'

'Got to spend money to make money, you've always told me. We have enough to cover this, even without borrowing more. And I'm pretty certain there'd be no issue with taking out a bank loan on the back of the business that'll come our way once the updates are complete. We're in a strong position.' Julia was puzzled. Usually it was Ian talking money, persuading her that a loan to bring forward development timescales would pay off in the long run. She'd always been a little more cautious with money. It was one reason their partnership worked so well.

Ian folded his arms. 'Yes, that's normally the case. I'm just not so sure this time. We don't have enough in the bank to cover costs without a loan. And is this the right moment to borrow more money? What if those new leads don't add up to anything?'

'You seemed very positive about them last week,' she reminded him.

'Can't we manage by paying Barry some overtime?'

'I'd have to do a lot of overtime too.' And hadn't she just decided that she was getting her work-life balance wrong? That she needed to spend more time with her family, focus on her relationship with Marc a little more?

'But it's doable, right?'

She looked again at the estimates. Not taking on anyone else would mean weekend working for months. And was it even fair to ask Barry? He had a lot on his plate at the moment, she knew. His wife was undergoing treatment for breast cancer, and his student daughter was undergoing a confidence crisis and needing a lot of support. No. She didn't want to ask Barry to do overtime, and put him in the awkward position of saying no. 'Actually, I don't think it is doable.'

'Well, what if we take on one more person? An all-rounder, to ease the workload for both you and Barry. Plus Tulipa could do more.'

'Her time is fully booked out for months on the designs, and she also needs to start looking at the next phase.' Julia realised she needed to be firm. The business was half hers, and she was the one with the expertise in development. She was the one who knew how many people they needed to get the job done. 'I'm sorry, Ian, one contractor just won't cut it. It'll have to be two as a minimum – a coder and a tester.'

Ian sighed and shook his head, peering at the figures on the PowerPoint slide. 'Well, I can try to shuffle some money around, I suppose, but it's not ideal.'

Julia was exasperated. He was not normally like this – where was his 'can do' attitude? 'Ian, I thought we had a very healthy bank balance? Enough to pay contractors the first couple of months, and then there'll be the existing licence fees coming in?'

'We've not got that much in the bank, no,' Ian said, and something about his tone worried her. She had only ever kept half an eye on the accounts. That was Ian's job, and generally he was good at it. Very good at it – another reason they'd been successful.

'What are you saying? We're not in trouble, are we?'

Ian laughed. 'Ah no. Not at all. Sorry, I didn't mean to worry you. Our finances are perfectly healthy. We just can't afford three contractors at the moment. But don't fret, I'll think of something. Meanwhile, if you can plan it around having just two extra bodies, and for fewer weeks, that will really help.'

'I suppose … Barry and I can pick up a bit of slack, Tulipa can take on some testing. We might get away with two people for eight weeks, rather than three for ten.'

'That's better,' Ian said, smiling now. That smile, Julia reflected, had generally got Ian whatever he wanted. People of both sexes melted when in its beam, and found themselves wanting to please Ian, to say yes to him. It was how he got half their clients.

'Right then.' She smiled back, happy that the issue was now resolved, even if it wasn't quite the way she wanted it. But that was how it always was, running your own company with a friend. Sometimes you had to compromise – to trust your partner and then work hard to make sure it all turned out well.

Julia had studied maths at university, but on gaining her degree she'd decided she'd like to work with computers, and had applied for a place on an IT graduate training scheme with a large retail company. They hadn't minded what degree you had, as long as you passed their aptitude test. Julia's logical mind had meant she found the test easy.

She'd then worked for four years in that company. Meanwhile, Ian, who she'd met during her first week at university – he'd been in the room next to her in her student flat – had gone to work for several companies in quick succession, but had not been happy at any of them.

'What I really want,' he said to her on one of their regular monthly meet-ups, 'is to run my own business. I've got all the correct skills for it. But I don't have a business idea that feels right.' They were sitting in a corner of their favourite pub in central London, a traditional old pub tucked away in a Soho backstreet.

'Something will turn up,' Julia said, patting his arm. 'I'd be terrible running a business. I can't really be bothered with all the admin and financial stuff. I much prefer designing systems and writing code.'

'We'd be a good team then,' Ian said, with a glint in his eye. 'Me running the business and you doing the real work.'

'Ha! Who'd be working for who?'

'We'd be partners. Equal shares.'

'Yeah, but think of all the responsibility. Not sure it's for me.'

'With responsibility comes reward, Jules. Money. Satisfaction. Control.'

‘Ha! I’ll take the money,’ she said, and raised her glass. ‘Cheers. Here’s to us one day making a million.’

He smiled, but didn’t join in with the toast. ‘I’m serious though, Jules. We could do it, couldn’t we?’

‘But what business would it be?’

‘Software, of course. Your speciality. You’d design and build some fabulous system; I’d go out and find customers for it.’

‘OK, yeah, just one question: what fabulous system would you like me to design?’

‘Whatever you like. Just bear it in mind, yeah? So when you come up with a winning idea that you’d be able to develop, talk to me, and let’s see if we could make it fly.’

Julia smiled and nodded. He wasn’t serious. It was just a pipe dream that would never happen. They moved on to talk about mutual friends from university – who was seeing who, who was getting married, buying houses, having babies. ‘I’m not ready for any of that yet,’ Julia said, although only a few days earlier she’d been on a first date with Marc, a man she’d met at a party. He’d been charming and fun, and she was definitely going to see him again.

‘Me neither,’ Ian agreed. ‘Only grown-up thing I feel ready for is being my own boss. Like Felicity is.’

‘Felicity? The girl with red hair from your course?’

Ian nodded. ‘Yes. Her parents decided to retire and have handed over their little haberdashery shop to her. Not saying I want to run a haberdashery shop, you understand, but running a small business like that would be great. Not a shop though. She says it’s been a nightmare getting to grips with everything. Her parents did everything on paper. Loads of ledgers and account books, and absolutely nothing on computer.’

‘Ugh.’

‘Yeah. She’s having to spend hours every day trying to find details of orders in all the little books they liked to fill in. She says it’s like being back in the 1970s. She wants to modernise everything, refit the shop and turn it into the kind of place younger people would go to buy craft supplies, not just somewhere your granny buys knitting wool. But first she needs to get to grips with the day-to-day running of the place …'

Julia's thoughts had drifted off as he spoke. A small shop, with no computer systems at all, that needed help … She thought about the systems she worked on in her job, and imagined how something similar could be built and adapted for small retailers. What would they need? A database of product information; a stock control system linked to point of sale; ordering and receiving functionality; a way of keeping track of customer orders; a set of financial reports … Something modular, that small retail companies could easily pick up and use whichever bits they needed, and plug in extra modules as required …

'Jules? Are you listening? Are you even still with me in this pub?' Ian waved a hand in front of her face.

She refocused her gaze on him and took a sip of her drink before answering. 'You know what, Ian, I might have just thought of a business idea. Something I could build, you could sell, and Felicity could use as our guinea pig customer. If you really are serious about setting up a company …'

By the time they left the pub that evening, they'd filled a small notebook from Julia's handbag, and also written on beermats and backs of pub menus. The business idea was taking shape. Julia had agreed to spend some time working out a potential design and what development software she'd need to build it. Ian was going to talk to Felicity, find out her needs and see if she'd be interested in such a system. In other words, they were going to work out if the idea had legs. And if it did, with a small business loan from a friendly bank and a couple of contractors to help Julia, then just maybe 'Julian Systems' – their two names merged together into one – could be born.

It was always Ian who'd driven things. She'd had the idea, she'd developed it into something sellable, but he'd been the one who created the company. Julia would have stayed forever in a safe job working for other people if left to herself. She had Ian to thank for pushing her into running their own business. It was rewarding, he'd been right about that, and it had paid off, bringing them both a substantial income for years.

*

'Package for you, Mum.' Oscar dropped a small parcel on the kitchen draining board, as he passed her at the sink.

'Oh! Don't put it there, it'll get wet,' she said. 'Put it on the table, would you? Anyway, what happened to you and Ryan doing the washing up?'

'That's on Tuesdays and Thursdays,' Oscar replied, as he grabbed a packet of crisps from a cupboard.

'I thought it was every day?'

'Nah.' A spray of crisp crumbs covered the floor as Oscar violently opened the packet. 'We decided two days a week was enough.'

'Who's we?'

'Me and Ryan. And Uncle Bob did say we should do it "a couple" of days a week, and a couple is two, right?'

'I suppose so … hey, sweep up that mess you made with the crisps!'

'Sure.' Oscar picked up a tea towel and spread the crisps around the floor with it.

'Not with that! Get the dustpan and brush!'

'Where are they?'

'Cupboard under the stairs, for goodness sake.' This was half the problem. Her sons at twelve and fourteen did not even seem to know the basics of how to clean something or even where things were kept. She'd failed, as a mother of sons. She needed to teach them how to keep house. Otherwise no self-respecting twenty-first-century woman would look twice at them when they were grown up. Who, these days, would marry a man who couldn't or wouldn't operate a Hoover?

To be fair to Oscar, he did a good job sweeping up once he'd found the brush, and even went around the whole kitchen with it. But then he stood in the middle with the dustpan seeming unsure what to do with his sweepings.

Julia sighed. 'In the bin, love,' and laughed as the solution dawned on his face.

Having finished washing the pans, Julia dried her hands and went to see what her parcel was. With a bit of luck it'd be the developed Box Brownie film. She sat down and opened it, and yes, it was a collection of snaps and the negatives, along with several brochures and fliers advertising the company's other services. She put these to one side and began looking through the little black-and-white images. There was also a memory stick with the pictures on. It'd be better to look at them on a screen. She grabbed her laptop, inserted the stick and clicked through the photos.

The first few were like the ones she'd already seen – there were a couple of shots of the same teenage girls she'd seen on other photos – she realised now one of them was her grandmother's old schoolfriend Ada. The girls having a picnic, clinking glasses together as though celebrating something, and on bicycles. And then a few that seemed to be from a different location. One of a tall young man, his face in shadow. A girl, standing in front of an imposing building, her expression one of amusement. Another that Julia recognised as her grandmother, by some bushes with what could be the same large house in the background, and then a clear one of the front of that house.

'I wonder where this is,' Julia said to herself. It wasn't anywhere she recognised. Maybe Bob might know. She had no idea of his work patterns but usually he'd reply to a text as soon as he could.

Got photos back from Grandma's camera. Can send you digital versions if you are free.

He phoned her back almost immediately. 'Hey, Sis. That's

amazing, yes, email me the pictures now and we can look at them together.'

'Sure, will do,' she said, cradling her phone between her cheek and shoulder so she could send him the email. 'Are you at home, then?'

'No. Hotel room in San Francisco. Bit bored, actually. It's raining, I've slept enough, and there are three hours to kill before I head back to the airport. So your text came at the right moment.'

'They should be on their way,' she said.

'And … yes. Here they are! Right then. You're on speakerphone so I can look at the pics on my phone as well as talk to you. Oh, Ada and those other girls again. Must be her schoolfriends.'

'Who's the young man with Grandma in photo number five?'

'Grandpa?'

'No. Too tall.' Julia clicked on another photo showing her grandmother with a different young man. 'That's him in number eight, though. That's definitely him.'

'You're right. The one in number five, she's got her arm round him, so whoever he was, they were close.'

'Any idea what that big house in so many of the photos is?'

'Let me see … hmm … it looks familiar somehow. Looks like …'

'Looks like what?'

'I'm just Googling … yes. Wow.'

'What? Tell me!'

'Are you on a laptop? Split your screen. Put the photo of the house on one side and on the other, Google for images of Bletchley Park.'

'Bletchley Park? Isn't that where …'

'Yes. The code-breaking headquarters during the Second World War. I told you I went there not long ago.'

'Blimey. So Grandma visited there, did she?' Julia was tapping away, bringing up images, and yes, there it was. A large country house that looked as though it had been built in Victorian times and suffered a bit by different owners adding parts to it in many different styles. But on many photos a copper dome at one end of the building was prominent, and an identical one was clearly visible on the black-and-white image. 'Wonder why she went there? Looks like a day trip, the way that other girl is posing in front of the building.'

'It wouldn't have been possible to make a day trip to Bletchley Park, back then. This must be during the war years. Those other photos of Grandma's had 1943 and 1942 written on the back of them, so this must be a similar time. Bletchley was kept top secret throughout the war. And after.'

'If she wasn't just visiting it, does that mean …'

'She must have been working there. Yes, I think that's exactly what it means. Wow.'

Julia felt a tingle of excitement. 'She never mentioned having worked there.'

'They all had to sign the Official Secrets Act. It was only in the 1990s that people began talking and writing about it. Unbelievably, there was talk of demolishing the house and redeveloping the site, when a group got together to preserve it and all its history. Honestly, Jules, it's a fascinating place to visit. Bet the boys would love it too.'

'You said that when you were last here. I've never been, but I quite fancy it, especially as you think Grandma may have worked there. What would she have done?'

'They employed hundreds of people there by the end of the war. Some civilians, some military. Girls from the Women's Royal Navy Service – the Wrens – worked there. I had a guided tour there. The girls were involved in some of the stages of code breaking. Setting up the machines, transcribing messages. It was a little industry in its own right by the end of the war. They reckon that the work at Bletchley Park probably shortened the war by about two or three years.'

'That's incredible! And you think our grandma was involved in that?'

'Well, given that she was certainly there at some point during the war years, it looks likely. She was really clever, if you remember.'

'Yes, especially at maths. Always thought that's where my logical mind came from,' Julia said. 'She got a first in maths from Oxford, which was pretty rare for a woman in her day.'

'That was after the war. She went to university quite late. I always wondered why.' Bob was silent for a moment as though remembering something. 'I asked her once, and she said her university place was deferred because of the war. I thought she'd meant that the college she had a place at was closed for the duration, but maybe it was because she was doing war work. At Bletchley Park.'

'That would make sense,' Julia agreed. 'How can we find out more about it? I'd love to know what role she played.' A memory suddenly came to her. 'Bob, do you remember how Grandma used to say no one was better at keeping secrets than her? I wonder if this was what she was referring to – that she'd kept her wartime role secret all those years?'

'Hmm, yes, it could have been. I always thought she was saying it to urge us to tell her our little childhood secrets but maybe not.'

Julia clicked back to the photos of Bletchley Park. 'Bob, the photo of Bletchley with a girl posing, do you recognise the girl?'

'Er, no. Don't think so. Do you?'

'Hold on.' Julia put the phone down on the sofa and fetched the box of photos Bob had brought. She pulled out an album. 'Just looking at Grandma's wedding album. Yes! I'm sure it's her!'

'Who?'

'That posing girl is Clarissa. I'm comparing with a photo of her as a bridesmaid at Grandma and Grandpa's wedding.'

'Clarissa!' Bob gave a short laugh of surprise. 'Well, I knew they met during the war but not that they'd met at Bletchley Park.'

'I'd so like to be able to ask her about this.' Julia sighed. 'If only we'd discovered this film and had it developed before she died.'

'She might not have talked even then,' Bob said. 'There are

many who worked at Bletchley who never said a word, even after the restrictions were lifted. That generation were often very private people.'

'Well, I can probably find out if she was in the Wrens or ATS at least. There must be records, even if they don't mention her work at Bletchley.'

'Keep me informed!'

'Will do.'

When Julia rang off, she gazed once more at the photos. She seemed to have given herself a research project to do, on top of all the other demands on her time. Well, that was clever. She'd fit it in, somehow.

Chapter 6

Pamela

The few short days between her interview and leaving for Bletchley Park went by in a rush. There was so much to do. People to see and say goodbye to, a kit bag to pack, train ticket to buy. Pam felt as though her feet barely touched the ground.

She managed a meet-up with Ada and Emily – they went to a Lyons corner house for tea and cake (there was only a plain Madeira sponge but it was better than nothing) to say goodbye.

'I can't believe you're the first of us to leave home!' Emily said. 'I thought it would be me, but I'm not off to London until the end of next week.'

'And I'm not going anywhere,' Ada said.

'Of course you're not, not now you've got your young man here!' Pam said with a fond laugh. Ada's relationship with the American airman seemed to be going from strength to strength. They met up every time Herbie was off duty. Pam felt lucky to have managed to pin Ada down for this meet-up, as too often lately she'd chosen to see Herbie over her friends.

Ada blushed. 'Sometimes I feel I should join up, the WAAF

perhaps. But they might post me anywhere. And I'd hate to be away from Herbie.' She looked down at her plate. 'After all, we might not have that long together. I want him to have the best life.'

She was referring to the very real danger that Herbie might be shot down on one of his missions, Pam realised. Soon Geoff would be in similar danger. Pam put her hand on Ada's arm. 'He'll be all right. He's a good pilot. And meanwhile, you are right. Make the most of every minute with him.'

'Thank you, Pam. I certainly shall.'

It was a fun couple of hours in the tea shop, but all too soon it was time to leave. Pam hugged her friends farewell. When she next saw them, it would be when she was home on leave. When she knew what her job was and had spent time working for her country. When Emily would have had some experience driving ambulances in London, helping victims of bombing raids. When Ada's relationship with Herbie would have progressed – maybe they'd even be engaged! They were all growing up and moving on to the next, exciting phase in their lives.

*

By the time Thursday came around, Pam was packed and ready to go. The last thing she'd put in her kit bag was her beloved Box Brownie. She caught an earlier train than she had for her interview. It was a fine summer's day and her feeling as the train steamed through the countryside was one of excitement and hope. What the future held she did not know, but she would be meeting new people, learning new things, doing her part for the war effort. A couple of years earlier it had seemed as though the outcome of the war was inevitable. Hitler's armies had rampaged so quickly through mainland Europe it had seemed only a matter of time before they invaded England. But the RAF had managed to gain the upper hand in the Battle of Britain, and London's spirit had not been subdued by the Blitz, and gradually hope had returned that maybe, just maybe, the tide might be on the turn.

On the second leg of the journey, she was sharing her railway carriage with a group of airmen who were loud and raucous but in a good-natured way. They were, one told her, on their way to a new posting at an aerodrome in Buckinghamshire. All had recently finished their training and were excited to be soon flying missions over Germany. Pam thought, inevitably, of Geoff who'd soon be doing the same thing. He'd enjoy the camaraderie, the banter with fellow pilots, the friendships that perhaps would be deeper and more intense between men who knew they might not make it back. She wanted to join in with the airmen: tell them that she too was about to take up a posting, about to do her bit for the war. But she'd signed the Official Secrets Act and knew she could never say anything, even when asked.

'Hey up, pet, where are you off to this sunny day?' One of the airmen had moved seats to sit opposite her. He had a friendly, open face.

'Joining the Wrens,' she replied with a smile. It was the truth, but was all she could say.

'Aw, girl like you should have joined the WAAF! We'd have loved to have you on our base, wouldn't we, lads?'

'Yeah, too right!' another one called, and Pam blushed a little and laughed. She remembered Clarissa saying there might be chances for romance for the Wrens stationed at Bletchley Park. Would she be ready for such a thing? Pam had never really looked twice at any boys, but since Ada had fallen in love with her American airman, Pam had begun to wonder if there would be someone out there for her, in time. She glanced around at the men in the carriage, being careful not to hold anyone's gaze for too long. Some were nice-looking, it was true. The one opposite her had a pleasant smile and a twinkle in his deep blue eyes that was rather appealing. As she watched him, he winked at her, in a teasing sort of way, the way Geoff might do.

Feeling herself blushing once more she averted her eyes and stared out of the window at the fields rushing by outside. It would soon be harvest time, the grain was ripening nicely. Here and there, groups of land girls could be seen, working in the fields. Overhead a pair of buzzards wheeled and swooped in the warm air.

'Sorry, pet. Didn't mean to embarrass you, like.' The airman opposite her spoke quietly so that only she could hear. She looked back at him.

'It's all right, you didn't. Best of luck with your new posting.' She smiled briefly at him, then looked out of the window again so he wouldn't think she was flirting. The base he and the others were heading to was nowhere near Bletchley Park, if her geography was correct. There was no point getting to know this young man, whom she would probably never see again.

'You too,' he said, before moving away, back to his original seat with three other airmen, across the aisle.

Pam felt a pang of regret. Maybe, if she'd been braver, she could have chatted more with him, given him a few moments of fun in female company, before he had to take his place in this war. For all they knew, he might be dead by this time tomorrow, if he ran into trouble on his first mission. It was a sobering thought, one that she pushed aside as soon as it arrived in her mind. We fight for tomorrow, but live for today, Geoff had said, when she'd hugged him goodbye and made him promise to be careful and come home to them. It was a good philosophy.

She realised that the train was slowing as it approached the next station, and she recognised the buildings. Bletchley, already! She stood and gathered her bags and got ready to leave.

'Aw, the train's going to seem a darker place without you, pet,' said the man who'd spoken to her earlier. 'Best wishes, love.'

She smiled and bade him farewell, and as she left the train the men broke into a rowdy chorus of 'We'll Meet Again' which made her laugh. She waved goodbye from the platform. What a way to start her new life!

No one was meeting her at the station this time. She'd been told to present herself at the security gate and show them the papers she'd been issued with at the interview. Nevertheless, she found herself looking around, in case that fair-haired young man she'd seen on interview day happened to be hanging around again, or if Mr Newman's assistant might be there. But there was no sign of either of them. It was hard work walking with all her kit in the heat of the summer's day but she was pleased somehow to be arriving by herself this time, able to take in her surroundings at leisure.

The short walk was soon over and she approached the sentry box at the gate and showed her papers.

'There's a few of you Wrens arriving today,' the guard said, ticking her name off a list. 'You're to go up to the main hall and report to reception there. If you hold on, just a moment … looks like there's another girl coming you could walk up with.' He was looking over her shoulder, and as Pam turned she saw that it was Clarissa, grinning broadly, who was approaching.

'Pamela Jackson! I thought it was you walking just ahead of me all the way from the station. I'd have called out if I'd been certain, but didn't want to make a fool of myself if I was wrong!' Clarissa caught Pam by the shoulders and kissed her cheek. 'Let me check in, then we can arrive together.'

Pam stood back to let Clarissa show the guard her papers, and then the gate was opened for them to walk up to the main house. 'Oof, I will be glad to be able to dump these bags somewhere!' Clarissa said, and Pam agreed.

Walking up the main drive Pam was struck once again by the number of people hurrying here and there between the huts. More people were sitting on the grass beside a small lake, presumably on their lunch break. Most were young, and there seemed to be as many women, many in the uniform of the Wrens, as men. Pam felt a surge of excitement once more that this was to be her world.

'Well, here we are!' Clarissa said, as they climbed the couple of steps at the main entrance. A sign pointed the way to reception, so they put their bags against a wall where there were already a few others, and went to report their arrival.

They were ushered through to a dining room to have a meal and a cup of tea while they awaited the other arrivals. The buzz of conversation in the dining room surprised Pam. 'With all the secrecy, I'd have thought everyone would sit quietly at the mealtimes and not say a word,' she whispered to Clarissa, who laughed.

'Listen, though. They're not talking about their work, are they?' And as Pam tuned in to a couple of nearby conversations, she realised her new friend was right. A table of Wrens were gossiping and laughing about who'd been seen with whom at the last dance. Two studious-looking men were discussing tactics for chess, and it sounded as though there might be a chess club connected with Bletchley Park. Another Wren was regaling her friends with a long, convoluted story about something that had happened at home while she was on leave.

'It could be a canteen in any workplace,' Pam said, and Clarissa nodded.

'Indeed. Hello, isn't that … what's his name, the chap who collected us from the station on Monday?'

Pam looked where Clarissa was pointing and nodded. 'Yes. Edwin Denham, his name was. Serious-looking fellow, with kind eyes, I thought.'

Clarissa smiled. 'You've summed him up well, but forgot to mention he was eyeing you up.'

'He was not! Shh. He's coming over.' Pam stifled a giggle as Clarissa made a gesture as though she was buttoning up her mouth.

'Hello, ladies, it's good to see you again. I hope you settle in quickly here at BP.' Edwin Denham gave a stiff little bow as though he was slightly embarrassed to have spoken to them.

'Thank you, Mr Denham,' Pam replied. 'I am sure we will. It's very exciting, starting a new job at a place like this.' She smiled at him and was amused to see he blushed profusely.

'Perhaps we'll be working in the same section. I'll look forward to seeing you both around.' He left them then, sitting at another table across the canteen.

'I told you he likes you,' Clarissa said triumphantly. 'He never even looked at me then, only at you. Do you like him too?'

'He's sweet,' Pam replied. 'A good sort. Yes, I like him.'

*

The afternoon was taken up with talks, a tour, the issuing of Wren uniform to those who didn't already have one. They weren't taken to every area at BP, just those they'd need to know. At last, when Pam was hot and tired and felt she couldn't fit anything more in her head, the new arrivals were told to collect their bags from the hallway and bring them out front to be taken to their accommodation. A battered old bus was parked on the gravel forecourt, awaiting them.

'Where are we to be billeted?' Pam asked Clarissa.

'Didn't they say it was to be in Woburn Abbey?' Clarissa replied. 'There's been so much information thrown at us today, I confess I wasn't quite taking everything in.'

'Neither was I. Woburn Abbey – sounds very posh!'

'It is,' Clarissa agreed. 'My parents were house guests there a few years ago. I don't suppose we'll be treated quite as well as they were.'

It was a short journey of around fifteen minutes, and as the bus drove through parkland amid herds of deer, Clarissa smiled at Pam. 'Yes, it's definitely Woburn.'

Pam was thrilled to think she'd be living in a stately home, and gazed out of the window in excitement as the bus drove the last half-mile up to the huge building. It was even more impressive than Bletchley Park. The bus drove around the side where a

Wren was waiting to greet them. They were led inside, through several rooms and corridors that were sumptuously decorated and furnished, and upstairs to a large room that had been converted into a dormitory. Each girl had a basic metal bedstead, bedside cabinet and chair. Curtains had been put up to separate the beds. The walls were covered with red silk, a reminder of the room's glory from before the war. Each new girl was allocated a bed, and Pam was pleased to find hers was next to Clarissa's.

'I hope we end up on the same shifts,' Pam said. 'Isn't it amazing to think we'll be living here?'

A girl who'd been lying on her bed reading a book laughed. 'You won't think that after you've been here a while. The plumbing in this place is atrocious. There's never any hot water. It's all a bit Victorian, and of course was never designed for so many people to be living here at once. The girls who are billeted in small private houses in the villages have much better conditions.'

It didn't matter to Pam. For the moment she was excited to be there and couldn't wait to get started. They were due to be collected by bus the next morning to return to Bletchley Park for their first day's training. Soon she'd be making a contribution, doing something real for her country. She still had no idea what her work would be. 'Something to do with intelligence,' Clarissa said. 'Though Lord knows what. We'll find out soon enough, I suppose. Meanwhile, I spotted a tennis court out there. Do you play? I wonder if there are any racquets we can borrow. It'll be fun!'

Pam had played a little at school, and yes, she agreed, it would be fun. There was another hour before dinner, so she followed Clarissa back through the enormous building taking care to memorise the route, and out to the tennis court. It was in use; four other Wrens were laughing and joking as they hit a couple of balls back and forth across the net, so Clarissa and Pam sat on a nearby bench to watch.

'I think I'm going to enjoy our life here,' Clarissa said, and Pam nodded vigorously in agreement.

Chapter 7

Julia

It was a couple of weeks before a free weekend loomed ahead in the calendar. The boys always seemed to have something on at the weekends that meant they could not spare a full day to do anything as a family. Football matches, friends' birthday events, extra-curricular school activities. Julia sometimes felt as though she was nothing more than a taxi service on Saturdays, ferrying the kids from one activity to another, though she had to admit Marc did his share, especially if it involved football.

But finally a weekend came around where nothing had been written on the family calendar. Julia checked with both Oscar and Ryan that they hadn't simply failed to fill it in, and was pleased to find they were both indeed free. 'I thought we might have a day out on Saturday, and take a trip to Bletchley Park,' she suggested over dinner mid-week. 'You know, the place where wartime code breaking took place. Do you fancy it?'

'Awesome,' Ryan said, punching the air. 'We did a project on codes at school. It's all just swapping one letter for another so you can do secret writing. Like an A becomes a G and B becomes K.'

'It's a bit more complicated than that,' Oscar said, scornfully. 'They had machines that changed the letter swapping so the first time A becomes G but then next time it becomes Z or something.'

'So are you both interested?' Julia asked. Ryan nodded enthusiastically and Oscar just shrugged, which was as close as a fourteen-year-old could get to agreeing with a parent, so Julia took it as a yes.

'Great!' She turned to Marc. 'It'll be lovely to have a family day out. I thought we could leave around ten. It'll take about an hour and a half to drive there. They have cafés, so lunch at Bletchley and maybe a pub dinner on the way home?' She smiled happily, looking forward to the day already.

'Oscar will order the most expensive steak on the menu, Mum, like he always does. I'll have a pub dinner if they do something with pasta,' said Ryan.

'I'm sure they will. Marc, how does that sound?'

'Hmm.' Marc was peering at the calendar function on his phone. 'Sorry, love. Not sure I can make Saturday. There's … um, a work thing on. A one-day course.'

'What? You hadn't mentioned it, and it's not on the calendar.' They had a strict system: everyone had to write their events on the shared family calendar no matter what. It was the only way Julia could keep track of her busy family.

'Ah, sorry. I put it on my phone calendar and forgot to copy it across. I'm sure there must be some way we could sync phone calendars rather than this old-fashioned manual method. You being an IT whizz and all, there must be a better way.'

'Marc, this has worked perfectly for years. We can all see at a glance what we're doing. Ryan doesn't have a smartphone yet, anyway.'

'Although everyone else at school has one. I'm like, the last. So embarrassing.' Ryan pouted.

'Next birthday, pet,' Julia consoled him. 'Marc, what about Sunday?'

'Tricky … there's a Six Nations match I want to see on that day.'

'And I'm at Luke's in the afternoon,' Oscar added.

'Jules, why don't you and the boys go?' Marc said. 'You don't need me. You'll have just as good a time. I'm not particularly interested anyway. To be honest, I'm not even sure why you're suddenly so keen?'

'It's because of those photos, isn't it, Mum? The ones with your great-great-grandma in or something.' Ryan looked at Julia for confirmation.

'My grandmother. Your great-grandmother,' she replied, nodding. 'Yes, those photos have piqued my curiosity about Bletchley's role in the war.'

'What photos?' Marc frowned.

'The undeveloped film in Grandma's old camera. I got it developed. Marc, I tried to tell you but …'

'But … I didn't listen. I suppose that's what you're going to say. What old camera, anyway? Do you tell me anything these days or is it all just secrets between you and the boys?'

Oscar and Ryan were staring at their plates, clearly embarrassed by their father's outburst. Julia sighed. 'I think you were watching the rugby when I tried to tell you about the old camera Bob found, that contained an undeveloped film of wartime photos Grandma took. It looks as though she may have worked at Bletchley Park for a while during the war, but never said anything about it. I want to find out more, and they do tours. It'll be interesting for the kids too.'

'Right, well, you take them if you want. Sorry, but I'm busy on Saturday.' Marc picked up his phone again and scrolled through pictures on Instagram.

He clearly wasn't interested in the slightest, Julia realised. To be fair to him, she knew that family history wasn't his thing so there was no point in pushing it. She was sure his claim of a one-day course was just an excuse – something he'd made up to get out of the trip – but confronting him about it would start a pointless row. Let it go, she told herself.

'OK, fine. Just you boys and me, then. Be ready ten o'clock Saturday morning. Oscar, that means up and breakfasted and showered by then, not just rolling out of bed at ten.' She nudged him to show she was teasing, and got an eye roll in response.

*

On Saturday Julia and the boys were up long before Marc, making it even more obvious to her that there was no course. He finally shuffled into the kitchen in his dressing gown just as they were finishing breakfast.

'Any left for me?'

'A bit of egg, if you want. What time do you start today?'

'Hmm? Start what?'

'The course?'

'Oh.' He glanced at the clock. 'Midday. You'll be gone by then.' He helped himself to some egg and a piece of toast. 'Hope you enjoy it.'

'I'm sure we will. Enjoy your course, too. There's some leftover curry in the fridge. You could boil some rice to go with it.'

'Oh. You mean for my dinner. Um, thanks.'

There was a clatter of plates, and she looked over to see Ryan busy loading the dishwasher. Not just his own plate, but he was actually looking around the kitchen and picking up everything that was dirty and needed to go in. That was a first. It was on the tip of her tongue to make some sort of snide or sarcastic remark, but she stopped herself. Catch them being good, was a parenting tip she'd heard years before.

'Hey, Ryan, thanks for doing that,' she said. 'Much appreciated.'

He grinned at her. 'Sooner it's done the sooner we can go, right, Mum?'

'Absolutely. Let's aim to leave in ten minutes.'

That made Oscar leap up from the table and go to his room to fetch his shoes, phone, and money, and Ryan was two steps after him once he'd finished with the dishes. Julia went to find her bag, phone and car keys and Marc followed her out to the hallway.

'So, yeah, like I said, have a good day. See you later.'

'Sure. I'll text you when we're on our way home.'

'Yeah.' He gave her a quick kiss on the cheek, and she went out to the car.

*

The journey to Bletchley was overall pretty enjoyable. The boys were on good form and spent half the time telling each other the corniest jokes they knew. Some of them made Julia laugh. She chipped in with her own favourite: 'What's brown and sticky?'

'A stick!' they yelled simultaneously, almost as though they might have heard the joke a hundred times before.

The drive passed quickly, and, following her satnav, Julia was soon driving onto the grounds of Bletchley Park, following signs to the visitors' car park. It was a sunny, pleasant day, and there were plenty of visitors already parked up. The grounds were pleasantly laid out, with neatly trimmed bushes and benches dotted around on lush grass, and a pretty little lake. They walked over to the main building, the manor house.

'Wow, awesome building!' Ryan said, looking up at the various gables and turrets and chimneys that made up the roof line. Julia wasn't so sure she'd describe it as awesome. It was such an odd mix of styles and features, and totally asymmetrical. Not pleasing to the eye, in her mind. And that green copper dome, it was distinctive and memorable, but did it add to the aesthetics? Not really, but of course it had been that dome that allowed Bob to recognise Bletchley Park in their grandmother's old photos.

'Well let's buy our tickets and get started,' Julia said, and they trooped over to the ticket office. The tours included the main house and several of the huts that still stood in the grounds of the house. Some were in disrepair but others had been restored and furnished as they would have been in the park's heyday during the war.

There was so much to see and do. They took a short break to have lunch at a café housed in Hut 4 but stayed almost all afternoon. Oscar was most fascinated by the story of Alan Turing and the breaking of the Enigma code, that had been widely used by the German Navy, particularly the U-boats. Julia enjoyed seeing the house, and imagining how it would have looked when in use as a country house by the Leon family before the war. There were displays showing photographs of the huge number of staff, both indoor and stable hands, that were employed in Edwardian times when the estate was known for its shooting and hunting parties.

But it was during the war that Julia's grandmother had apparently worked here, on the code-breaking activities known collectively as ULTRA. Julia peered at every photograph of rows of Wrens at desks, translating intercepted messages, wondering if she might perhaps spot Grandma in one.

Ryan had had the same thought, it seemed. As he gazed at one photo of a couple of Wrens setting up one of the Colossus machines, he gasped. 'What if, Mum, your granny was in one of these photos? Wouldn't that be totally awesome?'

'Totally, yes,' she said, with a laugh. 'But they employed hundreds here, over the war years. So the chances of her being in one of the pictures would be pretty remote. I don't even know what she did here – was she in any of the Forces or a civilian? She might have been employed in the canteen, for all we know.'

'Thought you said she was a maths genius?' Oscar said. 'So they wouldn't have had her making the teas. She'd have done something important in the code-breaking huts. Anyway, look. You can find out.' He was pointing at a board that advertised the Bletchley Park Roll of Honour. 'It's searchable by name. Bet you can find her on it, and it'll tell you what she did here.'

'Oh, that's amazing, well spotted!' Oscar grinned proudly as Julia noted down the website. 'I will definitely have a good look at that, when we're back home.'

'Do it now. You know, your phone has the internet on it and everything. God, Mum, for someone who's supposed to be good at IT, sometimes you're really slow. D'oh.'

'Less of your cheek, young man. Why don't you look her up, then? Her maiden name was Jackson. Pamela Jackson.'

Oscar perched himself on a bench and pulled out his phone, tapping into it with his thumbs. A moment later he brandished it triumphantly in front of Julia. 'There she is. Worked here 1943 to 1945, in the Newmanry. As a Colossus operator. Shame. I'd hoped she was on the Enigma team.'

'Let me see.' Julia took the phone from him and peered at the details. There wasn't much, but yes, there was her grandmother's name and the details Oscar had read out. So it was true, Grandma really had worked here, and never said a word about it.

'What is the Newmanry?' Ryan asked. 'And what's Colossus?'

'Well, let's go and find out,' Julia said, pointing at a sign that advertised a room dedicated to the Colossus story.

The Newmanry, they soon discovered, was simply the name given to the department headed by a man called Max Newman. It was dedicated to breaking the 'Tunny' code – encrypted teleprinter messages that were used extensively in the latter part of the war, by German High Command. It was a fiendishly complicated code, utilising twelve encryption wheels (compared to the three or four of 'Enigma'), but nevertheless a man named John Tiltman managed to find weaknesses and crack it. Because the code was favoured by the German High Command, the intercepted messages tended to be strategic rather than tactical, and therefore of enormous importance.

'Imagine, though, if you were decrypting a message and it turns out to say something like Invasion of Paris to begin at ten o'clock on Wednesday and you passed that on to our army so they could stop it happening,' Oscar said. Julia was pleased to see him getting caught up in the excitement of it all.

'Yes. Well, look, it says here, that overall the work that took place right here probably shortened the war by a couple of years.' This must be where Bob had heard that fact, she thought. 'And your great-grandmother was a part of it all.'

'Yeah. Awesome. But that Colossus thing in the picture, how on earth is that a computer?'

'It was probably the world's first. It read punched tape that had to be loaded up on this contraption they nicknamed "the bedstead".' Julia was paraphrasing from one of the display boards. 'It was designed by a chap named Tommy Flowers, who built the first one using parts from a telephone exchange. Lots of valves and switches. No silicon chips in those days.'

'He must have been very clever.'

'Yes, I think all the people who worked here were. It was a huge effort, but the prize – knowing what the Germans were going to do next – was immense.'

'Why didn't you know what your granny did in the war? I mean, I know my granny, Dad's mum, was a schoolteacher. She's always telling me stories about how things were in school when she was a teacher. Didn't you talk much to your granny?'

'I did, and she also told me stories of her time working after the war. I'm guessing she had to sign the Official Secrets Act, and she stuck to that right to the end of her life.'

'Says here they all signed it, and if they broke it, they could be sent to prison. Just for talking about their work! Good thing we don't have that now.' Ryan's eyes were wide as he read this from an information board.

'We do, stupid. We still have it. Like if you're a spy or something, or doing top-secret work for the government. They still have to sign it, don't they, Mum?' Oscar rolled his eyes at his brother.

'I believe so, yes,' Julia answered. 'Come on. There's a replica Colossus in the National Museum of Computing. That's on the other side of the car park, and I think you have to pay separately to get in, but we can go if you're interested?' She certainly was, especially if Grandma had been a Colossus operator.

'Yeah, let's!' Oscar was keen, and Ryan nodded. So when they'd seen enough of Bletchley Park itself, and the huts, they headed back across the car park and into the Museum of Computing, that had once been Block H where the Colossus machines had been housed. Once there they made a beeline for the replica Colossus.

'Why not an original one? Did they all fall apart or what?' Ryan asked.

'I don't know,' Julia answered.

'They were destroyed, it says here, except for one.' Oscar had found the information.

They stood for a moment marvelling at the contraption that took up most of the room. A huge metal frame, an enormous array of valves, a rack of wires on a plug board. It really wasn't at all obvious how it worked, but it clearly had worked well. There'd been ten installed at Bletchley by the end of the war, all working twenty-four hours a day.

'There's no screen, or keyboard, or mouse,' Ryan said, as he stared at the machine. 'How on earth does this thing do anything?'

Julia read the display boards. 'You set it up for a run using these cables and switches, and the input is read off a tape.' She pointed to the metal frame. 'This bit, that they called the bedstead because that's what it looks like, had the input punched tape set up round it. It could read one tape while they set up the next one. The output, which was a series of counts indicating what the encryption wheel settings were likely to be, was produced on this typewriter wired up to it.'

It was fascinating, gazing upon a replica of what must surely be the world's first functioning computer. Julia had already decided to buy a book or two on the subject. It'd be a way of finding out more about her grandmother's wartime role. There was a decent-looking shop on the site, that they could visit before they left.

'Listen to this, boys. Even after the Germans changed how they used their Tunny encoding machines so that they were changing the wheel pattern daily rather than monthly, the staff here were able to discover the wheel settings and decrypt the messages. By the end of the war, the various Colossus machines were decrypting every intercepted message, discovering all the wheel settings. Once they had the wheel settings, they could set up replica Tunny machines accordingly, type in the encrypted text and the original plain German text would be produced.'

'Awesome,' Oscar commented. 'Wish we could see it working.'

'Apparently they have tested this replica out on original World War Two messages, and it worked.'

'Cool. Imagine when they first built it and started using it. How would they know it had worked then?'

'I suspect they tested it on a known message. Before it was built, they were decrypting messages by hand, so they'd have had some they could use as tests. But yes, when it first ran and produced a result must have been an amazing moment.'

*

When they arrived home that evening, after a very enjoyable pub dinner somewhere en route, Marc was watching TV, a bottle of beer in his hand. The leftover curry was still in the fridge.

'Hey. We had a great day. How was your course?' Julia leaned over him and kissed his head.

'Oh, um, course was fine. Did the boys have fun today?'

'It was awesome, and we found out that our great-grandma operated one of the world's first computers!' Ryan was still buzzing.

'That's great. Hope you learned lots.' Marc turned off the TV and focused his attention on Ryan who was giving a convoluted account of how Colossus worked.

Later, when the boys were both upstairs, Julia turned to Marc. 'So, um, what did you have for dinner?'

'Oh, I ordered a pizza. Couldn't really face cooking.'

'I told you there was leftover curry. Well, no worries. Maybe I'll have it for lunch on Monday.'

Marc pulled her towards him to sit beside him on the sofa. 'Listen, Jules. I've booked us a table at Le Jardin de Michel. You've said the boys are old enough to be left alone, so just you and me, a date night, right?'

'Date night!' Julia remembered Ian's offer to babysit. A date night was exactly what her marriage needed. She snuggled into his arms, delighted at the idea. 'And at Le Jardin – I have wanted to try that place for ages. When's the booking for?'

'Friday.' Marc looked pleased with himself.

'Friday! Oh, but …'

'What?' Marc pushed her slightly away from him.

'Ian and Drew are coming for dinner on Friday. It's been written on the calendar for ages.'

'Oh, change it. They won't mind.'

Julia sighed. 'I can't. We already rescheduled it once when you had a cold last month. Can you re-book?'

'Doubt it. I was lucky getting that table – they had a cancellation. Usually you have to book months in advance.'

'Oh. I'm sorry, Marc. We'll just have to go there another time then. Maybe book somewhere else for the following week?'

'No, I think I'm busy then. Well, as usual, Jules, it seems you're prioritising your work and work colleagues over me. Fine, if that's what you want.' He stood up, stretched, and left the room.

Chapter 8

Pamela

Pam slept far better than she'd expected to, that first night. She'd feared that the noise of a dozen other girls snuffling, snoring, and coughing in the night might keep her awake, but she slept soundly and woke only when Clarissa nudged her toes.

'Up you get, Pam! Breakfast in twenty minutes then our bus will be here.'

She dressed in her new Wren uniform including her cap which bore a badge reading HMS Pembroke V. 'Even though we are based on land, we are part of the Navy and adhere to Navy traditions and use Naval terminology,' she'd been told when the uniform was issued. 'Our "ship" is HMS Pembroke V. And we work to "watches", not shifts. Your accommodation is to be known as your "cabin".'

Pam and Clarissa were outside with the other new girls in good time to board the bus for the journey back to Bletchley Park. There was no sign of the deer this morning although Pam looked intently for them as they passed through the parkland, where low-lying early morning mist made the grounds look ethereal. It would burn off in no time; the day promised to be a warm one.

Back at Bletchley, the girls were split into groups depending on where they were to be assigned. Pam was disappointed to find she was not put with Clarissa. The need for secrecy had been impressed upon them yet again, so she knew that if she was not doing the same work as her friend, she would not be able to discuss it with her. Still, there would be plenty of chances to talk about other things when they spent their leisure time together.

Pam and a couple of other new Wrens were escorted to a concrete hut known as Block F, where Max Newman, who Pam remembered from the interview day, awaited them. He peered at them through round spectacles and asked each of them their first names. 'I prefer to use your Christian names,' he told them. 'I think we work better together if we are more informal. Though you should all call me Mr Newman, of course.'

Pam and the others were directed to take their places sitting at rickety trestle tables in the sparsely furnished hut. In front of them was a blackboard, and Mr Newman took a place in front of it, chalk in hand.

'Like being back at school,' the girl next to Pam, whose name was Norah, whispered to her. 'Thought I was done with blackboards and chalk!'

Pam smiled at her but said nothing. She was excited at the idea of learning something new, and hoped it'd be mathematical. This was why she'd been picked, after all, because she was good at maths and had a logical brain.

And mathematical it was. Mr Newman gave a brief introduction: 'You will be working on code breaking. The Germans have begun using a new type of code for their communications, and we need to break it. The code is sent by teleprinter, using the teleprinter alphabet. Some of our remarkable men here worked out how the messages are encrypted, and how the German machine, which we call "Tunny", is constructed. It is fiendishly complicated, but by a combination of mathematics, mechanisation, and brute force we are able to decode some of their communications. You

Wrens in this block' – here he glanced around the room – 'will be involved in one part of the decryption process. You have been picked for your skills with maths. I am now going to teach you the teleprinter alphabet, and teach you how to "add" together two letters. This is just one part of the process, but a very important part. I expect you all to learn by heart the teleprinter alphabet and the letter combinations so that you can add them together in your heads.'

He picked up a length of teleprinter tape that was lying on a table beside him. 'You have two weeks of training before you will be put to work. By that time, I expect you to be able to read by eye, without reference, tapes such as these.' He handed the tape to the girl nearest him, who peered at it and passed it on. As it made its way around the room each girl who'd seen it stared back at Mr Newman with wide eyes. Some, Pam thought, looked daunted by the prospect. Others, like herself, were intrigued.

The tape was punched with holes in five rows along its length, with a sixth row of smaller holes that Mr Newman had explained were the sprocket rows for passing the tape through a machine. The larger holes in five rows were the encrypted message. In each position, there might be a hole, or no hole.

'We can represent this,' Mr Newman said, 'as a dot or a cross. Each letter of the alphabet can be represented by a combination of five dots and crosses. Thus the letter "A" is shown like this.' He turned to the blackboard and drew two crosses and three dots. 'It's a little like Morse code, but every letter or symbol always uses five crosses or dots, and no less. Here is "B".' He drew a cross, two dots and then two more crosses. 'On the tape, a cross is represented by a hole, and a dot by the absence of a hole.'

Pam was still holding the tape, and as she peered at it she saw that pattern running across it. Was that a letter B? She felt a rush of excitement as she passed the tape on to the next girl.

Mr Newman then handed out a sheet of paper to each girl on which was printed the whole of the teleprinter alphabet. 'You must learn all these by heart, so that you can read the letters fluently off a tape like the one that you are passing round. And now I will teach you how to add two letters together, using binary mathematics. This is one of the steps required in breaking the code.'

A little later, Pam's head was spinning after she'd learned that adding two of the same (such as two dots, or two crosses) produced a dot, whereas adding two different (a dot and a cross either way around) produced a cross. If you did this for the dots and crosses of each of the five positions of two letters, you could 'add' the letters together to produce a new letter. This, Mr Newman explained, was the start of unlocking the code. In time they would learn all the combinations, he told them, and would just 'know' that A plus B equals G, for example. Meanwhile, he gave them all a second sheet that contained a table of all the possible letter additions, for reference.

*

'Well,' Norah said to Pam, as they emerged blinking into the afternoon sunlight at the end of the day's training. 'How are we supposed to remember all that?'

Pam grinned. 'I suppose it will take practice. But isn't it lovely to be learning something new? I can't understand how adding the letters helps with breaking the code, though.'

'Maybe Mr Newman will tell us that tomorrow. It's fascinating, I agree. We've an hour before the transport back to Woburn. Do you fancy getting a cup of tea to drink sitting beside the lake?'

'Definitely!' Pam agreed. This was exactly what she'd dreamed of, when she first came to BP for her interview. Learning, friendship, sitting by the lake. She followed Norah into Hut 2, which served tea and, in the evenings, beer. They bought tea then went out to the lakeside where they found Clarissa sitting with a book.

'Clarissa, this is Norah. We're working in the same section. How's your first day been?' Pam introduced her two friends.

'Hello, Norah. Good to meet you. My day's been fine. My job seems to involve a lot of typing gobbledegook and reading German. That's all I can say, really. What about you?'

'Addition,' Pam said, and Norah grinned.

'Glad to hear you're making use of your maths abilities,' Clarissa said, with a laugh. 'Well, I'm delighted to report I've discovered there are to be ballroom dancing classes, held in the ballroom, no less! Right here at BP. I'm going to sign up. How about you two?'

'I have two left feet!' Norah said, but Pam nodded.

'I'd love to.'

'Excellent, I shall add your name to the list on the noticeboard. There's a girl in my hut who runs the class. She says there's regular dances in the Woburn village hall as well as some held here, so we've lots to look forward to.' Clarissa smiled at them both.

'I heard there's a dramatic society too,' Norah said. 'They put on plays, and local people come to see them. I fancy taking part in that.'

'It's quite a community, isn't it?' Pam sipped her tea and looked happily at her friends and then around the lake, where small groups of people were sitting on the grass. Would it be as good in winter, she wondered, when the weather wouldn't allow them to sit outside, and moving between huts and the main house might be cold and unpleasant. Still, it was only June so they could make the most of the rest of the good weather.

*

Although the journey back to Woburn was short, Pam managed to fall asleep on the transport, and woke up only when Clarissa nudged her just as the bus pulled up outside the Abbey.

Rubbing her eyes she followed Clarissa off the bus and around to the side entrance they'd been instructed to use. Passing a rose garden, she saw a young man busy snipping dead heads off the bushes. Suddenly Pam realised she'd left her gas mask on the bus.

'Darn it,' she said. 'Left something on the bus – I'll run back. See you inside.'

'All right,' Clarissa said, as Pam turned to hurry back to the bus before it left. As she approached it, its engine started and the bus pulled away.

'No! Wait, come back!' She waved frantically at the bus, hoping the driver might spot her in his mirror and stop, but the bus kept going. The young gardener saw her waving. He dropped his tools and ran after the bus, also waving and shouting. She suddenly realised she'd seen him before – he was the fair-haired young man from the railway station on her interview day.

Pam gave up running. She was hot, her skirt got in the way and her shoes weren't made for running in. She stood and watched in despair as the bus accelerated along the driveway. It wasn't only her gas mask. Tucked inside the case was her purse, containing all the cash she had. She'd probably get it back when the bus returned later, but she'd worry about it until then.

The young gardener hadn't given up. He was sprinting after the bus, and Pam saw his plan. He ran across the grass, cutting a corner. The bus would have to slow down at the bend, and the gardener would be able to get ahead of it and be in sight of the driver.

And it worked – he flagged the bus down just after it had rounded the corner. Pam hurried over to it, as the gardener spoke to the bus driver through the window, pointing back at her.

'Thank you, thank you! I left something inside,' she gasped, as she approached, and the driver opened the door for her. She quickly retrieved her gas mask and thanked the driver once more before getting off the bus again.

The gardener was standing by the side of the drive, grinning and panting. 'Everything all right, is it?'

She held up the gas mask. 'It is now! My purse is in here too. Thank you so much. I would never have caught up with the bus.'

'Ah, I was a good runner when I was at school.' He smiled,

wiped his hand on his trousers and held it out for her to shake. 'Frank Miller.'

'I'm Pamela Jackson. Nice to meet you, Mr Miller.'

'Oh, call me Frank, please. So, do you work here?'

'And you must call me Pam. Everyone else does. No, I don't work here, I'm just billeted here. We work at B—somewhere else.' She'd so nearly said Bletchley, and had stopped herself just in time. But did it matter? It was no secret that a lot of people – military and civilian – worked at Bletchley Park. 'They know we're here, they just don't know what we do,' Max Newman had said. 'And that's how it must stay.'

'Bletchley Park?' Frank asked, and Pam nodded. 'Ah, I thought I saw you there on Monday, at the station.'

'Yes, you did. And you? Do you work here?'

He grinned again, showing even white teeth. He was, Pam thought, probably the best-looking young man she'd ever laid eyes on. 'I do, yes. Trying to keep this garden looking its best. Only me here now – there used to be a team of gardeners but now it's just me. I do what I can.'

'Did the others get called up?' As she said it, she immediately regretted her words. Of course they'd have been called up. And some, who might have been Frank's friends, could have died.

'Mostly. Though one went voluntarily at the start of the war. I can't. Got asthma, see.' He shrugged as he said it, and she realised it wasn't something he wanted to talk about. Perhaps he felt guilty that all his fellow gardeners had gone off to fight for their country and he hadn't been able to. Pam had known someone from home like that, who'd been refused by the army due to his history of epilepsy. The fellow, a friend of her brother's, had said people spat at him on the street, assuming he was a conscientious objector.

'Ah. Well, you're doing a wonderful job here.' She waved a hand at the nearest flower bed, that was neatly edged and trimmed. It was good to see that some beds were still used for roses and hydrangeas and camellias. Elsewhere in the Abbey grounds the beds had been dug over and planted with vegetables, like so many other gardens across the country.

'I do my bit. So, are you heading inside the Abbey now? May I walk with you?'

'Of course.' She blushed a little as they turned to walk back up the driveway to the Abbey. It wasn't long until dinner time, and she needed to freshen up first. And find Clarissa.

'May I ask a question?' Frank said, as they walked.

She nodded.

'There are lots of you Wrens stationed here and being taken to Bletchley every day. What on earth are you all doing there?'

'Oh, you know. Secretarial work.' Well, Clarissa had said she was mostly typing, so in some ways it wasn't a lie. And they'd been told to say they were secretaries, if asked by anyone outside of BP.

He nodded, as though that made sense. 'I haven't seen you here before.'

'I'm new. Only just arrived yesterday. When you saw me on Monday I'd come for an interview.' Pam blushed a little and mentally kicked herself. Had she said too much already?

'They seem to need a lot of secretaries. There are more coming every week.'

'Yes, they seem to.' She smiled brightly at him and cast about for some way of changing the subject. 'Did you work here before the war?'

'Not really. I was at school, though I sometimes worked here in the holidays.'

'You're local then?'

He nodded. 'I was brought up by my aunt, in Woburn village. Well, here we are.' They had arrived at the side entrance where Pam needed to go in. Frank gave a little bow. 'I hope to see you again, Miss Pamela Jackson.'

She laughed at his formality. 'I'm sure you will. Thank you once again, Mr Frank Miller.'

At the door she turned and looked back. Frank was still

standing where she'd left him, watching her, smiling to himself. Pam felt a flutter of excitement. Clarissa had wondered whether they'd find romance at Bletchley, but it looked as though for Pam at least, romance might be closer still, right here at Woburn.

Chapter 9

Julia

Over the few days following her trip to Bletchley Park, Julia found she couldn't stop thinking about her grandmother's role there, particularly at 3 a.m. when she frequently lay awake fretting about anything and everything. At least thinking about that was better than dwelling on the little spat with Marc over his restaurant booking. Thankfully he seemed to have relented on that, and cancelled the reservation, agreeing with her that they could not put off Ian and Drew again.

It was around 3 a.m. one morning when she recalled she'd had a Christmas letter from Clarissa's daughter Caroline. In it, Caroline had mentioned something about compiling her family history, if Julia remembered correctly. They weren't at all close – Julia thought she had probably last seen Caroline at her grandmother's funeral, many years before. Grandma and Clarissa had been best friends most of their lives, and now their children and grandchildren were still on each other's Christmas card lists. Julia made herself a mental note to dig out that letter. With luck it would also contain an email address. Perhaps she could ask Caroline what she knew about Clarissa and Pam's work at Bletchley Park. It would also be worth asking her own father. Maybe he knew a little about it.

The following morning, during a coffee break, Julia took the opportunity to call her dad. He lived in Spain, where he'd been since Mum died so many years before. Julia didn't phone him often enough, she knew, but he'd never been a natural on the phone. They tended to call each other only when there was some real news, or something important to ask about.

He answered straight away. 'Hello, love. Anything wrong?'

'No, all good, thanks, Dad. How are you?'

'Oh, you know. Off to play golf in ten minutes. It's a hard life.'

'But someone's got to do it.' They both laughed at the joke they made on almost every phone call. Julia was glad her father was so happy and settled in Spain, although she missed him and wished the boys knew him better. 'Listen, Dad. I wanted to ask you something. Do you know anything about Grandma – I mean Mum's mum – and her role during the war? Bob and I were looking at some old photos he found and it turns out she worked at Bletchley Park, on the code-breaking operation.'

'Oh, interesting. No, I didn't know that at all.'

'Do you still have any old papers or photos or diaries, anything like that, that Mum might have kept relating to her mother?'

'Sorry, love. I dumped all that sort of stuff before moving to Spain. Remember I came here with just one small car-load of stuff, and my golf clubs took up most of the boot space.'

'Priorities, eh, Dad?'

'Indeed. You know, I don't recall any mention of what Pam did in the war, and I'm not even sure if your mother would have known she'd worked at Bletchley Park. They all kept everything so secret, that generation.'

'Yes. Remember Clarissa? We think she worked there too. You don't happen to have an email address for her daughter, do you?'

Dad gave a little chuckle. 'I didn't even remember she had a daughter. Sorry, love, I'm not in touch with that family at all.'

'Ah, no worries. I have a postal address for her at least. I was just wondering if she knew anything more about it all.'

'Well, let me know how you get on.'

'Will do.'

'Kids all right, are they? Marc all right? How's tricks with the business?'

'Yeah, all good, all good.'

'Well, must dash. The first tee beckons.'

'Have a good day. Bye, Dad.' As Julia hung up, she made a little promise to herself to try to see more of him. When they were together in person, they'd chat for hours, but he was often awkward on the phone. Maybe they could take a trip to Spain in the summer, as a holiday.

After the phone call, Julia looked through her overflowing to-do list. They had such a lot of work on. It was good to be busy, better than sitting around with very little to do. But she still wished they could take on three contractors as she'd originally planned. The two that Ian had eventually agreed to were due to start next week. Julia had interviewed several, and had ended up using one woman they'd used before – Maura – who Julia knew would turn in solid, error-free code, even if she wasn't the fastest at it. The other contractor was a young fellow named Rahul who had impressed Julia in his interview, but who had not yet much experience. Still, everyone had to start somewhere and she'd felt inclined to give him a chance. She looked through the list, trying to decide what to do next, but couldn't concentrate. Ian was in the office with her, currently leaning back in his chair and staring into space. Daydreaming, Julia thought. Interruptible.

'Ian?'

'Mmm?' He turned in her direction.

'Can I ask you something?'

'You just did,' he said, grinning cheekily.

'Seriously, though …'

'Sure.'

She watched as Ian rearranged his features into an expression of concentration. 'You've remembered about coming for dinner on Friday? With Drew?'

'Of course! Looking forward to it. Want us to bring anything?'

'Just yourselves.' She took a deep breath and Ian waited, looking expectant. 'The thing is, you know you said Marc and I should have a date night?'

'I did, and the offer's still there if you need a babysitter.'

'Marc had the same idea. He booked a table for Friday. He hadn't checked our calendar. So he's had to cancel and he's … well … a little uppity about it. I'm only telling you because I'm scared he might seem a little … off. On Friday. When you're there.'

'Jules, you could have rearranged with me and Drew. We wouldn't have minded.'

She shook her head. 'Ian, I didn't want to. It had been on the calendar for weeks, he knows our system, he should have checked. I'm sorry, I don't mean to be bringing you into all this, but I wanted to warn you in case he said anything snarky. You know what he can be like.'

Ian frowned. 'I've never thought of him as the snarky type.'

'He sometimes is. About the company.' She sighed. 'It's jealousy, I think. Because I earn more than him, and could be considered more successful than him. If I'm honest, I think he's a bit old-fashioned – thinks women should stay home and look after the house and the children. At most get a "little job"' – she made quote marks in the air – ' that brings in pin money. Not be the main breadwinner as I have been for years.'

'Hmm. Anything I can do to help?'

Julia shook her head. 'No, I don't think so. He needs to just get over himself. I mean, he benefits too from the success of our business. The house, the money, the lifestyle.' Not, she thought, that she ever had much chance to enjoy the money that had come with success. She was always working too hard. 'Anyway, for goodness sake don't mention this conversation to Marc, will you?'

'Oh God, Jules, as if I would!' Ian made a mouth-zipping gesture followed by a Scout's honour salute. She grinned. Of course he wouldn't. He was the one person she had always felt able to rely on.

*

On Friday evening she finished work at six on the dot, leaving the office even before Barry had. She'd have to go back through and lock up after he'd gone. Or send one of the boys to do it, which might be safer. She might be too tempted to sit down and do a bit of work on the way through, and there really was too much to do in the house preparing for the dinner with Ian and Drew.

First things first – feed the boys. They were both home for once, and she'd planned a quick pasta dinner for them that they could eat early, then get out of the way in their bedrooms. They hated being expected to join in with boring adult dinners and conversations. While they were eating she did a quick tidy of the sitting room and dining room, and ran the Hoover round. And then it was time to get on with the cooking. She'd gone for something simple but tasty: a retro prawn cocktail starter, a main course of chicken cooked with a spicy mango chutney sauce and served with mixed-grain rice, and a cheese platter to finish.

Marc arrived home from work just as she was putting the chicken dish in the oven. He crossed over the kitchen and kissed her. 'Looks good. When are they coming?'

'Dinner for eight. I expect they'll be here at a quarter to.'

Marc looked her up and down. 'You're still in your work clothes, aren't you?'

'I haven't had time to change yet, just about to go and do that. It'll only take me a few minutes. I know, you weigh out the rice and rinse it, while I change. Could you also set the table, please?'

'Sorry, love. Got to change myself – and make sure there's enough beer in the fridge as I know you often forget that.' He disappeared out of the kitchen as though to linger there would infect him somehow.

Julia let out the sigh she'd been holding and got on with what was needed, then yelled for Oscar to please come and help set the table, on promise of extra pocket money if he did a good job. 'We're having a starter, so two lots of cutlery each, and put out wine glasses and napkins too, please.' Oscar grunted in acknowledgement but went into the kitchen to do the job.

In their bedroom, Marc was lying on the bed, scrolling through Facebook posts on his phone. He hadn't yet changed. Julia bit her tongue before she said anything. She changed quickly into a pair of skinny black jeans, heels, and a floaty top that always made her feel special. She added a little bit more make-up than she usually wore. Marc wouldn't even notice, and Ian and Drew had eyes for each other only, so she was dressing up for herself. But why not?

Back downstairs, Oscar had done a fair job of laying the table and had disappeared back to his room. She finished it off, opened a bottle of wine and poured herself a glass, then put the starters on the table and arranged the cheese selection on a serving plate. The rice was in a pan waiting to cook. Everything was in hand. You could have it all – career and family – but you needed help. Most women had help from their spouses. She needed to rely on her sons. Thank goodness they were old enough to help, and beginning to understand that sometimes they needed to.

The doorbell rang, and at the same time Marc came downstairs, dressed more or less as he had been when he went up. Only his tie had been removed and the cuffs of his shirt turned up.

'Ian! And hello, Drew. Been too long since we saw you.' She kissed both of them, and accepted the flowers Drew handed her. Ian was clutching two bottles of decent wine. Both men nodded at Marc as they went through to the sitting room. They'd visited often enough to know the way.

There were the usual first few minutes of fetching drinks, putting the flowers in water, asking each other how they were. Drew nodded at the picture that hung above the fireplace. 'I always worry you've brought that out just because I'm visiting.'

'Don't be daft. I love it. You're so talented,' Julia told him. Drew was an artist, and managed to make a modest living selling his pictures.

'Yeah, who knew Drew drew?' Ian said, making the same joke he always made when the subject of his husband's occupation came up.

Marc seemed a bit distracted, Julia thought. He kept checking his phone, as though expecting a text at any moment. 'Marc, can't you put your phone away for the evening?' Julia hissed at him when the others were out of earshot. 'We don't let the boys have phones at the table, so why you?'

'There might be a problem at work. We're implementing an upgrade – you know how it is. Just need to keep an eye on it. It's not like you never do anything for your work in the evenings, is it? I bet you and Ian will end up talking about it later anyway.'

'Talking about what, mate?' said Ian, who'd just re-entered the room.

'Work,' Marc said. 'She's telling me off for checking on something at my work.'

'Ah, we won't mention the business at all this evening, will we, Jules? We spend enough time during working hours talking about it. And everything's going swimmingly at the moment, anyway. No worries that we'd need to discuss on a Friday night. It's all good.'

'Well, I'll drink to that,' Julia said, not sure if she was drinking to the idea of not talking shop that evening, or that the business was going well. It was, of course; their new designs had landed them some new contracts, albeit ones that weren't yet signed and were dependent on them delivering the enhanced systems.

'Yeah, no work talk tonight. This is a work-free zone,' Drew added. 'I need the break anyway. Been run off my feet with new commissions all week. Well, cheers.' He lifted his glass of wine, and they all clinked glasses, except Marc, who was still peering at his phone.

Julia frowned at him. Ian caught her eye and gave a little shrug, as if to say, let it go. He was right. Unless she wanted a row, in front of Ian and Drew, there was nothing she could do right now.

Drew seemed to have noticed the slight awkwardness in the room. He glanced at Ian, then tried to start up a conversation with Marc about rugby. 'Last Six Nations matches this weekend, isn't it? Who's going to win the championship?'

Julia smiled. Drew knew nothing about rugby. Even she was well aware that Ireland couldn't now be beaten, no matter what happened in the final three matches.

'Er, think Ireland already have it in the bag,' Marc replied, without looking up from his phone. He was tapping a message in with his forefinger.

'Ah, right. Cool. Will you be watching the matches?'

'Yeah. Hope so. Might go to a pub to watch the ones on Sunday. Better atmosphere than sitting in the front room with Julia scowling at me. I think she thinks I should spend the weekends doing jobs around the house. She doesn't get how bloody hard I have to work all week. Women, huh?'

Drew looked shocked for a moment, but then Marc laughed and nudged Drew with his elbow. 'Joke, mate.'

Julia also laughed. But she couldn't help but wonder if Marc might have actually meant it.

'Jules works hard all week too,' Ian said. 'I guess some jobs have to be done at the weekend because there's no other chance, and it's only fair to split them, right? We split everything straight down the middle.' He reached across and took Drew's hand, who smiled back at him.

'Two blokes together, you've no choice but to split the jobs.

But for us, well, Julia's the better cook. Honestly, there's no point me trying to do anything more complicated than frying an egg.'

'Maybe you should learn, mate,' Drew said quietly.

Marc stared at him, but said nothing.

'Well, come on, everyone. Starters are on the table – let's go through to the dining room. I just need to put the rice on, and I'll join you in there.'

'Right-oh,' Ian said, and led the way – the job that should have been Marc's, but he hung back to scowl at Julia.

'What's your problem tonight?' she hissed at him.

He shrugged. 'No problem. None at all. You spend all week with Ian, barely see me, then all Friday evening too. I feel like second best, Julia. You could have moved the dinner party so we could have had our date night, but no. Ian and your business first, as always.'

Julia battled with herself to stop the tears. He was still on about having to cancel the reservation, then. 'Now's not the time for this, Marc. Let's talk about it over the weekend, all right?'

'If you're sure you can make time for me.' Marc went through to the dining room.

She boiled the kettle and put the rice on the stove, setting a timer. There was a little part of her that wanted to just barricade herself in the bedroom and sob. But she had guests, and she'd do her damnedest to make sure they had a good evening. She took a gulp of her wine and went to join them in the dining room. Ian and Drew had waited for her, but Marc had already eaten half of his prawn cocktail.

'This looks lovely. Haven't had one of these since, ooh, about 1974,' Drew said, grinning.

'You weren't even born in 1974, idiot,' Ian said, giving him a playful punch.

'You're right though, it is a retro dish. I love it, and it's easy and quick. Enjoy!' Julia picked up her fork, right at the same moment that Marc finished his.

‘That was great. I’ll be back in a mo,’ Marc said, getting up from the table.

‘What’s up with him?’ Drew asked, when Marc had left the room.

‘I don’t know. He’s being a shit. Can we just ignore him?’ Julia said, her voice falsely bright.

‘Good idea. More wine?’ Ian smiled reassuringly at her and topped up all their glasses. He then launched into a long anecdote about something one of their friends had done, that had her roaring with laughter. Good old Ian. She could always rely on him to defuse any awkward situation.

*

The evening improved after Marc re-joined them for the main course. He seemed to make more of an effort, as though he’d realised he was behaving badly. Everyone relaxed as the wine flowed, and the evening ended up being a good one. Julia told Ian and Drew about her day at Bletchley, about what she’d discovered about her grandmother’s role during the war. Both men were fascinated and asked lots of questions, while Marc gave a loud and extravagant yawn.

Chapter 10

Pamela

There was a noticeboard affixed to a wall in one of the long corridors Pam used daily on her way to and from her cabin in Woburn Abbey. She and Clarissa made a point of stopping to check for new notices each morning as they made their way down to breakfast.

'Did you see that?' Clarissa asked, one morning about a week after they'd arrived at Woburn. 'A dance, in the village hall.'

'Ooh! When?' Pam peered at the handwritten poster her friend was indicating.

'A week Saturday – not long! What on earth shall I wear?' Clarissa flung the back of her hand against her forehead in a dramatic gesture and Pam laughed.

'I would bet my life savings that you own something more suitable than I do. But it doesn't really matter, does it? We just need to make the best of what we've got. I'm already looking forward to it.'

'So am I.' Clarissa hooked her arm through Pam's as they went down to the dining hall. 'We must make sure everyone knows about it. Norah who you work with, and Maggie and Amelia in my section. And the boys!' She giggled. 'Make sure you mention it to every good-looking fellow you come across. They'll all come if they know you're going to be there. We need plenty of men to dance with!'

Pam grinned and tried to imagine herself asking any of the fellows she came across in her day-to-day life, if they'd like to go to the dance. She tried, and failed. If only she had the kind of self-confidence Clarissa had, which was partly, she was sure, due to Clarissa's more privileged, upper-class upbringing.

They chatted all through breakfast about the dance, passing the news on to everyone sitting at their table. What to wear, what sort of music there would be, would there be alcohol, would there be transport to it, who else was going?

'It's in the village hall, just a short walk away so no need for transport,' a girl said, who'd been living at the Abbey a couple of months longer than they had.

'Oh! I haven't had time to explore yet,' Pam said. She had a half day off at the weekend; maybe she'd use that to walk around the local area and get her bearings.

'You must. It'll help you settle in, too,' the other girl said kindly.

A few minutes later, Pam was outside, waiting for the transport to Bletchley Park. Clarissa was telling her about a frock she owned that she was considering altering for the dance, when Pam noticed a familiar figure walking up the driveway, a spade hoisted on his shoulder. Frank spotted her and lifted his hand to wave.

Pam gave a tentative wave back, and Clarissa turned to stare at her. 'Who's that? He's lovely looking, isn't he?'

'He's a gardener here. His name's Frank Miller. Remember the other day, I told you I'd left my gas mask on the bus and a gardener helped me flag it down? That was Frank.'

'Oh! I'd pictured some wrinkled, crusty old man in dirty trousers.' Clarissa laughed. 'At least, that's what the gardeners left on my parents' estate are like. How lovely that here we have young, handsome ones!'

'Only him, I think. He said his colleagues have all gone off to the front but he has asthma so is excused from the call-up.'

'That's lucky for him,' Clarissa said.

'I got the impression he'd have liked to be able to do his bit,' Pam replied.

'Well, anyway, we must make sure he knows about the dance. It's not just for us BP staff – I'm sure there'll be locals at it as well, and that young fellow looks as though he'd be a wonderful addition. Although I must say, I prefer a man in uniform myself. RAF, ideally. All that smart navy serge, bringing out the blue of their eyes.' Clarissa gave an exaggerated sigh and gazed into the middle distance. 'We have to hope that somewhere in the vicinity there's an RAF base, and that those lads will come to the dance, and will take pity on us poor Wrens.'

The bus arrived, and the driver opened the doors and got out. 'Five minutes, ladies,' he called out, and went inside.

'Probably needs the lavatory,' Pam said, and Clarissa nodded. 'You get on. I'll be there in a jiffy.'

Pam climbed onto the bus and took a seat near the back, where they usually sat. Through the window she saw Clarissa hurrying across the grass to where Frank had begun digging over a flower bed. She gasped, realising that Clarissa was almost certainly telling him about the dance. She saw Frank smile broadly and nod, and then Clarissa ran back to the bus and took her seat beside Pam.

'Whew. I'm worn out, now! Anyway, he said he'd love to be there. I said I was your friend and you were definitely going, and his eyes lit up, I can tell you.' She turned and winked at Pam. 'I think he likes you.'

'Ah, piffle,' Pam said, but secretly she was delighted. She'd never have had the courage to ask Frank if he was going, and to now know that he was, and that maybe he liked her … Well. It was something to think about, all right. And perhaps she'd write about Frank in her next letters to Ada and Emily. Or maybe she'd just keep him to herself, for the moment.

*

It was hard to concentrate that day, and indeed every day between then and the day of the dance, but Pamela knew she must. There was a lot to learn, a lot to memorise and try to understand. Their job, Mr Newman had said several times, was essential to Britain's success in the war. Along with teams in other huts, if they could break these codes and read the German messages, they could save the lives of Allied servicemen. Pam had felt a thrill run through her, knowing she was training to do such an important job.

One day, they were taken through to another block and shown a machine. 'We call it the Heath Robinson,' Mr Newman said, 'after those cartoons in the papers I'm sure you'll all have seen.' Pam stood and stared at the contraption. A huge metal frame stood on end, looking like an upturned bedstead. Within it, bands of teleprinter tape were fixed around cogs and wheels. Attached to this was some kind of switch board, with dozens of knobs and wires and lights.

Newman explained how the machine could be used to shorten the work required to decrypt coded messages, and showed them a 'Tunny' machine with its twelve enciphering wheels and plug board. 'We wire this up according to the output from the Heath Robinson, and feed in the message tape.' It all made Pam's head spin, and she was thankful that Newman had emphasised that none of them would need to know or understand the entire decryption process. Each Wren would be assigned to one job. They had a test scheduled for the end of their fortnight training, and the results of that would determine which job they did. Pam liked the idea of working with the Heath Robinson – setting its tapes up, plugging and replugging wires, reading off the resulting counts to feed into the next run, but Norah shuddered.

'Can't see myself having anything to do with that monstrosity,' she said to Pam when they went for a tea break. 'I'd prefer the next step, with those Tunny machines. They look more manageable and from what Mr Newman said, more reliable.'

It was true that Newman had said the Heath Robinson suffered from frequent breakdowns. Mechanics were on hand with all shifts, to coax the beast into working.

One of the mechanics was familiar to Pam: Edwin Denham. He smiled shyly at her as Newman explained the workings of Heath Robinson. And later, while she sat by the lake with Norah and a cup of tea, he came out to join them.

'Mind if I sit with you?' he asked.

'Not at all.' Norah gestured to the ground, inviting him to sit with them. He hoisted up his trouser legs and crouched down, then sat on the grass, almost toppling over backwards as he did so.

'Whoops! I'm so clumsy, sorry.' He held out a hand to Norah to shake. 'Edwin Denham. I've already met Miss Jackson.'

'I'm Norah Clarke. Pleased to meet you.'

'Hello,' Pam said. 'I see you work with the Heath Robinson?'

'I do, yes. Rickety old thing. We're calling in an engineer, from the Post Office, to see if he can suggest improvements. When it doesn't break down it saves a lot of time and effort.' He gave a snort of laughter. 'Which is about one time in four.'

Pam began to rethink her desire to work with the machine. It would be frustrating if it broke down so often.

'You must be very patient,' Norah said, 'to keep fixing it so often.'

Edwin shrugged. 'It's what I do. It's the small part I play in all this.' He blushed a little then, and cleared his throat. 'Um, I don't know if you've heard, but there's a dance up at Woburn village, on Saturday. I believe you're probably billeted there? Are you planning to go, by any chance?' He looked mostly at Pam as he said this, but glanced over at Norah once or twice as though making an effort to include her in his question.

Pam smiled. 'Yes, I'd heard of it. I'm certainly going. Norah, I mentioned it to you the other day?'

'Yes, of course. Yes, I expect to be there too, though I'm not billeted at Woburn. It depends if they are laying on any transport to get Wrens from Bletchley to Woburn that night. I mean, at different times to the usual buses for the watch changes.' Norah shrugged. 'I'll try to find out.'

'Marvellous!' Edwin grinned broadly, as though Christmas had come early. 'I very much hope to see you there, Miss Jackson. And you, Miss Clarke.'

'Oh please, we are Pam and Norah,' Pam said. 'Look, even Mr Newman wants us all to use first names, except for himself. So let's not stand on ceremony. Yes, we'll see you there.' She sipped the last of her tea, as Edwin checked his watch.

'Oh, I must be getting back. Break time over.' He jumped to his feet with as little grace as he'd sat down, mock-saluted the girls and set off across the grass towards Block F.

'He likes you,' Norah said, nudging Pam's shoulder.

'Ah, he likes both of us,' she replied. 'He seems nice. A gentle sort, I thought when I first met him.'

'Yes. Gentle, honourable, and someone who'd be a great friend. Or perhaps more than a friend.' Norah winked.

Pam blushed. 'Not my type.' What was her type, she wondered, as she answered Norah. An image of Frank came into her mind – tall, blond, athletic despite his asthma. Edwin was slighter in build, with mousy brown hair and spectacles. The dance was just a few days away, and both boys were going to be there.

*

Pam was thankful it was summer and warm, so there was no need for stockings. Not that she even had any decent ones that she could wear to the dance. But she had a dress, the one she'd last worn to a dance back home, with Ada and Emily. That seemed such a long time ago now! She had some lipstick too, and planned to wash her hair and set it in rollers before the dance. Clarissa had promised to help and was also lending her a necklace of jet beads, that looked striking against the pale blue of her dress. They weren't working on the afternoon of the dance, so there was plenty of time to get ready.

Unfortunately, the elderly plumbing of Woburn Abbey was not quite up to the job of catering for dozens of Wrens all trying to bathe and wash their hair on the same day. The hot water ran out in no time, so for Pam it was a cold strip wash, then she leaned over the sink to wash her hair. 'This won't be much fun in winter,' she said to Clarissa, as she wrapped a towel around her head. 'I think if we have a dance in winter I'll wash my hair the day before. It won't look as nice, but at least I won't freeze my scalp off in the cold water.'

'Good plan,' Clarissa said. She fingered her own honey-blonde locks, regarding herself in the bathroom mirror. 'You know what, I'm thinking mine will do, if I brush it and pin it.' She shuddered. 'Can't face a cold hair wash. Perhaps I'll get up early tomorrow and pinch all the hot water then.'

'We'd not be much use on the front line, would we, with all our hair-washing needs,' Pam said wryly, and Clarissa laughed.

'No, darling, we wouldn't.'

*

They walked from the Abbey to the dance, which was held in the village hall, a short walk across the Abbey parkland past ornamental ponds, then along a lane into the tiny village. It was a beautiful evening, and the sun was still shining brightly as they walked, arm in arm, along with several other Wrens, all chattering excitedly about what the night might hold for them. Clarissa teased Pam about 'all' the men who'd be there for her. 'That handsome gardener Frank, and Norah tells me Edwin Denham has his eye on you too. Tell me, which do you prefer?'

Pam laughed. 'Oh, don't make me choose! They're so different. Frank's certainly better-looking and seems a real gentleman, but Edwin's a quiet, kind soul. I like them both! What about you, have you met anyone you like yet?'

'Oh, dozens and dozens!' Clarissa laughed, and shook her head. 'No, actually, no one yet. But I live in hope.'

The dance hall was small, in keeping with the size of the village. But it was thronging with people – airmen from nearby bases, other workers from Bletchley – both military and civilian, locals and of course almost every Wren billeted at the Abbey who was not on duty that evening. There was a palpable air of excitement as groups gathered outside waiting for their friends, and then went inside where a six-piece band was playing the latest hits. Already the dance floor was busy. Clarissa and Pam made their way to the cloakroom and left their coats, then somehow managed to get near to the bar. 'What'll you have? I'll pay,' Clarissa shouted over the music and hubbub to Pam.

'Gin and tonic?' she replied, it being the only drink she'd heard of. Ada had drunk gin and tonics at the last dance.

'Great choice, if they have gin,' Clarissa said. It seemed they were in luck, for a moment later she handed Pam a glass that even had a slice of cucumber in the top to garnish it. Pam sipped it carefully, liking the tang of the alcohol and feeling very grown up.

'Pam! You're here!' Norah wrapped an arm around Pam's shoulder and hugged her. 'Edwin's over there. We came on the same transport from Bletchley.' She indicated a table on the far side of the hall, where Edwin was standing holding a glass of beer, his other hand in the pocket of his brown suit jacket. He looked a bit out of place, Pam thought, as though he wasn't quite sure how to handle himself at a dance. She resolved to dance with him at least once. He worked hard. He deserved to have a night out that he enjoyed.

'Hi Norah!' she said, kissing her friend on the cheek. 'I'll go over to say hello to Edwin, too.'

'Yes, you do that,' Norah said, and turned to chat to Clarissa.

As Pam made her way over, dodging dancing couples and people fighting their way to the bar, Edwin caught sight of her and grinned, raising his hand to say hello. Unfortunately, it was the hand that held his beer, and he spilt a little of it over his hand and sleeve. Pam stifled a giggle as he pulled a handkerchief out of his pocket and began dabbing at it, spilling more in the process.

'Pamela Jackson, to be known as Pam. I am glad you are here.' She hadn't quite reached Edwin when Frank appeared at her elbow.

'Frank! Oh, hello! I – I didn't know you were coming.' She felt herself blushing and hoped it was dark enough in the hall for him not to notice.

He laughed gently. 'I think you did, Pam. Your friend – Clarissa, isn't it? – asked me if I was coming, and told me you would be here. I'm glad to have the chance to speak with you, get to know you a little, and dance with you, maybe. Speaking of which, would you like to dance right away? I love this tune.'

Without waiting for an answer, he plucked the glass out of Pam's hand, put it on a nearby table and took her hand, dragging her onto the dance floor. She cast an apologetic glance back over her shoulder at Edwin who was still dabbing at his spilt beer but then allowed herself to be caught up by Frank, his arm around her waist as he whirled her around in a foxtrot.

It was exhilarating. She'd danced with boys a few times before, back home, but never like this. Frank's shoulder felt warm and muscular beneath her hand. His grip was firm. His dancing was excellent; she allowed herself to relax as he led her in ever more complex steps, whirling around, using all the space on the dance floor. She knew there were plenty of other couples dancing but it felt as though there was only the two of them, as though the universe had shrunk until it contained only them. He kept his eyes – clear, startling blue – focused on her throughout. She was his world. He was hers.

The spell was broken when the band finished playing, couples parted and applauded, new couples came onto the floor and others left to return to their drinks or friends. Frank smiled at her, bowed and then brought her hand to his lips and kissed it. The old-fashioned gesture made her blush. 'Shall we dance some more later, Pamela?' he asked. 'You should return to your friends for now.' She nodded, feeling too overwhelmed to say anything.

She crossed the dance floor back to where Norah and Clarissa were waiting, then remembered her drink was on the table beside Edwin. She retrieved it, nodding at Edwin, and went back to the girls. Clarissa was grinning at her.

'You two looked so good dancing together,' Clarissa said. 'He's quite the catch, you know, and he seems to really like you.'

'I … I like him, too,' Pam admitted.

Norah squealed with excitement. 'And there's me thinking it was quiet old Edwin Denham you had your eye on. You're so pretty, Pam. You could have your pick of any of the fellows here.'

'Where is Edwin?' Clarissa said, and Norah pointed him out. He was still sitting on his own at another table.

'Ah, he looks lonely. I'm going to see if he wants to dance,' Clarissa said, and handed her drink to Pam to hold. A moment later she was pulling an embarrassed and reluctant-looking Edwin onto the dance floor.

*

It was a wonderful evening. Pam danced with Edwin once, with several other young men, and with Frank twice more. While dancing with others, she couldn't seem to stop herself from checking where Frank was, who he was dancing with, checking if he was looking in her direction at all. Once, she caught him watching her. She threw him a smile over the shoulder of the airman who was leading her around the dance floor, and received a smile and a nod in return. He really was so very good-looking, and charming. Her stomach gave a little flutter as she considered whether, possibly, just perhaps … he might be interested in her as someone to step out with …

At the end of the night, Clarissa and Pam queued to retrieve their coats. Norah, Edwin, and everyone else billeted in Bletchley had already left on their army transport buses. It was just Woburn locals and the Wrens from the Abbey who were left. Groups of Wrens were already walking back across the parkland.

'Pamela? May I walk you home?' Frank had appeared at her elbow.

'Oh! Yes, I'd like that,' she said. 'I just need to wait for my coat. I can meet you outside.'

Clarissa gave her a questioning glance when Frank had moved out of earshot. 'Shall I walk with you? Or hang back? Or I can walk back with some other girls if you prefer.'

Pam smiled at her friend. 'I'll be all right, if you can find others to walk with. He's a real gentleman. I'll see you back at the Abbey.'

'I shall require a full debrief,' Clarissa said sternly, and Pam laughed.

'Of course! See you later.'

Outside, Frank was leaning against the wall of the village hall. As Pam came out, he joined her. 'Did you enjoy your evening?'

'Very much so,' she replied. 'It's so good to be able to forget about the war for a short time, and just have fun.'

'Indeed.' He moved his elbow away from his side, inviting her to take his arm. She slipped her hand into the crook of his elbow, enjoying once more the feeling of warmth and strength that came from him. They began the walk back to Woburn Abbey, at a relaxed pace. Groups of Wrens passed them, chattering and giggling. Clarissa was with one group, and waved as she passed.

There was a full moon. Just as well, Pam thought, otherwise it would have been hard to see their way. Torches weren't allowed, under the blackout regulations. But the silvery moonlight was more than enough to light the way, along the lane and then through the Abbey parkland. By the time they reached the ornamental ponds there was no one else on the path; the others had all overtaken them.

'Shall we sit here, for a moment?' Frank asked, gesturing to a bench that overlooked the pond.

'Mmm, yes, why not. It's a beautiful night.' Pam sat down beside Frank. His arm was along the back of the bench, and it just seemed so natural to snuggle into him a little, allowing him to put his hand onto her far shoulder.

'I enjoyed dancing with you, Pamela,' he said. 'I hope there will be other occasions like this.'

'Well, you know where I live and where I work.' She turned to smile at him, wondering if he might kiss her, wondering if she would let him kiss her.

But he simply smiled back. 'Yes. For sure, I will see you around the grounds of the Abbey. You know where I work, where I will be every day.'

'I don't know where you live, though,' she said.

'Oh, just in the village,' he replied. He didn't seem to want to elaborate. It didn't matter. Pam couldn't imagine herself going to his home, not yet, anyway. They'd only just met. This damned war encouraged people to take things too quickly, to hurry relationships along rather than let them develop in their own time. Usually that was because the man was about to go off to war. But not in her case. Frank was exempt. She was glad of this – glad he wouldn't be suddenly taken from her, and that they had the time to let things develop slowly.

It was late. Pam found herself yawning. She tried to stifle it but Frank had noticed. 'I should get you back,' he said, standing up and pulling her to her feet. She allowed herself to stumble a little into his arms as she rose, and for a wonderful moment they stood, pressed against each other, arms around each other, under the moonlight. He'd kiss her now, she thought. He must. She gazed up at him, allowing her lips to part slightly. She'd never been kissed by a boy. Ada had reported it was a wonderful experience.

But again, he just smiled at her, released her, and then took her hand and led her back to the Abbey.

Chapter 11

Julia

Oscar seemed abnormally sullen the following week. He'd come in from school, kick off his shoes by the front door, drop his school bags and head to his room. Julia would follow the trail of debris there when she entered the main house after finishing work. He seemed not to have as many after-school events as usual. Come to think of it, she hadn't had to wash his football kit for a couple of weeks.

'You all right, Oscar?' she asked him, one afternoon. She'd purposely decided to take a tea break around the time he was due home from school, and was in the sitting room rather than the office when he came in, huffing and grunting.

'Yeah.' He threw his school blazer over an armchair, and went to the kitchen, coming back a moment later with a packet of crisps in hand. He flopped down on the armchair to eat them.

Julia took the fact that he'd decided to stay in the same room as her as a sign he'd quite like to talk. 'How was school?'

'Usual,' he replied, with a shrug.

'That good, hey?'

Another shrug.

'How's Marlon?' She hadn't heard him mention his best friend for a while.

'Dunno.'

Ah. That must be it. There'd clearly been a falling out. 'What's happened, Oscar?'

Oscar stared at her as though judging how much to tell her. Julia kept her face as open and sympathetic as she could. It was rare these days that the fourteen-year-old needed to confide in her, but this did look as though it might be one of those occasions. At last he spoke. 'I lent Marlon twenty quid. He wanted to buy a new PS4 game that his mum said he couldn't have.'

'Twenty quid?'

'Yeah. Well the game was actually about forty-five, but he already had the rest.'

'OK ...'

That shrug again. 'And now he says I never lent him the money. Says he earned it babysitting. Won't even lend me the game, that I half paid for!'

'Oh no. That's all wrong. You're sure when you loaned him the money he knew it was for this game?' Julia wasn't sure she entirely approved of him loaning his pocket money out like this, without asking her or Marc first, but perhaps now wasn't the time to discuss that.

'Yeah. We talked about it. I said I'd lend him the money if in return I could borrow the game, and he said that was cool. Now he's avoiding me and says I never lent him any money.'

'That's not like Marlon, is it?'

'He's changed. He took money off Nathan the other day, as well, and won't give it back. He goes round with Greg and Spudsy these days. I hardly talk to him anymore. Feel betrayed by him, in a way.'

'You thought lending the money might bring him back to you?'

'S'pose.'

'Want me to ring his mum and explain the situation, ask for your money back?'

Oscar stared at her, horrified. 'God, no, Mum. We're not little primary school kids, needing parents to sort things out for us.'

Julia was glad to hear it, but she'd felt the need to make the offer. 'Is there anything I can do?'

'Nah. I'll ask him for it back one more time. Nathan was there when I gave it to him so he'll back me up. Need to try to catch him without Greg and Spudsy around.'

'Why's that, love?' To Julia's surprise there was a glint of tears in Oscar's eye as he answered, but he kept his face turned from her.

'They'd back him up, whatever he says. And make life difficult for Nathan. And for me.'

'Ah. Yes, better to confront Marlon when those other two aren't there. I'm glad Nathan's on your side in this.'

'Yeah, he's sound.'

'Do you want to invite him round?' Maybe it was time for Oscar to develop a new friendship. He'd been friends with Marlon since starting secondary school, but now it seemed like Marlon was running with a bad crowd.

'What, like on a play date?' Oscar laughed. 'Mum, we're fourteen, not four. But thanks, yeah?'

'For what?'

Another shrug. 'Listening, and stuff. Not all mums do. Marlon said his mum never talks to him. Spends all her time with her boyfriend. Who's a creep.'

Aha, Julia thought. That was probably half the problem. She felt sorry for Marlon, but it wasn't anything she could do much about.

'Weird, though,' Oscar went on. 'Thought I could trust Marlon. But it turns out I can't. That's … you know … hard.'

Julia nodded, and patted his shoulder. 'It's tough when that happens. Maybe he'll come back around to you. Meanwhile, I'm glad Nathan's there for you.'

'I dunno. Even if Marlon, like, apologised and stuff, and paid me back, I don't know if it'd ever be the same. I could never trust him again. Maybe I've, like, outgrown him. When he's around Greg and Spudsy, he's so … immature.'

'Kids do mature at different speeds. You've been so grown-up lately. I'm really proud.'

'Why, 'cos I laid the table for your dinner party?'

She smiled. 'That, and other things. Look, just take the compliment, OK?'

'Yeah. Anyway. Two more weeks at school, then the Easter hols. What are we doing?'

'Doing? Oh … yes, normally we go away somewhere for part of it.' Julia realised that she and Marc hadn't so much as mentioned the school holidays at all. While the kids were mostly self-sufficient these days, and the advantage of having her workplace in the home was that she could combine childcare and work with ease, they usually took the chance to have a family holiday during each school break. 'Look, I'd better get back to work now, but I'll talk to your dad about the hols later, and we'll sort something out.'

'Yeah, great, thanks, Mum.' Oscar flashed her a smile as he got up and went back to his bedroom.

Julia returned to work pondering the conversation. She was pleased Oscar had opened up a little, but sorry he was experiencing the loss of what had once been a good friendship. The money didn't matter – she would find a way to make sure he wasn't out of pocket for long. He could do a few jobs for her and she'd pay him, to make up for losing that twenty pounds. And a holiday was a great idea. They all needed one. There was something about the period from Christmas to Easter – it always seemed so long and cold. Thankfully spring was well and truly here. A week away in the Easter hols would be lovely. She'd talk to Marc, and maybe they'd find a last-minute holiday cottage to book. She fancied the Lake District, to do some walking in the fells. Or perhaps somewhere in the west of

Ireland. Anywhere with beautiful scenery. Idly, she researched a few holiday cottages.

*

That evening, over dinner, she broached the subject. 'How about we have a holiday at Easter? I thought a week in the Lake District would be nice. There's a place in Glenridding. It's an old miner's cottage, small but cosy, and there are a few cafés and bars in the village.'

Marc nodded, and Julia was surprised to see he seemed receptive to the idea. 'Yes, that'd be good. We could both do with a few days off work. Bit of mountain walking, some fresh air. Family time.' He smiled at them all, and Julia was reminded of why she'd fallen in love with him.

'Boys, what do you think?' she asked.

'Will there be Wi-Fi at the cottage?' Ryan asked.

Julia laughed. 'Yes, it says there is, on the website details.'

'Cool by me, then.'

'Yeah. The Lakes are awesome. Thanks, Mum.' Oscar looked happy at the idea of getting away. It'd be a good break for him after his friendship troubles.

'Right then, I'll get it booked.'

She spent the evening booking the cottage, showing the boys the photos of it and where it was on the map. They also planned some walks and other activities. When that was done, Marc poured them each a glass of wine and handed one to her. 'Here's to our holiday. And the good news is, I have booked another restaurant for us. This time I checked the calendar and there's nothing on. It's on Wednesday.'

'Oh, that's wonderful. Thank you.' Julia clinked glasses with him, and settled on the sofa. A date night to look forward to, and a holiday. This was what had been missing in her life. As long as she could ensure the project work was on track with enough resources to meet their deadlines, before she went on holiday. Otherwise she knew she'd never be able to relax.

*

Ian had a few days off that week. They usually ensured that they never took holiday at the same time, so that there was always one or the other on hand to make any decisions. So when a query came through from Mannings and Co, it fell to Julia to respond even though usually Ian dealt with new potential clients.

Mannings and Co were asking if there was any chance of bringing forward the delivery date by two months. They were on the point of signing up but only wanted the new, not yet complete version of the system. They were offering a financial incentive if it could be delivered early, but also hinting that if that was not possible, they would need to look elsewhere.

'Typical,' Julia muttered to herself on reading the email from Mannings. 'Why does this have to happen when Ian's off?' She could deal with it, but it would take time and divert her energies away from getting the actual system coded. She called Mannings to discuss exactly what they were requesting, and promised that she would look into it and come back with a workable proposal before the end of the week. Ian was back on Thursday and she could run it past him before going back to Mannings.

So that was the priority for the day. Spreadsheets, time planning tools, estimates. Not her favourite part of the job but it had to be done. She roped in Barry to help with the estimates. His experience, as always, came in handy.

'If we had to complete the new version a month early, without reducing quality, what do we need to do?' she asked him.

Barry widened his eyes. 'Well, Julia, time, quality, and resource are the three variables when it comes to projects like this. They're in balance with each other. You don't want to reduce quality. You do want to reduce time spent on development. So that means you have to increase resources.' He studied the plans. 'I reckon you need at least two more contractors to do it, on top of the two we've just taken on. And then a bit of replanning to make best use of everyone.'

He was speaking sense, of course he was. She knew it. She'd also known what the answer would be. But Ian wouldn't like it. Maybe Mannings would pay some money upfront, that would help pay for extra contractors. 'Thanks, Barry. For now, we'll push on with our current plans. I'll talk to Ian on Thursday and we'll have to see what we can do.'

Barry nodded and left her office to get back to his own desk. Julia stared at the figures a little longer. If Mannings wouldn't pay anything upfront – and to be honest, she didn't really want to ask them to – the only other answer was a bank loan. She didn't like the idea of a loan; after the initial loans to set up the business and get it up and running in the first year or so, it had been self-financing. They had not had to borrow a penny, and had been able to pay themselves a decent salary.

She played around with ideas and figures for the rest of the day, but ultimately it would need to wait until Ian was back in the office, and they could talk it through. Mannings was too big a potential client to lose. They would have to come up with some way of meeting their deadlines.

*

It was a long, hectic week. So much to do, and so little time to do it all. Julia had had no time to look through any more of the things Bob had brought – the photos, letters, and books that had been Grandma's. Neither had she had a chance to keep investigating what Grandma might have done at Bletchley Park during the war. All she'd managed to do was dig out the Christmas letter from Clarissa's daughter Caroline. As she'd vaguely remembered, it mentioned family history research and she was delighted to see it also contained an email address. Julia sent a rather hurried message asking if Caroline had any information about her mother or Pamela working at Bletchley Park during the war. Maybe Caroline hadn't ever heard anything of this either, but it was worth a try.

Wednesday night came around, and Julia made sure she finished work in good time to make the boys some tea and get herself ready to go out. She dressed in a clingy black dress that had just a hint of sparkle in it; something she normally only wore for Christmas parties but she knew she looked good in it. She took care with her make-up, and dug a pair of heels out of the back of the cupboard. They were taking a taxi to the restaurant so there'd be no need to walk anywhere.

'Woo-oo date night – ugh!' Ryan put his fingers in his mouth and pretended to vomit. 'You guys are far too old for this.'

'Thank you, Ryan, for that. Make sure you do your homework, all right? Oscar's in charge while we're out.'

'You look nice, Mum. Don't listen to him. He's just a kid.' Oscar got a push from Ryan for that, and Julia had to step in to separate them.

'Come on, boys. Prove to us you're old enough and sensible enough to be left alone for a couple of hours, will you? Let's not start with a fight.'

'Sorry, Mum.' Ryan looked contrite. 'Hope you enjoy your dinner.'

'Thank you.'

'You ready, Jules? I think the taxi's here.' Marc called from the hallway.

Julia grabbed her jacket and handbag. 'Be good. Call us if you have any problems. We'll be back by eleven at the latest, and you should both be in bed by then.'

Oscar rolled his eyes. 'Yes, Mum. You have already said this a hundred times.'

She smiled and kissed them both. Ryan brushed the kiss away immediately. Julia followed Marc out to the taxi.

*

If she was honest, she was a little over-dressed for the restaurant Marc had picked. He'd been unable to re-book Le Jardin so had plumped for a new place they'd never been to before. It was a more casual place, with the waiters and some customers dressed in jeans. But who cared, Julia felt nice in her dress.

'Our first night out for just the two of us in ages,' she said. Years ago, they used to have a regular babysitter and go out once a fortnight at least, but that seemed to have all been forgotten about. For the last year or more, they'd only ever been out as a family on holiday, or separately.

'Well, let's drink to that,' Marc said, raising his glass to clink against hers. She smiled.

'This is how it should be, eh, Marc? And with the kids being older now, there's no reason we shouldn't do this more often. At least once a month. And it's only a few days until our holiday. Maybe one night in Glenridding we could go out for a drink, just the two of us?'

He nodded, thoughtfully. 'Maybe. Actually, about the Glenridding holiday …'

Something about his tone made her look up at him sharply. 'What about it?'

'I'm sorry, love, but I will have to leave early. I can't take the full week off work, there's too much on. I thought we could go up in two cars, then I can drive back early.'

'Oh no! When will you come home?'

'On the Wednesday, I think.'

'Oh, Marc! I've worked so hard to carve out this time for us!' With the project under so much pressure she'd felt guilty taking the week off but on the other hand, she'd wanted to put her family first. Why couldn't Marc do the same?

'Well, I tried to as well, Jules. But it can't be helped. At least I can come up for the first few days.'

'One day driving up, you'll have three days with us, and then you'll leave.' Julia tried not to sound petulant, but failed.

'Better than nothing. Isn't it?'

She forced herself to smile. This was their night out. She couldn't let this spoil things. 'Yes, of course it is.'

But it had spoilt the evening. The atmosphere between them felt forced for the rest of the evening, as though they were simply going through the motions. They were back home soon after ten, surprising the boys who scurried up the stairs to their rooms as though they'd been caught out.

Chapter 12

Pamela

It was a week after the dance before Pam had a chance to speak with Frank again, although she'd seen him from a distance a couple of times, working in the grounds as the army transport bus ferried her to or from Bletchley Park. Her watches were long now that the training was over, and she had little free time. There were three watches – daytime, evening, and night – and they rotated through them. A week later, Pam was due a full day off.

'It's perfect,' she said to Clarissa that morning. 'If it was more than a day, I'd feel obliged to take the train home to see Ma and Pa. But it's not worth going if I can't stay overnight. I'll be able to see Frank.'

'Is he not working today?'

'I don't know. If he is, I can still chat to him while he's working. If anyone comes, I can pretend I'm just out for a walk.' Pam smiled happily at her friend. She could spend the entire day out in the grounds of the Abbey. Even better, the sun was shining, the wind was still and it promised to be a glorious mid-summer day.

She dressed in her favourite cotton blouse and skirt, and took care to brush her hair, pinning it up at the sides and letting it fall in waves down her back. She contemplated adding a smear of lipstick but decided against it. She was, after all, just going for a walk in the grounds, wasn't she? She had breakfast with Clarissa as usual and waved her off on the morning bus, before setting out through the parkland. Where would Frank most likely be? Last time she'd caught a glimpse of him from the bus, he was near the park's road entrance, trimming some bushes. She decided to head over that way.

About halfway along the drive, she spotted a figure far off, walking over the grass from the direction of Woburn village. Was it him? She stood and waited until the figure drew nearer, and realised that yes, it was, and he'd spotted her and was jogging over towards her.

'Frank! Hello. I – I was out for a walk. I have a day off.'

He grinned. 'Hello, Pamela. And so do I. What a happy coincidence. May I join you, on your walk?'

'I would absolutely love that.' She smiled and took the arm he offered her.

'Let's leave the grounds,' he said. 'There's so much lovely countryside around here. I would love to share it with you.'

'All right. I have my walking shoes on,' she replied, glancing at her flat, sensible shoes that were actually part of her Wren's uniform.

'Good! Then we are ready.'

She loved the slightly formal way he spoke. The way he preferred to call her 'Pamela' rather than 'Pam'; no one since her much-missed grandfather had done that. The way he offered his arm for her to hold on to and pointed out any mud or trip hazards on their path. The way he smiled at her every time he turned to look at her. The piercing blue of his eyes, the fullness of his lips. He was a perfect gentleman, handsome, kind, and caring. And it seemed as though he was hers. What they were doing now – walking together on their day off – this was stepping out, wasn't it?

As they walked Frank asked her questions about her family, where she was from, what her brother was doing, what her father did. She steeled herself for questions about her own job, and was ready to repeat her response that she did 'secretarial work' at Bletchley. But no such question came, and for that she was glad. She wanted to get to know him, for him to get to know her. She wanted to share with him everything about herself, but she could not share any details of her work. So it was better that he didn't ask.

'And you?' she said, after she'd finished telling him about her deferred place at Oxford University. 'Did you always live in this area?'

He nodded. 'Pretty much. I grew up with my aunt and uncle. My mother died when I was young. She'd separated from my father before I was even born. I only met my father once, when I was a child. And then I heard he'd died a couple of years before the war.'

'Oh, that's very sad.' Pam could not imagine being brought up by anyone other than her parents.

'Not sad, really. Well, sad that my mother died so young, but I had a happy childhood with Aunt Flo and Uncle Harris. They were good to me.'

'Do you still see them often?'

'Alas, they are dead too, now. Both died just before the outbreak of this war.' He sighed. 'I am almost glad of it. They would not have liked to live through this. They were such simple, happy people. Good people.'

'They must have been, to take you on.' A thought occurred to her. 'Was it just you? Or do you have any brothers or sisters?'

He was silent a moment, as though working out how to answer her. She regretted her question, dreading the answer. Perhaps there was a brother who was, even now, fighting. Or killed in action.

Or a prisoner of war. 'I have … one brother. Older than me. But I barely know him. He was brought up by my father.'

Pam was about to ask why the family had split up – why hadn't his father taken Frank to live with his brother and father after his mother had died? It was an odd family arrangement. But something about the way Frank had hesitated in telling her of his brother made her think he did not want to discuss it further. So she kept quiet. Maybe, when they knew each other better, he'd tell her more.

They had reached the edge of the Woburn Abbey estate, and crossed through a small gate onto a lane. The fields on the other side of the lane were full of wheat, beginning to turn from green to gold. 'It's not long until harvest time,' Pam said, to change the subject. 'I love this time of year.'

Frank gazed across the ripened fields. 'So do I. The land producing for us, keeping us fed.' He reached out and plucked an ear of wheat, running his fingers up the stem so that the un-ripened grain fell away into his hand. He held it out to her. 'Look. This underpins all human civilisation. This simple seed, right here in my hand.'

She took a few grains from him and considered them. 'But with this war going on, humankind doesn't feel so very civilised, does it? Some of the things Germany has done to us – all that bombing of London, Coventry, Southampton, and everywhere else.'

'And some of the things Britain has done to Germany,' Frank replied. 'It takes two sides to make war.'

'But … Hitler started it!' She was amazed at his words.

'Oh, of course. I am not apologising for him, in any way. I am merely pointing out that not everything is black and white. Atrocities have been and will continue to be committed by both sides.' He stopped talking and turned to her, placing his hands on her shoulders. 'Let's not talk of the war, dear Pamela. We have so little time we can spare for each other. Let us make the most of it.'

She gazed up at him, and as she did, he bent his head to hers and kissed her. And there it was, the kiss that she'd so longed for on the night of the dance, here for her at last as they stood on the edge of a field of green and gold wheat, under the mid-summer sun, while somewhere across the continent war raged on.

*

It was probably because she was still dreaming about that kiss that Pamela managed to trip on the step at the entrance to their hut, the following day. Thankfully Edwin was behind her and managed to catch her before she fell.

'Oof, I nearly came a cropper there,' she said, as Edwin held on to her while she regained her balance.

'Are you all right? Did you twist an ankle?'

'No … I just was daydreaming and missed the step.' She smiled at Edwin. 'Thank you, my knight in shining armour.'

'Any time, my damsel in distress.' He blushed when he said this and let go of her. He'd seen her dancing with Frank, she knew. She'd danced with Edwin too, but only once, and much more with Frank. She thought Edwin had probably seen her take Frank's arm as they walked away from the dance hall too. He'd had an air of disappointment about him, as though he was resigning himself to only ever being her friend. But what a good friend he would make!

*

It became a habit – every time Pam's shifts gave her some time off in the day, Frank would ensure his time off coincided, and they would spend the time walking in the country, holding hands, talking, stopping every now and again to kiss. As summer ended, the wheat was cut and autumn began, Pam wondered how it would be during the winter, if on their days off the weather was too bad to go out walking. Frank was not allowed into the Abbey, and as yet, he had not invited her to his accommodation. She imagined, although he hadn't said, that he rented lodgings in a private house. Perhaps the landlady didn't allow him to have guests.

There was a tea shop in the village of Woburn, and they had visited it on a few occasions. But in the shop they could not hold hands or kiss or hug.

One sunny afternoon in early October, Pam decided to bring her camera out when they went for their walk. She had not used it since arriving at Woburn. 'I'd like,' she said to Frank, 'to take a few photos of you, if you don't mind? When I go home on leave I'll be able to show you off to my friends back home.'

'And may I take some of you? So that when you have the film developed perhaps you can pass one or two on to me?'

She blushed and agreed. They spent the afternoon finding the best spots in the grounds, the most attractive backdrops. It was Pam's last film, and she had not found anywhere locally where she could buy more, so she was careful to ensure each snap was as good as it could be. She took one of Frank by a rose bush he was particularly proud of, that was still blooming profusely even though it was late in the season. And for another, they stood under an enormous sycamore tree in full autumn plumage, held the camera at arm's length, and pointed it back at themselves, laughing all the while.

'I bet that won't come out,' Pam said, as she wound the film on ready for the next picture.

'Oh, but it will be marvellous if it does!' Frank said. 'You know, I've been to Bletchley town, but of course I can't get near to see the big house where you work without a pass. I'd love to compare it to this place. Is it as grand?'

'No, not as large,' she replied. 'And not as beautiful, as they have added so many extra huts in the grounds.'

'Whatever for?' He sounded surprised at this.

'It's where most of us work.' She glanced over at him, hoping he wasn't going to ask anything about her work.

‘So many of you.’ He stared at the horizon for a moment, then turned to smile at her. ‘I’d love to see the big house, and the gardens. I know there’s a lake. I’d love to compare it with Woburn!’

‘Oh, the grounds here are so much nicer than at Bletchley Park, believe me.’

He looked thoughtful. ‘Do you think you might, I mean, would you take your camera to work one day, and take a snap of it for me? I expect you’d like a photograph of it yourself, for your collection.’

‘I would, yes. But I’m not sure I’m allowed to take my camera there.’

‘Hmm. I suppose not. It’s all very hush-hush there, isn’t it? There are so many rumours flying around about what goes on there. I know you tell me you’re a secretary, and I’ll never ask for details, but you’re not, are you?’

It was only Frank asking. Her boyfriend. Pam knew she’d never break the Official Secrets Act, but there was no point pretending she did secretarial work when he knew she didn’t. ‘No. But I can’t say more than that,’ she replied. A small part of her half expected to be struck by a bolt of lightning as she confirmed his suspicion, and she felt part relieved and part disappointed when nothing happened.

Frank smiled at her. ‘You have such integrity. I won’t ask any more questions.’ He pulled her into his arms and kissed her, deeper and longer than ever before, and all she could think of then was him, his warmth, his love for her. And she knew she was in love with him too.

*

It was at Bletchley the next day that Pam had an idea. She would like a photograph of BP for her collection, she thought. And her parents would love to see a picture of the grand place where she worked. The problem was taking her camera to work. But every day the Wrens had to take their gas masks with them. It was a rule, though not entirely strictly observed, that all personnel at BP should carry their gas masks in cases with them at all times. That day, in the canteen, she noticed one girl open her gas mask case and take out a powder compact to repair her make-up.

'Tell me,' she said to Clarissa who was sitting beside her, 'do you stick rigidly to the rule of carrying your gas mask everywhere?'

To her surprise Clarissa threw back her head and laughed. 'Oh, dear no. I did for the first week. And then I realised that the gas mask cases are never checked during inspections, and a couple of girls in my section confirmed that. So now the case is just an inconveniently shaped handbag. Look.' She opened hers and showed Pam the contents. A hairbrush, a purse, a handkerchief in a little pouch, a packet of cough lozenges.

In return, Pam opened hers, to show her gas mask, and both girls laughed some more.

But, Pam thought, this was how she could do it. Her Box Brownie camera would fit nicely in the gas mask case. She could bring it on a sunny day and take a few snaps. Just pictures of the main building and the grounds. She'd be careful not to show the huts or any personnel, or anything that gave any sign of what their work here was. She could get the film developed, and then present Frank with a set of pictures – of herself, Woburn Abbey, and Bletchley Park. It would be lovely too, to show Mum, Dad and Geoff where she worked. As well as Miss Osbourne – it was because of her she was working here at all. And Ada and Emily, although she suspected they'd be more interested in the pictures of Frank.

She'd had plenty of news from home, of course. Weekly letters from Mum and Dad, occasional letters from Geoff, Ada, and Emily. Geoff was stationed much further north, doing his initial flying training, and apparently loving every minute of it. Pam hoped his training was comprehensive. The longer it took, the longer it'd be before he was flying dangerous missions over enemy territory. Ada was still seeing her American airman Herbie; he had thankfully managed to stay safe. Emily was driving ambulances in London, a job that was immensely tiring and stressful but so rewarding, as she reported in the only letter she'd had time to write to Pam. It was good to hear from her friends and brother, all doing their bit for the war effort.

*

Pam had to wait a few days before there was a day of decent weather. There was no point taking her camera on an overcast, grey day. At last on Friday she woke at Woburn to blue skies and bright sunshine. The perfect opportunity. After dressing, she lifted her gas mask case onto her bed, removed the mask which she stowed under her clothes in her bedside cabinet, and tucked her camera, out of its case, in the gas mask case instead.

Clarissa returned from the bathroom just as she was doing this. 'What's that?' she asked, and Pam reddened.

'Oh, I'm just …' She wondered whether to make something up, and decided against it. After all, she wasn't doing anything wrong. There was no rule that said you couldn't take photos of the house, and that was all she was going to do. 'I'm taking my little camera to work today. I thought I'd take a few snaps, of the house and the lake. Nothing else,' she added hastily. 'Nothing secret.'

'What do you want with those photographs?' Clarissa asked.

'Just to show BP off to my parents, when I'm home next.'

'Are you sure you should be doing this?'

'It's all right, Clarissa, honestly. I'll take the pictures discreetly and I won't take any that might be compromising or give away any secrets. And none of people except for myself. I wonder if you'd take one of me outside the main entrance?'

Clarissa smiled. 'Of course I will. Sorry if I sounded suspicious. It's this blasted Official Secrets Act. I'm so terrified I'll accidentally break it and they'll have me in chains in the Tower of London before I know it. You're right there's no problem in taking a picture of the house. There have been pictures of it in newspapers and books before now anyway, I'm sure. Before the war, I mean.'

That made Pam feel better about it. Frank could have seen those pictures. All the same, she decided not to tell Clarissa that it was Frank who'd asked her for the pictures.

On arrival at Bletchley Park, as usual their security passes were checked at the gate and then the bus was waved through. Pam kept a tight grip on her gas mask case as they drove up the driveway and parked outside. She couldn't help but think that at any moment a guard was going to pounce on her and demand she hand over her camera. It wasn't until she had settled down to her work, with her gas mask case hung over the back of her chair in its usual place, that she felt she could relax.

She took the photos during her lunch break. There were very few people about, and she approached the house from behind a clump of bushes, taking her camera out and getting it ready while still hidden in them. She stepped out and took a photo of the house quickly, feeling shaky even though she kept telling herself she was doing no harm. Photo taken, she hurriedly put her camera back in her gas mask case and turned to go, only to find herself bumping into another person. She gasped and put a hand to her face, then realised it was just Clarissa, laughing fit to burst, with Edwin grinning awkwardly by her side.

'Oh, that was funny! I am sorry, Pam. We shouldn't have crept up on you. But you're making yourself look guilty, hiding behind hedges to take your photos. I mean, that's exactly how a spy would do it, isn't it? Come on. You wanted one of yourself. Now go out there by the steps, and smile.' Clarissa took the gas mask case from her and pushed her out into the open.

Sheepishly, Pam went to stand where Clarissa had said. Her friend had walked out in front of her. 'Back a bit, left, now then, Pam, shoulders back and smile!'

But Pam found it hard to relax for this photo. Edwin was standing with Clarissa, watching. A couple of men were walking past behind them, discussing something. And young Mimi – a local girl who delivered messages from hut to hut – was cycling past and waving at them. Clarissa paid them no heed, and took the photo. 'Now one of you two,' she said, pushing Edwin gently to stand alongside Pam. 'So you can show your parents who you are working with.'

She took the photo and handed the camera back. 'There. That should be a good one. Take one of me?' She walked out in front of the house and struck a pose as though she was a cover girl for a magazine.

Pam laughed and took the snap. 'I think that's captured your spirit nicely!'

'Good!' Clarissa grinned. 'Now, then, I do believe it's lunchtime, and I was told there's toad in the hole. I also heard a rumour of spotted dick for pudding.' She linked arms with both Pam and Edwin and led them across to the canteen.

Chapter 13

Julia

There never seemed to be any time for anything outside of work these days. Once again Julia couldn't help but wonder if she had the whole work-life balance wrong – but if she did, what could she do? Running a business took a lot of time. Worst of all, she'd had no time for the boys that week. The day before, Ryan had been distant and cold to her, and it was only after she'd gone to say goodnight to him that he'd told her why. 'It was our project presentation day today. Loads of parents came. But not you.'

'Oh no. Your "Romans in London" presentation? You worked really hard on that.' Julia was trying to recall if she'd known about the presentation. Had it been in her diary? She'd been so distracted with work. She sat down on the bed where Ryan was tucked under his duvet and put a hand on his shoulder.

'Yes. That. Mum, you said you'd be there.' Ryan turned over to face the wall. He was trying not to cry, she realised.

'Did I? I'm so sorry, Ryan. I must have failed to put it in the diary.'

'It's on the family calendar.' His voice was muffled under the duvet.

She had no excuse. If it was on the calendar, she should have known about it. 'Oh, Ryan. What can I say? Work's been a bit frantic lately, and with Ian away, there's even more for me to do. But I shouldn't have forgotten. Did the presentation go well?'

He shrugged in response, then reached out a hand to turn off his bedside light. She was dismissed. She dropped a kiss onto his head, and apologised once more, promising she would never let it happen again. Then she left the room, kicking herself. She'd always promised herself, the kids came first. She wouldn't let her career, her business, get in the way of her being a good mother. Running the business from home had worked well for this – she'd been able to attend Christmas concerts, sports days and the like. But now, she'd failed Ryan. She'd missed this important event, and he was rightly furious at her.

*

Julia had never been a great sleeper. She tended to wake in the middle of the night and find herself running through work problems in her head, working out solutions and hoping she'd remember them when at her desk later in the day. As long as she'd had a few hours before waking up and worrying, she was good. But that week was terrible. She found she was taking hours to get to sleep, and then waking after only a couple of hours, and fretting about how to bring forward the project timescales, how she'd let down Ryan, and Oscar's friendship troubles.

At last, the day of Ian's return to the office rolled around. He'd only taken a few days but it had seemed like forever. Julia had booked an hour in his work diary to go through their plans. Hopefully he'd be more receptive to taking on more contractors this time. She felt exhausted before starting work; she'd finally nodded off at around six o'clock after brooding for hours on

Marc's decision not to come to the Lake District for the whole week, only to be woken by the shrill ringing of her alarm clock at seven. She had to then get back to Mannings by the end of Friday, and then she had her holiday, thank goodness. She was in dire need of it.

Ian was late to the office, arriving only ten minutes before their scheduled meeting. He apologised, saying he and Drew had been so late back the previous night from their short break holiday that he'd felt the need to lie in. 'Or I'd be trying to function on only six hours' sleep,' he explained, with a winning smile.

For once his smile didn't work on Julia. She'd only had about three hours' sleep in total, yet she'd been in the office since eight o'clock. 'Right, well, sort yourself out then we have our meeting in ten minutes. Lots to discuss about the Mannings contract.'

'Oh ye Gods, I see I have no fewer than forty-nine emails as well. I was only off three days, and there's only four of us in this company. Can I just get on top of these first, before we talk finance?'

'No.' Julia was not in the mood to negotiate. He'd known she'd booked this meeting, and it was his own fault he'd come in too late to go through his emails first. She went to fetch herself some coffee from the office kitchenette then returned to her desk for the meeting. It didn't take long to run through Mannings and Co's requirements and put to him the options she'd come up with. 'Can't see Mannings agreeing to fund our development costs. So we need a bank loan, unless the business has more money squirrelled away somewhere that I don't know about.'

'There's some money in a high interest account. Look, it's all in my monthly finance report.' Ian pointed to a figure on a printed copy of his report, that Julia had on her desk. He sounded petulant, as though she was accusing him of some wrongdoing.

'That sounds good. Have we enough to take on at least two more contractors for six months?'

'Yes, sure. As I said last time. Didn't they start this week? Maura and who was it, Rahul?'

'Two more as well as them, so we can bring the dates forward. Ideally three, Barry suggested.'

Ian laughed. 'What on earth are you doing with all these people, Jules? We've done projects bigger than this with just the four or us, haven't we? Why do we suddenly need eight on this one?'

'To achieve the timescales Mannings need! Otherwise we'll lose them, and that's a very lucrative contract.' Julia ran her hands through her hair. What was wrong with Ian? He seemed to be being deliberately awkward about this.

'Well, I can tell you now, we can't pay two further contractors. I've had to work hard to make sure we can cover the two you've taken on, but no more.'

'Oh.' Julia ran her hand through her hair. 'Well then, like I said, the other option is to take out a bank loan.'

Ian shook his head. 'Adding monthly interest payments to our outgoings really won't help, Jules.' He sighed. 'Truth is, money's a bit tight in the business at the moment. As soon as we get the new version out there and licence payments from the new contracts start rolling in, we'll be fine. Just a bit of a hump until then.'

'Which we must get over by borrowing. Come on, Ian. It makes sense. And any bank's going to be happy to lend to us when they see the projections, with Mannings included.'

He sighed and shook his head. 'I don't like borrowing, Jules, you know that.'

'I know. Neither do I, but right now it's the only way I can see us getting through this. We'll come out the end stronger, and isn't that what it's all about? We'll have grown the business. You know it makes sense, right, Ian?'

Their discussion went back and forth along these lines for the entire hour and a half scheduled for the meeting. By the end Julia felt drained. Ian had been immovable on the subject of a loan. Julia was wondering about her own, personal money. Maybe she'd need to pour some of that into the business to get them over this hump? But why should she, unless Ian did too?

Anyway, she didn't have much. Marc had no savings and she'd never wanted him to put money into the business. It was entirely hers and Ian's enterprise. For now, they had no solution, but Ian had agreed to take over communication with Mannings and Co. He'd have to anyway, as she was on holiday for the next week. Maybe she shouldn't go away at such a critical moment, she'd wondered, but she also knew she was desperately in need of a holiday, the boys deserved one too, and there were only going to be more critical moments ahead as they progressed with the system development.

'What are you going to suggest to Mannings?' she asked Ian, sounding tired even to herself.

'Don't worry. I'll talk them into backing us,' he said, with his engaging smile firmly back in place. Julia wanted to believe that he could do it, but right now, she felt so tired she simply nodded, and they ended the meeting and went off for their lunch breaks. Julia's was spent napping on the sofa in the main house, something she never normally let herself do.

*

The issue with Mannings and Co had not been resolved by the end of the week, but Ian assured her it was all in hand and he'd have it sorted by the time she returned from her holiday. She'd never felt so ready for a break. A week in the Lake District among the mountains would soothe her soul.

When Saturday came, she and the boys were packed and ready to go by nine o'clock. Marc was driving up in his own car, as he had to drive back alone on Wednesday. 'A short but perfectly formed break for me,' he'd said with a smile, as he waved them off. 'Drive carefully and I'll see you up there this afternoon.'

The end of the week would be, she realised as she headed up the M6, the first time she'd been away without him. The first holiday where they had set off together but not come back home together. That thought caught in her throat a little, and to take her mind off it she pushed a CD into the car's stereo – the soundtrack to Hamilton. The boys had watched it a few times and they all enjoyed singing along.

Their holiday cottage was along a lane just outside Glenridding, a little way up a valley from Ullswater, but within walking distance of the village. It was an old miner's cottage, built of dark grey slate, with an impressive view of the Helvellyn range from the upstairs windows. It was comfortably if cheaply furnished, and the boys quickly picked their rooms and explored the place. Julia unpacked the food she'd brought and made herself a cup of tea. She took it to the little sitting room and chose a chair that faced out into the small back garden, where a swathe of daffodils on a grassy bank was brightening up the day. Back home, further south, the daffodils were all finished now, but here they were in full bloom still. As she sipped her tea she reflected on how rarely she was able to do this at home – just sit, drink tea, and contemplate a view. That was the trouble with running your own business, from your own home. You could very rarely switch off from it entirely. She tried not to resent it – it paid the bills – but sometimes she couldn't help feeling that life was more stressful than it needed to be.

'Mum! Are we going to sit around here for the rest of the day or are we going out?' Ryan came barrelling into the room and threw himself across the sofa.

'Let me drink my tea, and we should wait here until Dad arrives. Then we'll go and explore. I'm not driving anywhere though. Driven far enough today.'

'Hurry up with your tea!'

'Go and check out the garden if you're that keen to get outside. Just let me have a few minutes to recover from all the driving, OK?'

Ryan took up the suggestion, and opened the patio door to go out. He left it swinging wide open of course, but the day was mild and Julia enjoyed the gentle breeze that blew in.

It wasn't long before the doorbell rang, and Julia answered it to find Marc standing on the doorstep, looking a little frazzled from the long drive. She kissed him and put the kettle on. Tea and a rest looking out at the view would revive him, as it had for her.

'What's the Wi-Fi like here?' he asked, as she handed him a cup of tea.

'It's fine. You won't be out of touch with your work or anything.'

'Good. What's for dinner?'

'I thought we could go out and explore the village, and maybe have dinner in a pub. To save me cooking after all the driving.'

'Oh. Yes, I suppose.'

Julia raised an eye at his grumpy response but put it down to residual stress from driving. The Lake District would soon work its magic on him. They had three full days together before he needed to leave. The weather forecast was good, there were mountains crying out to be climbed, the boys were already having fun chasing each other around the garden and all their work worries could wait. Julia at least was determined not to even think about projects or clients or contractors, and she hoped Marc would do the same. Family time was so important, and they had far too little of it.

*

The next few days were good. So what if Marc spent more time than she'd have liked checking messages and emails on his phone whenever he had Wi-Fi or a good phone signal. So what if he spent more time chatting to the boys than to her? That was just as important anyway. So what if he turned away from her in bed, saying he was too tired after the day's walking, for any intimacy. They were together, and she was not thinking – much – about work.

'It's been nice, having this family time,' she said to him on Wednesday morning as he packed to leave.

'Yes, very nice.' He was distracted, already checking his phone.

'How long do you think your big project is going to take? I feel like we hardly see you these days.'

'Now, you know what it's been like for me these last few years,' he replied. 'You can't complain – you have always worked long hours and left me babysitting. Now it's my turn to spend more time working. It's just how it is, Jules.' He zipped up his bag of toiletries and shoved it into his holdall.

Babysitting. They were his kids too, so 'parenting' was a more accurate word, but Julia decided, yet again, to let it go. 'When we're all back home again, I think we need to talk about this, Marc. Maybe there's some way we can carve out more time for us. We're both busy, but we ought to be able to manage our time a little better than we have done lately.'

He sighed, and put his arms around her. 'Yes. We should.' He kissed her forehead. 'Well, you have fun for the rest of the week. Take care.'

'We will. Drive carefully, won't you, and ring me once you're home.'

'Sure.' He kissed her again, zipped up his holdall, then went to say goodbye to the boys. Julia was left feeling a little tearful after the brief, tender moment.

It was only after he'd gone that she realised what the date was. The anniversary of their first meeting. The day on which they would usually share a bottle of Martinborough Pinot Noir and go outside to look at the stars if it was a clear night, remembering that long-ago party when they'd met. This would be the first year they'd missed doing that. Marc had forgotten. And so, she realised with a jolt, had she.

*

Julia was determined that she, Oscar, and Ryan would make the most of the remainder of the week. That day they climbed Helvellyn via a route that took them along a river valley, then up over the magnificently named Dollywaggon Pike and Nethermost Pike. She'd always loved those mountain names. The boys were on good form, though they looked across at the rocky scramble of Striding Edge with longing. 'Another time, boys,' she said. 'When it's less windy and you're a little more experienced in the fells, we'll do it then.'

At the top they huddled in a stone shelter eating the sandwiches she'd made. Oscar pulled out his phone.

'You're as bad as Dad,' Ryan said, 'always wanting to check your phone.'

'Is there even a signal up here?' Julia asked.

'Yeah, there is here. Not on the way up though. Got a couple of texts I need to reply to.' Oscar tapped away on his phone.

There was something contagious about phone-checking, and Julia felt the urge to pull hers out. There'd be no reception again until they were back at the cottage.

She had a few emails and messages from the team at work, but those could wait. There was also an intriguing email from Caroline, saying she certainly had some information on Clarissa and Pam's wartime activities, that she would scan and send over soon. There was also a text, from the company's bank. An automated text, that she'd set up to warn her if the funds in the main account fell too low. She'd received such texts before, but only when she'd expected to, when they'd had a large outlay. She hadn't been expecting it this time. While there was still reception at the top of the mountain, she attempted to log into the company's main bank account, but it timed out. She'd have to wait until she could use the Wi-Fi at the cottage.

Chapter 14

Pamela

At last, in mid-autumn, Pam's first three-day leave was granted. She had not yet used up the film that was in her camera, so she had not been able to get it developed. She'd have to rely on describing Bletchley Park to her family – just the grounds and the house, of course. Not the work. There was so much she wanted to tell them. And Ada and Emily as well. She'd written home to tell her parents which train she would be on.

'I'll miss you,' Frank told her, during a snatched moment after Pam had got off the transport bus the day before.

She laughed. 'It's only a couple of days. We often go several days without seeing each other.'

'I know.' He sighed. 'But then I know where you are; I know you are either here at Woburn or just a few miles away at Bletchley. This time you will be far from me.' He wrapped his arms around her and kissed her.

'Come on, lovebird,' Clarissa called, 'it's dinner time!'

'I'll see you when I get back,' Pam said to Frank, giving him one last kiss.

'You certainly will,' he said with a smile.

*

Early next morning Pam took a transport bus to Bletchley Park and asked the driver to drop her off in the town. She caught a train home, excited to see her family and friends again.

Mum had a cake waiting for her on the kitchen table, when she walked in. 'I saved our sugar rations for weeks to make this,' she said proudly, as Pam kissed her hello.

'It looks delicious,' she replied. 'It'll be lovely to have some homecooked food for a couple of days. The canteen food is a bit hit and miss, if I'm honest.'

'I can't wait to hear all about it,' Mum said.

'What is it you do there?' Dad asked, as he took a seat at the table and accepted the cup of tea Mum passed him.

'Ah, just … secretarial work, really,' Pam replied.

'Secretarial? You with your mathematical brain? Anyone could be a secretary. Why on earth did you give up your university place to be a secretary?' Mum sounded aghast, but Dad shushed her.

'I'm imagining, but not expecting Pammy to confirm or deny it, that there's more to it than that. I suspect she may have been told not to talk about her work.'

'What, even to her family? Her parents?' Mum stood with the teapot still in her hand, sounding indignant.

'Even to her family.' Dad's tone admitted no further argument on the matter, and Pam smiled at him gratefully, receiving a wink in return. It'd be easier all round if they asked no questions.

'What I can tell you about is where I'm living,' Pam said, in an effort to give her mother something she could pass on to her friends. 'I'm billeted at Woburn Abbey. It's a stately home. If you can imagine it, they've converted some of the grandest rooms into dormitories for Wrens. It's quite fabulous. There are even deer roaming in the parkland around the Abbey.'

'Living in a grand house, how wonderful!' Mum's eyes were shining. 'You'll be slumming it back here with us – I wonder how you'll cope?' Her tone was teasing.

'Actually, Mum, in some ways it'll be so much better. The plumbing at Woburn is terrible. The hot water runs out so quickly. I am looking forward to having a good long soak in the bath here, rather than a cold stand-up wash.'

Mum laughed. 'Oh, how funny! We imagine the upper classes living so finely in their big houses and here's you saying they don't have enough hot water.'

'Grand bathrooms, but dated plumbing, I think.'

Over tea and cake she answered all their questions about the Abbey, its grounds, the village of Woburn and town of Bletchley, and the Bletchley Park building itself. 'And do you work inside the big house?' Mum asked.

'Well, not quite. I go in for meals, but there are a number of temporary huts in the grounds and I'm in one of those.'

'Goodness,' Mum said, gazing into the distance as though trying to imagine it all. 'I can't think why they need so many Wrens and others. I won't ask you any more about it.' She gave Pam a spontaneous hug. 'I am so proud of you, you know, whatever it is you are doing. And Geoff too. To think, both my children away and fighting for the country in their own ways.'

At the mention of Geoff, Pam felt guilty for not asking after him sooner. She'd been so excited to see her parents again and tell them her news. Although she hadn't yet mentioned Frank. 'How is Geoff? I had a letter two weeks ago from him but nothing since.'

'He's fine. He's almost completed his training. He's been up there, in the sky, flying an aeroplane.' Mum shook her head as though in disbelief. 'I do find that hard to imagine, what it must be like up there looking down on all the little houses and fields.'

'Any news on when he can come home?' Pam asked.

'He gets two days after finishing his training and before he starts flying missions,' Dad answered. There was a brief pause, as Pam contemplated what it would mean for Geoff, when he began taking part in active missions. 'He'll be redeployed to a different base as well. We'd been hoping,' Dad went on, 'that your leaves would coincide, and we could have a few more days as a family again.'

'There will be other occasions, I'm sure. When the war's over, at least.' If, please God, Geoff survives, Pam added silently.

'Yes. Let's hope so.' Dad cleared his throat. 'Anyway, he's enjoying the flying. Good at it, too, he says. He's to fly fighters, escorting bombers.'

Pam pressed her lips together and nodded. Escorting bombers didn't sound like a very safe activity. She'd hoped that somehow he'd be involved on missions far away from the real action. She'd heard of WAAF girls who flew planes from one airfield to another, all within Britain. But of course, they wouldn't waste a newly trained RAF pilot on that sort of job.

'Well, anyway, more cake?' Mum said brightly. Too brightly. Pam could tell she was battling tears at the idea of Geoff flying into danger, over enemy territory.

'Thank you, I would love a small piece, but do save plenty for tomorrow.'

'Ah, love, you'll have left by teatime tomorrow, though,' Mum said.

'But you'll be here. This isn't just for me.' Pam accepted the quite sizeable piece her mother passed her, nevertheless. It wasn't often she ate cake these days.

'Any other news?' Dad asked her. 'Made any friends up at Bletchley?'

Pam smiled, and then told them about Norah and Clarissa. 'They both work at BP. Clarissa lives at Woburn with me. I also work with a chap called Edwin. He's nice.' She blushed a little before continuing. 'And then there's Frank. He's … a young gardener at Woburn, and we've become friendly.'

'Aye, aye,' Dad said, winking. 'Friendly with Frank the gardener, is it? Handsome chap, is he?'

'Well, I like him, yes. I sometimes go for walks with him on my afternoons off.'

'Hmm, well I hope you are not getting too friendly.' Mum pursed her lips. 'He's only a gardener. I'd hope for something better for you. Why's he not in the Forces, anyway?'

'He has asthma. And there's nothing wrong with being a gardener.' Pam felt cross. Why did Mum have to spoil things? 'Anyway. If you don't mind, I'd like to go and see if I can catch up with my friends for the rest of the afternoon.'

'Yes, love. Sorry, I didn't mean anything against your young man. I'm happy if you're happy. Lord knows we need to take hold of our chances of happiness when they arise, while this blasted war goes on.' Mum patted her arm, and Pam squeezed her hand in return.

*

Emily was away in London, but Ada was at home, and suggested they go out to a Lyons corner house for tea and cake while they caught up with each other's news. 'One can't have too much cake,' Pam laughed, thinking about the one Mum had made for her.

It was lovely catching up with Ada, who was looking bright-eyed and happy. Shyly, she showed Pam a delicate engagement ring Herbie had given her. 'Thing is, we're still so young and the war's still on, so we are not telling anyone just yet. Only you. Keep it secret, will you?'

'Of course! And congratulations! What a pretty ring.' Pam told Ada a little about Frank. 'He's very special to me.'

'Oh, Pam, that's wonderful that you've found someone too. Have you told your parents about him? Or are you keeping him a secret for now?'

'I've mentioned him.' Pam smiled at her friend. 'Tell the truth,

I have enough secrets to keep without adding that one to the mix.' Ada frowned and looked as though she was about to ask something, but Pam held up her hand. 'Forget I said anything.'

'All right. Just answer me: are the secrets to do with your work?'

'Yes.' Pam pressed her lips together to show that she would say no more, and Ada, thankfully, changed the subject, chatting about a dance she and Herbie had been to recently.

'Emily was home that weekend and able to come. She looks exhausted, poor thing.' Ada sighed. 'I just hope this war doesn't drag on too much longer, for her sake. And Herbie's, and your brother's, of course.'

Pam nodded. 'We're all doing our best to end it, believe me.'

*

The two days' leave passed all too quickly and soon it was time to return to Bletchley. Pam hugged her parents goodbye and promised to return soon, and next time she'd bring photographs of her friends, Frank, Woburn, and Bletchley. She took the familiar train journey, feeling excited to be returning to her work and friends and of course to Frank. At Bletchley station she alighted and walked up the road to BP. She could get herself a cup of tea at the canteen there, and then catch a transport bus back to Woburn later on.

In the canteen, she ordered tea and a slice of buttered toast, and then looked around for an empty table to sit at. Her eye fell on Edwin, seated by himself near a window. He waved when he saw her and pushed a chair out for her.

'Hi, Edwin. Mind if I join you?'

'Please do. I've just sat down.' He glanced at his watch. 'I've got twenty minutes. You've been on leave, haven't you? How was it? I … I missed you.'

'It was lovely. Hard not to be able to tell Mum and Dad anything about my work, but they were suitably impressed that

I live in a stately home, though less so when I said I was sleeping in a dormitory with five other girls.'

He laughed. His face lit up when he laughed, she noticed, making his usually plain features seem quite handsome. 'This war has a lot to answer for. And if nothing else, it'll be a story to tell your children and grandchildren in years to come. Oh yes, I used to stay at Woburn Abbey a lot when I was young, don't you know?'

It was Pam's turn to laugh at his affected accent. 'Yes, I'll enjoy that. It's probably the only thing I'll be allowed to say about my time working here, isn't it?'

He nodded, serious now. 'Yes. It's odd, knowing we've got to keep quiet about all this for our whole lives. But that's war for you, I suppose. Careless talk costs lives, and all that. You don't know who you can trust.'

'Apart from the people you work with.' She smiled at him. 'Like you and Norah. It's nice to have friends working in the same block.'

He gave her a shy smile in return. 'I'm honoured to be considered one of your friends, Pam.'

Chapter 15

Julia

When they returned to the holiday cottage Julia had meant to phone Ian about that worrying text from the business's bank, but it slipped her mind. The boys were tired and needing food, and there was that interesting email from Caroline that she'd been pondering on the way down the mountain. In the end, it wasn't until after nine o'clock, with dinner eaten and cleared up and a glass of wine in her hand, that she remembered. She called Ian's mobile but it went straight to voicemail, so she tried his home number. Drew answered.

'He's not here, Jules.' Drew sighed. 'He'll be out till quite late, I imagine. He left his phone here and I had to turn it off. Too many people were ringing it.'

'Including me. Sorry to have disturbed you, Drew. There's something pretty important I need to discuss with him. If he's back before eleven, say, can you ask him to ring me please? On my mobile.'

'Oh yes, you're on holiday, aren't you? How's it going? Glenridding, isn't it? I love that place!'

'It's beautiful, yes. Marc had to leave this morning though, for work. But the boys and I had a fabulous walk up Helvellyn.'

'We did that the last time we were there. I love the Lakes. Just being there makes everything feel better, doesn't it? Honestly I'd buy a place up there if we could afford it.'

Julia laughed. 'You'd have me visiting every chance I got.'

'Hey, maybe relocate the business up there?'

'Tempting! But we'd lose Tulipa and Barry, and would be much too far away from all our clients.'

'Ahem, there are phones, and emails, and even video conferencing, these days. You don't need to be in the same room as your clients for a meeting. Oh go on, Jules. Do it! I can paint anywhere, and actually it would be so inspiring to be up there.' Drew tailed off for a moment before adding, quietly, 'And it'd be better for Ian, I'm sure.'

'Better how, Drew? Is there something wrong?'

'Ah, no. I just meant, being in the mountains is better for everyone, isn't it? There's … nothing wrong. Nothing you need worry about. OK, so I'll ask Ian to call you if he's back before eleven. Enjoy the rest of your week.'

'And to call me tomorrow morning if he's back later …' Julia added.

'Sure thing. Bye, then.' Drew hung up, and Julia was left pondering. Something about the way Drew had spoken made her worry there was something wrong with Ian. It was unusual, she thought, for him to be out late on his own. He and Drew had always done everything together. Was their relationship in trouble?

*

A call from Ian finally came just before eleven that evening. He sounded as though he'd been drinking. 'Hey, Jules, whassup? Drew said you needed me! Ha! I am glad someone does!'

Julia told him quickly about the text from the bank. 'Just

wanted to check you've got it in hand, and there's nothing going wrong. I had a look at the account, and can see lots of money being shuffled to another account — I guess the higher interest one you spoke about? But you've moved too much out, I think?'

'Ah, might have, yes. Never fear, Ian is here, and I shall move it back forthwith. Henceforth. Tomorrow. Whatever. Hic.'

'A mistake, then?' He never normally made financial errors.

'Mistake? Moi?' Ian laughed. 'You accusing me of getting something wrong, Jules, my darling?'

'Well, it's not normal to let the account fall to that level. I mean, it wouldn't even cover the next payroll for Tulipa and Barry, let alone the contractors. And us. So something went amiss.'

'You know what, I think I moved the money the wrong way. I will move it back. Fear not. Your wish is my command, I am your fairy godthingie, and I will fix it first thing.'

She couldn't help but laugh at this, even though a part of her was still irritated by the needless worrying he'd caused her. 'All right, then. I think you need to get to bed now.'

'Mmm, with the fragrant Drew. I think you are right. Mwah, lovely lady, enjoy your hols.' Ian rang off, leaving Julia with a smile on her face. He could be so exuberant out of work, and he seemed on such good form, compared to his mood during their last few meetings. The old Ian back again. She was reassured; she'd been worrying for nothing.

*

The following evening, after a day spent climbing Place Fell on the opposite side of Ullswater and a meal in a pub on the lakeside, Julia arrived back at the holiday cottage to another email from Caroline:

Hope you have a Google account. I thought this would be the easiest way of sharing, as otherwise the attachments to an email would be enormous. Back in the 1990s Mum wrote a memoir. It was the days before digital publishing and she only ever had a few copies made for her immediate family. I've started the process of scanning each page and uploading them to a Google folder I have shared with you. I hope it's all readable, let me know if not. Anyway, let me know if there's anything of interest in there for you. It's been a while since I read it myself. I'll do the rest of it as soon as I can but so far I've done her early life and the start of her days at Bletchley Park.

A memoir! Clarissa had actually written a memoir! Julia felt a surge of excitement. Surely it would mention her grandmother. The two had been such close friends. She clicked on the link, and opened up the first image. It was a scan of a type-written page. Back home, she could print all the pages and staple them together as a little booklet, but for now she'd need to read on screen.

As Caroline had said, the first pages covered Clarissa's early life, her pre-war childhood living on a small country estate in Hertfordshire. Reading them, Julia formed a good impression of the young woman from a privileged background.

I remember my parents going on occasional weekend visits to both Woburn Abbey and Bletchley Park. My siblings and I would be left in the charge of our governess, quite jealous that our parents were at parties without us. Of course I had no idea that during the war years I would end up living at one of these grand houses and working at the other! My parents found it most amusing. Their own home was thankfully not requisitioned, but they did take in a large number of evacuees from London and their lawns were dug up to grow food.

Julia read through these sections quickly. It was all fascinating stuff that she would reread at leisure later, but for now she was impatient for mentions of her grandmother. She skipped through to the parts dated 1943, when Clarissa had joined the Wrens and then had been sent for an interview at Bletchley Park, due to her fluent German gained at a Swiss finishing school.

I met another girl that day, a mathematical genius. Of course it was Pamela Jackson, as she was called then. We hit it off instantly and I knew we would always be friends. A few days later, I found myself following her from the station to Bletchley Park when we arrived on our first day. I caught up with her at the sentry's gate at the entrance, and we were inseparable from that moment on.

Julia smiled, imagining the two young women from the photographs linking arms and giggling as they walked up Bletchley's driveway.

She read on. There were descriptions of dancing classes in the ballroom at Bletchley Park, games of tennis at Woburn Abbey where it seemed both Clarissa and Pam had been billeted, and numerous social events. There was even a little bit about Clarissa's role in the code-breaking effort.

We are finally released from our oath of secrecy, after all these years. Many who worked there (including darling Pam!) say they will still never breathe a word of what went on, but I want to set it down here, for my children and grandchildren, and for future generations. I'm proud of the small part I played in helping win the war, and I shall write about it here, so that when I am gone the memories are not lost.

She went on to describe how her job was to type in what seemed like random letters into a replica Tunny machine, after the wheel settings had been determined.

This as if by magic stripped out the encryption to produce plain German text. If you could call it plain German – of course, it was all military mumbo-jumbo with lots of acronyms and figures and abbreviations. But sometimes there'd be an absolute gem, and we'd shout out and pass the intelligence to our superiors and go back to our billets happy, knowing we may very well have saved countless lives. It was the most wonderful feeling.

Julia smiled reading this. From her visit to Bletchley she had a good idea of what Clarissa's job had entailed, but it was lovely to read a first-hand account of it. She read on, to a section about a dance at Woburn village hall.

Pamela had her pick of young men that night, as I recall. Frank and Edwin in particular. Had she known what would happen later, how everything would turn out, would she have acted differently? I never asked her that, and I know she does not like to talk about the war years so I cannot even ask her now. We shall never know.

'Bit cryptic, Clarissa! I hope you are going to tell us what happened to Pam later,' Julia muttered. Annoyingly, that was the last scanned page Caroline had sent so far. 'Hurry up and send the rest, Caroline!' She looked again at the names of the young men her grandmother had danced with on that long-ago evening. 'Grandpa and another chap, who I guess is the one I don't recognise in the photos – Grandma had her pick!'

*

The weather forecast for Friday, which should have been their last full day in the Lake District, was appalling. Torrential rain and gales all day. 'We should cut our losses, boys, and go home,' Julia said to them in the morning. 'There's no point staying – we'd be stuck inside all day.'

'I'll be able to see Nathan on Saturday if we're home, so it's cool by me,' Oscar said, and Ryan seemed happy enough with the plan too, so they packed quickly and set off. It wouldn't hurt, Julia thought, to get back to the office before it closed for the weekend, and have a quick chat with Ian.

The journey home was long and tedious. She found herself in nose-to-tail traffic, hemmed in by hundreds of articulated trucks. It was a slow crawl for much of the M6 and M1, and by the time she got back to their home in west London it was almost six o'clock and Julia felt tired and frazzled from the journey. The boys were hungry and bored, and had spent the last hour of the trip doing their best to annoy each other. As Julia pulled into the driveway, she noticed Marc's car was missing – he was presumably still at work. Ian's was nowhere to be seen either, and only Tulipa's bike locked to a fence post indicated who was in the building.

'Boys, bring in the luggage, will you? I'm going straight online to order us a takeaway to be delivered. Pizza or McDonalds?'

'KFC,' Oscar said, and Ryan nodded his agreement.

'Right then,' she said, unlocking the front door. She perched on a chair in the hallway to place the order, which would be with them in about twenty minutes and not a moment too soon. Then she went through to the office to let Tulipa know she was back.

'Ian around?' she said, though she knew he wasn't.

'Haven't seen him all day,' Tulipa responded, with a shrug. 'Hey, how was your holiday? I thought you'd come back yesterday, actually. Could have sworn I saw you having dinner in Giorgio's. Well, I saw Marc anyway, and assumed you'd be with him.'

'Er, no. Well, Marc came back on Wednesday, but the boys and I only got back just now.'

'Oh, well, must be my mistake, then.' Tulipa looked away as she said this.

'Anyway, yes, lovely holiday. Lots of mountains climbed. I'm going to be feeling it in my knees for days.'

'That's good. Not about the knees, I mean, that you enjoyed it. So … I was about to head off, unless you wanted an update first?'

'Ah, no. It can wait until Monday. You get going, I'll lock up the office then. Have a good weekend.'

'Cheers. Bye, then.' Tulipa strapped on her cycling helmet, shoved a few things in her rucksack, and left the office.

Julia tidied up a little, locked the office outer door and went through to the main house. The food would be arriving soon. The boys had dumped bags and rucksacks in the hallway, and she called them back downstairs to take their own ones up. 'And unpack, put your dirty things in the linen basket … you know the score.'

'Can't I do it tomorrow?' Ryan whined.

'Where's Dad?' Oscar asked. 'Did you text him to tell him we were coming home today?'

'Er, yes. I did. I think?' Julia put a hand to her forehead. She'd meant to, but the decision to come back had all been a bit last minute.

The doorbell rang. 'That'll be the Uber Eats driver,' Julia said, and the boys cheered and ran down the stairs.

Julia felt better after eating. They'd had a brief stop around eleven that morning at which she'd only had a coffee, so it had been a long time with no food. She sent Marc a text to say they were home. He'd turn up sooner or later.

*

Or so she'd assumed. She'd had no reply to the text, and there was no sign of Marc by 10.30 when Julia decided to go to bed. Still no sign of him when she woke at midnight, needing the loo.

A text was waiting on her phone in the morning, to say he hadn't seen her text till after midnight, and had spent the night at a mate's rather than be at home on his own, as he hadn't realised she'd come back early. He'd see her in the morning.

Chapter 16

Pamela

Life had slipped back into a comfortable routine since Pam's visit home. There was excitement when a Post Office engineer named Tommy Flowers visited to discuss his plans for a new machine that would replace the Heath Robinson. He was working day and night, he said, to get it built and tested.

Pam spent break times with Norah, Edwin, or Clarissa – whoever was off when she was. They no longer took cups of tea to sit by the lake as it was now too cold and wet to do so. Pam had heard that the lake froze over in the winter, and people skated on it.

There were social events, all held at Bletchley Park which meant that unfortunately Frank was unable to attend them with her. He encouraged her to go to them anyway, and always asked about them, listening intently to her tales. It was sweet of him, she thought, to show such an interest. There was a dramatic society that had put on a show, another dance, a chess club that Pam had joined and was doing well in, and the ballroom dancing classes.

Walking around the Bletchley Park lake with Edwin one cold

but bright morning, Pam slipped on a patch of mud. 'Are you all right? Let me help.' Edwin offered a hand to help her up. 'Are you hurt?'

'Only my dignity,' she said, allowing him to pull her up. 'You are constantly having to catch me, it seems.'

His hands were surprisingly warm in hers. 'If you fall, someone must catch you,' he said. 'Your Frank doesn't know how lucky he is.' He muttered this last part, as though he wasn't sure he wanted her to hear it. She pretended she hadn't, brushed herself off, and recounted an anecdote Clarissa had told her the previous evening, which made him relax again and laugh.

When her watches allowed it, Pam still saw Frank as often as she could. If the weather was bad, they'd go into Woburn village and have tea at a café. Frank had still not allowed her to come to his lodgings, although he had once pointed out where he lived – in an attic room just off the main street, above a haberdasher's shop. His landlady ran the shop and lived above it, with Frank on the top floor. Pam made a careful mental note of the address, in case she ever had need to call on him at home.

He seemed distracted one day. They were sitting in their favourite café in Woburn, but he kept gazing out of the window rather than at her. She'd been talking about her watch pattern for the next few weeks, and the unwelcome news that she would be on duty at Christmas.

'And so, at Christmas it doesn't look as though I'll be able to go home at all,' she said. 'My next leave isn't until mid-January. What will you be doing at Christmas? I hope there's a dance on, that we can both get to. That'd be fun, eh, Frank?'

'Mmm? What was that, sorry?'

'I said, it'll be nice if there's a dance on in Woburn over the Christmas period.'

'Ah. Yes, let's hope so. Will you be going home to see your parents?'

She sighed in exasperation. 'No, I just told you, I'll be working.'

'Oh.'

'And you?'

'Hmm? I won't be working. I suppose I'll just be on my own. Maybe I'll be able to see you at some point before or after your shift on Christmas Day?'

Pam wasn't sure how to answer that. She would be working the evening watch, from four o'clock until midnight, and they'd been told there would be a Christmas dinner in the canteen earlier in the day and celebrations for all those at BP. It'd be fun to spend the day before her watch with Clarissa, Norah, Edwin and the others. 'Maybe,' she said, noncommittally. 'In your flat?'

'Ah, no, I don't think my landlady would allow it.'

'Well, the cafés won't be open.' That was it settled then, they wouldn't be able to see each other on the day.

Frank pulled a face. 'This is the problem allowing girls to work. It means you're not able to be with your boyfriend even on Christmas Day.'

'Allowing girls to work? What do you mean?'

Frank gave a lopsided smile. 'Oh, nothing. I suppose I'm a bit of a traditionalist. I mean, imagine a woman trying to run a business!'

Pam bristled at this. 'Women can do almost any job a man can do. We're proving that, during this war. Look at me, my job's very technical and I'm just as good—' She broke off, suddenly terrified that she'd give away something about what she did at Bletchley.

Frank was laughing and winked at her. 'Of course you are good at your job, whatever it is. I'm only teasing you.'

Was he really just teasing, or was this what he really believed? She couldn't let the topic go. 'Women have to work. Who else would do all the jobs while the men are off fighting a war?'

'Well, right now, I suppose you need to do your bit. But after, it'd be better to go back to how things were before. After all, someone needs to look after the home and the children, and women are much more suited to it than men.'

Pam felt a pang of irritation towards Frank. She liked that she was doing something useful, and felt that she would be happy to keep working, at least until she had children. Why shouldn't women work? One thing this war was proving was that women could do most of the same jobs men could. But she realised that if she said this to him now, they'd end up arguing, and she didn't want that. She changed the subject back to that of Christmas plans.

'Have you no family you can go to at Christmas? There must be someone. Your brother?'

He glanced at her and frowned. 'No, I won't be able to see my brother. That's for certain.'

'Oh. I'm sorry.' He'd never quite told her what his brother did. Pam didn't like to ask. It could be something secret, like she did. Maybe Frank himself didn't know.

'What's your brother's name? I don't think you've ever told me. And yet he's your only living relative, I think?' She knew so little about Frank.

'He is, yes. His name's Wo—Wilfred. He's older than me. We were not brought up together, but when we met as adults we got on very well.' Frank stared at something in the middle distance. 'I wish we had been brought up together. I think we would have been great friends. I like and admire him immensely.'

'Do you have a photo of him?'

'I do.' Frank paused for a moment, then took out his wallet and pulled a much-creased photo out from it. 'This was taken some years ago. Before the war. W-Wilfred sent it to me.'

Pam took the picture from him and peered at it. It showed a young man, whose features were very like Frank's yet somehow not as handsome. He was standing on a street outside a small house that had some sort of flowering shrub in its front garden. He was wearing an ill-fitting suit, and grinning at the camera.

'He looks just like you,' she said, and Frank smiled.

'Yes, we are quite alike.'

She looked at it again. 'But you are the more handsome.'

Something at the edge of the photo caught her eye. Just behind Wilfred was a street sign. Only half of it was visible, his body obscured the other half. She held it close, frowning. The right-hand part of the street name read Straße. German for 'street'. 'Where was this picture taken?'

Frank frowned and snatched the picture back. 'Oh, just … outside my brother's house.'

'Where? Only I noticed that …' She pointed to the street name. 'It's in Germany, isn't it?' She said this last in a whisper. 'Did your brother live in Germany before the war? Was that why you hardly saw him? Where does he live now?'

Frank opened his mouth as though to answer, then stopped himself. 'Come on. Let me pay the bill and we shall walk.'

Pam was about to object, then realised that if his brother lived in Germany, perhaps he didn't want to tell her in a public place, where the walls might have ears and people might jump to conclusions about him. She nodded, and put on her coat, hat, and scarf ready to leave.

Outside, Frank offered his arm as he always did, and led her through the village streets and along the track that led to the Abbey. He didn't speak until they had reached the bench beside the pond, and there was not a soul to be seen.

'Please, let's sit a while.'

'All right,' she said, shivering a little. But he clearly had something he wanted to tell her, so cold or no cold, she was going to sit and hear it.

He remained silent a moment longer, staring into space. At last he turned to her. 'My brother's name is not Wilfred. I am sorry I lied. It is the only lie I have told you. The rest … is just omission.'

'So what is his name?'

'Wolfgang. And my name, originally, was Franz. Franz Müller. But I've been called Frank Miller almost all my life, so that was not a lie.'

'Wolfgang, and Franz. What are you telling me?'

'My father … he died in 1937.'

Pam waited. She already knew his father had died before the war. And his brother – Wolfgang – had visited him. Had he come from Germany?

'He was … German. But my mother was English. Half English, anyway.'

'You're part German?'

'Yes.' He swallowed hard.

'Were you born in Germany? Is your brother still there?'

Again, a silence, as though he was deciding how much to tell her. 'Wolfgang was born in Germany. When my mother was pregnant with me she came to England, to visit her sister – my Aunt Flo. The marriage was not going well. She left Wolfgang with my father. She decided not to return until after her baby was born. And then she stayed some more, and then she got ill and died, and so I was brought up here with Aunt Flo and Uncle Harris. Wolfgang remained with my father.'

'Did he never want to come to fetch you back? After your mother died?'

'He did. He came once when I was about six. But Aunt Flo persuaded him I was better off here, and in any case I don't think he could afford to bring up two boys alone.'

'So you're—'

'I'm English. My brother is German. This is how we see ourselves.'

Pam felt silent, letting that sink in. He was half German. He was in danger of being put into an internment camp. 'Do … do the authorities know?'

'I was born here, to an English mother, so I have a British birth certificate,' he answered quietly. 'Pamela, it changes nothing. I love you.'

She smiled and took his hand. But it did change things. She couldn't help but wonder – was this the real reason he had not signed up? Was his asthma just an excuse? She'd never seen him wheeze or cough. But he must have a doctor's certificate that excused him from being called up. Oh, how she hated this war! It was making her distrust the man who loved her. He'd never said he loved her before, she realised. Should she say the same thing back? Did she love him?

'Pamela? You trust me? I am on the side of the British, in this war.'

'And your brother? In Germany?'

Frank sighed. 'He makes his own choices. I have not seen him since before the war of course. He visited me once after our father's death.'

Pam remembered that Frank had said he'd enjoyed his brother's company, when they'd been together as adults. And now they were on different sides. There must be some conflict in Frank's mind, whether or not he wanted to admit it. It was as well he had not been called up to fight. But what of Wolfgang? 'Frank, is your brother in the army? Is he fighting on the other side?'

Frank looked away, gazing across the lake. 'No. He is not in the army.'

'Good. Then he will stay safe, and when this is all over, you'll be able to see him again.'

Frank turned back to her and smiled. 'Yes, I very much hope so. He is a good man. Well, this is enough talk of it all. May I just request you to not tell anyone – about my German heritage, I mean. It's of no consequence to me, but there are those who might … make things difficult for me.'

'Of course.'

'Thank you.' He leaned towards her and kissed her, and while the kiss lasted it didn't matter whether he was English or German or from Outer Mongolia, or whether they'd disagreed about Christmas and women working. He was Frank, he was her boyfriend, and he loved her.

They walked back through the village. Passing the Post Office, Frank stopped. 'I just need to pop inside, to send something,' he said, as Pam looked questioningly at him. She followed him inside and they queued for a short while behind a tired-looking, middle-aged woman who was posting parcels to her sons on the front line.

'In good time for Christmas,' she said to the Post Office clerk, with a forced smile. 'It'll be hard not to see them again this year. But I live in hope that next year the tide will turn, and the whole thing will soon be over.'

'It's all we can do,' the clerk agreed, and Pam gave the woman a sympathetic smile as she turned away from the counter.

Frank stepped forward and pulled a letter out of his pocket. 'I need to send this, to my aunt in Switzerland,' he said, passing it over.

Pam frowned. He had not mentioned relatives in Switzerland, but she supposed as he was half German and Switzerland bordered Germany, it was quite possible he'd have relatives on his father's side there. But the impression she'd got was that he was not in touch with anyone on that side of his family, other than his brother, who was in Germany.

She bit her tongue. In front of the clerk, it was not a good idea to ask. But she caught sight of the address, and it was to W. Müller, at an address in Switzerland.

As they left the Post Office, Frank took her hand in his and whistled happily as they walked through the village, back towards Woburn Abbey. 'I feel better for having told you about my background,' he said. 'I don't want there to be any secrets between us.'

'Neither do I,' she said, but her thoughts were still on that letter, which wasn't to an aunt, she was sure. It was to his brother, who he'd said was in Germany. Why would he have posted something to Switzerland?

She put it out of her mind, for the moment, so she could focus on enjoying the rest of her all-too-brief afternoon with Frank. But there was much to think about, from his revelations. He was German. Müller, not Miller. Franz, not Frank. But then, she reminded herself, so was her boss. Max Newman's father had been German. He'd been interned during the Great War. The family name was originally Neumann, anglicised after the Great War. Mr Newman, who'd been a theoretical mathematics professor at Cambridge had not thought he would be allowed to do war work initially, until he'd been called upon to come to BP and help set up the code-breaking function. He'd told his entire section all this, during one lunchtime talk. 'Better you hear the truth directly from me, rather than listen to any rumours that might circulate. I am, of course, not a spy,' he'd said, fixing each of them with his steady, calm gaze.

The country trusted Mr Newman with the most secretive, critical work. Frank was only a gardener.

*

'Is it possible,' Pam asked Edwin the next day, as they walked from Block F up to the main building for their lunch break, 'to send letters to Germany, right now?'

'To friends or relatives on the front line? Of course it is,' he replied. 'Is it your brother? I thought he was in the RAF and stationed in England.'

'He is, and no, not him. There's no one I want to write to. I was just wondering about it. I mean, if someone here had a distant relative, or old friend, in Germany – could they write to them?'

'All mail going overseas is censored, of course. And I don't think any can be sent to enemy countries at the moment.'

'So you'd have no way to stay in touch with someone in Germany?'

'No.' Edwin scratched his chin. 'Unless, I suppose, you sent the letter via a third party, perhaps someone in a neutral country.'

'Like Switzerland.'

'Yes. If you knew someone in Switzerland, you could send a letter there to be forwarded to Germany. The letter might still be censored leaving England, but it would be possible to send it.' Edwin looked at her quizzically. 'Why are you asking?'

'Oh, no real reason. I was awake in the middle of the night and just started pondering it. At 3 a.m., believe it or not!'

Edwin laughed. 'Oh, I have 3 a.m. thoughts too! Mine tend to revolve more around work. Better methods of keeping the Heath Robinson running.'

'At least you're pondering something useful. My mind goes off on flights of fancy about all sorts of rubbish.'

'In the cold light of dawn I usually realise my 3 a.m. ideas are indeed all rubbish,' Edwin replied, and they both laughed again.

But Pam had her answer. It was clear to her that Frank was staying in touch with his brother Wolfgang by sending letters to some intermediary in Switzerland. It was fair enough, she supposed. Why shouldn't he keep in touch with his only remaining relative? It wasn't their fault they'd ended up on opposite sides in this darned war. It wasn't as though either of them was actively involved in the war. Frank was merely a gardener, and he'd said that Wolfgang was not in the army. Maybe he too had asthma and was excused from fighting.

Chapter 17

Julia

On Saturday, when they'd thought they'd be still driving home from the Lake District, the boys decided to spend the day with their friends. Oscar's new friendship with Nathan seemed to be doing him good – he was in much better spirits these days. Nathan was the kind of straightforward young man Julia approved of. He wouldn't betray Oscar's friendship the way Marlon had. That was as it should be.

Marc sent another text to say he was doing some Saturday morning overtime then going to a local rugby match with his work friend, and he'd be back by five. Julia grumbled to herself that she seemed to be last in his priorities list but reminded herself he had not expected her back until the evening. So why shouldn't he have made other plans? Anyway, she had the day to herself.

Checking her email, she found a message from Caroline to say she'd uploaded more scans of Clarissa's memoir to the shared folder. Good, that dictated what Julia was going to do for the next couple of hours. She settled herself on the sofa with her laptop and a cup of tea and began reading.

Clarissa described her first Christmas at Bletchley Park: *a working day like any other, but with added paper hats and plum pudding in the canteen.* In January apparently the lake at Bletchley Park had frozen over, and anyone owning a pair of ice skates made use of it.

I was lucky enough to own a pair which I picked up on a visit home. Every girl whose feet were within a size or two of my own borrowed them, and a couple of the smaller chaps did too. They were quite worn out by the time the ice melted! It was such fun. Only one person came a cropper, skating when the ice was beginning to melt. His foot went through, but thankfully he was near the edge of the pond where it wasn't deep, and able to wade to safety. I'm afraid all those who saw him simply laughed.

We felt then, in the early spring of 1944, as though the tide of the war was beginning to turn. The end was distant yet, but we had hope that soon it would be within sight, and that the Allies would win. That, as you might imagine, spurred us on considerably so that we all worked harder and faster than ever.

Although it wasn't my section and Pamela wasn't supposed to talk about her work, we were all aware that some new machines had been installed that were helping break the Tunny codes faster. Certainly, the numbers of messages coming through to the Testery for the final stage of decryption were increasing dramatically in numbers. I didn't mind – the harder I had to work, the nearer we were to the end of the war. That's how I looked at it anyway.

Julia smiled at this. She had only sketchy memories of meeting Clarissa a few times in her childhood, but she remembered her positive, upbeat attitude well.

When she'd read through everything Caroline had scanned, Julia decided to flick through Grandma's photos again. She spent a while looking at the wedding album. Her grandparents had married in the late 1940s; Grandma had worn a mid-calf dress with a thick lace veil. Grandpa looked as proud as punch, as though he couldn't quite believe his luck that she'd married him.

'You were a lovely man, Grandpa. You deserved your beautiful, clever wife,' Julia whispered to the photograph of the two of them on the steps of a church.

In the box from Bob there were also bundles of letters. Julia flicked through them. One in particular caught her eye. As she read it her eyes widened. She needed to share this with Bob. She picked up her phone and called him, hoping he'd be available and not on a flight somewhere over the ocean.

He answered immediately. 'Hey, Sis, good to hear from you. Great timing, I'm on a couple of days off. I've been in Devon, sorting out the house. Not had chance to put it on the market yet but I'm getting there. How are things with you?'

'All good. Back from a few days in the Lake District.' No need to tell him Marc had come home early. Added to Marc not being there when Bob had last visited, it made it sound as though their marriage was in trouble. 'I've been in contact with Caroline – you know, Clarissa's daughter. Clarissa wrote a memoir and Caroline, bless her, has been scanning it page by page and sharing it with me. Do you have a Google account? If so, I can add you to the shared folder so you can read it too.'

'I haven't, but for that I'll create one. How wonderful that she wrote a memoir! Does she say much about Bletchley Park and Grandma?'

'Yes, there's quite a bit. I haven't received all of it yet. But I was looking through some old letters in that box you left me and there's one from Clarissa to Grandma that's intriguing. Let me read it out to you. It's dated 1992 and is obviously from around the time she wrote the memoir.' Julia picked up the letter and began reading.

'I know you think that even now we should remain quiet about what we did during the war, but Pamela darling, almost fifty years have gone by. It's time, I think, that our stories were told. To that end I have occupied myself lately writing a memoir – a brief account of my time at Bletchley Park. My intention is to get a few copies

run off, that I can give to my children and grandchildren, so that they can know and understand what I did during the war. I think it's important that it is no longer covered up. I understand a Trust has been formed, to try to protect Bletchley Park itself, and there is a rumour it may even be opened to the public, to educate them about the immensity of our achievements there. When I think of Ralph Tester, John Tiltman, Max Newman, Alan Turing and all those other geniuses, not to mention all we Wrens, the civilian code breakers, and all the others – we need to be remembered too, darling. I would love you to read my memoir and approve it, for of course you feature in it quite significantly. I would also like to write about that rather dramatic and frightening little episode you were involved in. Darling, I want to write this with your approval but I will go ahead without it, if necessary, because I think it simply must be done. If you like, I will send you copies when it is printed, for your daughter and grandchildren.'

'Grandma must have declined the offer of copies,' Bob said. 'What a shame.'

'Yes. But did you hear the bit about the "frightening little episode" – what on earth does that relate to?'

'You said you hadn't read the whole memoir yet. Hopefully Clarissa did write about it.'

'What if Grandma refused permission and Clarissa decided to leave that bit out?'

Bob laughed. 'Then we will never know. Grandma's instinct for secrecy will have won.'

Julia groaned. 'I don't think I can bear to know that something dramatic happened and not know what it was!'

'Well, you will just have to wait until you receive the rest of the memoir, and keep your fingers crossed. Anyway, how are the boys? Did they enjoy the Lake District? They're old enough now to do big walks up the mountains, aren't they? Talking of being old enough, are they keeping their promise of helping you more around the house?'

She chuckled. 'Whatever you said to them that day worked wonders. They're much better. And yes, they did enjoy their holiday.' They chatted on for a bit longer, until Bob said he needed to leave to get to a dentist appointment. He promised to text details of a Google account as soon as he'd set one up.

*

Marc arrived home just after five o'clock, as he'd promised. He gave her a quick kiss as she stood chopping vegetables ready for the evening meal. 'All right, Jules? Did the boys enjoy the last couple of days? Why did you come back early?'

'Hello, Marc. Yes they did. I told you in a text, I think – the weather was appalling on Friday so there was no point staying. The boys were able to go out with their mates today instead.'

'Oh, yeah, you did write that.' Marc picked up a letter that had arrived for him, that Julia had left on the kitchen table, and opened it. 'Hmm. No I don't want double glazing, thanks, Anglian.' He dumped the junk mail in the bin and headed through to the sitting room.

'Pasta bake all right for dinner?' she called after him.

'What? Oh, yeah, sure.' There was the sound of a newspaper being rustled and the TV being switched on. Any moment, Julia thought, he'd come back through to the kitchen for a beer. She was right, he did, but he said nothing to her. As he walked out, she realised he had not looked her in the eye since he'd come home. She sighed. On holiday, in the Lakes, and just before then on their date night out, she'd thought they were moving in the right direction, taking steps to bring back the sparkle in their marriage. Now it looked as though they were going the other way. He'd only been in the house five minutes but he seemed cold and distant.

She put down the pepper she'd been chopping, wiped her hands on a tea towel and followed him through to the sitting room. 'Everything all right, Marc?'

'Hmm? Yeah.'

'Doesn't look like it, from here. What's wrong?'

'Nothing. Tough couple of days at work, that's all.'

She leaned over him to kiss the top of his head. 'I'm so sorry. Is there anything I can do?'

He shrugged and lifted her hand off his shoulder. 'No. Nothing. Are the boys in? I'll go and say hello to them.'

'They've been out with friends. I told them to be home by seven for tea.' She glanced at the clock. 'They should be back any moment.'

Right on cue the front door banged and Oscar came in, closely followed by Ryan. They were deep in conversation about the latest release of a video game one of Oscar's mates owned. 'Oh, hi, Dad,' Ryan said, on spotting him.

'Hey. Good time on holiday?'

'Yeah. Had to come back early because of the weather. But I reckon Mum was pining for her job, anyway. You working parents, honestly.' Oscar gave an exaggerated eye roll which made Julia laugh, but Marc's expression was stony.

'Jules, if your work gets in the way of the boys having a decent break from school, don't you think something's wrong?'

'Marc, you're the one who had to leave on Wednesday! Your work was getting in the way of the holiday far more than mine!'

'But you're their mother.'

'And the main breadwinner in this family!' Not this old chestnut, again. But yes, it seemed so.

Marc slammed his hand down on the coffee table. 'You're their mother, their primary caregiver. Or you should be. But as Oscar just said, sometimes your little business venture gets in the way of your responsibilities. You should hand it over to Ian to run. He's more than capable. Let him buy you out. You could just take an ordinary salary as an employee.'

'Mum, I never meant …' Oscar began, looking mortified that he'd inadvertently caused this row.

'It's all right, love. Your dad doesn't mean it. We share the parental duties. Sometimes one of us has to work harder than the other. This week it was just unfortunate that we both had busy periods at the same time. And no, I have no intention of selling my half of the business to Ian. We're a good team. Now then. Dinner in ten minutes. Oscar, can you set the table please?'

Over dinner Marc asked the boys about the walks they'd done, and more or less ignored Julia. Afterwards he went to watch TV, leaving her to clear the dishes. She decided to have a soak in the bath, with a glass of wine to hand. Her mood had swung downwards again, because of him. Best to keep out of his way.

They'd rowed in the past, of course they had. What couple hadn't? They'd rowed about Julia's business on more than one occasion. The more successful it was, the more Marc seemed to resent it.

One memorable row had ended with Marc storming out of the house and coming back three hours later, soaked through. He'd been walking the streets, he said, and it had begun to rain, and he'd just kept going until he calmed down. And then he'd come across a florist's shop, bought a huge bouquet, called at the off-licence next door to it and bought a bottle of good wine, and come home to apologise. They'd opened the bottle, talked for hours and worked things out. It was something Julia had always been proud of: that they talked and resolved issues rather than letting them fester.

That was how it used to be. Could it be like that again?

The following day Marc took the boys out to a laser quest site. He seemed to have completely forgotten about their row. Maybe she should just forget it too.

On Monday morning the boys were back at school and everything was returning to normal, more or less. Marc had announced over breakfast that he had been sent an email offering him a last-minute place on a course that week. It would enhance his skillset, give him a better shot at promotion and more pay. 'I'm sorry it's short notice, Julia, but I really think I should go on the course. It starts this afternoon. The company was going to send someone else, but he's sick, and they've offered the place to me rather than lose it.'

'No problem, Marc. If it's good for your career you should do it. So what time do I expect you home tonight?'

'Um, well, the course is residential. I'll be back at the end of the week.'

She was a little taken aback – it was very short notice for him to be going away. But it didn't matter; the boys were old enough to sort themselves out when they came home from school. 'Fine, all right. Well, I need to get to work now so I hope you enjoy the course.' She gave him a quick kiss and went into the office.

*

Julia was able to get on with her work uninterrupted that morning. Ian was out at meetings with clients all day, and not due to come to the office at all. They had so nearly got Mannings and Co to sign up; they were on the last push. If they could guarantee they would be able to deliver the enhanced version of the system to Mannings' timescales, Mannings had agreed to help fund the development. But they wanted detailed plans and estimates, and proof that they had the resources to be able to deliver on time. Ian was out on a charm offensive to try to talk them round.

And Julia was doing what she did best: getting on with the design and build. Writing specifications, assigning tasks to the contractors, discussing solutions with Barry. It was good to feel progress was being made, though they were still too short-staffed to meet the accelerated timescale. If Ian's negotiations paid off, Mannings would fund the extra contractors and they'd be able to deliver on time.

The day passed quickly, and it was only as Tulipa left for the day that Julia remembered that tomorrow was the company's pay day. It was Ian's job to ensure the business's current account had enough money in it to cover everyone's salaries, but the financial hiccup while she'd been on holiday was still bothering her. She quickly logged into the company's current account to check, and was horrified to see it was low – definitely not enough to cover the payroll. What was Ian doing? Why hadn't he transferred money in from the other account? Maybe he had and it just wasn't showing up yet. She tried to log in to the newer high interest account to check, but there seemed to be something wrong with the log-in details he'd sent her. After three attempts at putting in a set of letters from the password she was locked out.

In a panic, she picked up her phone to call Ian. He'd said to trust her, to leave the finances to him, but it being the day before the payroll and not enough money to cover it surely meant she had reason to check it with him? She needed to talk to him.

And then she changed her mind. If it was simply that the money wasn't yet showing in the current account, she'd look a fool, again. He'd told her to trust him. Could she not just do that? The pay run was at ten the following morning – that was when salary payments came out of the company account and went into the staff and contractors' bank accounts. She could check in the morning. The money would be there then, and if it wasn't ... well, she'd have to do something fast to fix it then. Ian was due in the office, so he'd be able to deal with it if necessary.

She locked up the office and went into the main part of the house, working out ways to take her mind off it for the evening. That wasn't going to be easy, with Marc away as well. There was a book she'd bought on her visit to Bletchley Park. Perhaps she could read some of that, if there were no more scans from Caroline to look through.

Chapter 18

Pamela

It was almost Christmas. Pamela had been kept so busy at work, she had barely had time to see Frank since his admission of his German heritage. She was still processing it, trying to get used to the idea, telling herself it didn't matter. And really, it didn't, did it? Mr Newman was half German and that didn't bother her. Was she being prejudiced towards Frank, and if so, why? She couldn't quite put her finger on it, but something didn't feel right.

She told herself not to be so silly. He was still her Frank. He'd said he loved her. He'd been born and brought up in England, and his mother was half English. He was Frank Miller, not Franz Müller. But his brother – his brother had been brought up in Germany. How odd to have a family split like that! Of course, Frank was not as close to his brother Wolfgang as she was to Geoff. He'd only ever met him a couple of times, he'd said. Once as a child when his father brought Wolfgang over, and then again in 1938 when Wolfgang had come for a visit.

That day, two days before Christmas, was cold and dark. Pamela felt as though she'd barely seen daylight for weeks. She was sitting beside Clarissa, as usual, on the bus as it approached Bletchley Park, her mind already on the day's work ahead.

'Isn't that your Frank?' Clarissa said, just as the bus turned onto the BP driveway.

'What? Where?' Pam leaned over her friend and peered out into the gloomy morning light. A figure was standing near a tree at the end of the drive. 'Yes, I think it is. What's he doing here I wonder?'

'Hmm. He should be over at Woburn, raking up leaves or something.' Clarissa frowned. 'Pam, it's not the first time I've seen him over here. Last week, I walked into Bletchley village during my break, and he was lurking behind that same tree. I was going to say hello to him, but as soon as he saw me he scarpered. I thought perhaps he was waiting for you.'

'No. We'd made no arrangements to meet at all last week.' The bus had reached the hall now, and the girls climbed off. 'Should I run back to the gate, and ask him why he's here? I mean, maybe he has a message for me or something …' Pam stared back the way they'd come.

'He'd leave you messages at Woburn, like he usually does,' Clarissa replied. 'And it doesn't explain what he was doing last week.'

'Oh. Well, I suppose I don't have time to run back now. I'll see him tomorrow in any case, and I can ask him then.'

Clarissa nodded, unsmiling. 'Be careful, Pam.'

She turned away, to go to her own hut, before Pam had chance to reply. What had she meant, be careful? What was there to be careful of? He was Frank, her Frank, and he loved her. But what was he doing lurking by the BP entrance gates?

Minding his own business, she supposed. And she should mind hers. No, she wouldn't ask him about it, she decided. It would sound as though she didn't trust him.

*

There was another dance at Woburn, just before Christmas. Clarissa wasn't able to go, as she was on watch that evening, but Pamela attended. Frank of course was going, and walked her across the parkland to the village. It was a cold, frosty evening, and Pamela had her coat pulled tightly around her. Frank's arm was around her shoulders as they walked, and she was grateful for the extra warmth.

At the village hall, a familiar figure was standing outside, finishing a cigarette. Edwin looked up as they approached, and nodded guardedly at Pam.

'Hello, Edwin,' she said. 'You've met Frank, haven't you?'

'Not properly,' he said, dropping his cigarette and holding out a hand to shake.

Frank ignored the offered hand. 'It's cold, Pamela. Let's get inside quickly.' He tugged her towards the door.

'I'll see you inside,' she called over her shoulder to Edwin. 'Perhaps we'll dance, later?'.

Edwin nodded and gave a half-smile.

Later, she looked for Edwin throughout the evening, hoping to have a chance to dance with him, hoping he wasn't standing lonely in a corner somewhere. But somehow she didn't spot him at all. Either he'd managed to keep out of sight, or he'd gone home very early, she wasn't sure. But she had Frank, whom she danced with all night and who had eyes only for her.

At work the next day Edwin asked her if she'd enjoyed the dance, but apart from that he seemed a little cold and distant towards her. When she mentioned this to Clarissa later, her friend looked at her sadly. 'Poor old Edwin. I hope he finds someone special soon, now you have Frank.'

*

Christmas, when it came, was just another day. Better food in the canteen, paper hats worn while at work, small presents exchanged with friends, a parcel from home containing a hand-knit cardigan and scarf and a jar of jam, but otherwise, just another day, another evening watch. A day on which she could not see Frank. Her days off and his didn't coincide until just before New Year, when they were finally able to meet up and go for a walk. It was bitterly cold that day, with a chill wind, frozen mud underfoot on all their favourite paths. Pam had her new scarf wrapped around her head and face. Frank's head was bare.

'Aren't you cold?' she asked him, partway through the walk. He'd seemed distracted all day.

'Not particularly,' he replied, though he looked it.

Pam shrugged, and then slipped a little on a puddle that had iced over. She gave it an experimental kick, and the ice held her weight. 'Look, this has frozen solid,' she said, as Frank watched, quietly. 'I wonder if the lake here or at BP will freeze solid? I heard last year people at BP went skating on it.'

'Do you skate?' Frank asked.

'Never tried it,' she replied. 'Do you?'

'I have a pair of skates somewhere. I used them last winter on the lake here, just once or twice. There weren't so many Wrens stationed here then though, so I had it to myself.' He turned to her. 'It'd be more fun skating with others.'

'I have no skates,' she said.

'Maybe you could borrow some? Or maybe I could come to Bletchley Park and skate on the lake there? Do you think you could get me through the gates, if it was only to be in the grounds?'

'Oh! N-no. I don't think so. Everyone has to have a security pass to get past the gate.' Pam was astonished that he would even ask, but of course, Frank had no idea what went on at BP. He'd have no reason to know about the security there.

'Is there no other way in? A back gate or something?' He tilted his head on one side and grinned. 'Just so I can skate – there's no harm in it!'

'Frank, no. There's no other way in that I know of, only past the sentry post that is always manned, and they always check our passes.'

'Lot of security for a bunch of secretaries.' Frank had turned away and muttered this, half under his breath. Pam decided to let it go. They were in danger of having another argument, and she didn't want that to happen.

She tucked her hand into the crook of his arm. 'If I can borrow some skates, perhaps you can teach me to skate on the little lake here? If it freezes solidly enough, of course. I shall ask Clarissa if she has any. Or the other girls staying here. Maybe they'll all come skating on the lake here anyway.'

'It's not that important,' Frank said.

Pam felt rebuffed. She'd tried to cheer him up by suggesting skating at Woburn, but he'd dismissed her suggestion out of hand, even after asking her, more or less, to break him into BP! She inwardly shrugged. It wasn't worth getting upset over it.

'Pamela, I have a suggestion for you,' he said suddenly, his voice bright and cheerful. 'On our next full day together, which I think is Saturday, how about you and I take a trip to London? We can go by train, we can do a bit of shopping, have tea somewhere special. Would you like that?'

'Oh! Yes, that sounds very exciting! I've not been to London since before the war … is it far, on the train from here?'

'Not at all. I haven't been for a while, but I used to go quite regularly. I should like to take you, Pamela. A proper date. I feel we've exhausted the delights of Woburn village and surroundings, pleasant though it is. I'd like to do something special, with my special girl.'

Pam smiled happily and cuddled close to him, against the biting wind. He turned her towards him and kissed her. That was enough to warm her up and make her forget their little argument. And she had a day trip to London to look forward to!

*

Pam could hardly wait until Saturday and the day trip to London. They were lucky with the weather – it was one of those bright but cold winter days, when as long as you're well wrapped up you don't mind being outside at all. 'Perfect day to drink hot chocolate in cosy cafés,' Clarissa said as she waved Pam off. 'Have fun.'

Pam had taken the usual transport bus to Bletchley but then she walked on to the station. She had her gas mask slung over her shoulder – the case contained her actual gas mask this time, not her camera. She was due to meet Frank at the station. She'd wondered for a moment if he would ask if he could come with her on the transport bus, but of course that passed through the checkpoint at the gates before letting people off. She'd been steeling herself to say no, that wasn't possible, to him, but thankfully he didn't ask. He used a bicycle whenever he needed to go further afield than Woburn village and the Abbey, and just as she arrived at the station, he pedalled up alongside her, flushed from the cold nine-mile ride.

'All set?' he asked, as he locked his bike to a railing outside the station. 'Looking forward to it?'

'Absolutely!' she said, taking his hand as they walked into the station to buy their tickets.

The journey took under an hour, bringing them into Euston station. It was spent chatting about their day ahead, where they would like to go and what they wanted to do. Pam hadn't been to London for some time; her last trip had been before the war with her parents, when they'd visited the Natural History Museum and been awed by the dinosaur bones displayed within. But Frank seemed to know the capital much better, and had plenty of suggestions of things they could do. She wondered whether she should have written to Emily and asked to meet up, but Emily was no doubt busy, and Frank had wanted it to be a day for just the two of them.

It was a fabulous day, which seemed to pass far too quickly. Everywhere they went there was evidence of bomb damage.

'They've had it so hard here, compared to Buckinghamshire,' she said to Frank, and he nodded.

'Yes, certainly. It must be hard to live in London now.' Pam thought suddenly of Geoff, whose job it now was to accompany bombers on their raids in Germany. Bombers who would be inflicting this sort of damage on German towns and cities. War was such a waste – of buildings, of time, of life. But someone like Hitler had to be defeated, whatever the cost.

They spent the day walking through parks, looking in shop windows, sitting in cafés for lunch and afternoon tea. It was fun to be somewhere different, exploring new streets with Frank. They walked holding hands, or arm in arm, and Pam enjoyed the feeling of Frank's warm body pressed to her side.

All too soon it was time to head back to Euston for the return journey. As they took the underground from Leicester Square to Euston, Frank seemed on edge. At Warren Street, the station before Euston, he suddenly stood up, kissed Pam and said, 'I'll meet you at Euston. There's something I have to do quickly first. I'll be there in twenty minutes, in plenty of time for our train. Maybe you should get a cup of tea, and I'll see you at the station café?' Without waiting for an answer, he jumped off the train just before it left.

Pam stared after him, open-mouthed, as the train pulled away for the last part of the journey. Why on earth had he suddenly abandoned her like that? She felt very alone, for a moment. A woman opposite leaned across and patted her knee. 'Don't worry, love,' she said. 'Your fella's probably run off to buy you a bunch of flowers or something. My Archie's always doing funny little things like that. You'll see, he'll turn up at Euston with a huge bouquet. Or chocolates.' She sighed, looking wistful. 'Chocolates. Now there's a thing. How I'd like to have a really good box of them, right now. I've not had any decent ones since 1939.'

Pam couldn't help but smile, although she was still confused by Frank's actions. It wasn't like him to be suddenly spontaneous. He was more of a planner. But there was nothing she could do. The tube train pulled into the station and she alighted, went up the escalators and across the concourse to the coffee shop where she took a seat near the window and ordered a cup of tea, as Frank had suggested. From there she had a good view of the concourse and would see him approach. Checking the station clock, she could see there were twenty minutes before the next train to Bletchley, and there was another one less than half an hour later, should they miss the first. She could relax and wait for him.

It was only fifteen minutes before she spotted him, making his way across the concourse from one of the street exits. She frowned as he approached. He was carrying a suitcase, not flowers or chocolates, and from the way he was holding it, leaning slightly over, it looked to be heavy. She stood up and left the coffee shop, leaving the remains of her cup of tea.

'Frank! What on earth is that?'

'Oh, just something a friend has asked me to look after. It … it's why I had to run off. I suddenly remembered I'd promised my friend I'd pick it up when I was next in London. He lives near Warren Street so I knew there was just time …' He smiled, that winning broad grin she'd grown to love. 'I'm so sorry, Pamela, to abandon you like that. I only just remembered and there simply wasn't time to explain. Come on. Our train's just come into the platform.' He grabbed her with his spare hand and hurried her over to the platform gates. A few moments later they were sitting on the train, just the two of them in a small compartment.

Pam looked across at him. Frank had put the suitcase on the floor, between his feet, and was keeping a hand on it. 'What's in the case?' she asked, again.

His expression hardened. 'Things belonging to a friend, as I said. I'm to store it for him.'

'Clothes? Books?'

'Just … things. I'm not even sure. I'm not about to go poking through my friend's belongings, am I?'

Pam fell silent for a few minutes as the train pulled out of the station. 'Who's your friend?' she asked, once the train had picked up speed.

Before Frank could answer her, the ticket inspector slid open the door to their compartment and checked their tickets. 'You want to store that case up on the rack?' he asked Frank. 'I can give you a hand ...'

'No, it's perfectly all right here,' Frank answered. His voice sounded pleasant enough but there was an unusual glittering in his eyes, as though he was fighting to keep control. 'I'll move it if the compartment fills up too much.'

'Right you are, sir,' said the inspector, and he left.

Pam looked at Frank expectantly, awaiting the answer to her question.

'What?' Frank sounded irritated, on edge.

'I was just ... wondering who the friend is that you're storing that for. Is it someone you've talked about?' Pam knew it wasn't. Frank had never spoken to her about anyone other than their mutual acquaintances at Woburn, and those brief mentions of his family.

'No. An old friend, from ... way back.' He turned to face her, unsmiling. 'Look, I don't question you, about what it is you do at Bletchley, even though I know for certain you're no secretary. You have your reasons for not telling me, and I respect that. So do me the honour of respecting me, and stop the constant questioning. The case contains things belonging to a friend, and I am storing it for him, and that's all there is to it.'

'Oh! Sorry. I'll ... say nothing more then.' Pam bit her lip to stop the tears that threatened to fall, and turned her face away to stare out of the window. It was getting dark and there was little to see other than their blurred reflections, but it was better than facing him. They'd had a wonderful day, but now it felt spoilt, and all because she hadn't been able to stop herself asking nosey questions. It really was none of her business. For all she knew,

Frank might be engaged on secret war work that he wasn't able to talk about, just as she was. He'd respected the fact she couldn't talk about her job, and had never asked her for any details. So she had no right to question him either.

About halfway through the journey Frank took her hand, raised it to his lips and kissed it. She turned back to him, and gave a tentative smile.

'I'm sorry, Pamela,' he said. 'I shouldn't have snapped at you. Friends again?'

'Of course we are.'

'Come and sit beside me, then.' He patted the seat beside him, and she moved across. His arm went around her shoulders and pulled her in tight, but she couldn't help but notice his other hand stayed on the handle of the suitcase. Whatever was in it must be important to him. She couldn't imagine what it was, and it was no use dwelling on it. He'd made it clear he'd say nothing more about it. He was right – she kept secrets from him, and she must accept that he might keep some secrets from her.

Chapter 19

Julia

Ian didn't show up for work the next morning. There was a minor crisis with Ryan, who'd hurt his knee playing football the previous day so he needed a lift to school, and with Marc away on his course it fell to Julia to do it. So it was after nine before she was able to sit at her desk and check the accounts.

She had a bad feeling about it as she logged in to the bank's website. With Ian not in the office, and not answering his phone, there was only one explanation. Something had gone badly wrong.

And she was right. The account balance was even lower than it had been yesterday. Nowhere near enough to cover the pay. Salary payments to their employees and contractors would bounce.

She swore, and punched in Ian's number again. No answer. She tried his home number. It rang for ages, and eventually Drew answered, sounding out of breath as though he'd run indoors from his garden studio.

'Yes, Ian's here. Still in bed I think.' Drew sounded as though he was suppressing fury, a fury Julia assumed was directed at his partner.

‘He’s not answering his mobile. Is something wrong? Is he sick?’ As she asked the question, she knew she was clutching at straws. Had he genuinely been sick, either he or Drew would have called her to let her know.

‘He’s not physically sick, no.’ Drew took in a deep, shuddering breath. ‘But it’s fair to say he has problems.’

‘Oh God. Drew, I’m sorry, whatever it is. But it’s affecting the business, too. There’s not enough money in the current account to pay our staff today.’

‘Shit. I didn’t know it had got that bad.’

‘We had loads of money in there. He moved a lot into a high interest account, and was supposed to move it back before today. I need him to do that right now. I don’t have access to it.’

There was a silence, and Julia could hear Drew tapping a fingernail on something, as though weighing up his next words. ‘Jules, come round. Talk to him. Maybe it’s all right, and he can transfer that money …’ But the way Drew spoke made her fear the worst – that the money was gone. Gone where? How?

‘All right. I’m on my way.’ She hung up and swore again. What was going on? ‘Barry, something’s come up. I’ve got to go out for a bit. Maura and Rahul are due in for a catch-up. Can you stand in for me? Just check they’re happy with everything and know what they’re supposed to be doing. I’ll be back … later.’

‘No problem, Julia.’ Barry gave her a thumbs-up.

She went through to the house to grab a jacket and her car keys, and a moment later was on her way to Ian and Drew’s house. They lived in a bungalow that had a large garden, the scene of many a summer barbecue in years gone by. Drew had his artist’s studio in a garden room that was tucked beneath a spreading oak tree.

It was Drew who answered the door and ushered her through to the sitting room. ‘I’ll fetch you some coffee, and let Ian know you’re here.’ He was tight-lipped as he ducked into a bedroom.

Julia could hear a muttered conversation and then the sounds of someone getting up and using the en suite bathroom.

Drew didn't look her in the eye as he went through to the kitchen and came back with a coffee for her. 'He'll be a couple of minutes. I'll be in my studio … if you need me for anything.'

'Drew? What's going on?' she asked.

'You need to talk to him,' was the only answer Drew seemed willing to give, as he went out through patio doors to his garden studio.

Julia sat in silence for the next ten minutes, waiting for Ian. Eventually he appeared, wearing a T-shirt and jeans, his hair wet as though he'd just had a shower. He was unshaven and there were dark circles beneath his eyes. He fetched himself a coffee and sat down in an armchair at the opposite end of the room to Julia. 'Sorry, Jules. Late night, barely slept before six. Must have turned my alarm off in my sleep.'

'It's not you being late for work that's brought me here, Ian,' she said. 'You know what day it is, right?'

'Er, Tuesday, I think? Am I right?' He flashed her a weak attempt at his trademark smile.

'Tuesday. Twenty-fifth. Which means …'

'Payroll.' He clapped a hand to his head. 'Did I not transfer the money?'

'You did not. And I can't get into that account. I must have got the password wrong. Got locked out. Can you move the money across now?' She looked at her watch. 'Right now? So the payroll payments don't bounce.'

'Er, yeah. I guess.' He got up and went over to a desk where a laptop sat closed. It took him ages to open it, start it up, navigate to the banking website. Before entering log-in details he turned back to her. 'Look, I'll do it. You don't need to stay. Get back to the office – isn't it team meeting time? Make my apologies and I'll be there this afternoon.'

'I'll stay here while you transfer the money, Ian. In case there's some problem.'

He sighed. 'You don't trust me, do you? After all these years!'

'I do, Ian. But just in case … let me see the money transfer. I hardly slept too, when I realised you hadn't done it yesterday.'

He turned back to his laptop but didn't do anything. She got up from the sofa and went to stand behind him.

'What, you're going to actually watch over my shoulder?'

'Yes. And I want you to write the password down for me. I was obviously getting it wrong this morning.'

He sighed, but still made no move to log on to the site. 'Jules, with you there …'

'For God's sake, Ian! Just make the bloody transfer will you, then I will go and leave you in peace!' Out of the corner of her eye she saw Drew, over in the garden studio, looking back at the house with concern.

Ian sighed again and bashed at the keys. It took him two attempts to get the password right too, and although she couldn't see what he'd typed in, from the movements of his fingers it was clear it was nothing like the password he'd told her. Almost as though he'd meant for her not to have access to this account.

And when the statement appeared, with the current balance in bold at the top, she gasped. The account was almost empty. 'Where's the money?' For a brief moment she wondered if perhaps he'd already made the transfer to the current account, and the money was safely there. But Ian was shaking his head.

'Where's the money, Ian?' she said again, her voice sounding shrill even to herself. 'What have you done with it?'

'It's … gone. I was going to put it back. Honestly, last night, I tried …'

'Last night? What do you mean? Have you spent it? What on?'

'No, I didn't spend it, as such … and honestly, Jules, this wasn't meant to happen … I was going to put the money back, just as soon as I'd …'

'You took the money out. You did something with it. Ian, it's our company's money. My money. What did you do with it?'

'Horse racing.' Drew was at the patio door, standing with his hands on his hips, his face taut with anger. 'He bet on horses with it. And lost. Just as he's done with all our savings. I've tried to help, but he won't admit he has a problem.'

'Betting? You've gambled away our company's money?'

'I borrowed it. I was on to a sure thing, a definite winner. I wouldn't have put it on anything risky.'

'And yet, you lost? So it was risky?' Julia could not believe what she was hearing. Of all the possible explanations, she'd never have guessed this. It was the first she'd ever heard of Ian gambling, although they'd occasionally run little office sweepstakes when the Grand National was on.

'It should have been a sure thing,' Ian repeated, shaking his head as though he'd been cheated.

'There's no such thing,' Drew said. 'Julia, I don't know what to say. I've tried to stop him. But he sneaks out when I'm not looking, leaves his phone behind, places bets. Goes to casinos too. And gambles online.'

'I only use casinos to try to get the money back,' Ian said, sounding indignant. 'Odds aren't good at casinos.'

'Fuck's sake.' Julia felt her fury rising. 'You lost money through gambling, so gambled more to try to get it back?'

'It's what gambling addicts always do,' Drew said. 'They need the hit. They need to place bigger and bigger bets, to get the same rush.'

'How can it be a rush when they keep losing? I don't understand it!'

'Neither do I.' Drew entered the room fully, closed the patio door and sat down. 'I'm glad this is out in the open now. He needs help. When I realised he was dipping into the business account – which was only last week, by the way – we had an enormous row about it. I said he should talk to Gamblers' Anonymous, or one of the other groups that can help, but he won't listen.' He looked at her sadly, and then gazed at Ian. Julia saw love and compassion in his eyes.

'Ian, do you accept you have a problem?' Maybe this was the place to start. Julia didn't know much about addiction but she'd heard that the first step in dealing with it needed to be the addict themselves seeking help.

Ian shrugged. 'Sometimes I probably go a bit far. But this is just a streak of bad luck. It'll turn around soon. Honestly, Jules, if that horse had come in, like it was supposed to, you'd never have known a thing. The money would be back in the business account. And I'd have repaid what I took from our savings.' He nodded to Drew. 'It's so bloody unfair.'

'So bloody stupid, you mean. Ian, you can't take the business's money like this!'

'I didn't take it, Jules!' Ian made quote marks in the air around the word 'take'. 'I borrowed it, and was going to put it back with interest.'

'It's not yours to borrow. It belongs to the business. To us.'

'I've always handled the finances.' Ian sounded petulant now.

'Not anymore, you don't. You can't be in control of those bank accounts if you're using the money to feed your gambling addiction. We're going to have to change the account so that we both need to approve any outgoings.'

Ian had the grace to look sheepish at that. 'I understand why you want to do that. I am sorry, Jules. This wasn't meant to happen.'

'Too bloody right it wasn't. Now, how are we going to cover the payroll?'

'When's that due?' Drew asked.

Julia looked at her watch. 'About ten minutes ago.' She pulled out her phone, and as expected, there were several notifications saying payments from the business current account had bounced. She needed to do something, and fast, before the staff and contractors discovered they hadn't been paid. Barry and Tulipa would probably understand and accept a short delay, but the contractors – who would blame them if they just left, or sued the business?

She looked at Ian. 'We'll have to cover it ourselves, this month. Can you transfer some personal money into the account?'

He shook his head. 'I've nothing.'

'Borrow on a credit card?'

'They're maxed out.'

Drew put his head in his hands and groaned. 'I didn't know about the credit cards. Jules, I don't think we can help.'

'Not your fault, Drew,' she said quietly. What an awful situation he was in, but it sounded like he'd had no idea of the extent of the problem.

'I should have told you sooner. I thought we could sort it out, as a couple. Until I realised he'd used business money …'

'Ian, you've got to get help for this, do you see that?'

'Fuck off. Both of you. Leave me alone.' Ian got up from the chair where he'd been sitting and stormed out of the house. Drew ran after him, and Julia heard some shouting and then the sound of a car starting up. A moment later Drew was back inside.

'He's gone, who knows where. You'd better block the business accounts, if there's any money left in them. I've got a couple of grand in a personal savings account, if that'll help …'

'Don't be daft. The business is nothing to do with you, you have no liability. I'll sort something out.' Though she had no idea what.

'On his behalf, I'm sorry.' Drew took her hand and squeezed it. 'I'm furious, but also mortified he's done this to you.'

'He's done it to you, too.'

'I know. Maybe this is crunch time. Maybe he'll realise now that he needs help. We'll get through this, one way or another.'

'We'll have to. Look, I need to go. Lots to sort out. I hope … I hope Ian comes back soon.'

'Yes. He will, eventually. Good luck, Julia.'

'You too.' She kissed his cheek. Ian didn't deserve him.

As she drove back to the office, Julia worked through her options. First, she needed to protect what little money was left in the company's bank accounts. Set them up so that Ian couldn't access the money without her authority. Second, she needed to ensure the staff and contractors were paid, if at all possible. Tulipa's flat purchase and Barry's student daughter were dependant on that. It was a good thing Tulipa's pay rise hadn't yet been finalised. She had money in a personal account, but not enough. She'd have to ring the bank, try to arrange an overdraft. It was about fire-fighting this month; somehow, she had to get the salaries paid, and then figure out what to do next. How much money was coming in, and when. Whether Mannings and Co might agree to bring forward their payments to help finance the development – if she could talk them into it without revealing their financial problems.

Just how much had Ian gambled away? How bad was it? That was the first question to answer.

Back at the office Julia shut herself away and got busy checking the true financial status of the company. She cursed herself for not staying on top of it, but it had always been Ian's department. She'd left it to him, while he'd left the technical side of things to her.

She discovered the numerous withdrawals Ian had made over the last few months, from both business accounts. But it was worse than that. She called the bank, and discovered a loan he'd taken out, using the business as collateral. The first repayment was due in days, and there was no money to cover it. The bank would not give her an overdraft.

And then an email arrived, from Mannings and Co. In it, with great regret, they confirmed they could not provide finance to develop the new version of the system, and as Julian Systems could not meet their preferred timescale they had decided to buy a different system from another company.

There were no payments due in from client companies for

the next three months. But they had outgoing payments, for the development software they used, due within a week. It was a perfect storm.

Julia felt her blood run cold as she entered all the figures she'd found onto a spreadsheet. The gap was widening. She checked her own bank account, and the joint one she and Marc used for household expenses. If she emptied both, she could cover Barry and Tulipa's salaries this month, but not the contractors'. That would leave her and Marc and the kids nothing to live on other than Marc's salary, until the business was back in the black. She checked her credit card limits. Maybe she could draw out cash on those to cover it. What about the contractors? And the loan repayment?

She put her head in her hands. This was too big for her. There was no way she could meet the company's debts.

There was a tap at the office door. She looked up to see Barry peering around the door, Tulipa behind him. 'Julia? Are you all right? I thought we were having a team meeting? Maura and Rahul have arrived …'

'Oh. No. I mean, yes, there was one scheduled, but no, we're not going to have it.'

'What's wrong? Where's Ian?' Barry's face was filled with concern.

'Ian's not coming in today.' She could not keep the note of bitterness out of her voice.

'What's happened?' Barry came fully into the room, and closed the door behind him. 'Julia, I've worked for you for what, six years now? There's something not right. Is it anything I can help fix?'

He'd have to know soon. He'd spot the lack of salary payment soon enough. 'Barry, I'm sorry. It's … well, the thing is … there's no money. I think—' Oh God. She didn't want to say it, but it was the truth.

'You think …?'

'I think … we're bankrupt.'

'What?' Barry sat down heavily on Ian's chair. 'I thought we were going from strength to strength. We took on Maura and Rahul, and you were talking about more contractors to meet Mannings' dates?'

'Mannings have pulled out. And the business's money has … gone. We're in real trouble. Barry, look, I'm going to cover yours and Tulipa's salaries this month, at least as much of it as I can. But then …'

He stared at her. 'You really mean it? You can't even cover our wages?'

'Not at the moment. And I – I don't know what to do.'

'Doesn't Ian normally handle the financial side?' As he spoke, realisation dawned on Barry's face. 'Oh … I see, I think.'

'Yes. Ian has, for want of a better phrase, royally fucked up.'

'Ah.' Barry leaned forward, elbows on his knees, and regarded the floor for a moment. Then he looked up. 'Listen, Julia, remember I used to run my own business for a while? I've a little experience in this. I wound it up in the end. If I can look at the accounts, maybe I can help …'

'Thank you. That would be helpful. But I can see no way out of this.'

'If that's so, then at least I can help you get the ball rolling in terms of liquidating the company.'

Liquidating. What a horrible, ugly word.

Chapter 20

Pamela

In January, there was much excitement in Pam's section at BP, when a huge machine they dubbed the Colossus was delivered. It was to replace the Heath Robinson, and would be far more reliable, so its designer and builder Tommy Flowers promised. Pam remembered meeting him when he'd come to visit some months earlier. He'd been asked then how to improve the notoriously unreliable Heath Robinson and had obviously decided it was better to start again and build something new.

The Colossus was delivered in pieces but quickly assembled. Like its predecessor there was a huge frame on which the punched tape was mounted. But if she'd thought the Heath Robinson had a lot of valves, this had far, far more. 'I thought valves were fragile, and failed easily?' she said to Edwin, who'd helped construct the machine.

'Mr Flowers says the problems are when you keep turning them off and on again. His idea with this machine is to keep them on the whole time. There's to be a test this afternoon – I can't wait to see how well it does.'

Pam smiled. 'Me too. I've news for you, Edwin. I applied to Mr Newman to see if I could work on the new machine, and he's said yes. I'm going to be one of its operators. And so I'm allowed to be present during the test today.' She'd been sitting on this news for a couple of days, unable to believe her luck. Ever since seeing the Heath Robinson for the first time she'd wanted to work with it directly. Imagine a machine that could do thousands of computations each minute, so much faster than a human? And now imagine one that could do that more reliably, without constantly breaking down?

Edwin's eyes were shining. 'That's wonderful, Pam. And I'm going to be working with this machine too. I'll be working out the settings and telling the Wren operating it – that'll be you! – how to connect it up. I'm delighted we'll be working so closely together.' He blushed suddenly, as if embarrassed to have said this, and picked up his coffee cup to hide behind.

*

The test, later that day, was an astounding success. The Colossus was set up to decode a message that had already been decoded using the old methods. It ran successfully the first time, as soon as it was switched on, and produced the correct answer within minutes. The same test was run again, and produced the same response, to applause from all present. It was warm in the room, Pam noticed. The machine had no fewer than 1,500 valves, mounted on horizontal racks she'd been told had come from telephone exchanges. They cooled by convection.

'It's probably a bit naughty,' she said to Edwin later, 'but I can't help but think hanging damp clothes above the racks of valves would be a wonderful way of drying washing.'

He snorted with laughter. 'Pam, you wouldn't dare bring your wet washing here and hang it over Colossus! What if it dripped?'

'I said "damp", not dripping wet! You're right though, I

wouldn't dare.' It'd be nice to be working in a warm room though, especially during the winter. Her mind turned for a moment to that conversation with Frank about skating. He hadn't mentioned again wanting to skate on the BP lake, thankfully. But neither had he mentioned skating at Woburn, even though the pond there was well and truly frozen, and a couple of Wrens had ventured out on it the previous weekend. Clarissa had brought some skates from home and was lending them to anyone with the right sized feet.

*

The day after its installation and test, Colossus was put to work in earnest. Pam was shown in detail how to operate it – how to load up the tape onto one of the sets of pulley wheels (the machine had two sets, so that one tape could be loaded up while the other was being read). How to plug in the cords in the switchboard and rotate the wheels to the required setting. How to read off and interpret the output counts, printed on a typewriter that was connected to the machine, and use those to set up the next run. It was all very complicated, but over the months Pam had pieced together knowledge of the Tunny code-breaking operation, and she could see that this machine would remove one level of encryption from each message, and it would do so quickly and efficiently.

The messages would then be passed through to another section, where the remaining encryption would be tackled by hand. The Tunny machines had twelve wheel settings. Once these were all known, the replica Tunny machine in Mr Tester's section where Clarissa worked would be set up, and the encrypted message typed in. Out would come plain text German.

This was the theory then. If it worked, and worked well, they would be able to decrypt many more German transmissions than they had to date. They might be able to discover German military plans, and pass the intelligence on, allowing the Allied forces to take action against it. It was an intoxicating idea, that their work here in the concrete huts with this odd-looking machine, might alter the course of the war, and alter it in their favour.

*

In February a letter arrived for Pam, from her brother Geoff. In it she was delighted to read that he had been moved to a different RAF station, at Turweston, Buckinghamshire, and it was nearby! It was just a bus ride away. 'I don't have any leave for some time, and when I do I should go home to Mum and Dad,' he wrote, 'but if you have any half days off perhaps you could visit me here? It'd be grand to see you.'

Pam wrote back immediately, with details of her watches so that he could tell her when would be a convenient time. She knew he mostly worked nights, escorting bombing raids flying out over Germany. He replied the next day with a suggestion, and Pam decided to use her next free Saturday afternoon visiting Geoff. It would mean missing out on seeing Frank, but he'd understand. This was her brother, and she hadn't seen him for months, and given his job, who knew how many more occasions there'd be when she could spend time with him? She sent Frank a note, explaining she wouldn't be able to see him that week but arranging to meet him the following weekend.

'I can't wait to see Geoff,' she told Clarissa on the bus a couple of days before. 'He's such a lovely fellow. I'm proud that he's my brother.'

'Wish I had a brother,' Clarissa said, with a sigh. 'It must be lovely.'

'It is, though I do worry about him, of course, being in the RAF.' Pam had a sudden thought. 'Clarissa, are you working on Saturday afternoon? If you're not, would you like to come with me, to see Geoff?'

'Oh! I couldn't – surely you want him to yourself, a bit of family time?'

'Geoff's the friendliest person you could ever meet. He always says, the more the merrier. I'm sure he'd love to meet you. I've told him quite a bit about you in my letters.'

'Well, if you're sure …' Clarissa smiled, and Pam realised she was delighted by the idea. They spent the rest of the journey to BP that day making plans for the weekend, deciding on small gifts to take to Geoff, whether to wear their Wren uniforms or civilian clothes, what they would do with the four hours they would have in his company.

'Let's leave that up to Geoff,' Pam said. 'He'll no doubt have some ideas, and of course it'll depend on the weather.'

*

Saturday turned out to be fine, and the two girls set off. As usual they took the army transport bus to BP and walked back to the village to catch a bus to Brackley and another to the RAF base. It was only a five-minute journey to the nearest stop to the base. 'We could have walked that,' Clarissa said.

'We'll know next time. Look, there he is!' Geoff was waiting at the bus stop, looking smart in his RAF uniform and Pam was pleased they'd decided to wear their Wren uniforms. He waved vigorously when he spotted them. Pam hurried off the bus and into his arms, relishing the bear hug he gave her.

'So good to see you, Sis! Let me look at you.' He pushed her gently away, admiring her uniform. 'You look fantastic.'

'So do you! Geoff, this is my good friend Clarissa. She was at a loose end today so came with me.'

'Clarissa! Pam's written about you in several letters. Good to meet you.' Geoff grinned broadly and shook Clarissa's hand, and Pam was intrigued to see her friend blush a little, and stutter as she answered him.

'It's lovely to see … I mean meet you. Pam's told me lots about you too.'

'Well, ladies, I'm glad the weather's good today, and not as cold as it has been lately. Shall we walk? I thought I'd take you onto the base, we can get tea at the mess, meet some of the lads. We can have a walk later via the village and then back to your bus stop. There's a Lyons Corner Shop there that usually has cake so we can pop in there if there's time.'

'Sounds perfect!' Pam glanced at Clarissa, who nodded her agreement to the plan. But Clarissa's eyes were on Geoff, she noticed.

As they walked the short distance along a lane bounded by high hedgerows and through a checkpoint onto the RAF base, Pam and Geoff caught each other up on all their news since they'd each left home the previous summer. 'Hard to believe we are where we are, isn't it?' Geoff said, as he signed the two girls in at the gate.

'It is, indeed.' Pam watched as he entered details on a form, and then followed him across an open grassy space towards a cluster of corrugated iron sheds. 'Your security is less than we have,' she said. 'We wouldn't be able to sign you in like that.'

'Oh? What is it you do at Bletchley Park? One hears rumours it's all very hush-hush ...'

'Hush. We're all secretaries,' Clarissa told him, with a wink, and he laughed.

'All right, I see. I won't ask. Anyway, look. There's my hut – I sleep in there with seven other men.' Geoff pointed to the nearest shed. The door was open and two men were leaning against the wall, smoking, watching them approach. 'All right, Alston? Smithy?' Geoff said, raising a hand in greeting.

'All the better for seeing these two beauties,' one of the men said. 'Your sisters?'

'This one is' – Geoff indicated Pam – 'and this is her friend. They're both out of your league, Smithy, so don't be getting ideas.'

Pam giggled as Smithy made an elaborate bow and blew her a kiss. Geoff hurried them past, apologising. 'They don't see many women here, bless them. Just the ATS girls who fly planes between airfields, and the girls who run the mess.'

'Do you have dances locally?' Clarissa asked him.

'Not since I've been here, but I heard they did last summer. What about you?'

'Yes, last summer there were some at both Bletchley and Woburn.'

'Pammy, you'll have to let me know when your next dance is on. I reckon I could borrow a motorbike and come over for it. Would that be allowed?'

'Certainly – the dances are often in village halls rather than on the Bletchley estate itself, so there's no issue with security.'

'There was one last year at BP that we both went to,' Clarissa put in.

'Oh yes! Well, we'll be sure to let you know when the next one comes round. It'd be lovely to have you there.'

'Thank you. So, here's our mess hall.' Geoff held open the door to a larger hut, that was filled with men sitting at tables, playing cards, drinking tea, reading newspapers. There was a general hum of conversation. In a corner, a darts match was in progress. Geoff indicated an empty table, and the girls sat down while he went to fetch them cups of tea.

'It all seems very relaxed here,' Pam commented to Geoff when he returned to the table. 'I thought there'd be people rushing about and planes taking off and landing.'

'It's relaxed between missions. But if enemy aircrafts are spotted approaching and we're scrambled, it's all pretty hectic then. The lads are good, I think, at making the most of the quieter periods in between.'

As Geoff spoke, Pam noticed he addressed himself mostly to Clarissa, who was leaning forward slightly, towards him, a half-smile on her lips. Her eyes rarely left his. Pam leaned back in her chair, giving them space. She was happy for them both, if they liked each other. Geoff deserved happiness. So did Clarissa. She, herself, had Frank. It was lovely that her friend and brother had hit it off so well.

*

The afternoon passed all too quickly, and although Pam felt she hadn't had as much time chatting to Geoff as she'd expected, it had been fun, and the potential romance between Geoff and Clarissa was an unexpected bonus. As they sat in the Lyons Corner Shop near the bus stop, Pam disappeared out to the ladies' to give her brother and friend a few minutes alone to say goodbye, or to make arrangements to meet up again. She smiled happily at herself in the mirror as she washed her hands. She wouldn't begrudge them any time together. For herself, she could always come to see Geoff on her own, on a day when Clarissa was on watch. 'Anyway,' she told herself, 'I've had him to myself for nineteen years. Time someone else had a share, and who better than Clarissa?'

She checked her watch. It was almost time for the train. As she went back into the café, she noticed the lovebirds were leaning towards each other, their foreheads almost touching, holding hands above the table. They broke apart when they noticed her approach, and Pam pretended she hadn't noticed.

'We've got three minutes,' she said. 'Best get going.' She held out her arms to Geoff for a hug. 'I'll try and come again in a fortnight, if that's all right with you?'

'Lovely. I'll write with suitable times. Hope you can both come again.'

'We'll wait to hear.' Pam kissed her brother and left the café. Clarissa came out a moment later, looking unusually flustered.

'He's lovely, your brother,' she said, as they boarded the train.

Pam just smiled quietly to herself, and imagined a future time, the war over, and herself as bridesmaid, Clarissa as her new sister-in-law.

*

The week after visiting Geoff, Pam was back to her usual routine of seeing Frank when she wasn't covering the day watch. It had been a fortnight, and after the unpleasantness on their way back from London when he'd run off and come back with that mysterious suitcase, she wasn't sure quite what footing their relationship was on now. But when she met him, at the front of the Abbey's main building, he was all smiles and charm, her old Frank restored to her.

'Pamela! Lovely to see you again.' He pulled her towards him and kissed her. 'I hope you had a lovely time with your brother last week? You must tell me all about it. Let's walk, shall we?'

It was like the early days of their relationship. The day was mild and they walked for miles around the extensive parkland that surrounded the Abbey, stopping to watch the herd of deer run across a field in front of them. 'Beautiful, aren't they? And they have no idea a war is going on,' Pam said. 'Wouldn't it be lovely to be running free like them?'

'We could run, if you like,' Frank said. He caught her hand and pulled her across the field, laughing. They reached a woodland glade and stopped there. Pam was gasping for breath, a stitch in her side.

'Oh, you crazy boy,' she said, as he gathered her into his arms and kissed her.

'You beautiful girl,' he whispered, as they broke apart a few moments later. 'I can't imagine life without you. Will you … do you think you might … marry me? When the war is over, and we can do it properly, in a church, with a hundred guests and a feast afterwards?'

'Oh!' Pam clapped a hand to her mouth involuntarily. He was proposing! She had not expected this, especially not after their London trip. He wanted to marry her! Was it what she wanted too? Three or four weeks ago, she'd have instantly said yes, but now … she'd had a glimpse of another side to him, and she had the feeling she didn't know him as well as one ought to know someone one plans to marry.

He was waiting expectantly, smiling at her. How was she going to answer? She loved him, but she needed to know him better, for longer, before she could agree to marry him, didn't she?

'Frank, I … I'm honoured, I really am. We haven't known each other long enough, though, and with the war still on …' His face fell as she spoke, and she hurried on, not wanting to take away all hope from him. 'I mean … I'd love to marry you, in time, but I am not sure now is the right time to actually … get engaged, or anything. I think we should … hold off a little. Go on as we are, until things are different.'

'You're not saying yes.' He tilted his head a little to one side. 'But you are also not saying no. That is enough for now, thank you, dearest Pamela.'

She felt guilty that she had disappointed him, but she had to stay true to how she felt. This was the biggest decision of her life, bigger even than deciding to come to work at BP rather than take up her university place. And it was a life-changing decision. Not something to be rushed into. She would think about it, over the coming weeks. She'd try the idea out, in her mind. Herself as Mrs Miller. Or Mrs Müller. After the war, might he want to revert to his German name? Would he want to go to live in Germany, near his brother? Would he allow her to take up her university place, to have a job, to make full use of her abilities?

'Let's not say anything to anyone, for now,' she said, placing a hand on his arm. 'We'll keep it to ourselves, until things are more … settled.'

'Of course.' He gazed away from her for a moment, at a blackbird pecking in the ground at the edge of the field. 'Though I cannot wait for you to say a definite yes, and for us to tell our families. Your brother would be delighted, won't he?'

She smiled. 'Yes, he would. Maybe he too will be getting engaged before too long.' She told him then about how Geoff and Clarissa had got on so well. 'In fact, I do believe she's going to see him again tomorrow.'

'Without you, and so soon!'

'They must take every chance they can. I told you Geoff's in the RAF. Who knows what might happen? It's so frightening, knowing every time he goes up in his plane might be the last.'

Frank nodded, serious now. 'I know. I know just how it feels – it's the same for Wolfgang.'

'The same?'

'He too flies aeroplanes,' Frank said, quietly.

'He … I thought you said he was not in the armed forces?'

'Not in the army. He's in the Luftwaffe. I only heard this recently.'

Pam took a step back and turned away, fixing her gaze on the horizon across the fields. Frank's brother in the Luftwaffe, Geoff in the RAF. They might be up there now, right now, attempting to shoot each other down. It was a horrible thought. 'I can't … I don't know what to think about that. How does it make you feel? Your own brother, on the other side?'

Frank took hold of her arms and pulled her back towards him. 'I am glad I have asthma, Pamela. I am glad I am not fighting, for it means I do not have to pick a side and fight against my brother. I only need to tend to these grounds, keep the garden tidy and productive, and wait for the war to end, one way or another, so that my girl will marry me.'

'Not pick a side? You live here in England, you have always lived here!'

'Yes, and my brother has always lived in Germany. This accident of birth … it means nothing. One merely supports the country to which one has most ties.'

'I'm not sure I agree,' she said, once more pulling away from him. 'There's been bad from both sides in this war, certainly, but without a doubt it is the German side most at fault. It is Hitler and his despicable Nazis, and whatever happens he must not prevail! We must defeat him, whatever the cost.'

'Even at the cost of your own brother?'

'My brother makes his own decisions.' Pam dashed away a tear.

'And, Pamela, as well as bad on both sides, there is good too. Not all Nazis are "despicable" as you put it.'

'They are!'

'My brother is not. He is a good and honourable man. Yet he joined the Party in 1938.'

'What!' Pam couldn't believe it. Not only was Frank's brother in the Luftwaffe, flying planes on missions against her country, but he'd joined the Nazi party, which she was sure could only be full of monsters.

'He joined for what he believes are good reasons. For his Fatherland. To bring Germany back to prosperity. We can't pretend to understand what it has been like for people in Germany since the last war. I am sure Wolfgang is doing what he thinks is best, just as we are, too.' Frank sounded defensive.

'And now he's at war against us. Against you.' Pam shook her head. She wished Frank had not told her this, about his brother. It was horrible, knowing it, but not knowing how to handle this knowledge. 'Let's not talk of it anymore. We only have another couple of hours together, until next week. Can we try to enjoy them?' She felt confused. He'd proposed, then told her his brother was a Nazi! She needed to think about it all. Not just his proposal, but the other things he'd said. She suddenly, perhaps unfairly, felt very unsure of him.

Chapter 21

Julia

Barry's frown grew deeper and deeper as he looked through the company's accounts and peered at bank statements.

'Go on, then. What's the verdict?' Julia asked, when at last he leaned back in his chair and sighed.

'You're right, I'm afraid. The company is insolvent. There's not enough money to pay the debts that are due right now. Julia, I'm so sorry.' He rubbed his chin, in the way he often did when trying to solve a knotty coding problem. But there was no amount of computer code that could get them out of this problem.

'What am I going to do? I need to pay your wages – yours and Tulipa's, at least, somehow. And the contractors. And the bank loan. Maybe I'll be able to sell the software we've built to another company – how do you even go about doing that? I'll need to say something to our clients. If we're bust, we can't support the software and they'll need to implement something different. I'm going to have to lay off Rahul and Maura …' She was pacing back and forth in the little office as she spoke, the problems building up in a tsunami in her head.

'Julia, please sit down. Listen, it'll be all right …' Barry began.

'How can it be all right? We're bust! Bankrupt! Bloody Ian!' She was in danger of losing it, she knew. In front of Barry. So unprofessional, but right now she didn't care. She wanted to rant and rage and scream and shout.

'Listen to me,' Barry was saying. He caught her arm as she paced past, and stopped her walking on. 'You know I wound up the business I used to own? Well, I was never actually insolvent but wrapping up a company that's still solvent is much the same process. The important thing is that you don't have to do everything yourself. You find an insolvency practitioner, and they take over. They'll work out what assets you have and how best to dispose of them, and they'll pay off company debts in the right order. They pay themselves first, of course. But they're on your side, trying to do what's best for all parties.'

'Getting someone like that in would make it all seem so final.' Julia slumped down in her chair, leaning back.

'But when a company's insolvent, the sooner you get them in the better. Otherwise you might end up liable for more costs yourself.' Barry shook his head. 'I can't believe this has happened, but honestly it's the only thing you can do. It's the responsible thing. They might even find a solution that allows the company to keep trading.'

'How on earth do you find a … what did you call them?'

'Insolvency practitioner. Or IP. Well, let's look online, shall we?' Barry smiled and began tapping into his laptop. 'OK, so there are several based in this area. I'll send you the links and you can choose whichever one you like the look of. As I said, the sooner you get this ball rolling the better.'

'Thanks, Barry. I really appreciate your help.' Julia felt so pathetic, so small. She vaguely remembered reading something about how to wind up a company years ago. When she and Ian had first set up the business, she'd read some books on how to run a limited company, but had skimmed over all the parts to do with insolvency. That was never going to happen to them, was it?

'No problem. You gave me a job when I needed it most. You've paid me well. I'm going to be sad to leave, but it is what it is.' Barry spent another minute on his laptop then folded it up and stood. 'Well, I've sent you those links. I'll leave you alone now.' He walked to the door of the little office then turned back. 'You might want to tell the others now what's happened. The sooner they know, the sooner they can … start job-hunting.'

Barry closed the door softly behind him, leaving Julia staring at it. Oh God. She had to tell them. It wouldn't be as bad for the contractors – annoying for them, of course, and they'd be out of pocket, but they'd pick up other work soon enough. But for Barry and Tulipa … Tulipa had her house deposit she was saving up for. Her flat purchase was supposed to complete this month, but without this month's salary it might not be able to happen. And Barry was supporting a daughter at university. It'd be tough for him to lose a month's pay. Maybe more than a month, if he couldn't get another job quickly.

It was all too much. Too sudden. Fuck Ian. How dare he let this happen? How dare he steal the company's money? She could probably take him to court. But what was the point? Suing him was pointless as his only wealth had been the company. At least her house was safe. It was a limited company so anything in her own name rather than the business's was safe. But then with a jolt she realised that without her own salary from the business, and the rent the company paid her for the office space, she would not be able to pay the mortgage. Marc's salary wasn't enough to cover it either. They'd have to sell up.

She groaned, her face in her hands, as she realised the implications of it all on her family. And then she looked towards the door. Out there were four people waiting for her to go out and tell them what was happening. Barry might have dropped a hint, but it was her job to break the news. She took a deep breath, dabbed at her eyes with a tissue, and went out to the other room.

They listened silently, with shocked, solemn expressions. As soon as she'd finished talking, Rahul picked up his rucksack, put a few personal items in it and walked to the door. 'I guess this is it, then. Thanks for the opportunity. This could have been so good.'

Maura too put on her coat. 'If ever … you're working somewhere that needs contractors … remember my name, hey?' She nodded and followed Rahul out of the door.

With only Tulipa and Barry left, both watching her with sympathetic expressions, Julia sat down on one of the comfortable chairs in the break-out area. 'I'm so, so sorry, guys. This should never have happened.' Before she could do anything to stop herself, she began to cry. Huge fat unstoppable tears rolled down her cheeks.

'Oh, Julia. It's so awful. But things will work out.' Tulipa pulled her chair over beside Julia and wrapped her arms around her, allowing Julia to sob on her employee's shoulder. It felt cathartic to just let it all go. In times past she'd have cried on Ian's shoulder, but it was Ian who had caused all this.

Barry too offered sympathy, standing behind the two women, patting Julia's shoulder. She caught his hand and squeezed it. 'I am so sorry, you two. I had no idea this was on the cards. Tulipa, I realise this might affect your flat purchase. And Barry, your daughter … If I could do anything to help, I would … I'll look at what's in my personal account …'

'You'll do no such thing,' Barry said, firmly and Tulipa was also shaking her head. 'The IP will handle selling assets and paying debts, including what's owed to us. Might take a while but I'm sure we'll get it in the end, if a buyer can be found for the software. Meanwhile, what's in your personal account is your own, and you'll need it to live on for a bit.'

'Where did the company's money go?' Tulipa asked, gently.

Might as well tell them, she thought. 'Ian, it turns out, has a gambling problem.'

'Oh.' Tulipa looked away, then turned back to Julia. 'My dad gambled. There are organisations that can help gamblers and their families. I will send you some links.'

'Thank you. Right now, I'm afraid I can only feel fury towards him, not sympathy.' Those links might be helpful for Drew, she thought.

'That's understandable. But believe me, you'll feel better once an IP has been appointed,' Barry said.

'You're both amazing.' It was all she could say. She stood and left the office, going through to the main house. The boys were just coming home from school. She called them into the sitting room and told them the news.

Ryan just shrugged. Oscar looked more concerned. 'Will you get another job?'

'I'll have to,' she said.

'Working for someone else rather than running your own company?'

'Yes.'

Oscar gave her an uncertain smile. 'But that's good, isn't it? A job you can just leave at five o'clock each day and forget about, rather than having to work in the evenings and weekends. Like, a job with a steady salary. Isn't that easier?'

She smiled at her elder son. 'Yes, I suppose it is. Thank you for looking on the bright side.'

'What does Dad say?' Ryan asked.

She reddened. 'I ... er ... I haven't had chance to talk to him yet. He's away on that course, remember.'

'Wow. You told us before him. He won't like that.'

Oscar was right. He wouldn't like it.

Julia decided she couldn't tell Marc over the phone, or even hint there were problems. This needed to be a face-to-face discussion, when he came home at the end of his course. It affected him too – obviously it did if they ended up selling the house, or perhaps renting out the office space to someone else. She'd just have to live with it herself for the next couple of days. He'd been so excited about getting the place on this course, the opportunities it might lead to in terms of better work and more pay. She couldn't spoil it for him, however much she felt the need to talk to someone. But to be honest, Marc was not really the person she wanted to talk it through with. It'd be more of a duty than a help, telling him and working out what they as a family would do about it. She couldn't imagine he'd have much sympathy. He'd be angry about having to move house and having less money as a family. And she hated to admit it, but she could easily imagine Marc being secretly pleased that her business had failed and he was now the principal breadwinner. He'd always been jealous of her success.

She spent some time researching insolvency practitioners and booked an appointment with one that had good reviews for the next day. That done, she pottered about for the rest of the day, preparing a meal, cleaning up, tidying the sitting room, putting some washing on. Anything to take her mind off the fact she was losing her business. And, she realised with a sigh, quite possibly losing her best friend too. How could her relationship with Ian survive this? She certainly would never be able to trust him again. Of course you couldn't be in business with someone you didn't trust. Could you be friends with them? Maybe. It was too soon to tell.

The boys were surprisingly helpful. She'd thought they might barricade themselves away in their rooms and keep out of her way. But they made themselves available, offering to help, looking for little tasks they could do. Ryan found a duster and began dusting all the vases and ornaments in the sitting room. Oscar fetched the ironing board and set about ironing his school shirts. Julia was quietly impressed, and proud they were stepping up when she needed help.

She spent the rest of the evening taking photos on her phone of each of her grandmother's snaps. It was a cheap way of digitising them. Once uploaded to her laptop, she could zoom in on details and faces. She organised them by who was in them and roughly when they were taken, as far as she could work out. The earliest ones were from the Box Brownie, and then there were more from the late 1940s and onwards, that appeared to have been taken with a different, more sophisticated camera. Probably the old Leica her grandfather had proudly kept for many years.

It felt like a bit of a pointless task, but it was absorbing, and kept her mind off her worries. Oscar looked over her shoulder at one point, and gestured at the photo of Bletchley Park. 'That's where we went, isn't it? So cool that my great-gran worked there. Hope you're going to find out more about her.'

'I'm hoping to,' she replied.

'You'll have more time, anyway, now you don't have to work.'

'Hmm. I'll be busy for a while yet. The company has to be properly wound up. And I've got to go job-hunting.'

'Yeah, but there'll be more time. A new job can wait.' Oscar spontaneously kissed the top of her head, then ran out of the room as though he'd embarrassed himself.

Julia was left rubbing the spot he'd kissed, wondering if one consequence of all this might be a closer relationship with her sons. She hoped so. It was true that her work-life balance had been out of kilter in recent years. And here was the perfect opportunity to reset it and get it right. 'Bear that in mind, Julia,' she told herself, 'when you are looking for a new job.' Nothing too stressful. Nothing that would keep her working when she should be spending time with the boys, who were growing up far too fast.

Chapter 22

Pamela

Spring was at last in the air, bringing with it new life. There were several fawns spotted among the deer herd at Woburn; there were house martin nests under the eaves at the Abbey, the parent birds often flying close to Pam's cabin window; there was blossom in the hedgerows and baby rabbits in the fields. And it felt as though the tide might be about to turn in the war. There'd been a day when a partially decrypted message was passed as usual from Pam's section through to the Testery for the second stage of decryption, and a couple of hours later an almighty cheer went up from the girls there. Pam and Edwin had been unable to stop themselves from opening the door between the two sections.

'What's going on?' Edwin asked, and it was Clarissa herself who answered.

'I've just finished inputting that last message into our Tunny, and got the plain text out. It's a corker! Yet to be translated but even my German's good enough to get the gist of it.' She grinned at them. 'Can't tell you what, of course, but put it this way – we're going to save many lives now we know Himmler's latest instructions.'

'Well done!' Pam said, giving her friend a hug. 'Proud of you!'

'Ah, don't be silly, it's a team effort. But I do feel proud of what we're doing here.'

Pam nodded. 'Yes, me too. We're doing a great job. Shame we can never tell anyone. They'll never know about our part in the war.'

'We'll know it, and we can be quietly proud of it all our lives. And maybe one day we'll be allowed to talk or write about it.'

Pam shook her head. 'I don't think I ever would.'

'Ahem, back to work, ladies.' They hadn't noticed Max Newman come through behind them.

'Sorry, Mr Newman,' Pam said. 'I just wondered what the roar was all about.'

But Newman's eyes were twinkling behind his horn-rimmed spectacles and it was clear he was as delighted as everyone else at their achievement.

Pam followed Edwin back through to their section and got to work on the next message tape to be loaded up onto her Colossus. There were several in action at BP now, but she was proud to have been one of the first Wrens to work on them. 'Isn't it wonderful,' she said to Edwin, 'to be playing such an important part in the war?'

'It certainly is.' He smiled. 'I feel quite sorry for people who aren't able to fight and don't have jobs like ours. Must be hard. Like your Frank, and his asthma stopping him from joining up.'

'Hmm. I'm not sure he'd have wanted to join up anyway.' Pam thought of how conflicted Frank seemed, with his brother in the Luftwaffe but his life and friends all in England.

'A conscientious objector?' Edwin looked puzzled.

'No. Something different.' Suddenly Pam had an overwhelming urge to confide in Edwin. Since hearing about Wolfgang being in the Luftwaffe, she'd found herself questioning Frank's patriotism more and more. She needed another perspective on it. Edwin, with his calm, practical nature, would be able to advise her. He'd no doubt tell her not to be so silly, to enjoy Frank's company, and stop worrying about it.

'What is it, Pam?' Edwin looked concerned, and Pam realised she'd been frowning and biting her lip.

'Can I talk to you? Somewhere quiet, private. Not here.' Mr Newman might come in at any moment.

'Of course. Look it's only five minutes until our tea break. We could walk through the grounds, away from the huts. We'll find a quiet spot somewhere.'

'All right.' Pam forced a smile to her face and got on with the tasks that needed doing before they could go for their twenty-minute tea break. The next message tape was loaded up and ready to go.

A few minutes later they were walking past Bletchley's lake and on to a circuit of gravel paths. There were a few others out for a walk but no one going in the same direction as them. 'What can I help you with, Pam?' Edwin asked, gently.

'It's Frank.' She blurted this out, before she lost the courage. She did need to talk to someone about this, she knew, but it wasn't going to be easy.

'Frank? Pam, are you sure I'm the best person to talk to? Wouldn't one of your girlfriends – Clarissa, or Norah perhaps? – be better? I mean, if something's gone wrong in your relationship …'

'No, it's not that. It's … more complex.' She turned to Edwin. 'I think you are the right person. And I can rely on your discretion, can't I?'

'Of course.' He frowned and looked at her expectantly.

'So, the thing is, I've found out a few things about Frank, and I'm … a bit unsure of him now, if I'm honest.'

'Unsure … how? He hasn't hurt you, has he?' Edwin looked as though Frank would have him to answer to, if he had.

'No, no. I'm just unsure … where his loyalties lie.' She took a deep breath. 'Frank's half German. He was brought up in England, but his father was German.'

'Like Mr Newman.'

'Yes, but his brother was brought up in Germany. And his brother is … in the Luftwaffe.'

'Oh. I see. And is Frank in touch with his brother – oh, that time you asked about sending letters to Germany?'

'Yes. Frank writes to an address in Switzerland, but it's his brother's name on the envelope, so I think someone must be forwarding them on.'

'He was seen, wasn't he, hanging around the gates at Bletchley?' Edwin rubbed his chin. 'Clarissa told me.'

Pam nodded. 'Yes. And ages ago, he asked me to bring my camera here, and take photographs. So he could see where I worked, he said.'

'I remember. Clarissa took one of you and me. Did you give him those photographs?'

'No. The film is still in my camera, undeveloped. I never used it up.' She felt herself redden. If she'd given Frank those photographs, she might be guilty of breaking the Official Secrets Act. How could she have been so stupid?

Edwin must have had the same thought. He stopped walking and caught hold of Pam's arm. 'Pam, you haven't told him anything about your job, have you?'

She shook her head vigorously. 'Nothing at all. I wouldn't. I said I was a secretary, just as we were advised to. He suspects there's more to it – everyone local suspects – but I have not said a word. Anyway, he's never really asked me about it. He knows I can't talk about it.' To her dismay, tears came. 'Edwin, you have to believe me! I was stupid with the camera, but I would never, ever breathe a word of what goes on here!'

'It's all right, Pam. I believe you. So, what do we have? A half German gardener, who knows nothing of what happens here, who may be writing to his brother who is in the Luftwaffe. His letters will be read by the censors before they leave our shores, so he can't be passing on any knowledge, even if he has any, that way.' Edwin smiled. 'He's almost certainly innocent of any wrongdoing, Pam. Do you trust him?'

'I don't know anymore! I … I love him, I think. I thought I trusted him. But I am not certain he's innocent. His brother's a member of the Nazi party as well as being in the Luftwaffe. There's the problem of the suitcase, too.'

'Suitcase?'

'He collected it when we went to London that day in January. He says he's looking after it for a friend.'

'Does he still have it?'

Pam shrugged. 'I don't know. I've never been to his lodgings. I haven't asked him about the case. We argued about it at the time, so I haven't dared bring it up. Why, what do you think it is?' Edwin was looking seriously concerned now.

'Probably nothing. But … I'd love a peek inside his lodgings. Do you know where he lives?'

'Yes, but …'

'It'd be interesting to see if that case is still there, and what's in it,' Edwin said. Then he turned to Pam and smiled. 'But don't be worrying about it. Like I said, it's probably nothing. You love him, trust your instincts. He's more English than German. He's not his brother.'

'Thank you.' Pam was silent as they walked on, wondering: did she trust Frank? What exactly were her instincts telling her about him? He loved her, she loved him, but love didn't necessarily mean trust, did it? Could you love someone without trusting them; could you love someone and still at some level wonder whether they were a traitor or not? If she genuinely had doubts about Frank, should she be reporting him? Who to? And what would that mean for him?

She knew very well what it would mean. He'd be arrested, questioned for hours, probably interned. She could not do that to him, not without absolute proof that he was a danger to the British war effort. And she didn't have that, did she? She only had a few misgivings, a few oddities that could easily be explained away. In all likelihood, Frank was innocent of any wrongdoing. Reporting him could harm him and would almost certainly mean the end of their relationship.

*

She was distracted for the rest of the day, mulling over her conversation with Edwin, going round and round in her head, wondering whether Frank could possibly be a traitor or not. Edwin had to check her work – more than once she set up the plug board wrongly. He seemed to understand that half her attention was elsewhere, though she tried to focus. Her job was important. It was vital they decrypt as many messages as possible; each one could mean saving hundreds, even thousands of Allied servicemen's lives. They were making a real difference to the war.

And was Frank making a difference too, in the opposite direction? She had to know for sure. It wasn't something she could simply ask him outright: Frank, I love you, but are you secretly working for the Nazis? No. The answer was as Edwin had hinted: she needed a look inside his lodgings. She needed to know what was in that suitcase. If it was indeed a friend's personal belongings, perhaps this friend had gone off to fight and had nowhere else to store his things. But if that was the case, why hadn't Frank simply told her the truth? He was hiding something. The more she thought about it, the more she convinced herself.

Well, she knew where he lived. One way or another she needed to find out what he had in that suitcase, or at least see if there was anything in his lodgings that would confirm – or deny – his innocence.

*

Pam made a decision to use an afternoon off to get inside Frank's lodgings, one way or another. She had not yet worked out how she'd accomplish this but there were several days before she'd get the chance to try, and several nights when she would no doubt lie awake thinking about it. She could always ask Edwin for advice. The one thing she knew was that she implicitly trusted Edwin, with all her soul.

Why didn't she feel that way about the man who'd asked her to marry him?

But before her next free afternoon came around, a letter arrived that changed everything. It was from her mother, and in it she wrote that they had received a telegram, reporting that Geoff was missing in action. Shot down over France, believed killed.

The post had arrived at Woburn during her working hours, so it was on her return from BP that Pam picked up the letter. She opened it immediately, and read it as she went up to her cabin. When she got to the devastating news she crumpled to the floor, on a half landing partway up the stairs. Geoff, shot down, missing, believed killed. Simple words but somehow they made no sense, not all together like that, not when they related to her brother. How could this be – Geoff, with his open face and expression of constant amusement, Geoff with his broad shoulders and handsome features, Geoff who'd been there for her all her life, looking out for her, cheering her on? Geoff who'd fallen in love for the first time, with her friend Clarissa.

At the thought of Clarissa, Pam put her head in her hands. Not only did she have to deal with her own shock and grief at this news, she also had to tell Clarissa.

'Pamela? What's the matter?'

A warm hand on her shoulder. Pam looked up, to see a girl she barely knew, Margaret, looking down on her with concern. Pam waved the letter vaguely, unable to find any words.

'Oh no. Bad news from home? Oh, love. Come on, to your feet, and let's go and find somewhere to sit, and a cup of tea.'

Margaret held out a hand and Pam took it, allowing herself to be hauled to her feet. She didn't want to talk, didn't want tea. All she wanted was to curl up somewhere on her own and sob, but she recognised that the staircase was not the right place. If she went to her cabin, Clarissa would probably be there. And for now, she wanted to put off that moment of telling her friend the awful news. Let Clarissa have a few moments more of happiness. She'd planned to go and see Geoff again on Sunday. She would be devastated to hear of his loss.

Pam let herself be led by Margaret into a room that had been set up as a common room. There was a tea urn at one end, and Margaret fetched Pam a cup, after helping her to sit in a sumptuously upholstered armchair. 'Now then, do you need to talk?'

'My brother.' Pam managed to force out the words. But she could not bring herself to make it into a full sentence, that would render it the truth. She couldn't.

She didn't need to. It was happening all too often, to everyone. 'I'm so sorry,' Margaret said, her eyes filled with sympathy.

There was nothing more she could say, Pam realised. Nothing more to say. She found herself appreciating the quiet presence of the other woman, whose hand held hers firmly, as if to say, we'll get you through this. She sat there, sipping her tea, letting memories of Geoff from across the years play out in her head. To think she would never see him again … no. She could not think that. She could not bring herself to think that. Missing, presumed killed – was there space for hope there? Even a tiny space … She looked at Margaret. 'He was shot down. Missing, presumed k—' She couldn't say that word. Not about Geoff. 'Is there a chance, do you think?'

'Oh, love,' Margaret said, squeezing her hand, and Pam realised from the look in the other girl's eyes there was no chance.

'I have to find Clarissa Morton.' It was time to break the news.

'Your friend?'

'Yes, and my brother's sweetheart.'

Margaret's shoulders slumped on hearing this. 'I think I saw her, upstairs. Shall I fetch her? Or come with you?'

'It's all right.' Pam forced a weak smile to her lips. 'You've been very kind. I must find her and tell her …'

'If there's anything else I can do …' Margaret's voice tailed off, and she ended with a small shrug. Pam understood. There was nothing anyone could do, in these circumstances. You had to offer, but there was nothing you could do that helped.

'Thank you.' Pam pulled herself together, and went in search of Clarissa. There was half an hour before dinner, and somehow she expected that neither of them would make it. At least they'd be able to find somewhere quiet and alone while everyone else was in the dining hall.

*

'No!' Clarissa cried out, when Pam broke the news. 'No, not Geoff! So young, so brave!'

'I know. It's all so unfair.' Pam let the tears stream down her face, as they were streaming down her friend's face too, and reached over to pull Clarissa into her arms. They had each other, they could help each other through this. What would her parents be feeling? They had dreaded this day – her mother especially had wept when Geoff signed up for the RAF. She had, perhaps, a mother's intuition that this is how it would end. 'I'll go and see my parents, on my day off. I must. My mother …'

'Will you tell them about Geoff and me?' Clarissa gazed at her through her tears.

'If you want me to. I imagine Geoff may have written home about you anyway. He was not one to keep secrets.'

'I'd … I'd like to meet your parents some time. Not this time, it should be just your family. But perhaps on your next visit home, you'll take me? I'd like to meet them.' Clarissa bowed her head and whispered the next words. 'We might have become sisters, in time, you and I. I know it was only a short while, but already I knew I loved him.'

There was no answer Pam could give to those words. She gathered her friend into her arms and held her tight, hoping that grief shared might be grief lessened.

Chapter 23

Julia

The next day, the day after the one she thought she would always look back on as the worst day of her life, Julia dressed carefully in the morning, putting on a smart black skirt suit and her favourite pink top under the jacket. She added make-up and a pair of heels. It was rare that she dressed like this, but she had a meeting with the insolvency practitioner, and she wanted to make a good impression. She didn't want him to think that just because her business had gone under, she was letting herself go too.

'You look nice, Mum,' Oscar said, as he shovelled cereal into his mouth before school.

'Thank you, pet,' she replied with a smile.

He regarded her for a moment and then nodded. 'Good luck today.'

That was all it took. Her fourteen-year-old son wishing her luck as she began the process to wind up her business. Tears sprang to her eyes. 'Oh no. Here we go. Knew I shouldn't have put mascara on.'

'Don't you have waterproof stuff?' Oscar asked, handing her a tissue.

'Yes. It'll still smudge if I have to rub my eyes.'

'Sorry, Mum.'

'It's OK.' She smiled and gave him a quick hug. 'I appreciate you wishing me luck. Today's not going to be easy.'

'Does Dad know yet?'

'No. I think I should tell him face to face, when his course is over.'

'His course, oh yeah, that,' Oscar said, frowning.

Something about his tone made Julia think Oscar knew something she didn't. She was about to ask him, but then decided against it. It was enough that her business was going under. One thing at a time.

'Can we have a lift to school?' Ryan had come clattering down the stairs. 'My knee still hurts a bit from football.'

Julia thought for a moment. There was nothing much she could do beyond pulling out paperwork ready for the meeting with the insolvency practitioner. He wasn't due to come until ten o'clock. The other staff wouldn't be coming to the office, and there was no point her continuing working on the system. She might as well take the kids to school. 'Yes, all right. We'll leave in ten minutes, OK?'

'Yesss!' Ryan punched the air and ran off to get his school bags ready.

Oscar tilted his head on one side, gazing after his brother. 'Mum, I know that we'll have less money, and a smaller house and all that, but, like, if you have a normal job working for some other company, you'll probably end up with more time to spend with us, right?'

Julia smiled. 'It's quite possible. As long as I can find a local job, or one that lets me work from home some of the time.'

'That's easy enough in IT, isn't it?'

'I hope so. Right then, in the car with you.'

She dropped the boys at school, came home to clean up the kitchen and then went through to the office. It felt empty and cold. Usually by this time Tulipa would be there and Barry would be about to arrive. But not today. She pulled out some files she knew they'd need, and arranged a couple of chairs in the little break-out area, for the IP and herself to sit on for their meeting. Funny to think that the business was about to be wound up and that this might be the last ever meeting in the office. It didn't seem real.

There was an email, from Tulipa, with the promised details of organisations to help gamblers and their families. A helpline, and apps you could use to block access to gambling websites and gambling transactions from a bank account. 'Good stuff, Tulipa,' Julia said to herself, as she forwarded the email to Drew. Some of it might help.

Her phone rang, just as she was putting a pot of coffee on. It was Ian. 'Hey, Jules. I'm … sorry. Really. What's the plan? Do you want me in the office today?' His voice sounded upbeat, but forced. Julia guessed Drew had made him phone her.

'No. I really don't want you in the office, Ian. You understand that we are insolvent, right? I have someone coming in later this morning to start the process to liquidate the company. I don't yet know what that will involve, but what I do know is that I want to do it myself, without you.'

'Shit. Do we have to liquidate?'

'We can't pay our debts, Ian. That's the definition of insolvency. So yes, we do have to.'

'But you don't want me there?'

Julia sighed. If Ian came to the office today, she couldn't be held responsible for her actions. 'I think it's better if you don't.'

'I think Barry's expecting me for a meeting though,' Ian said, a little petulantly.

'No, he's not. Barry's not here. Neither's Tulipa.'

'Why not?'

'Because they no longer have jobs, of course!' Honestly, he was being so obtuse. Or was he simply in denial?

'You told them?'

'I had to. Their wages haven't been paid. And like I said, I've called in an insolvency practitioner. Look, Ian, I've got to go, to prepare for that. Don't even think of coming here – I would probably throw things at you. As a director of the company you'll be kept informed at all steps.'

'All right.' There was then a muttered conversation, as though Drew had said something to him. 'Drew wants to know about the house.'

'My house? As I understand it, as we're a limited company, my house is safe. Though I might well be selling it anyway as I won't be able to pay the mortgage and I don't need the office space.'

'I mean my house.'

'Also safe, as far as I'm aware. I'll be in touch.' Julia hung up before he could say anything more. She could sue Ian, she realised. He'd appropriated company funds. If she sued him, his house certainly would be in danger. But it would be unfair on Drew, whose only crime was falling in love with a man who'd developed a gambling addiction. No, she wouldn't sue Ian. She liked Drew. And, despite it all, Ian was still her friend. Maybe, with the business gone, and given time to let the dust settle, they could still have a friendly relationship.

*

The front doorbell rang a couple of hours later, and Julia went through to answer it. A smartly dressed woman in her fifties was on the doorstep. 'Madeleine Rowstone, of Rowstone Derby. You contacted us about Julian Systems' insolvency.' She held out her hand to shake.

Julia was taken aback; she'd assumed, for no good reason, that the insolvency practitioner would be a man. 'Of course! Thank you, come on in. The company offices are through here.' She led the way through.

'Ah, should I have come to a different door? I wasn't sure …' Madeleine indicated the side door.

'It doesn't matter.' It really didn't. Of all her concerns, which door to use was right at the bottom. 'Coffee?'

'Yes please.'

Julia indicated the seats she'd arranged ready for the meeting and fetched the coffee. Madeleine was already pulling folders out of her briefcase and passed Julia a pile of leaflets. 'These explain the process. There's a lot to take in, but I will talk you through it and will advise you at every step of the way. I'm here to help, and to get the best possible outcome for you, your employees, and your creditors.'

'OK. Thank you. It's all been a bit sudden. My business partner was in charge of the finances. I had no idea …'

'Is your partner a director in the company?'

'He is, but he's not joining us today. He knows what is happening.'

Madeleine regarded her carefully. 'I see. Well, let's get started. My job is to take control of the company, settle any disputes, sell its assets and use the funds to pay creditors, which includes employees, any outstanding tax bills, and of course, our own fee. At the end, I will deregister the company from Companies House. So I need to see your financial statements.'

Julia nodded, and passed her the relevant paperwork. The morning passed quickly as Madeleine worked through, getting quickly up to speed with the business's financial situation. She was sympathetic but efficient and Julia was surprised that very quickly she began thinking of the IP as an ally rather than a foe.

'Well, it looks as though you have a decent asset in the form of the software you've developed,' Madeleine said, with a smile. 'I should think we will be able to sell that. Once all debts are paid off, if there's any money left, it goes to the shareholders – in your case, that means the directors. You and your partner.'

Julia nodded, and they carried on working through the list of debts. Peering at some banking paperwork, Madeleine frowned. 'This director's loan. Is that you or your partner?'

'What?'

'It looks like one of you has borrowed money from the business. There's a property address that was put up as collateral. 57 Hawthorne Drive. Does that mean anything to you?'

'That's Ian's address. My business partner.' Julia was confused. What had Ian done?

'He's taken a loan against the business, using his house as security,' Madeleine explained. 'I will need to contact him to recover that money.'

'He hasn't got any money. He won't be able to pay it back.'

Madeleine looked at Julia over the top of her glasses. 'Then I'm afraid his home will be at risk. Your own is safe.'

'Oh God. Poor Drew.'

'Who is Drew?'

'Ian's husband.'

'It's tough on family, when this kind of thing happens. What did he take this loan out for?'

Julia sighed. Time to come clean and explain about the gambling. She outlined what had happened and how she had only found out yesterday. Was it really only yesterday? 'That's what I meant by saying it all happened very suddenly.'

'It's often the way,' Madeleine said, with sympathy. 'Well, I'll need to take some of this paperwork away, and I'll get going on finding a buyer for your software, and I'll also need to start proceedings against your business partner to recover that loan. It's all going to take several weeks. If your employees are in financial trouble as a result of this, they can apply to the National Insurance fund. It pays out a basic minimum amount, which should help them. I'll send them the details. So I think we are done here, for today. I'll get going, and I will be in touch tomorrow, when I should have made some progress. Meanwhile, you do something relaxing for the rest of the day. I know how difficult this all is. I hope your husband is looking after you.'

Julia forced herself to smile and nod at that. If she said anything, made any kind of response, she felt as though she'd end up crying on Madeleine's shoulder. The urge to confide in Madeleine how up and down her marriage had been lately, and let the calm, efficient woman sort that out as well was almost overwhelming, but thankfully she kept quiet. The insolvency practitioner was there to help, but not to provide emotional support, after all. 'Thank you. I'll hear from you tomorrow then.'

Madeleine shook her hand. 'Yes. You've done the right thing, Julia. Be comforted by that knowledge at least.'

*

Once Madeleine had left, taking with her boxes of paperwork, Julia realised she had no work to do. What an odd feeling! After so long running her own business when there was always something to get on with, here she was once again during working hours with the kids at school and feeling at a loose end. She went through to the main house and changed into a more casual outfit, then pottered about for a bit. But the house was clean and tidy, she'd done all that before Madeleine arrived. She could, she supposed, start job-hunting. Or contact estate agents to value the house. But how could she do either of those things when she still had not had the chance to talk to Marc?

She felt tears prick at her eyes at those thoughts, and at the knowledge that soon she would have to tell him. What would his reaction be? She had no idea, but she wasn't looking forward to the conversation. They ought to be a team – they once had been a team, but recently had drifted so far apart. Whether they'd ever be able to get back to the strong and stable marriage she'd thought she had was another question she didn't want to dwell on right now.

She needed something to take her mind off it all. She checked her personal email and was delighted to see an email from Caroline saying that she had scanned a bit more of her mother's memoir.

I am sorry it is taking so long. Our scanner is old and cantankerous and needs coaxing to do each page. I wish I'd just taken photos on my phone, it might have been easier, but I have started doing it this way so I shall finish. Mum always said I was stubborn. I always said I got that trait from her.

Julia smiled at this, sent a quick reply to say thank you, and opened up the Google folder. There were only a few more pages, but she read them slowly, taking in every detail and trying her hardest to forget that she'd lost her business.

If she'd hoped these pages would cheer her up, she was to be disappointed. Clarissa wrote of the day when Pam received news that her brother Geoff had been shot down over France. She wrote at length about the agony they'd both felt – Clarissa had been dating Geoff at the time. Both girls were devastated.

We knew of course that war could take anyone, and a fighter pilot was probably more at risk than anyone else, but neither of us had ever dwelt on the idea that it could happen to Geoff. Not Geoff, with his sunny smile and bubbly personality, his handsome features and strong shoulders. Never Geoff. But there it was, written in Elsie Jackson's spidery handwriting, posted in a black-edged envelope. We knew many people at Bletchley Park who had lost loved ones, who would know exactly how we were feeling, but how could they really know? This time it was our loved one, our Geoff, and the devastation we felt was immense.

Julia leaned back in her chair for a moment, trying to imagine how it felt to receive such news. She had already known about Grandma's brother being shot down during the war but reading Clarissa's account of hearing the news put her own woes into perspective. What was losing a business compared to facing the loss of a brother or a boyfriend? As Clarissa had said, so many people lost loved ones during the war, so many family members snatched away with no chance to say goodbye. So many families broken into pieces, through no fault of their own, with no choice in the matter. 'We're lucky, this generation,' she told herself. 'We've not had to face a war or anything like it. Long may that continue.'

She read on, and came across another section that made her gasp, but this was one she felt she could relate to.

It was right around this time that poor Pamela became unsure if she could really trust her boyfriend. She'd lost her brother, and one would expect to lean on one's young man at such a time, but there were a few things he had said and done that had made Pam suspicious of him. What a terrible time it was for us. And for Pam, it was to get worse before it got better.

'Oh, Caroline! How can you end it there! And, Grandma, don't I just know the feeling.' Julia snapped shut her laptop in frustration. Damn Caroline's dodgy scanner! Or was she leaving it on a cliffhanger on purpose? There was nothing for it but to be patient and wait for the next batch of pages.

Chapter 24

Pamela

Pam managed to rearrange her day off so that she could go see her parents on the day after she'd heard of Geoff being missing in action. They'd appreciate her visiting as soon as possible; she was their only remaining child. Mr Newman was sympathetic when she told him what had happened. 'So many brave souls being lost. I am sorry, my dear. My condolences to your parents as well.'

She managed to post a letter to Frank. She'd have to work on the day they'd arranged to next meet up, to cover for the extra day off. In it she told him briefly of the news about Geoff, in unemotional terms. She still wasn't sure how much she trusted him.

Her visit home was brief but emotionally draining. Her mother clung to her, sobbing, while her father looked ten years older and empty, as though his soul had been sucked out of him and discarded. 'Tell me there's still a chance,' Mum said to her. 'You with your secret job, your inside knowledge. Perhaps you know more than the rest of us. Perhaps you know if there's still a chance for him?'

Mum's expression of hope broke her heart, but all Pam could do was shake her head. 'I don't know anything more than anyone else, Mum. I can't imagine there's much hope. His plane was seen being shot down.' She'd been shown the official telegram that had arrived, with its awful news given in stark, short sentences.

She did what she could for them – passing the news on to people who needed to know, shopping for them, cleaning the house so that her mother could rest and forget about it for a few days at least. She offered to clear some of Geoff's things from his room but Mum shook her head. 'No, love. I want to leave his room just as it is. I go in there, and sit on the bed sometimes, and it helps me feel closer to him.'

Ada called round to see her, and Pam fell into her arms, sobbing, allowing Ada to comfort her the way Pam had tried to comfort her mother and Clarissa. You needed someone a step removed to help you through grief like this. Someone who knew and understood, but who was a little less affected by the loss, who could lend you their strength. She knew though, even as Ada held her and rubbed her back, that while she was offering sympathy Ada would not be able to stop herself thinking of the very real possibility that she too might lose someone she loved.

Pam told her parents a little about Clarissa. Mum nodded. 'Yes, your brother wrote and told us he'd met a wonderful girl. I think she was going to see him at every opportunity, wasn't she?'

'Yes. I think so. Clarissa's lovely. She said she'd like to come and meet you some time, in the future.'

'That would be very nice,' Mum said, but without conviction. It was too soon, Pam realised, for her to contemplate meeting the woman who'd stolen her son's heart.

*

As she got off the train at Bletchley on her return journey, with her mind still full of her parents and their loss, she was astonished to see Frank waiting by the station entrance. She hadn't told him which train she would be taking back. For a moment she hung back – he hadn't spotted her yet. What was he doing there – was it yet another event that might be construed as suspicious? He was reading something, a letter, she thought. He was frowning over it, and as she watched he screwed it up and shoved it angrily into his pocket. That was when he noticed her, and raised a hand in greeting as he walked over to her.

'Pamela. I've been waiting here a while. I was hoping you'd be returning on that last train. I was waiting to meet you, to find out how things are? How are your poor parents?' His voice was strained, missing its usual jolly tones.

'Hello Frank. Thank you for coming to meet me.' She took his arm and gave him a brief kiss, on the cheek. 'My parents are as well as can be expected. They've taken the news hard, but they will come to terms with it in time, I am sure. They are resilient.'

'And you? How are you taking it? You loved your brother so much.'

'I did, yes.' And he may have been shot down by your brother, she wanted to add, but she stopped herself. It was highly unlikely, and even if it was the case, it wasn't Frank's fault. It wasn't Frank who was in the Luftwaffe.

'I loved mine too.' Frank let go of her arm and pushed her away a little.

'Loved?'

'You are not the only one to lose a brother, it seems. I have had a letter. My brother's aeroplane was shot down in flames. He did not bail out. This happened a couple of weeks ago but the news has taken this long to reach me.'

'Oh, Frank, I am so sorry.' Pam's hand flew to her mouth. They had both lost a brother, albeit men fighting on opposite sides. They were still their family. Though she had, of course, been much closer to her brother than Frank had been to his, whom he'd hardly ever met.

'Shot down. By the RAF. By your brother's colleagues. By Geoff himself, for all I know.' Frank turned to stare accusingly at her.

'That's so unlikely,' she said. But hadn't she, just a moment before, had the same idea that Wolfgang might have shot Geoff's plane down?

'But possible. Your Geoff was still alive, still flying when mine was killed. It could have been him. We shall never know.'

'No, you're right, we have no way of knowing. So there is no point dwelling on it. I am sorry about your brother, I truly am, as I hope you are sorry about mine.' She realised he had not said he was, at any point. He'd asked after her parents and how well she was taking it, but had never actually said he was sorry for her loss. Was he? Or was he secretly celebrating one fewer RAF pilot in the skies? And now, seeing her loss as payback for his?

His expression softened. 'Yes, I am sorry about your brother too.' He sighed. 'This damned war. It is pushing itself between us, taking our loved ones. My brother. My only family. I had hoped we would be able to get to know each other better, when all this is over. Now I never will know him.' He whispered that last sentence. Pam tried to take his arm again, to give him some comfort though she knew all too well anything she could say or do was inadequate. 'Frank? I know it's hard, when you've only just found out, but ...'

'But nothing. There is nothing to be done, is there? We are at war, people die. Our brothers have died, for their countries. We are lucky, you and I, Pamela, that we will not be called upon to lay down our lives. We should be grateful, I suppose.' He looked down at his feet and then raised his eyes back to hers. She saw a deep, profound sadness there. At last he wrapped his arms around her and held her close. She tried to derive comfort and strength from the embrace and hoped she was able to give some back. They both needed it to get them through this.

After a minute he gently pushed her away. 'You should get back to Woburn now. I have a few things to do here and then

I shall cycle back. Shall we meet again next time our days off coincide? Perhaps we'll have got over our losses a little by then. If that's ever possible.'

'Of course. Very well. I'll see you a week on Saturday.'

'Yes. Until then.' He gave her a brief kiss, then turned and walked away, towards the centre of Bletchley village, the opposite direction to the one Pam needed to take. She watched him walk away. Everything felt changed.

She turned and began the familiar walk up the lane to BP, to catch the next army transport bus back to Woburn Abbey. Frank had just lost his only family member. He'd only just heard the news. It was understandable for him to lash out at the nearest person. It was only natural. She should give him the benefit of the doubt, and when he'd had a little time to begin to come to terms with it, he'd return to his old self. And she would trust him once again, and they would move on together, supporting each other through these difficult times.

But first, to be completely sure she could trust him, she needed to know what was in that suitcase. A vision of Edwin's kind, concerned face came into her mind. She'd like to see him, she realised. He'd be at work, in BP. Maybe she could pop in and join him for his tea break? He was such a good person to talk to. She'd told him everything about Frank, she could tell him this too, and see if he could advise her at all.

Pam hurried past the sentries at the gates to BP, waving her pass at them. Edwin. She needed to see him, as soon as possible. She glanced at her watch as she hurried up the driveway, jumping out of the way of an army transport bus that was leaving the grounds. It was just about Edwin's teatime – he was on the day watch that day. If she hurried, she'd catch him coming out of the hut.

And indeed, there he was, shrugging his jacket on as he descended the steps from the hut's entrance. She began to run, calling out to him. 'Edwin! Hold up, I'm coming!'

He turned, looking surprised to see her. Without realising she was going to do so, she ran into his arms, flinging hers around his neck. 'So glad I've caught you. Do you mind …? I'd like another chat with you, somewhere private.' She looked him in the eye as she said this, so that he would guess it was about Frank.

'Not at all,' he said, gently unwinding her arms from him, and then tucking her hand into the crook of his arm as they walked away from the main building, around the back, into the parkland. 'I heard about your brother. I am so sorry. You went to see your parents, I believe? How are they?'

'Yes, I did go, for a twenty-four-hour pass. They are … suffering, as you might expect. But proud, I think, that Geoff played his part in the war.' Pam dashed away a tear as she said this.

'And you?' Edwin's voice was soft.

'I am coming to terms with it. It's like I always knew this could happen, from the moment he joined up.' She took a deep breath. 'But, Edwin, the reason I need to talk to you … I'm not the only one who's lost a brother.'

'What do you mean?'

She told him then what had happened just minutes earlier, outside the railway station. 'He's blaming the RAF. Of course, they're the ones who shot his brother down. He blamed my brother. The way he was talking, I think … I fear …'

'You're doubting his loyalty to Britain even further?'

She nodded. 'Yes. And I was thinking about what you said … about that suitcase and what might be in it, and how to determine one way or another whether he can be trusted. I've got to be sure of him, if we're to have any kind of future together. I was working out a plan, before I had the letter about Geoff, of how to find out.'

'What are you planning to do?'

'Get into his lodgings. Somehow. When he's not there.'

'How?'

'I'll go when I know he's at work. I'll find his landlady – she runs the shop below his lodgings. I'll make up some excuse about why I need access, and hopefully she'll let me in. I'll find the suitcase, say that he's storing things for me that I need, and open it.'

'That might work, if she'll let you in.'

'Frank has said she's very strict and he's not allowed any visitors. But if I tell her he's my fiancé …'

'He's not, though, is he?' Edwin had tensed up at this.

'He did ask me to marry him.'

'And you said yes.' Edwin phrased it as a statement, a fait accompli, rather than as a question.

'No. I – I didn't give him a definite answer. I sort of … hedged it. I said we needed to wait until after the war was over. It was a while ago; at the time I thought I could trust him, I thought I loved him …'

'But now you don't.' Again, a statement, gently put, rather than a question. And as he spoke, she realised the truth. She did not love Frank. She had been smitten by his charm, his good looks, his attentions to her. But you could not love someone you didn't trust one hundred per cent. You could not be married to a person you doubted. Whatever happened, whatever she found in Frank's lodgings, or didn't find, their relationship was over. She would tell him so, after she'd checked that suitcase.

It was odd, but now that she'd made up her mind and had a plan, she felt lighter. As long as she didn't think about Geoff, her loss, she could almost call herself happier.

'No, I'm not sure that I do,' she answered Edwin. 'And now I should go back to Woburn. It's been a long day. Anyway, you need your tea break.'

'Just one thing, when will you go to Frank's lodgings?'

'I'm not sure.' She thought for a moment. 'Tomorrow – I'm on the day watch. If I go straight back at four o'clock, I should be able to be at his lodgings before he returns from work. He stays working at the Abbey until it's dark, which is about half past six now.'

'I'm working then too. We can refine your plan in our lunch

break.' Edwin stepped forward and gave Pam a spontaneous hug. 'Take care, dear Pam. And be careful, if you see him.'

'I will. Thank you, Edwin. You've helped a lot. As always.'

'Anything for you,' he said, and instantly blushed to his roots. Pam pretended she hadn't heard and turned away, waving, as she walked back to the front of the main building. There'd be a bus to Woburn leaving shortly.

*

Pam did not see Frank again that day. They had not arranged to meet, and she did not search him out in the grounds of Woburn. She kept out of his way.

The following day, she was back at work, on the day watch. Everyone offered condolences at her loss, but they were all careful to keep their expressions of sympathy brief, for which she was grateful. If anyone had said too much, she would only cry. And she was far from being the first in the section to lose a loved one. She wouldn't be the last, either.

She talked her plan through with Edwin again as they took a stroll around the grounds after lunch. They didn't dare say a word about it while they were in the hut, even when alone in the room housing the Colossus, for fear of being overheard. 'Keep it between us for now, but if you discover anything suspicious in his rooms, you will have to report it. You do understand that, Pam?'

'Yes. I do.'

It was strange. In some ways she was hoping she wouldn't find anything incriminating in Frank's lodgings. She could then end things with him, and relax, knowing she'd done her duty. On the other hand, she found herself half wanting to find something that proved his disloyalty, to prove her suspicions, show that her instincts had been right. She felt distracted all day, and was only too glad when four o'clock came round and she could leave.

'I'll tell you what happens tomorrow,' she said to Edwin as she left.

He caught hold of her hand and gave it a squeeze. 'Good luck and be careful.' He had another few hours to work before the end of his shift.

The journey back to Woburn felt as if it lasted ages. Clarissa was not on the bus; she was working a different watch that week, so Pam sat alone. As soon as they reached the Abbey she got off and walked through the parkland towards the village, hoping she would not bump into Frank on the way.

She was in luck. He must be working on the vegetable patches on the other side of the Abbey, she thought. She hurried through the village to the building he'd indicated once, so long ago it seemed now! He had rooms above a haberdasher's shop. The landlady ran the shop and lived on the first floor, and Frank's rooms were in the second-floor attic. At that time of day, the shop was still open, and a middle-aged woman with grey hair scraped into a bun was standing behind the counter, attending to some paperwork.

Pam took a deep breath and entered the shop. A bell jangled loudly above her head, startling her a little. The woman at the counter raised her head from her paperwork and scowled at her, as though annoyed to be interrupted. 'Can I help you?'

'Hello. My name is Pamela Jackson. I am a … friend of Frank Miller who I believe rents rooms on the second floor here? You must be his landlady.' She'd fixed a bright smile to her face and held out her hand for the other woman to shake, which she did, still frowning.

'Yes, Mr Miller is my lodger. What do you want?'

'It's a little bit awkward,' Pam went on, still smiling, trying to get the landlady on her side. 'Frank's looking after something for me, but I need it in a bit of a rush. Is there any possibility of you letting me into his rooms? I would only be a minute.'

'Let you into his rooms? And you someone I don't know from

Adam? You could be a common thief!' The woman folded her arms across her chest.

Pam gave a little laugh. 'Oh dear, I was worried you might think that. Actually, Frank is my fiancé, believe it or not. We haven't quite made things public, but he asked me a few weeks ago, and when things are more settled in the world we will get married. He's such a lovely man, don't you agree?'

'He's a quiet enough lodger, I suppose. Gives no trouble.'

'That's my Frank.' Pam treated her to a bright smile. 'He'd do anything for anyone.'

'Look, miss, you'll have to prove you know him, before I let you in. Like I said, you could be anyone.' But the woman's tone was softening. Another push and Pam would be in.

'Well, his name's Frank Miller, as I said, and he works as a gardener up at Woburn Abbey. He's not been called up due to his asthma. I met him up at the Abbey – I'm billeted there while I work nearby. I'm a Wren.'

'A Wren! Oh my dear, you should have said. My name's Mrs Sparsholt. So pleased to meet you, and I'm sorry I was suspicious at first. A previous lodger, you see, brought all sorts of unsuitable girls back here. Mr Miller hasn't brought anyone at all, as I told him not to after that last lad. But you Wrens I think are absolutely marvellous, doing all the jobs you do. Come on, let me close the shop a moment and I'll take you up.'

'Oh, thank you, Mrs Sparsholt. But if you tell me the way I can find it myself, no need to close the shop.' As Pam spoke, another customer came in and began browsing a display of buttons on cards.

Mrs Sparsholt glanced over at the new customer. 'Very well, since you're a Wren, I know I can trust you.' She opened a drawer under the counter and pulled out a key. 'Here you are. The door will be locked as he's still at work. Go back out to the street, and down the side alley, round to the back. There's a green-painted door. Open it with this, go straight up the stairs to the top – that's Mr Miller's room.'

'Thank you so much. I shan't be long.' Pam took the key and darted out of the shop before Mrs Sparsholt had second thoughts. But the customer had already picked a card of buttons and was approaching the counter to pay, so her attention was diverted anyway.

The side alley was narrow and dark, and opened onto a small courtyard at the back. Opposite the alley was a coal store and an outside lavatory. The paint on the door was peeling, but the window beside it was clean and hung with neat net curtains.

Pam put the key in the lock and turned it. It unlocked easily, and opened onto a passageway, from which stairs led up. She went up, past the first-floor doors that would open onto Mrs Sparsholt's rooms, and up a narrower set to the attic. At the top was another door, painted brown. Here it was at last. She paused for a moment. What if she'd got it completely wrong? What if there was nothing to be suspicious about, and it was all just her overactive imagination? She almost turned and went back down the stairs, but then decided that as she'd come that far, she might as well look for the suitcase. If nothing else it'd put her mind at rest. Where might the suitcase be? In a wardrobe, or under the bed? She was considering where to search as she tried the door, expecting it to be locked. It wasn't. The first thing she noticed was that the curtains were partially drawn. And then she noticed the bed, which was under the window, and pulled out from under it the suitcase, lying open and empty.

And finally, she noticed Frank, sitting at a dressing table with a set of headphones on and a radio set in front of him.

Chapter 25

Julia

The day after Julia's meeting with Madeleine, the IP, she had a few tasks to do related to winding up the business, but they didn't take long. She spent a lot of the day doing small jobs in the garden, prepared a homemade lasagne for dinner, and then curled up on a sofa with a book. She'd hoped Caroline might upload more of the memoir, but although she checked several times there were no more emails and nothing more in the Google folder.

Seven o'clock arrived – their usual dinner time – but there was no sign of Marc returning home, although he'd said the course was due to end by four o'clock and it wouldn't take him more than an hour or so to get back. Julia sent him a text. After ten minutes with no reply, she sighed, and called him. No answer, so she left a voicemail, and served up the lasagne to the boys and herself. Marc's portion was left in the oven. The pasta would dry out but that was too bad.

At eight, with the dishes cleared and washed up by the boys, she decided to call him again, but discovered her phone was out of charge. She plugged it in and borrowed Oscar's instead. This time, Marc answered.

'Hey, son. Everything OK?'

'It's not Oscar. It's me. I thought the course finished today? Are you coming home any time soon? There's something I need to talk to you about.'

'What is it?'

'I really don't want to discuss it on the phone. What time will you be back? Your dinner's in the oven, but we've eaten.'

'Ah, it's all right, I've eaten too,' he said. There was something odd about his tone – it was as though he was trying not to laugh at something. In the background, Julia could hear another person. A whisper. A giggle.

And then the sound was muffled, as though Marc had covered up his phone, and there was a definite laugh and a 'shh'.

'Where are you?' she asked, when Marc came back on.

'In the office. Had to call in after the course to deal with a problem.'

'Who else is there?'

'Oh, just … Liam. The new apprentice. Trying to make an impression, I think.'

Another giggle, quickly suppressed, one that sounded more like a woman than anyone who'd go by the name of Liam. Marc hushed the other person.

But then the woman spoke aloud, obviously with the intention of letting Julia hear. 'More wine, darling?'

'Who is that?'

'L-Liam, like I said.'

'Offering you wine using a woman's voice? In the office? Calling you darling?'

'Ah, no. OK, listen, actually I'm at a colleague's house. Discussing, um, the project. With a glass of wine to ease things along. The darling part was a joke. Didn't want to say in case you jumped to conclusions …'

More giggling, then the woman's voice again. 'She'd not be wrong, though.' Quietly said, but Julia heard it clearly enough.

'I wouldn't be wrong if I jumped to conclusions? Consider the conclusions reached. Don't fucking bother coming home tonight, Marc. Just stay with your girlfriend – that's what she is, isn't she? For fuck's sake. What a week.'

She stabbed at the phone to hang up, not wanting to hear another word from him. Ian, and now Marc – she'd thought she could trust them but both had betrayed her horribly. Her business gone. Her marriage in trouble. No, it was over too. She realised that there was no way she could carry on with Marc, knowing that she couldn't trust him.

This affair had probably been going on for some time, she realised now – all those late nights 'working', those missed meals, the 'overtime' that had called him home from the Lake District early. And Tulipa's comment about seeing him in Giorgio's the other day. She could see it so clearly now. All of that had been lies. What about this week – the course he was supposedly on? Had that been a lie too? Had he actually been away with his mistress?

And then she thought about the way Marc had always been jealous of her company's success – back in the days when it had been successful. How he'd resented the fact that she'd always earned more than him. He'd hated that it was she who'd been able to put down the deposit on the house, and she who paid the bulk of the mortgage and bought most of the items for the house. Marc's salary had only at best been half of hers.

She padded over to the fridge and pulled out a half-empty bottle of white wine. Pouring herself a glass she sat on the sofa and tried to make some decisions. It was clear that she'd need to start job-hunting. And that without the business and if her marriage really was over, then the house was too big. She would get valuations done and put it on the market. And she could apply for a mortgage holiday in the meantime, to reduce her bills. It was all going to be a big change. A huge change – she'd be a divorcee, a single parent.

There was a tap at the door of the sitting room, and Oscar came in. 'Are you finished with my phone? Is Dad coming home?'

As she gazed up at her son, trying to work out what to say to him, the floodgates opened. Julia felt herself crumple, for the hundredth time that week. She grabbed at a tissue from a box beside the sofa but there was no hiding it.

'Oh no, Mum, what is it? Is it the business?' Oscar sat beside her and put his arm awkwardly around her shoulder.

'It's that … and …'

'Dad?'

She nodded.

'Have you found out, then?'

She stared at him. 'Found out?'

'Oh … nothing. I just thought as you were crying, and he's not here again, perhaps you knew …'

'I think I know. I think he's been … seeing someone else.' There. She'd said it, to her fourteen-year-old son. 'Did you know?'

Oscar looked away and shrugged. 'Didn't know, exactly, but I heard him on the phone to someone once when you were out … I wasn't eavesdropping, honest, but couldn't help but hear, and it sounded like he was talking to a … girlfriend. Anyway, what else would he be doing when he's out so much and is so horrid to you when he's here? I'm old enough to work it out. Didn't know if I should say anything to you or not.' He shrugged again. 'I guess I was hoping I was wrong and it'd all just go away.'

'Does Ryan know?'

Oscar shook his head firmly. 'He's too young to worry about that sort of thing. So, what's going to happen? Are you and Dad going to split up?'

Julia took her son's hand and squeezed it. 'We'll need to talk about it, but yes, I think it is likely. But look, let's not say anything to Ryan just yet. Not until Dad and I have decided what's going to happen.'

'All right. It's tough for you, isn't it? The problem with the business and now Dad.'

She bit her lip to stop herself wailing. Instead she took a deep breath and dabbed her eyes with the tissue. 'It is, yes. I'm sorry, Oscar. It's all going to be a bit rubbish for you and Ryan too.'

He patted her arm. 'We'll be all right. We're young. We're always being told the young are resilient. I think it means we bounce.'

She smiled at him. 'Yes. But listen, whatever happens, we'll be all right, you know? We'll probably move from here, and I'll get a new job, but we'll stay in this area and there will always be enough money. I promise.'

Whatever happened, she'd keep those promises. The boys came first.

*

An hour or so later, when the wine was finished and Julia was debating with herself whether to open another bottle to properly drown her sorrows, she heard a key in the door. Both boys were thankfully upstairs – Ryan in bed, Oscar with headphones on playing some sort of online computer game with Nathan. So, Marc had decided to come home, had he, rather than stay with his mistress? God how she hated that word. She debated getting up to meet him in the hallway, but decided to stay put, in the sitting room, on the sofa. Let him come to find her.

From the sounds of things, he took his time removing his coat, kicking off his shoes, taking something upstairs where perhaps he looked in on the boys. Avoiding her. But he couldn't do it forever. At last he returned to the hallway, and she heard him let out a huge sigh just before he entered the sitting room. She did not look up at him.

He took a seat in an armchair opposite her. 'Jules. It's not what it looks like.'

'Not what it looks like? What is it, then?' Julia was amazed to find herself acting so calm. She'd always imagined that she'd have shouted and screamed in this situation, but she felt almost clinically cold. She wanted an explanation. She wanted the truth, and then she wanted to work out a way forward.

'It's … it was … a mistake.' Marc sighed and sat down heavily on an armchair.

'A mistake?'

'Yes. And it only happened two or three times. Four max. I was going to tell her it was over. Then you rang.'

'You're admitting an affair?'

He raised his head to look at her and nodded. 'Jules, I am so, so sorry. As I said, it was a mistake, I never should have … it was when you were so busy with work, I never seemed to see you. There was a work do. I drank too much and she was all over me. Honestly I couldn't do much about it …'

'Are you saying she raped you?'

'Rape? Good God, no.'

'But you couldn't stop her? No, Marc. You mean you couldn't stop yourself.' Now the anger came. Red hot waves of it, bursting out through every pore. 'Marc, I'm working all the hours I can providing for this family and you're off philandering with some woman from the office who makes eyes at you? And your excuse is you never seemed to see me? What is it, out of sight, out of mind, eh? Listen to yourself. Have you any idea how … how despicable this all sounds? A one-night stand I might have … got over, but you said you've been with her several times. You shagged her, then you went back to her for more, lying to me about where you were, over and over. This is it, Marc. This is the end.'

'The end? What do you mean?'

'I mean, you've been unfaithful and broken our marriage vows. I can't forgive that. I can't get over it. Our marriage is over.'

Marc slipped off his chair and onto his knees in front of her. 'No, Jules, please don't say that! I was stupid, so stupid, but it's over. Like I said, I was going to tell her it was over. We're a family, Julia. I made a mistake, I was weak, I shouldn't have let it happen.'

'But you did let it happen. Fuck's sake, Marc. I can't trust you. How can I stay married to a man I can't trust?'

'I'm … sorry, so sorry, Jules.'

She looked down at him, still grovelling there by her feet. Pleading with her to forgive him, and save their marriage. Desperate to keep his family together. Telling her the affair meant nothing, that it was a mistake, it was over. She stared down at him, looked deep into his eyes and saw nothing there that she could trust. Nothing, she realised, that she loved, anymore. Not now. Not after this.

She stood up and moved away from him, opening the door to the sitting room. 'Get out, Marc. Go back to her, if she'll have you. I don't care. Get out of my house. Our marriage is over.'

He opened his mouth as though to say something more, but must have thought better of it. After all, there was nothing more to say, was there?

A minute later the front door slammed shut, the sound reverberating around the house with an air of finality.

Chapter 26

Pamela

Frank's back was to the door, so he didn't spot Pam immediately. And with the headphones on, presumably he hadn't heard the door open. She stood frozen to the spot for a moment, her mind frantically working out what to do. Should she sneak out quietly, leave the key in the lock downstairs, hurry back to BP and report what she'd seen? Or confront him, ask him what the hell he was doing?

She could see what he was doing. He was tapping out a message in Morse code, while reading off a pad of paper in front of him. She could just about see what was written on it, but it was gibberish. Code, then. Who was he reporting to – the English or German command? As she stood there, barely able to breathe, he finished tapping, twiddled with the dial on his radio set for a moment until he was satisfied with the frequency he'd found, and then he began speaking into a microphone. In German.

It was enough. There was no doubt about where his loyalties lay now. The safest thing for her was to creep out and report him. She took a step back towards the still-open door behind her. A floorboard creaked loudly, and Frank whipped around in his chair, tugging his headphones off. 'Pamela! What the devil are you doing here?'

She gasped as he jumped up from his seat, across the room, and pulled her inside, slamming the door closed. He pushed her roughly towards the bed, where she stumbled over the open suitcase. 'Frank, I – I was just passing and wondered if you were in, and your landlady in the shop said to come on up …'

'No, she didn't. She doesn't know I'm here. You're spying on me.' He waved his hand at the radio equipment.

'Not spying, no!' It was true – she hadn't come here to spy on him. Not really. She'd only wanted to find out what was in the suitcase he'd brought back from London. Well, now she knew.

'How long were you standing there?' His eyes were full of fury as he stood over her, his hands on his hips.

'I'd only just entered.'

'If you thought I was here, why didn't you knock at the door?'

'I did, just a little tap.' An outright lie, but now her focus needed to be on saving herself. For she suddenly realised she was scared of Frank. Very, very frightened, of what he might do.

'And when there was no answer, you just walked in? How did you get through the door from the yard? I locked it behind me when I came in, so Mrs Sparsholt wouldn't realise I was here.'

'Um, I … I …' She had no answer to that. He grabbed her roughly and rummaged in her pockets.

'You have her key. So you didn't expect me to be here. What were you planning to do?'

Her eyes flickered to the radio equipment and back to him. 'Frank, I …' She was still lost for words. All her planning, all her thinking through what she was going to do once she was in his lodgings – she had never once considered what she would say if he caught her here. 'Why aren't you still at work?'

'Oh, so you did think I'd be out? And you wanted to snoop

around, is that it? Find out what was in the suitcase I was storing for my friend?'

She nodded. He'd guessed. There was no point lying, denying.

'And …' He leaned in closer to her, his hands gripping her upper arms, his face just inches from hers. 'What were you going to do, once you'd discovered what was in it?'

'Frank, I thought it'd be clothes, books, just personal things. But I couldn't stop myself worrying that it wasn't …'

'Worrying I might be a spy?'

Pam felt her mouth open and close, but no words came out. Yes, that was precisely what she was worrying.

His expression softened for a moment and he sighed deeply. 'Pamela, I care about you. I honestly do. We have had some good times together. All this' – he gestured to the radio – 'it's nothing. Nothing at all. I was passed the radio set by my friend to hold, and thought I would have a little play around with it. I probably shouldn't have.' He shrugged. 'I can see how you might think it was suspicious.'

'I'm not suspecting anything,' she said, quietly. If that was the way he wanted to play it, she'd go along with it, and maybe she'd be able to get out of here, away from him, and let the authorities check out his story.

'Oh, but you are, Pamela.' He'd changed again, harsh now, and once again he stood over her. He grabbed her face, squeezing her cheeks, and tilted her head backwards, staring into her eyes. 'You are thinking that I was only interested in you so I can find out what's going on at Bletchley Park, so I can give all your precious secrets away to the German war effort?'

'Frank, you're hurting me,' she tried to say, but he was pressing so hard on her cheeks her words came out mangled.

'Hurting you? Not as much as you'll hurt me, if you report what you've seen and heard. Oh Pamela, what am I going to do with you? Why did you have to come here, and spoil everything? I can't let you go. I can't let you give me away.'

'I won't.' She tried to convince him with her eyes, that he could trust her, that she'd keep his secret. She pulled his hands away from her face. He allowed that, but held her wrists tightly. 'Honestly, Frank, I won't say a word. Just … don't hurt me, please.'

'I love you, Pamela. I did want to marry you – that day when I asked, and you wouldn't answer. You hurt me then. We could have been engaged, waiting for this war to end, and no matter which side wins, we could have had a life together. Here or in Germany.' He sounded sad, regretful. For a moment she felt sorry for him. 'You always suspected me, I think, from the moment I told you my father was German. Didn't you?'

'No, I didn't, I honestly didn't,' she said, trying to sound genuine. 'But will you tell me – how long have you been …' She nodded towards the radio set. How long, she wanted to say, have you been betraying the country you were born in, your mother's country, the one where you grew up?

'You know I only picked up the case in January. Before then, only cryptic letters via Switzerland.'

'Why?'

He shrugged. 'Doing my bit, for the Fatherland. Ha! For me, it really is my father's land.'

She suppressed a gasp. After his earlier attempts at a denial, his insistence he was only trying out the radio set, he'd now admitted that he was a spy. He must have realised she hadn't believed him. 'What information have you been passing on?'

'Wouldn't you like to know!' He bent over her again, still gripping her wrists firmly. 'Oh, Pamela. Why did you have to come here today? You've ruined everything. We were good together. We might have had a fine marriage with lots of children.' He took a deep breath. 'Look, we have a choice now. We can stay together; it can be like it was in the beginning between us, and we can marry, later on. But only if you keep quiet about what you've seen and heard here today. And help me out.'

'Help you?' Her voice emerged as a squeak.

'Tell me what you're doing at Bletchley Park. What all you girls, and all the other people are doing. Round the clock, isn't it? All those hundreds – thousands, is it? – that go through the security gates every day. What do you all do?'

'I can't, Frank. I can't tell you.' How on earth did he think for even a second that she might break the Official Secrets Act, especially knowing he was a spy?

'Your choice, Pamela, is between me and your country, it would seem. You told me you loved me. Now you choose. And choose wisely.'

'There's no choice, Frank. I can't spy for you, and that's what you are asking.'

'Then it's going to end badly for you.' He slapped her then, hard, around the face. She screamed in pain, but at least he'd let go of one of her wrists in order to slap her, and that allowed her to grope around for anything she could use as a weapon, to free herself. Her hand alighted on a heavy book that had been open on the bed and she lifted it and smashed it hard into the side of his head.

'Argh! Playing dirty, are you? Stupid little bitch.' He yanked her to her feet and pushed her roughly against a wall. 'You know what else was in that case?' He was trying to hook the case towards him with a foot, while not letting go of her. 'A gun. I'll finish you off. It didn't have to be like this, Pamela. You could have come along with me. We'd have worked well together.'

As he spoke, he bent down, reaching into the case with one hand. But Pam had heard something else, that he apparently hadn't – footsteps on the stairs outside.

'There's no need to shoot me,' she called out, loudly, warning whoever was coming up that Frank had a gun.

The door crashed open, and it was Edwin, looking hot and flustered. 'Gun in the suitcase!' she yelled, and Edwin kicked the case out of Frank's reach, across the room.

'Let her go!' Edwin shouted. 'I've called the police. They'll be here any second.'

'Bitch! You've been cheating on me, with him! That weedy little runt!' Frank let go of Pam then, and lunged at Edwin, who neatly sidestepped, causing Frank to fall to the floor. But once there he reached again for the case, scrabbling around in the base of it.

'He's trying to get his gun!' Pam squealed. Edwin caught her hand and yanked her towards the door.

'Go down, get help. Now!'

'Thought you'd called—' She broke off as Edwin gave a tiny shake of his head, realising that he must have lied about calling the police. She hurried out of the room, glancing back to see Edwin kicking out at Frank once more, trying to keep him away from the suitcase. She was torn – should she stay and help him, or do as he'd said? That gun – what would happen if Frank got hold of it?

'Pam, go!' Edwin's shout helped her decide, and she ran down the stairs, out of the house and back down the alleyway.

'What on earth is going on up there?' Mrs Sparsholt had come out of her shop and was gazing up at the windows to Frank's room above.

'Do you have a telephone? Call the police!' Pam urged her, but the woman stood her ground, arms folded.

'Who else is up there? I thought I saw someone go down the alley. An intruder! Well, our Frank'll see him off, won't he? Lovely strong lad, he is.'

'No, you've got it all wrong …' Pam started to say, and at that moment there was a loud bang, a gunshot, and both women screamed.

'Was that …?' Mrs Sparsholt's hand had flown to her face.

'A gun. Yes. Listen, Frank's a German spy. I just found out. The other man is my colleague and we can trust him. Call the police. I'm going to see …' She pushed Mrs Sparsholt towards the door of her shop and ran back along the alley. Who'd been shot? Please God, don't let it be Edwin! With a jolt she realised she cared far more about Edwin's safety than about Frank's, even though until very recently she'd thought she loved Frank. No time to stop and consider what that meant right now. She was halfway up the stairs when Edwin appeared at the doorway.

'Edwin! Thank goodness you're safe, I heard the gun …' She was terrified at what she'd see in the room behind him.

'Yes, it went off in the struggle but he's not hurt, I tied him up.'

She saw now that Edwin had tucked the gun into his coat pocket, and that Frank was sitting on the floor, his hands tied behind him to the frame of his bed. His feet were also tied. He had a few cuts on his face and a rapidly swelling eye. A bullet was lodged in the heavy wooden desk Frank had been sitting at when she arrived.

'You bitch! You brought this bastard here. We could have sorted it out together, Pamela, you and I. He nearly killed me!'

'We could never have sorted it out, Frank,' she said. 'Never.'

'Sweetheart, untie me, please.' He'd adopted a wheedling tone. From calling her a bitch to calling her sweetheart, within seconds!

She shook her head. 'You're staying right there.'

'Come on, Pam. We have to get back to BP and report this.'

'Yes, of course.'

Edwin had picked up a key that lay on the desk beside the radio set. As they left, he fitted it into the lock of Frank's door and turned it. 'Right then, he's not going anywhere. Is his landlady safe?'

'I asked her to call the police.'

They found Mrs Sparsholt dithering in her shop. 'Don't go upstairs,' Edwin told her. 'He's a dangerous man. We're off to report him.'

'How will we get to BP?' Pam asked. 'Come to think of it, how did you manage to turn up here?'

He nodded at a motorcycle parked along the street. 'I borrowed this and came to Woburn, when you left BP. I watched you go into the shop and then round the back, and I waited outside. Came running when I heard you scream.'

'That was when he slapped me,' she said, touching her sore cheek.

'So come on, jump up behind me.' He'd straddled the motorcycle and was nodding at the pillion.

'Well, this is a first,' she said, but climbed on anyway and wrapped her arms around his middle. It felt good, secure and safe. Edwin started the engine and drove off, carefully but quickly, along the lanes that led towards Bletchley.

She had time, on the back of the bike, to consider her own position in all this. There'd be questions, plenty of them. Why had she been consorting with a German spy? When had she first had suspicions? What, exactly, had she said to him? She would have to be completely honest and give as detailed an account as she possibly could. Edwin would back her up. The authorities would question Clarissa, and Edwin too – all her friends. She felt a pang of guilt for dragging them into all this. but how could she have known? A surge of gratitude for Edwin who'd saved her coursed through her, and she wrapped her arms a tiny bit tighter around him, resting the unhurt side of her face against his back for a moment.

It took only minutes to cover the distance back to Bletchley, and soon they were hurrying into the block that housed the Newmanry. 'Mr Newman will know who we should speak to,' Edwin had said to Pam as they'd parked the motorcycle. 'We'll speak to him first.'

Max Newman was in one of the Colossus rooms and listened to their story with a worried expression. 'You must speak to Commander Travis about this. He can send the Military Police to arrest this man. Hurry. You know where his office is?'

Pam had never been to the Commander's office, but she knew where it was in the main building, so she nodded, and with Edwin close behind ran across to the big house, inside and up the stairs. She had a quick word with the Wren who served as the Commander's secretary, who then tapped on the door to his office and showed them in.

It was a fraught few minutes as they explained what had happened, and how a potential German spy had been left locked in his room and tied to a bedstead over in Woburn village. Commander Travis's expression was sombre, and he fired a few brief questions at them, before picking up the telephone and speaking urgently to someone.

'A team of Military Police are heading over there right now and will arrest this man. We also of course need to question the two of you in detail, and anyone else who had dealings with this man. Wait here.'

'Sir, I have the key to the room he's locked in,' Edwin said, fumbling in his pocket and passing the room key to the Commander who took it without a word and left the room. A guard entered as he left and stood by the door.

'We're under suspicion,' Edwin said to Pam. 'Although we restrained him and reported him, they'll be worried we might have previously been collaborating with him, and then changed our minds.' He took Pam's hand and squeezed it. 'Just remember, you have done nothing wrong. Be strong.'

The wait for the Commander to return seemed to stretch to eternity. His office had clearly once been the nursery of the house, and was hung with Peter Rabbit wallpaper. Such an important office, such serious business went on in here, and yet there was this childish, frivolous wallpaper. At a different time, Pam would have chuckled at the incongruity of it all.

At last, Commander Travis returned. As Edwin had predicted, they were each taken to separate rooms for questioning. Pam sat in front of a grand desk, before a senior Wren, a member of the Military Police, and Travis himself. She was questioned for what felt like hours, as it fell dark outside and her stomach began complaining that it was well past dinnertime. She was asked to detail exactly how she met Frank, and what he had told her about himself.

Partway through, a telephone call came through for Commander Travis. After taking it, he turned back to her. 'Well, Miss Jackson, I can now confirm Frank Miller is in custody and being taken to a secure location for questioning. Now let's go back through everything. I want to know what happened on every encounter you had with him.'

She answered as completely as she could again, although she couldn't remember every single one of their meetings. 'We were … stepping out, sir. We met up as often as we could, on our days off.' And she realised she would have to admit to the seriousness of their relationship. Better they hear it from her than from Frank. 'Sir, he asked me to marry him one time.'

'And what was your answer?' Travis leaned forward, frowning.

'I wasn't sure, so I said neither yes nor no, but that we needed to wait until the war was over.'

'And at that time, did you suspect Mr Miller at all, of being a traitor?'

Pam took a deep breath before answering. 'I knew he was half German. But that is not a crime. I knew his brother was in Germany, in the Luftwaffe, and that worried me but as he'd told me they'd been brought up separately in different countries, and that he barely knew his brother, I did not think it would be likely to make him a traitor. But …' She took another deep breath.

'Go on.'

'I saw him post a letter addressed to his brother to Switzerland. And I saw him hanging around the gates at Bletchley, staying hidden behind bushes as though trying to see who goes in and out. And he asked me to take photographs of where I work …'

'Did you?'

She blushed as she answered. 'I took some. One of the main house. None of the huts or anything else.'

'Did you give them to him?'

She shook her head. 'No. I have not used up the film, so it is still in my camera.' Thank goodness she hadn't. This could have got her into a lot of trouble, even though she knew her photograph would not have given away any secrets. It was just a shot of the house.

'What about the radio set?'

'I'd wondered what was in the suitcase he collected on the day we went to London. He said it was personal items belonging to a friend, and he got cross when I asked him more about it. I think that's what made me really begin to suspect something might be wrong.'

'Why didn't you report it then?'

Pam swallowed back tears. It wouldn't do to look weak and tearful. Answer honestly, she told herself. You've done nothing wrong. 'I considered it. I discussed it with Edwin Denham, then. I didn't think there was enough evidence, and because of our relationship I thought I should be sure, before getting Frank into trouble that might not be justified. So I decided to try to get a look at the contents of that case first. That's why I went there today, when I thought he'd still be at work.'

The Commander nodded. That was, she thought, a good sign. A sign that he believed her, and that her decisions had been the right ones. But then he leaned back in his chair, arms folded. 'It was very dangerous, what you did. If he had a gun, as you say, then you might have been killed. You should have reported your concerns and we could have followed up on them, discreetly.'

'I am sorry, sir. It was a dilemma and I thought I was doing the best thing. I hadn't for a moment thought that he might have a gun.'

'Well. You and Denham are safe, and the traitor is now in our custody and we will soon find out exactly what he's been up to.'

'Sir, what will happen to him?'

'Interrogation, and then internment. He'll be taken elsewhere – it won't happen here. We will aim to find out what information he passed on, and where he acquired the radio set.' Travis's expression softened for a moment. 'Miss Jackson, I doubt you will ever see him again. You will do well to forget all about him, and in time I am sure you will find yourself a new young man, one more worthy of you.'

'What will happen to me?'

'You will return to work tomorrow, of course. You are a skilled Colossus operator, so Max tells me, and we cannot afford to lose you.'

'Thank you, sir.' Her response came as a whisper, and at last her tears fell.

Chapter 27

Julia

Julia had spent the couple of days since throwing out Marc job-hunting, registering with IT employment agencies, compiling a CV. Anything to take her mind off the fact her marriage was over. The more she thought about it, the more she knew that whatever Marc said or did now, whatever he promised, it was over. For too long he'd sneered at her achievements to hide his jealousy. He'd expected her to do all the work in the house as though she was a traditional housewife. And now this ultimate betrayal. Well, no more. Her marriage was beyond saving. In some ways, she just wanted to get it over and done with now, so she could move ahead with the next phase of her life. As an employee, not a business owner.

As a single mum.

They'd eaten and were debating whether to play a game or put a movie on, when she heard a key in the lock. 'Boys, I think that's your dad. Go and say hello to him, but then you'd better go upstairs while I talk to him.'

'About the company going bust?' Ryan asked.

'Yes, that, and other things, pet.' She hadn't found the words to fully explain things to Ryan yet. He'd asked why Marc hadn't come home at the end of the week and Julia had fobbed him off with a vague answer about the course being extended.

Oscar caught her eye and then pushed Ryan towards the door. 'Come on, Ry.'

She heard them greet Marc in the hallway, Oscar sounding cautious. It broke her heart. Whatever happened she wanted the boys to continue to have a good relationship with their father. A minute later there was silence, and then Marc was there, in the sitting room, standing near the door with a suitcase in his hand. 'Hey, Jules.' He had the grace to look sheepish as he said it.

'Hello. I suppose you need clean underwear? She doesn't do your washing yet, I'm guessing?' It was a petty snipe, but she couldn't help herself.

He blushed and put his case down by his feet. 'God, Jules. What a way to greet me. But yes, as it happens. I wanted to see the boys and pick up some more clothes.' He sighed. 'And talk to you. See if there's any way … any hope for us?' He sat down opposite her and gazed at her sadly. There were bags beneath his eyes that hadn't been there a few weeks ago, she thought. As though he hadn't been sleeping well.

She shook her head. 'No, Marc. I can't be married to a man I don't trust, and who doesn't respect me or our marriage vows.'

'So that's really it, is it?'

'Yes. That's it.'

He gave a little shrug. She interpreted it as indicating acceptance, rather than dismissal.

They sat in silence for a minute, just watching each other with sadness. So this was how a marriage ended. The anger Julia had felt a couple of days ago was gone, and in its place a profound sense of sorrow that what had started out with joy and hopefulness and love had descended into this.

It was Marc who looked away first. He patted the arm of his

chair. 'I'll need my share of the value of the house. You'll have to buy me out.'

'No, we'll sell it.'

'What about your offices? I assumed you'd want to stay here because of the business.'

She told him then about the insolvency. He listened without commenting, his mouth falling slightly open.

When she'd finished, he shook his head in disbelief. 'What a bastard Ian is. How could he do this to you?'

'Betray my trust, you mean?' Julia raised an eyebrow. 'I don't know. How can anyone do that to someone they care about?'

He opened his mouth to answer, and then seemed to realise there was no good answer he could give. He let out an enormous sigh. 'Fair point. OK. So … where do we go from here?'

'I'm getting the house valued. I'll put it on the market as soon as possible. You'll need to sign things, no doubt. I'm obviously looking for a new job and will also find a house suitable for me and the boys. In this area.'

'I'll stay local too.'

'With … her?'

'Her name's Libby. For now, yes. I don't know about the long term.' He raised his eyes to hers. 'She's not you. I'm a fool.'

'Yes. You are.' At least he realised what he'd lost. 'Go and see the kids, tell them … whatever you want, but be aware I'll tell them the truth. Oscar has guessed anyway. He's been a great support to me. I'll find a solicitor and will let you know who it is.' She paused, then looked back at Marc. 'Let's do this amicably, if we can. It'll be better for the kids, less stressful all round, and God knows I don't need any more stress than is absolutely necessary.'

He was quiet for a moment, staring at her, and then gave a small, sad smile. 'Yes. Amicably.' He stood up and stretched. 'Well, I'll go and pack some things, then.'

'Yes.' As he left the room she called after him. 'Come and say goodbye, before you leave?'

He nodded, picked up his case and went upstairs. Julia leaned back in the sofa and stared at the ceiling. So this was how a marriage ended.

*

Fifteen minutes later he was back down. 'Well, this is it,' he called to Julia, who went out to the hallway, where his suitcase sat by the front door. Oscar and Ryan were at the top of the stairs, white-faced, watching.

'OK, so, I'll be in touch,' she said. 'About a solicitor and everything.'

'Yes.' He was standing a metre away from her. Close, but the gap between them was a chasm, uncrossable. 'I'll see you, next Saturday. When I pick up the boys.'

He must have promised them a day out or something. She nodded. 'All right.'

He cleared his throat. 'So. I'll, um …' He gestured to the front door.

'Yes.' But he didn't move. She met his eyes and saw the sadness there. Fifteen years of marriage, ending right here and right now. With a whimper, not a bang. But ending it was definitely the right thing to do.

'Still friends?' he said, and she guessed that was to reassure the kids as much as anything else.

She nodded, and that was enough. He stepped forward and put his arms around her, leaning his chin on the top of her head. The hug that was so familiar, that they had shared so many times, that had always made Julia feel as though she'd come home. And in that hug, and the way he gave her a gentle squeeze which she returned, there was an apology, an acceptance of her decision, and a promise that yes, they would remain friends, and one way or another the future would work out for both of them.

'All right, then,' he said, as the hug ended and he stepped back. Julia was too choked to respond. Marc picked up his case, glanced up at the boys, and left the house. Julia quietly, gently, closed the door on him, and on their marriage.

When Marc had gone, Oscar and Ryan came downstairs. Both looked solemn, and Ryan had clearly been crying. She pulled them to her and held them tight. It wasn't often Oscar submitted to a hug lately, but today he did. 'Dad told you, right?'

Ryan nodded. 'He said you and he had had a good marriage, but even good things come to an end. Like your business too.'

'He said we'd see him at weekends and can stay with him overnight on school nights sometimes, when he's found himself a flat,' Oscar added.

'He said he was sorry.'

'He said it'll all be better in the end, once everything is settled.'

Julia nodded at each statement. 'He's right, about all that. Everything will be better in the end. I promise you.'

*

There were a number of emails Julia needed to deal with that evening, after Marc had left. A couple from Madeleine asking for a few more details on Julian Systems' clients. She responded quickly to those, feeling strangely relieved that decisions were out of her hands. It was odd; she'd have imagined hating the loss of control, but instead found it liberating. Now, she just wanted the software sold and the business wound up as fast as possible, as long as Barry and Tulipa weren't left out of pocket.

There was an email from Tulipa as well, checking in, asking how she was and whether there was anything Tulipa could do for her. Julia sent a friendly reply. Not yet, but further down the line when the insolvency process was nearer completion, she resolved to organise an evening or lunch out with Tulipa and Barry. It'd be nice to stay in touch. For now, she'd decided not to tell them about the breakdown of her marriage. They'd be devastated for her, and she didn't want that.

As she was replying to Tulipa, another email arrived. It was from Caroline, saying she'd uploaded more pages of the memoir, including some that were about Pamela. Julia was glad to read this email. Something really meaty to take her mind off her problems. She poured herself a glass of wine and then settled down to read the memoir. As she read it, she came to a section that made her gasp, then reach for her phone and call Bob.

'Any chance you might have some time off in which you can come to visit?' she asked him. 'I have so much to tell you, and none of it is suitable for a phone conversation.'

'Very cryptic!' He laughed – she'd managed to keep her tone upbeat. 'As it turns out, yes, I have a few days off week after next. Want me to come to visit? Is that all right with Marc too?'

'I'd love you to come.' Julia decided not to say anything more or answer the question about Marc. If she said anything, she'd blurt it all out and end up sobbing over the phone. Better that it wait until Bob was there, with her.

They arranged a date, and Julia hung up smiling. Something to look forward to. And the boys would be pleased to see their Uncle Bob too.

*

Things seemed to move quickly over the next few days. Julia chose an estate agent and put the house on the market. She decided against having a 'for sale' sign. It would only lead to neighbours calling to see what was happening, and as yet she didn't feel ready to tell the world about her changing circumstances.

The estate agency, however, already had people on its books who were after that kind of house, and sent people around to view it immediately. By Saturday evening there were three offers on the table. All she had to do was speak to Marc and then pick one. By Sunday evening a buyer was lined up: a developer who had plans to split the house into three flats. Julia quite liked the idea of it having a completely new format once they had gone.

She phoned her father to catch him up on her news. 'Oh, pet. What a lot of awful things happening all at once. Do you want … I don't know if it'd help, but do you want me to come over? Anything I can do?'

'Ah, thanks, Dad. That's a kind offer but no, I don't think there is anything much you can do. You stay right where you are, and as soon as I've got things sorted I'd like to bring the boys over for a holiday. Can't be certain it'll be this summer, but we'll see.'

'That would be wonderful! Or you could come for Christmas, or New Year. We always go to the beach for a barbecue on Christmas Day.'

She smiled. 'I think we'd rather like that.' It would be a goal to aim for. It would be good for the boys to see more of their grandfather.

Towards the end of the week Julia was called for a job interview, with a small IT consultancy. She arranged the interview for the following Monday. At this rate, she thought, by the time Bob arrived for his visit she'd have a whole new life sorted out for herself.

The thought of going for an interview was daunting – mainly, Julia realised, because she had not done such a thing for so many years. Not since she was straight out of university, a fresh-faced graduate who was not expected to know anything much about the job she was applying for as it was a graduate training scheme. For the last fifteen years it had been she who'd interviewed others. Still, she put her best black suit on, a hint of make-up, and made sure she had a proper breakfast. Both boys wished her luck as they left for school. She left a few minutes later, driving westwards into Berkshire to the company's offices in a converted country house. If she was offered the job, she'd have to get used to this commute. But the good thing was, she pointed out to herself, she'd be travelling in the opposite direction to most commuters who'd be heading in towards London rather than out of it.

It was a sunny day and a not unpleasant drive, especially the last section through the Berkshire countryside. Julia arrived in good time for the interview feeling confident and more relaxed than she'd expected to be.

She parked in a staff car park around the back of the building, from where she could see pleasantly laid-out grounds with lawns and benches. It'd be a good place to spend coffee breaks in the summer. As she went in through the old entrance hall her thoughts turned to Bletchley Park. Her grandmother had worked in a building like this, all those years ago. She must have felt a little overwhelmed when she first turned up there. Julia walked over to the reception desk, feeling as though her grandmother was right there beside her, cheering her on. It gave her courage.

She was early, and there was time for a coffee before the interview. As she'd hoped, she was offered the opportunity to take the coffee outside, through a door from the back of the hallway that led to the lawns. 'Someone will come to find you there at half past,' the receptionist told her. Julia thanked her and took her coffee to a bench in the sunshine.

Right on time a young man in a suit came out to fetch her and take her upstairs to an office that had been created by partitioning what must have once been a grand room. It still had an ornate ceiling rose and large marble fireplace.

*

Half an hour later, Julia returned to her car, feeling thoughtful. The interview had gone well. There'd been two interviewers, and it was clear she had the right experience and skills, although the consultancy did not work in retail. They were interested in her technical knowledge. She'd be working in a team, doing some coding but also quality checking other people's work. She'd be a perfect fit for the job.

The company had not said very much about what systems they built, or who their clients were. Just one thing had been mentioned – one of their clients was the Ministry of Defence, and if Julia were to take the job, she'd be required to sign the Official Secrets Act.

'Just like you, Grandma,' Julia muttered to herself.

Chapter 28

Pamela

It was odd returning to work the next day, as if none of it had ever happened. Clarissa asked her about it over breakfast. 'I heard rumours that Frank was arrested? Can that be true? What on earth for? Are you all right, Pam?'

'It's true, yes. And it was Edwin and I who alerted the authorities.'

'You and Edwin? But why?'

Pam told her friend the full story. Clarissa would probably have to answer some questions too. 'And yes, I'm all right. I would have broken things off with Frank soon anyway, I think. He'd shown another side to himself that I didn't much care for.'

'You are better off without him. And tell me, how are your parents? I have been thinking of them, since the news about Geoff.'

Geoff's loss seemed like a lifetime ago, so much had happened since. The reminder of it hit Pam like a punch to the gut, and she had to swallow hard before answering her friend. It had only been a couple of days since they'd heard the horrible news, after all. They were both still raw from it.

*

Work helped. Concentrating on setting up the Colossus correctly for each run took her mind off it all, and she was almost able to forget the events of the last few days. By unspoken agreement, Edwin didn't mention any of it either, apart from checking that she was all right and that the questioning had not been too much of an ordeal.

Just before lunchtime Mr Newman came in to see both Pam and Edwin. 'You two had a bit of excitement yesterday, I hear?'

'We did, sir,' Edwin replied.

'You did well, I understand, in restraining him and preventing anyone being hurt. Commander Travis wants to see you again, Pamela, if you could pop in during your lunch break.' He smiled. 'Don't worry. It's nothing bad.'

And indeed it turned out to be just a few more questions. Now that Frank had been interrogated, there were a few points the Commander wanted to check with Pam. He also gave her an update on what Frank had told them.

'You deserve to know, I think, Miss Jackson. It seems that just before the war began, Miller's brother visited him here in England and persuaded him then to do what he could for Germany – what he called the Fatherland. Miller had written letters with hidden messages to his brother throughout the war, but had never had much of interest to write about.' Travis looked Pam in the eye. 'Until he met you and began suspecting that Bletchley Park might be important in some way to the war effort, although he had no idea whether it was or not. That's when it was arranged for him to pick up a radio set so that he could more quickly pass on intelligence if he did discover anything of interest. Fortunately, you told him nothing.'

Pam felt herself break out in a cold sweat. She had not broken the Official Secrets Act, but nevertheless Frank had guessed there was secret work going on and might have informed his German handlers of that. 'I heard him speaking German on it,' she said, recalling those moments when she had stood frozen just inside Frank's room.

The Commander was smiling at her. 'You will be pleased to hear, Miss Jackson, that Miller admitted he'd gained no useful information to pass on. His best guess was that BP was being used to sew uniforms for troops, and this is what he'd fed to his handlers. He said he could not think of any other reason to employ so many girls. Clearly, he did not think women could manage work of any importance.'

Pam was relieved Frank had not managed to pass on any information. 'Thank goodness.'

'Indeed. We can now put this episode behind us and get on with the important job of winning this war.' He nodded at her. 'You are dismissed, Miss Jackson.'

'Thank you, sir.' As she left the office, her knees felt weak. It was such a relief that no damage had been done by her liaison with a German spy, but how close it had come to being disastrous! If BP was targeted by German bombers, that could be the end to all their endeavours and an end to ULTRA intelligence.

She vowed, as she walked to the canteen for lunch, to work harder than ever. What they did here at BP was paying dividends, saving lives and would lead to Britain and her allies winning the war, she knew it.

*

There was a letter waiting for Pam when she returned to the Abbey from BP a couple of days later. Another letter, with her father's handwriting on the envelope. The last letter had contained the awful news about Geoff. Pam's stomach turned over as she opened it. What could have happened now? She found herself praying. Please let Mum be all right. And Dad. Please let it not be bad news.

As she read the letter, she gasped and grinned broadly. Not bad news. Not bad news at all. The very opposite!

'What is it, Pam?' Clarissa asked.

'I think – oh, I think you'd better just read it. It's from my father.'

Clarissa gave Pam a puzzled glance and took the letter from her. She read it quickly. 'Whoop! Oh, Pam, this is the most marvellous news! So he managed to safely eject, parachute down, and is now in the hands of the French Resistance! Oh, Pam!' She flung her arms around Pam and the two girls jumped up and down with joy.

'It's unbelievable! He's injured, and it might take a long time for him to get home, but he's safe!'

'The Resistance are marvellous. Lord knows how they got this message out, but they did. They'll look after Geoff, fix him up, move him up the line and get him home. Oh, isn't this just the best news!'

It felt to Pam like a turning point. As though things were beginning to work out. She dared to hope that fortunes would change and the end of the war would soon be in sight.

Chapter 29

Julia

It was a busy week. Julia began house-hunting and by Friday she'd placed an offer on a three-bed semi-detached house just one street away from their current home. It was a good bit smaller, and of course did not have the attached annexe, which was why she'd been able to afford it. The offer had been accepted. The new place backed onto a park, through which the boys could take a short cut on their way to school, and they pronounced it better than the old house. Oscar's friend Nathan lived on the same street. Then on Friday Julia heard back from the job interview, and it was good news. They were offering her a job. She didn't see the email until too late on Friday to reply so it would have to wait until the following week. It wouldn't hurt to have a weekend to be sure this was the right job for her, though. She'd applied for several others, one of which was much closer to home. There'd only be a ten-minute commute, although the pay was less.

And finally, it was Saturday and Bob was due to arrive by lunchtime. The boys were with Marc – the first of their days out with him. He'd arrived at ten o'clock to collect them, much to

Oscar's disgust; he'd wanted a longer lie-in. Julia had offered Marc coffee while they waited for Oscar to get showered and dressed. 'Bit odd, you offering me coffee in my own house,' Marc had said. Julia had let the comment go, and changed the subject onto whether it was likely to stay fine all weekend and what time Marc would bring the boys back. 'Bob's coming. I just need to know if they'll be here for dinner or not. It's no problem either way.' Actually, she'd have preferred them to be home for dinner with their uncle but it was Marc's only day with them all week so she was prepared to forgo this. Keep the peace, she told herself. It'll be worth it in the long run. She'd been careful not to ask Marc what his living arrangements were.

'I'll bring them back before seven, for dinner,' he'd replied. 'Say hello to Bob for me.'

'Will do.' And then Ryan had come downstairs, closely followed by Oscar who was still half-asleep despite having had a shower, and after the boys ate a hurried bowl of cereal each they'd left Julia alone.

In days gone by she'd have relished the opportunity to go and do a bit of work. But now she just found herself missing the boys, and pleased they'd be back in time for dinner.

Bob arrived at midday. He took a small suitcase up to the spare room. In the new house, Julia thought, there wouldn't be a spare room. She'd need a sofa bed, or else one of the boys would have to move into the other's room for a night when Bob came to stay. They wouldn't mind that.

'So, Sis! You've news, you said? Where are the boys, and Marc?'

'All out together. The boys will be back by dinnertime.'

'And Marc?'

'Let me get you a coffee, and we'll sit out on the patio as the weather's good, and I will tell you all my news, from the beginning.'

*

Somehow, she managed it without crying. Bob let her talk, let her tell the tales of the end of her business and the end of her marriage in her own words, in her own time. At the end he reached out and took her hand in his. 'Oh, Julia. What a lot to happen, all at once. You know you can always call on me, right? For anything you need – whether it's childcare for a few days, a loan, a shoulder to cry on or just someone to talk to.'

'Thanks. I'm surprisingly OK about it all. I think because I'm already taking steps to sort my life out – we have a buyer for this place; I've found somewhere to move to that the kids love; I've had a job offer ...'

'A job offer, already? That's good going!'

She told him then about the job.

'What sort of work is it – what do they build?'

'I don't really know. They were a bit cagey. I'd have to sign the Official Secrets Act.'

'Wow! Just as our grandmother probably had to.'

'Yes, she must have, working at Bletchley Park. And talking of Grandma, I've found out quite a lot more about her. Caroline's sent me loads more of Clarissa's memoir. We're so lucky to have this, and it turns out our great-aunt was quite the writer, too! There's still more to come. The last part I read was from 1944, when they'd just heard that Geoff had been rescued by the French Resistance.'

'Oh yes, I vaguely recall he was in the RAF and was shot down in the war. He walked with a limp, I seem to remember.'

'Yes. He'd already started dating Clarissa by then. It was Grandma who introduced them. But listen to this bit.' Julia fetched her laptop, found the relevant scanned page from Clarissa's memoir, and began reading.

'In 1944 there was a bit of excitement involving Pamela. Her sweetheart – the young gardener named Frank I mentioned earlier – well it turned out that he was German! She'd found this out but not told anyone, to avoid anyone treating him any differently. But then it all came out that he was sending cryptic messages to his

brother who was in the Nazi party. Pamela surprised him at his lodgings when he was using a radio set. There was a set-to, and a gun was fired but thankfully no one was injured. Pamela was rescued by Edwin Denham, whom of course she married after the war, and Frank was captured by the Military Police and interned. We were all questioned about what we knew of the gardener, to ensure no one had told him anything of what we did at Bletchley Park. Of course, no one had said a word about it, not even Pamela, thank goodness.'

'Wow,' Bob said, when she'd finished reading. 'Quite a story! And, wait, Grandpa rescued her? Did he also work at Bletchley Park then?'

'I think he must have done. Hold on, we can find out.' Julia opened a new tab and typed in the Bletchley roll of honour website address. She searched for Edwin Denham. 'Yes! Look, he was in the Newmanry, the same section as Grandma. He was a Colossus engineer. They must have worked together.'

'So now we know how they met. But first she was dating this German chap. Grandpa had to wait for his chance.'

'And then he rescued her! I'd love to know more about how that happened. A gun was fired – oh, Clarissa, couldn't you have said who fired it at least!' Julia laughed. 'That's the thing about researching the past. There's only so much you can find out. Whatever the people who were present thought it worth recording or reporting, and even then you are sometimes scuppered by what they were allowed to tell.'

Bob nodded. 'Yes, indeed. And it's unbelievable to think the whole place was scheduled for demolition at one stage. If it wasn't for a group of people who understood its significance it would have been razed to the ground and a housing estate built instead.'

'A lucky escape.'

'For both Bletchley and Grandma, I think!'

'She knew this fellow was German and didn't say anything.' Julia rubbed her chin thoughtfully. 'He's the young man in the photograph, I think. I suppose Grandma wanted to protect him first, after all, being German in itself wasn't a crime.'

'Not at all. I read that Max Newman, her head of section, was himself of German background. His name was originally spelt Neumann.'

'All this secrecy. I don't know how Grandma and Grandpa lived with it, all their lives. So much they didn't talk about. I mean, I'd want to always be able to be open with my kids about what I do, and would want to proudly tell my grandchildren if I'd had a part in something important. The thought of keeping quiet for decades, or even all my life, is horrible.'

Bob was grinning at her, his head slightly tipped to one side. 'You're going to decline that job offer, then?'

'Am I?' She frowned.

'You've just more or less said you'd hate having to sign the Official Secrets Act.'

'Have I? Well …' She thought back on what she'd just said. He was right. It wasn't just a theoretical idea of having to keep quiet about her work. If she took this job, she'd really have to do that. She wouldn't be able to tell Oscar or Ryan anything about it other than in the vaguest of terms. She wouldn't be able to talk to Bob about it either, or anyone else.

And … what could it be that was so secret, for the Ministry of Defence? Some sort of spy software? Intelligence gathering and analysis? Or … something like missile guidance programming? Could she really be a part of that? Could she go to work every day knowing that computer code she'd written might in the future lead to the deaths of other people? As she considered this, she made a decision. That job was not for her. She wanted a simpler life. A job she could just get on with and leave behind at the end of the day, not worrying about it, yet still able to talk about it to whoever she liked. A job that was local, that would allow her to get to events at the boys' school. Who cared about the salary, as long as there was enough to live on?

'You look as though you're making a decision?' Bob prompted.

She nodded. 'I am, I think. I'll decline that job. I think you're right, it's not for me. I've rather had enough of secrets lately.'

'Have you had other interviews?'

'Not yet, though I've applied for a few. One's promising – it's local, lower paid but shorter commute.'

'Sounds good.' Bob smiled at her. 'Whatever job you get, I'm sure it'll all work out for you. You've a habit of making sure things work out. Proud of you, Sis.'

Chapter 30

Pamela, May 1945

For the last few weeks, as spring came to Bletchley Park in all its green and gold glory, it had felt like it'd be only a short time before the war ended. So near, and yet soldiers were still dying. Pam was working harder than ever. With the end in sight, it made their efforts seem even more worthwhile. There were ten Colossus machines installed now, all working round the clock decoding messages, and their design had come on so that now all twelve Tunny wheel patterns were found by machine, not just the first five settings. And this was despite the fact that since just after D-Day, the Germans had begun changing their wheel patterns daily rather than monthly.

'Do you think they have any idea we're reading all their communications?' Pam had said to Edwin one sunny morning as they relaxed beside the lake with a cup of coffee.

He shook his head. 'If they did, they'd have changed the way they encode messages. I don't think they can have a clue that we are reading practically everything they send.'

'And they can't have been decrypting our side's messages. Or we wouldn't now be about to win this war.' Pam leaned back on the grass on her elbows and sighed. 'I'd love to know the truth of it all. I'd love to read a book about the efforts of both sides to decrypt each other's messages. I know, I know, it's all top secret and none of us who know what's gone on here will ever be allowed to talk about it let alone write a book. We won't even be able to tell our children or grandchildren of the part we played in the war.'

'Would you like to have children?' Edwin regarded her quizzically. Over the last year they'd become closer. Firm friends. The one thing Pam was not looking forward to, when the war ended, was leaving BP and no longer working with Edwin every day. She'd miss him terribly.

'Oh yes. Not yet, though. When this is all over, I want to go to university. I was offered a place at Oxford to read mathematics but deferred it so I could come here. If the offer's still open I want to take it up. To think I might be there this autumn! Two years later than originally planned. And then I'd like to work for a few years in industry, using my degree. Or perhaps stay at the university, doing research. Eventually I'd like to marry and have children. And then perhaps work again. One thing the war has proved, is that women can do all the jobs men do, just as well.'

'They certainly can. Equally as well, and often better.' He smiled at her, and Pam was briefly reminded of the very different attitude towards working women that Frank had had. 'I know what you mean,' Edwin continued, 'about not being able to tell our children what we did. But we can quietly be proud of what we've accomplished here. And whenever we meet up, you and I, Norah, Clarissa, and anyone else we worked with, we can talk about it to each other.'

'Do you think we will?' Pam rolled onto her side and gazed at him. 'Meet up, after it's all over, I mean.'

'I'm sure of it. This – the work, this place, you – have all been such an important part of my life.'

The way he was looking at her, the way he'd placed a little

emphasis on the word 'you' made her wonder. How important was she to him? Come to that, how important was he to her? She tried to imagine a future away from BP, seeing Edwin only once or twice a year as part of a reunion meet-up, writing occasional polite letters to him. And she felt her heart sink. That was not the future she wanted. She glanced at him. He was still looking her way, a half-smile on his face. She realised – had she always known it? – that she wanted a future with Edwin in it. Close by. Near enough to see him often. In her life. Part of her life. She felt herself blushing, and looked away. Well, the war wasn't over yet, and they still had work to do, together, here at BP. There was no point wondering about what the future would hold just yet.

*

On the way home that day, Pam had almost the same conversation with Clarissa. 'At least when we leave here I won't stop seeing you,' she said. 'I'm hoping you'll be a regular visitor.' Geoff had taken months to get home the previous year, only able to return after the Normandy landings had taken place and the Allies had secured a route to the Channel. After a visit home and an emotional reunion with Pam and her parents, he'd returned to his RAF base, working a desk job as his injuries did not allow him to fly. He would always walk with a limp. Clarissa had been a regular visitor to Turweston ever since, and Pam was hoping they would one day be sisters-in-law.

'I'm sure I will be,' Clarissa said. 'If your brother does not propose to me soon, I swear I'll propose to him. I don't see why it should always be the men who get to pop the question.'

Pam squealed with delight and hugged her friend. 'Do it! How wonderful!'

Clarissa grinned. 'I shall. And you and Edwin – do you think you will keep seeing him? He worships you, you know.'

'Oh, I'm not sure, does he?' Pam tried to laugh it off but

underneath she was delighted by what Clarissa had said.

'Absolutely. I suspect he's too shy to say anything to you.' Clarissa looked thoughtful. 'He might wonder if you still carry a torch at all for Frank Miller. Do you?'

'Not at all.' Pam gave a little shudder. 'We had some good times at the start, and I thought I really cared for him. But there was nothing deep about it. I liked his looks, and I was flattered he liked me, and life was so new and different and exciting here. But I see now the relationship would never have lasted, whether or not he'd turned out to be a German spy. We had different values. I do feel I had a lucky escape.'

'Edwin rescued you.'

'He certainly did. I shall be forever grateful to him.'

'Tell him that, Pam. I'd love the two of you to be as happy as Geoff and I are.'

Pam smiled and hugged her friend. For the rest of the journey home, she allowed herself to imagine situations with Edwin in which they declared their feelings for each other. In which they kissed, the way she had kissed Frank. Looking back, she sometimes wondered what she had seen in Frank. She had been taken in by him, in so many ways. Thank goodness she'd never developed that film, those photographs of Bletchley Park. She had still not used up the film, and if she was honest with herself, she knew she never would. She didn't want to see the pictures of Frank, to be reminded of him. She wanted to look forward, not back. Forward to a future that she hoped would involve Edwin.

*

A few days later Pam had popped out from Block H to visit the ladies'. Her route back took her past a hut filled with teleprinters. Their constant clacking as they printed off incoming coded messages intercepted by listening stations and sent on to BP by teleprinter had been a background sound ever since

Pam had arrived at Bletchley Park. Today though, something was different. The girls working in that room were standing around, puzzled. 'They can't all have broken at once,' she heard one girl say. It was odd, it being so quiet.

'What's happened?' she asked a girl who'd come out of that hut, looking puzzled.

'The machines have all stopped. There are no more incoming messages. We've sent for Mr Tester to see if he knows what's wrong.'

Pam felt a rush of joy. There could be only one reason why the incoming messages had stopped. It must mean that no more were being sent, which in turn meant that the listening stations were no longer picking up any German traffic to send on … because there was none … because the war was over. She didn't dare say this to the girl, in case she was wrong. Instead, she hurried back to Block H, where she'd been working that day with Edwin. If the war was indeed over, she wanted to share the moment with Edwin. She broke into a run as she approached the hut. All around people were coming out of their huts, aware something had happened, not yet sure what, and not daring to believe it.

Edwin was still in with the Colossus, setting it up for its next run. A reel of teleprinter tape sat ready to be loaded up.

'Edwin! I think … something's happened. Have you heard?'

'Heard what?'

'The teleprinters have stopped.'

'Stopped?'

'No more incoming messages.' She watched as the implications of that dawned on Edwin's face, and he broke into a broad grin.

'It's over. Oh, Pam, it's all over. The war's over!'

She wasn't sure how it happened but it did. She was in his arms, hugging him. They were squeezing each other tight, her head against his chest, both laughing, jumping up and down a little as they held on to each other. And then, as though reacting to a hidden cue, they stopped jumping and she tilted her head to look up at him, and he bent a little and they were kissing. Deep kisses that somehow were far more meaningful in every way than the ones she'd shared with Frank, sending a thrill that reached right through her. The war was over, and Edwin was in her arms, and somehow, in some way, they would build a future together. She knew that, instinctively. This was no wild, celebratory kiss. This was the start of something important. The start of a new life. The start of forever.

But the kiss had to end eventually, and when it did, Edwin pulled her outside. 'Let's go outside and see if it's true.'

She nodded and they hurried out, holding hands. In front of the main building, people were singing and dancing and hugging each other.

'Looks like it is!' Pam said, and they hugged and kissed again.

'Pam! Edwin!' Clarissa had spotted them and came running over. 'The war's over! At last! Our boys have done it!'

'And we've done it, too,' Pam said, kissing and hugging her friend. She was about to say something more when she heard something far off. She turned to Edwin and Clarissa. 'Listen.'

In the distance, church bells were ringing, joyously pealing up and down the scale, a sound they had not heard since the start of the war.

*

The few weeks that followed seemed surreal. The war had been part of their lives for so long that it was sometimes hard to believe that it had ended. Pam found herself waking up in the morning, remembering with a start, and smiling happily to herself. She'd then remember the kisses she'd shared with Edwin and smile even more broadly. There was no need to ever explain her constant grin because everyone was the same.

There was still work to be done, though not much. Already many Wrens and other personnel had left BP. There were no more messages to be decrypted. Instructions had come from Churchill's government that BP was to be largely shut down, and the Colossus machines destroyed, with just one being kept but taken to another site. Only work decrypting Japanese codes was still going on, and would continue at BP until the war in the Pacific was over too.

Pam was involved with the dismantling process. 'It seems a shame,' she said to Edwin. 'These wonderful contraptions helped us win the war. Surely they could be used in some other way? With a bit of programming and a few alterations, couldn't they be general purpose computational machines of some sort?'

He nodded. 'I'm sure they could. And let's hope that's what they plan to do with the last one.' There'd been ten Colossi in total, since that first one arrived in January the previous year. Ten, working around the clock. Pam was proud to have been a small part of the huge endeavour to decrypt German messages, and even more proud that she'd been an operator on the very first Colossus.

As they disbanded on the last day, with the final parts of the machines boxed into crates and awaiting trucks to take them away, Max Newman called his team together for one last time. They stood in the now-empty Block H to listen to what he had to say.

'You have all played a crucial role in the war, and have undoubtedly led to our success, as well as helping shorten the war. Without our efforts, the war would almost certainly have dragged on for many more years. During the Battle of Britain, Mr Churchill said about our brave RAF fighter pilots, that "never had so much been owed by so many to so few". He could quite easily say that about us. But he won't, for our work here is to remain a secret, and for the last time, I must impress on you all the importance of never speaking to anyone about what we did here. I know it will be hard, for all of us. As leaving here will be. We are all losing the most interesting jobs that we will ever have. I thank you all, and wish you well, whatever you plan to do next.' He swallowed hard, as though emotion threatened to engulf him, nodded, and left the room as the team broke into spontaneous applause – both for Mr Newman and each other.

'Well, that's that, then,' Edwin said as he and Pam walked back to the main building. Pam's train home was that afternoon, and her luggage was already waiting at the station. They had time for one last cup of tea beside the Bletchley Park lake, for old times' sake.

'He's right, old Newman,' Edwin said, 'about how we'll never have a job as interesting again. I'm glad the war's over, of course, but still sad to see the end of all this.'

'What are you doing next?' Pam asked Edwin. She knew that for now he was returning to his parents in Sheffield for a fortnight or more.

'See my folks, and then I'll be heading southward. I have a new job lined up.'

'Oh really? Where?' She prayed it would be somewhere near enough that they might be able to meet up occasionally. They'd spent so much time together. She couldn't imagine her life without him in it, but how that was to be managed she had no idea. She still longed to be able to take up her place at university in the autumn.

He smiled at her and pulled her to him in an embrace. 'Oxford. At the university, to be precise. Working in an electronics research lab.'

'Oxford?' She whispered the word.

'Yes. Oxford. Where you will be in due course. I didn't dare tell you I had applied for a job there, in case it didn't work out. But it has.'

'We can be together.'

He smiled again, his eyes warm and full of love and hope. 'We certainly can.' As he kissed her, the future stretched ahead of them, bright, shining, and peaceful.

Chapter 31

Julia

The other job Julia had applied for – the local one that didn't pay so well – brought her in for interview, were impressed by her, and offered her a job on the spot. Julia thought about the offer for all of ten seconds. 'You don't have to decide immediately,' the interviewer, a pleasant-faced middle-aged man, said with a laugh as Julia accepted it. But he looked amazed and delighted. 'Can you start next week?'

'I certainly can,' Julia replied, pleased that she would be able to report some security to Oscar and Ryan, happy that one thing at least had stabilised.

'Excellent. Stay for lunch and meet some of the team.' The interviewer made a quick phone call, and a woman of around Julia's age, who introduced herself as Chloe Davidson, came into the office and took Julia on a tour of the building before lunch.

'You used to run your own business?' Chloe said, as they queued in the staff canteen. Staff canteen! No more rummaging around the kitchen to make her own lunches, Julia thought.

'I did. Unfortunately we had some … financial problems and became insolvent.'

'Aw, shame. Must have been good to be your own boss.' Chloe looked thoughtful and then turned back to Julia. 'Though actually, if I'm honest, I'm not sure I'd want that. There's something to be said for having less responsibility, knowing you don't have to do everything yourself. I rather like clocking off at five-thirty on a Friday and knowing that's it until Monday morning.'

Julia smiled. 'You've got it in one. It's hard work. The rewards can be great, but right now I definitely prefer the idea of a job like this one, that I can leave at the end of the day and go home to my kids.'

'Kids?'

'Two boys, twelve and fourteen.'

'Oh, much like me then. I have a sixteen-year-old girl and a thirteen-year-old boy. And no husband, since I threw him out last year.'

'We do have a lot in common, then.' Julia liked the openness of this woman. Perhaps here was a new friend in the making. That would be nice. She could do with a new friend. Someone who only knew her in this new, post-Marc, post-Julian Systems incarnation.

As though Chloe had read her mind, she grinned at Julia. 'You're starting Monday? Fancy a drink after work then?'

'That would be marvellous!' The boys were old enough to be left for a couple of hours. She could leave them a pizza with instructions on how to heat it up, for their tea. A drink out would be a lovely way to end her first day at the new job.

*

And so in under a month since Julian Systems became insolvent, Julia found herself with a steady income, working for a medium-sized company that had its own in-house IT department and needed to modernise and update their suite of systems. There would be plenty of work ahead for her to get stuck into – exactly the kind of system design and coding work she most enjoyed. And she'd be able to have flexible hours, working from home a couple of days a week, with time off as necessary for school events.

When she told the boys, over dinner on the evening after her interview, Oscar immediately got up from his place, came round to her side of the table and leaned over to hug her. Ryan joined him. 'Mum, I'm so pleased for you. Pleased for all of us. Love the idea you're working nearby.'

'I was always working nearby. Very near, when I was just in there!' She gestured towards the door that led to the old office.

'That was too near,' Ryan said. 'You could never get away from it. You were kind of always working, in your head if not actually at your desk. Remember when you missed my presentation?'

'Mmm. I think you're right, I was. I'm sorry. Especially about the presentation. But those days are gone, and I promise things will be different now.'

'Work to live, eh, Mum, not live to work?' Oscar said with a wink.

'Absolutely. Got it in one. And if it's OK with you guys, I want to go out with a new friend from work on Monday, just for a drink after work. Will you be all right on your own for a couple of hours? I can leave you a pizza …'

'Course we will. When I'm round at Nathan's, we always cook our own dinner. Pizza, or sometimes we heat up a curry his mum's made and cook rice to go with it. Cooking's easy. And I can teach Ryan.' Oscar glanced at his younger brother.

'Yeah, no problem, Mum,' Ryan said.

'Thank you.' Julia felt quietly pleased that her sons were growing up into such supportive, independent young men. They'd dealt with all the upheaval so well.

*

Things progressed well over the next few weeks. The company software was sold and most of the debts paid off. There was no spare cash for the directors but at least the staff had been paid.

'So, best of luck with your new job,' Madeleine said, as she shook hands after their last meeting. 'I know it's sad circumstances but I have enjoyed working with you on this. I hope all goes well for you from now on.'

'I think it will. Thank you,' Julia replied. If she was honest, once the company name was removed from the register at Companies House, she felt nothing but relief. The responsibility was over. The worry was gone.

Her new job was also going well. A Monday night drink after work with Chloe and sometimes one or two other women, had quickly become a regular event, one that Julia looked forward to immensely. It was something she'd missed out on — having female colleagues who weren't her employees, with whom she could have a moan or a giggle about work. Julia had begun to wonder if Chloe might get on well with Bob. When he next visited, she resolved to introduce them. It would be quite something if they hit it off. Grandma had introduced her brother to a work friend, and ended up with her as a sister-in-law. Julia smiled at the idea of this bit of history repeating itself, even if she had ducked out of repeating the part about signing the Official Secrets Act.

The house sale and purchase were progressing nicely. With a developer buying the old house, and the new place being a probate sale, there was a very short chain and Julia was able to control everything. Marc seemed happy to just sign papers she pushed his way. 'Glad it's going to sell quickly. I could do with my share of the money, so I can buy myself a flat,' he'd said, on one occasion when he was dropping off the boys. He'd been living with his new girlfriend, but it wasn't working out, Oscar had reported. 'I think Dad wants his own place. Libby makes him do too much housework.'

Julia had to laugh at that. 'I'm glad he's learning how to do it at last.' Maybe that's where she'd gone wrong – she hadn't insisted that Marc do his share. She'd thought that having it all meant she needed to do it all, too. And she'd got the balance wrong, for years, without realising it.

'We do more than Dad ever did, don't we?' Ryan piped up.

Julia ruffled the top of his head. 'You certainly do, these days.' The boys now looked after their own bedrooms, loaded and unloaded the dishwasher, and took it in turns to clean the bathroom they shared.

And then there was Ian. He and Drew had also had to sell their house, at a knockdown price to the bank, to pay back the director's loan. Drew had thought long and hard about how to help Ian, how to stop him gambling, and in the end had decided a change of location to somewhere completely different might do the trick. 'I can work anywhere,' he'd said to Julia on the phone just before they moved. 'And I quite fancy working somewhere beautiful. We're off to the Lake District. We'll rent, initially, and buy a small place when we can. It'll be in my name.'

'Sounds perfect,' she'd said.

'And, Jules? Ian said to tell you you'll be very welcome to bring the boys and come to stay. They might have to sleep on the floor, but there'll be a bed for you.'

'Thank you.' Julia managed to choke out a reply. Ian had been her best friend for over twenty years. What he'd done was hard to forgive, but he had an illness, an addiction. Thankfully he also had a loving partner who was doing all he could to cure him of it.

'We want a place we can do up. I'm thinking that giving Ian a project might keep him out of trouble, give him a new focus. As long as there's a corner where I can paint, and ideally a garden where I can build a studio in time, I'll be happy.'

'Is Ian going to get a job?'

'He says he'd like something low-key. Maybe he'll work in a bar or restaurant. I make enough, and I have savings – we don't need much income. It's probably better if we have less. Life will be simpler and less stressful.'

'He's lucky to have you, Drew.'

'I know. And I keep telling him that. We'll be all right. But come and visit us, yeah?'

Julia smiled. 'Yes, I think we will. Would the May half term be OK for you? I know it's short notice but …'

'Yes! We move this Friday – you can come up any time from Sunday onward. We'll make it work!'

Something to look forward to. A few days in the Lakes, reconnecting with her old friend, surrounded by mountains. Actually, Julia thought, she had a lot to look forward to. A life rebuilt in a simpler, more sustainable way. More time with the children who were fast growing up. A life where she no longer tried to have it all and do it all. And no more secrets.

Author's Note

The idea for this novel came about when I was sorting out our attic prior to moving house, and came across not one but two Box Brownie cameras. One of them had been my mother's and I have no idea where the other came from. Sadly, neither had a half-used roll of film inside. But what if there was? my writer-brain thought, and what if the photos when developed raised questions about my family history?

At the back of my mind I'd had an idea to write a novel set at Bletchley Park for some time. I knew I'd love doing the research for it. Combining the two ideas was the starting point for this novel.

I wanted, so much, to visit Bletchley Park, take a tour, go to the Museum of Computing and learn all I could about it all. After a thirty-year career working in IT, I knew I would love all of this. Unfortunately the Covid-19 pandemic got in the way and by the time I finished writing the novel, I had not been able to visit. It was closed throughout the lockdowns and is too far from my home for a day trip. My descriptions of Bletchley Park, town, huts, and museums all had to be researched online and in books. If I've got anything wrong, I apologise.

The characters in the historical sections of the novel are all fictitious with the exception of Max Newman, Commander Travis and Tommy Flowers whose brilliance in designing the Colossus computer cannot be overstated. Too often the Colossus story is overlooked in favour of Alan Turing's achievements in breaking the Enigma code. With this book I wanted to focus on the lesser-known but equally important efforts of those involved with breaking the Tunny code.

One day soon I will get to Bletchley Park and see it all for myself.

Acknowledgements

I found this a difficult book to write, but with enormous help from my editor Dushiyanthi Horti it's ended up being a book I can be proud of. Thank you, Dushi – I could not have done this one without you!

Thanks are also due to everyone else in HQ who has helped produce this book – copy editors and proof readers, cover designers, marketing department and everyone else. All do a fabulous job and I love being part of the HQ family.

Thank you to my son Connor McGurl who helped me thrash out the plot on our many lockdown walks during the summer of 2020. It helps so much to have a sounding board for ideas. Thanks also to my other son Fionn and husband Ignatius for their support as always during the writing process. Love you all, and if there is anything good to say about the pandemic it's that it meant the four of us all lived together again for a few months, unexpectedly.

Finally, thank you to all my readers everywhere. Thanks for continuing to buy my books! I love hearing from you, and I hope you enjoy this one as much as the others.

Keep reading for an excerpt from *The Lost Sister* …

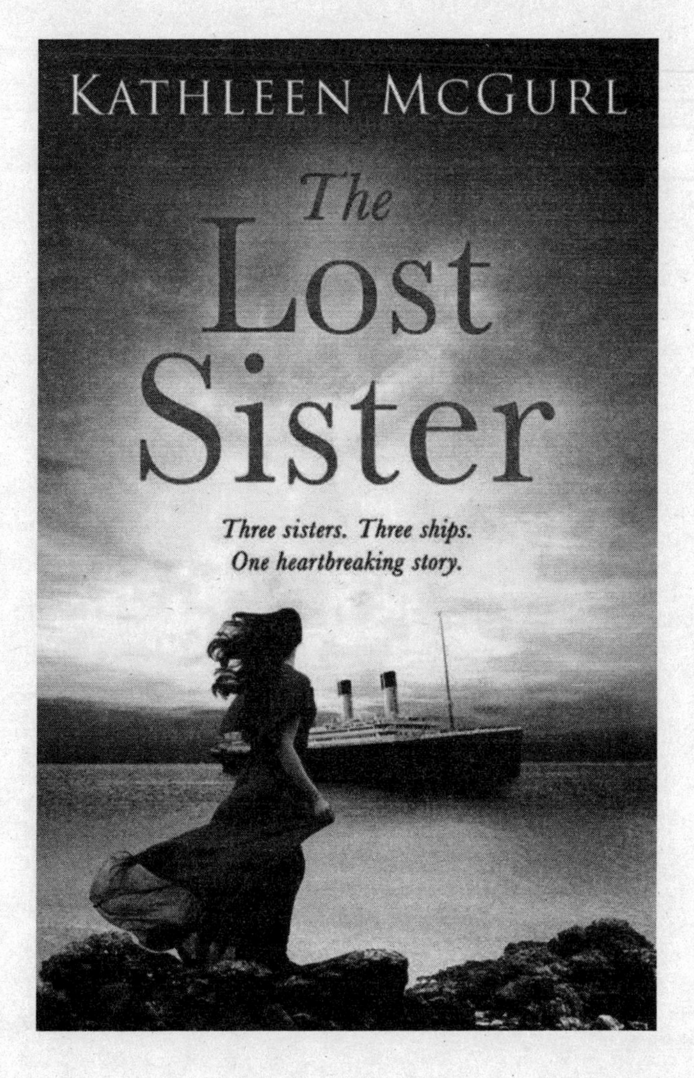

Chapter 1

Harriet, 2019

How she would ever thin down her possessions enough to allow a move into a much smaller property, Harriet had no idea. She wandered from room to room, touching ornaments, stroking the backs of armchairs, running her hand along polished tables and sideboards. Everything was infused with so many memories of her seventy years. The little Toby jug on the mantelpiece that had been her mother's and she remembered loving as a child. The dining room table and chairs that she and John had saved up for in the early years of their marriage, determined to buy decent furniture that would last them a lifetime. The large, squishy sofa, much more modern, bought only about ten years ago and so comfortable and perfect for stretching out on when reading a book. It would never fit in the kind of two-bedroom bungalow her daughter Sally thought she should buy. Neither would the dining table. But how would she ever part with them? And all this stuff was just downstairs. Upstairs she had four bedrooms and a study filled with more stuff. And then there was the attic – huge, and filled with endless boxes of who knew what.

That's what they were due to start tackling today: the attic. Sally had suggested it when she'd phoned the previous evening. 'I'll go up there with you, Mum, and we'll just do it bit by bit. Once we get started you'll find it easier but I know how daunting it must feel.'

'Are you sure you can spare the time, love?' Harriet had asked. 'What about Jerome?'

'He's doing well today. He's in school, and he should be well enough to go to school tomorrow. So I'll have time. See you around ten; get some chocolate croissants in for me from McKinley's bakery, will you?'

'Sure, of course, love,' Harriet had replied. And now the croissants were warming in the oven, the coffee was made and at any moment Sally would arrive and they'd have to get started on the attic, going through the forty years' worth of junk and memories that were stored up there. Outside it was a blustery March day, raining on and off. The perfect day to tackle an indoor job, even one that was likely to be difficult and emotional.

The doorbell rang and Harriet rushed to answer it, smiling as she greeted her eldest daughter, the one who'd stayed living close to her home in Bournemouth, the one she saw every week, who'd supported her when John died so suddenly and throughout the nine long months since, as Harriet adjusted to life without him. And all this even though Sally had so many troubles of her own. She gathered her daughter into a hug and kissed her cheek. 'Hello, darling. Thank you so much for coming round to help.'

'No problem, Mum. If I'm honest, it's good to have a few days when I'm not just looking after Jerome. Did you get those croissants in?'

'Of course! I was outside McKinley's before it had even opened. We'll have coffee and pastries first, before going up into that hideous attic.' Harriet gave a fake shudder at what was ahead, and Sally laughed.

'You know what, I reckon you'll quite enjoy it once we get started, Mum. It's quite cathartic, throwing out rubbish.'

Harriet nodded, and poured out the coffee. It wasn't the rubbish she was worried about finding up there. It was the memories. 'I'm sure it is. Anyway, sit yourself down and tell me, how's my little grandson?'

'On good form.' Sally took a mouthful of warm pastry and had to immediately reach for a paper napkin Harriet had piled on the table, to mop up some escaped chocolate from the corner of her mouth. 'Wow, these are as excellent as ever. He's at a point in his treatment cycle when he has more energy than usual, enough to do a few days in school. I'm so glad. A bit of normality for him, a chance to play with his friends; and for me, a chance to do something else other than constantly change the DVDs while he lies on the sofa.'

'Poor little mite. Is the chemotherapy working?' Six-year-old Jerome had been diagnosed with an acute form of leukaemia a couple of months earlier. It had knocked them all for six. It just seemed so unfair.

'I'm really, really hoping so, Mum.'

Harriet glanced at her daughter. Sally's voice had cracked a little and there was a tell-tale glistening in her eyes. Time to change the subject, then. She knew that Sally hated showing how vulnerable she was, and found it hard to talk about Jerome's illness. Even in the early days when he'd just been diagnosed, she'd struggled to put into words what the consultant had told her. Half the point of today was to give Sally a chance to take her mind off Jerome for a few hours. 'Shall we get going then, if you've finished your coffee? I've pulled the loft-ladder down already.'

'OK. Let's do this.' Sally stood up abruptly and rubbed her eyes, which Harriet pretended not to notice as she led the way out of the kitchen and upstairs. The hatch to the loft was above the landing, and they had to duck around the ladder. 'You go up first, Mum, and be careful.'

'I'm perfectly all right on the ladder, love,' Harriet said. She might be seventy but she was fit and active, doing Pilates every week and cycling everywhere. Even so she climbed the ladder with care. It'd be mortifying to trip and fall with Sally here. Her daughter would never forgive her.

She flicked the light switch as she emerged into the attic. It was a large space, boarded over, and with a murky skylight set into one section of the sloped roof. There was very little free floor space – boxes were piled on top of boxes, carrier bags tucked into corners, small pieces of furniture stored haphazardly. John's set of golf clubs leaned against a chimney breast. Half a dozen framed pictures were balanced against the golf clubs. Boxes of Sally's and Davina's old schoolbooks were tucked deep under the eaves. Three boxes of books and bric-a-brac she'd once sorted out to sell at a car boot sale that somehow she'd never got round to doing, were stacked in the middle. A pile of crates that she'd brought from her own mother's house twenty years ago, meaning to sort them out, had never got further than her own attic and now sat in what had once been intended as a clear walkway through the space.

'Well. Where shall we start?' said Sally, as she emerged through the hatch and stood beside Harriet, hands on hips, gazing about her and trying unsuccessfully to hide her astonishment at the amount of stuff there was to deal with. 'This is, I hate to say it, even more cluttered than I remember.'

'I know. But I kind of know where things are – there's sort of a system,' Harriet said, sounding uncertain even to herself. 'Over there's Christmas decorations. All that lot is from your nan's house. Stuff relating to you and Davina is in that corner. Photos and slides and the projector and whatnot over there.'

'What's this pile?' Sally had her hand on a precariously stacked pile of boxes. The bottom one had 'old stuff' helpfully written on the side in marker pen.

'No idea,' Harriet had to admit. She had a horrible feeling the 'old stuff' box might have remained packed and sealed since she and John moved out of their last house and into this one, nearly forty years ago.

'Well then, shall we start here?' Not waiting for an answer, Sally heaved the top box off the pile, opened it and peered inside. 'Vases. Salt and pepper shakers in the shape of church towers. A picture of the Coliseum.'

'Ah. Mum's old bits and pieces. I thought it was just that pile.' Harriet gestured to boxes that sat on top of an old travelling trunk. 'But yes, we can start here.'

'So what's the plan?' Sally asked, holding the cruet set. 'One pile for keep, one to go to charity or car boot sale, one to go to the tip? And only keep what's valuable or really sentimental?'

Harriet smiled. Sally was so much more efficient than she was. Her daughter's house was always tidy and clutter-free. 'That sounds good to me. For a start, you can put that cruet set in the charity pile. I always loathed it. Mum bought them when on holiday in York many years ago.'

'I quite like them,' Sally said, 'but I'm not keeping them.' She looked around her, found an empty box that had once held an old cathode ray tube television set, and put them in. With a marker pen she pulled from her pocket she wrote 'Charity' on the side, then held up an ugly green glass vase with a crack down one side.

'Bin,' said Harriet, and Sally nodded. That was put into a different box.

They progressed quickly through the first pile of boxes, and by the end Harriet was pleased to find she was only keeping two small items: a pie funnel in the shape of a blackbird that she remembered her grandmother using, and a framed photo of her parents in their wedding outfits. The boxes marked 'For the Tip' and 'Charity' were full. 'Let's get these downstairs to give ourselves more space, have a cup of tea and then get back to it,' Sally suggested.

Harriet agreed, and stayed in the attic while Sally went down, then passed the boxes down to her daughter. 'The deal is,' Sally said, 'you need to dispose of these boxes as you go along. So when we're finished today, drop those off at the charity shop and those at the tip before you do any more sorting.'

'Yes, boss,' Harriet said, making a mock salute. It was always easier to just go along with whatever Sally suggested. She had to agree with the sense of the system however. Little by little, bit by bit, was the only way, as Sally had told her. And actually, it was cathartic. With five boxes sorted there was a long way to go, but it was actually quite fun doing it with Sally. It'd be harder once they got to things that held all the memories of her life with John, she suspected. Though most of that was downstairs still, anyway. She'd be better off doing that herself, taking her time over it, enjoying the memories as she sorted through. Sally would make her rush it too much, and there'd be a danger she might throw away things she'd later regret.

After a reviving cup of tea (and after Sally had eaten another chocolate croissant), they returned to the attic.

'What next?' Sally asked.

Harriet looked around. It hardly looked as though they'd done anything, despite having worked for a couple of hours. 'I suppose that lot. Keep going with Mum's old stuff. Unless you want to tackle your old toys?'

Sally laughed. 'Don't say you've still got our old dolls up here! Surely they could have gone to a school fete or something?'

Harriet shrugged. 'I always meant to. But then …' She sighed. 'Davina had her daughters, and I suppose I thought I'd keep the dolls …'

'In case she ever turned up here with your other grandchildren in tow?' Sally snorted. 'Unlikely. She's so bloody selfish. Those kids must be, what, eight and ten by now? And you've never been allowed to even meet them?'

'I know, I know.' Harriet waved a hand to stop Sally saying anything more. If she dwelt too long on the facts, she inevitably found herself sobbing. It hurt, it really did – the way Davina had left home as a teenager and cut off all contact other than occasional calls from a withheld number. How she'd let Harriet know by postcard about the birth of her first grandchild, two months after the event. How ten years on, she still had not met little Autumn, or her sister Summer. And that horrible day … the event that had hardened Davina's resolve to stay away. The estrangement wasn't entirely down to Davina's selfishness, if she was honest. They'd all played a part in it.

But Sally kept talking. 'Has she even called you recently?'

'Not for a bit, no,' Harriet had to admit.

'Does she know? About Jerome, I mean?' Sally's tone was confrontational.

'No. I haven't had a chance to tell her.'

Sally rolled her eyes. A muscle twitched in her jaw as though she was trying to get her anger under control. A moment later she sighed and shook her head. 'You're right, Mum. We'll not think about her anymore. Let's just get on with sorting out Nanna's things. Right then. This box next.' Sally opened a box marked 'Ornaments' and they continued the process of separating them into keep, charity, and tip piles.

Three boxes later they had finished all of Harriet's mother's stuff. Harriet was pleased to find she had only decided to keep half a dozen items from it all for sentimental purposes.

'So now, this? What is it, some sort of travelling trunk?' Sally patted the trunk that the boxes had been stacked on top of.

Harriet nodded. 'That was my grandmother's sea trunk, I think. Mum had it stored in her attic and after I cleared her house, I just moved it here.'

'What's in it?'

'No idea. I've never looked. It's locked, and I don't have a key. But we'll never manage to get it downstairs and out of here. Maybe we can just push it to a corner of the attic and leave it here when I sell up.'

Sally stared at her mother, an expression of utmost horror on her face. 'Absolutely no way, Mum. We are not just leaving this. There could be some real gems in here. What do you mean, her sea trunk?'

'My grandmother worked on board ocean liners when she was young,' Harriet replied. 'I guess this is what she packed her stuff in, to take on board ship. Grandpa worked on them too – it's where they met.'

'Yes, there are labels on it – White Star Line. That rings a bell,' Sally said, frowning as she peered at the sides of the trunk.

'That's the one. Gran worked on the Olympic, which used to sail back and forth across the Atlantic from Southampton to New York.'

'Hmm. But you say you don't have the key?'

'Not anywhere I know of. Shame.' Harriet ran her hand across the top of the trunk, feeling its scratched and battered surface. Finding it had piqued her curiosity about her grandmother's early life. As a child she could remember sitting on her grandmother's knee, listening enraptured to tales of life at sea. She'd loved gazing at Gran's wrinkled and powdered face, watching her eyes light up as she told her stories. She could remember the feeling of Gran's arms wrapped around her, the smell of her perfume and powder, the gentle sound of her voice. But she couldn't remember much of the detail of Gran's stories – just vague impressions of her talking about her job as a stewardess on board ocean liners, being run off her feet by spoilt and demanding passengers.

And now here, in her attic, was Gran's old sea trunk. Harriet sighed. How she'd long to see inside it!

'Mum?' Sally was on her knees in front of the trunk, looking closely at it. 'Thought you said this was locked?'

'It is.'

'No, it's not. It's just held by a catch that's a bit stiff. Look.' Harriet watched as Sally prised open the catch then pushed the lid up with both hands. It made a cracking sound as it rose, as if decades of dirt that had sealed it were being broken, but then it was open, the lid leaning back on its hinges, and the contents of the trunk exposed for the first time in many decades.

Dear Reader,

We hope you enjoyed reading this book. If you did, we'd be so appreciative if you left a review. It really helps us and the author to bring more books like this to you.

Here at HQ Digital we are dedicated to publishing fiction that will keep you turning the pages into the early hours. Don't want to miss a thing? To find out more about our books, promotions, discover exclusive content and enter competitions you can keep in touch in the following ways:

JOIN OUR COMMUNITY:

Sign up to our new email newsletter:
http://smarturl.it/SignUpHQ

Read our new blog www.hqstories.co.uk

https://twitter.com/HQStories

www.facebook.com/HQStories

BUDDING WRITER?

We're also looking for authors to join the HQ Digital family!
Find out more here:

https://www.hqstories.co.uk/want-to-write-for-us/

Thanks for reading, from the HQ Digital team

HQ

USA TODAY BESTSELLER
LANA KORTCHIK
DAUGHTERS of the RESISTANCE
A novel of World War II
BENEATH a STARLESS SKY
TESSA HARRIS
KERRY BARRETT
The Secrets of Thistle Cottage
The truth can be dangerous in the wrong hands.
The War Girls
Can their friendship survive the darkest days of war?
ROSIE JAMES
THE USA TODAY BESTSELLER
Terry Lynn Thomas
HOUSE OF LIES
The Forgotten Gift
What would you do to protect the ones you love?
KATHLEEN McGURL